Ft. Leavenworth
Liberty
PAWNEE FORK
Westport
Independence
Council Grove
CIMARRON R.
ARKANSAS R.
CANADIAN R.
MISSISSIPPI R.
SABINE R.
NUECES R.
RIO GRANDE
Mier
Palo Alto
Resaca de la Palma
Reynosa
Monterey
Matamoros
Saltillo
GULF OF MEXICO
Tampico
Querétaro
Guadalupe Hidalgo
Chalco
Jalapa
Puebla
Cerro Gordo
Vera Cruz
Taxco
Ciénaga Grande
Orizaba
Chilpancingo
Acapulco

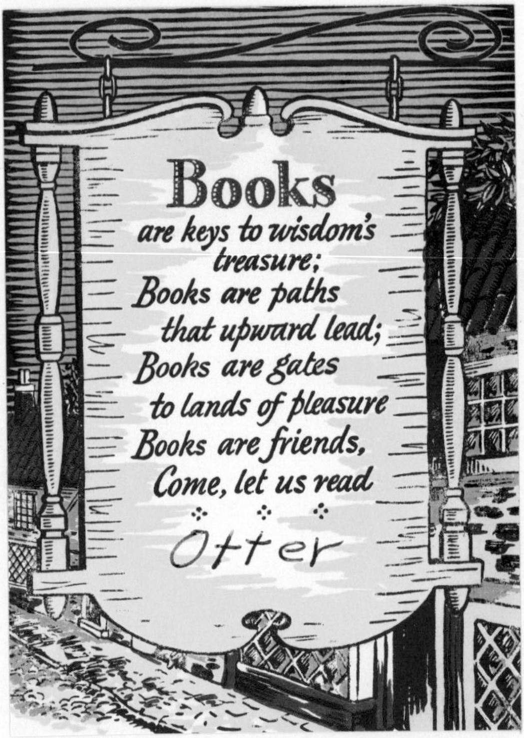
Books
are keys to wisdom's treasure;
Books are paths that upward lead;
Books are gates to lands of pleasure
Books are friends, Come, let us read
Otter

TWO ROADS TO GUADALUPÉ

By Robert Lewis Taylor

TWO ROADS TO GUADALUPÉ

THE AMAZING MISTER CHURCHILL

A JOURNEY TO MATECUMBE

THE TRAVELS OF JAIMIE MC PHEETERS

CENTER RING

THE BRIGHT SANDS

WINSTON CHURCHILL

PROFESSOR FODORSKI

THE RUNNING PIANIST

W. C. FIELDS: HIS FOLLIES AND FORTUNES

DOCTOR, LAWYER, MERCHANT, CHIEF

ADRIFT IN A BONEYARD

Two Roads to Guadalupé

ROBERT LEWIS TAYLOR

DOUBLEDAY & COMPANY, INC.
Garden City, New York, 1964

With the exception of actual historical personages, the characters are entirely the product of the author's imagination and have no relation to any persons in real life.

Library of Congress Catalog Card Number 64–17916

Printed in the United States of America

PART ONE

I

When I went to bed, the sky was clouded over, lightning fluttered on and off, very nervous and jumpy, gusts of wind swirled up strong and then died, and thunder grumbled along steady on the horizon toward the river, where most of our storms come from. It was what they described as a "wild night"; I was glad to pull the covers up tight and finish off the day. It hadn't been much of a day anyhow. I'd got a licking for practically nothing—making a rabbit trap from out of a book, where these people in Burma dig a pit, covering it over with rushes, and set up some sharpened stakes in the bottom, for tigers and elephants and such. When they came to lift out Hyacinth, our colored darky houseman, after he'd gone to throw away laundry water, he was only very slightly injured, not seriously punctured by the stakes, but with one leg sort of twisted under and back, what they called sprained. But he took on so, everybody lit into me like the furies, as usual. And did they ask whether I'd been trying to catch some rabbits so's we could have a nice stew? Not at all. They charged right ahead, selected a wicked-looking slat from a pile, peeled me down, and gave me what for, out in the smokehouse. Here lately, I hadn't done *anything* right, and frankly, I was ready to get out. But I'll come to that soon.

I slept fretful and uneasy, because the house rattled so loud in the wind it woke me up every half-hour, I reckoned. I'd just got to sleep nice and deep, dreaming a comfortable dream about another kind of trap, where those selfsame people, traveling now in Borneo, strung a concealed loop in the ground, with one end fixed to a bent-over tree, and by George, there was Hyacinth, dangling upside down by his sprained leg—done a-purpose on this round, you can bet, and I hoped it taught him a lesson to stay on the path, and not branch out when emptying tubs.

Well, all of a sudden I sat bolt upright. A scream had near about split my ears. It rose up again and again, hair-raising and horrible, and at the same time I heard some commotion, like a chair turned over and a window banging shut, down below. You could make it out even over the wind and rain that was tearing at the roof. Then there were shouts and a lot of racket, and I bounced out of bed in a hurry. But I'd forgot to put on a nightshirt, and I wasted a couple of minutes drawing one over my head, then I barked my shin, confound the luck, on a stool they'd shoved in there so I'd sit down to take off my Sunday shoes, and not do it with one toe on the other heel, muddying them up.

It was in my mother's room; I never saw such a sight. Her scalp was laid back from her forehead, showing the pink naked bone, and blood was everyplace you looked—soaking into the pillows, running down the sheets in little pools, and even spattered on the walls and floor. Along with my sister and half-brother, my father was there from his room next door, and he was holding her down, trying to calm her. Also the darkies were wringing their hands in the doorway, scared out of next season's growth. But Annice, the cook, was still in bed in the kitchen, sleeping right through, which didn't seem likely, so this mess was cleared up pretty fast. She was a poor feeble-minded half-wit, pretty enough, but more white than black, which my father claimed made bad blood. He said white blood was too risky to try on anything but whites, who were used to it and could stand it, for the most part.

Anyhow, they got the blood stopped flowing, with cold towels and an all-around lifesaver of a commodity called Jew David's Hebrew Plaster, and sent a boy galloping through the storm for Liberty, to fetch Dr. Ferguson, a new doctor that had set up there and was doing a lot of fine work on what people said was the fairer sex. I took it to mean along the order of towheads and albinos. I'd read his advertisement in the Liberty *Tribune* only the week before. It was educated, and gave assurance:

Dr. E. S. Ferguson,
Physician, Surgeon & Obstetrics,
Having permanently located in
Liberty, Mo., offers his professional
services to the citizens of that
town and vicinity.

He will pay special attention
to inflammatory and chronic diseases of women and children. He
promises to treat them without the indiscriminate use of Mercury as has heretofore been practiced by the profession.

His charges will be made to conform
to the hard times.

Office in the brick building
of Mr. Estes (upstairs, rear).

April 20, 1846

My uncles and their families had reached our house, now, from their places around the bend, and with my father and my half-brother Blaine, they questioned Annice. At first, my uncles, who were tall, straight, sober Kentucky men, fierce and bad to cross, were inclined to go at it rough and quick, but my father took Annice by the shoulders, pushed her back in the bed, and exchanged some words in tones too low to catch. Then he nodded, straightened up, looking at us over his shoulder—pretty tired and sad, it appeared to me—and said, "McClintock."

After that there was a dreadful scurrying around of saddling up, snatching down rifles from the walls, and unchaining dogs. I wouldn't been in McClintock's shoes for a stern-wheel Missouri River steamer. He was our farm overseer, a whiny, mean, shifty fellow who was, as my father once said, lower than the ignorantest Negro on the plantation. But his hand at growing hemp was a kind of miracle; even our neighbors said so, jealous or not.

"The horses are all here—he's cut for the river," my father called from the back yard, and then some know-it-all told me to hike upstairs and get back in bed. I barely had time to grab a rubber coat out of my closet and shinny down the sycamore tree before they were off in a clatter of mud, and some cusswords, too, here and there. Our dogs were laying to their work, raising a pow-wow that a person might hear in Halifax, humping along and baying as happy as if they were on the right scent. They were nice dogs, always friendly and willing to eat, never cranky about their food, but pinning down quail and turtle doves was more in their line. Human people never got dog-run around here; there wasn't any occasion for it.

My uncles had lanterns, and what with the lightning that snaked down now in ugly forks, with the constant fluttering stopped, you could see well enough.

I hadn't got time to saddle my paint pony, but went after them lickety-split, bareback, and could have caught them perfectly easy but didn't wish to appear forward. The trail led back between hemp fields and corn patches, then through a woods of black walnut and oaks and black ash, and then down along the bank through thick cottonwoods to a sandbar where McClintock kept his skiff tied up, for fishing. And sure enough, he'd only started and was out maybe fifty yards in the river.

"Hold up, McClintock!" ordered my father, and one of my uncles sent a shot that splunked the water in front of his boat, but not very far, by George.

McClintock hesitated on his oars and called out something, but a regular rouser of a thunder clap came along just then and nobody understood him. What's more, the horses were stamping and switching around, frisky to get going again. They were all studs, meaner than copperheads.

"Pull back to shore, you scoundrel, and don't waste time about it!" my father cried. I never heard him in a humor that meant business plainer.

In the next lightning flash, we could see him trying to make up his mind, but my Uncle Allen smacked a bullet right into the boat on the forward water line, so then there was nothing for it except to crawdaddle in before he sunk.

Well, they hauled him out of that boat like a sack of wheat, and if I was to tell the truth, they roughed him up some. Then they hustled him along back to the house, with me still following behind. There'd been some talk lately about me taking too much on myself, as they called it, and I disliked to appear important.

Every lamp was on in our big old house, and the family women were all there, and darkies, and Dr. Ferguson from Liberty. He was a fussy, solemn stringbean of a man, bearded, with bushy black hair, yellow gold cheaters, and a habit of saying, "Hmm, hmm, let's see, now," or sounds to that effect. But he buckled right down, got some catgut out of his carpetbag, and sewed my mother's head up, after washing her and saying it wasn't serious and then giving her what he said was a medium strong hypnotic. I noticed that he first scraped off the Jew David's Hebrew Plaster and threw it out of the window, with his nose kind of turned up. This was an amazement to me, for our family swore by it, as well as by the man that invented it (he having got the prescription from a relative in the Bible, so he stated) and also Garlichs & Hale, the druggists that sold it in Liberty. And did Dr. Ferguson fish up a bottleful of Mercury, which was the custom just then, as mentioned? He did not, and one of my uncles, later, said it was a credit to him, but my brother Blaine said the occasion hadn't arisen, that nobody but a jackass would apply Mercury for a scalp wound. That was just like him; he was a scholar, and read books all the time, though perfectly normal in other respects, and was always blowing up this or that solid old saying or belief.

I was anxious about my mother, of course, but there were too many people in there, and besides, I was interested in all that uproar in the kitchen. So I crept back—the kitchen was separate; you got to it by a roofed-over passage—and they had McClintock tied to a chair by about a hundred feet of rope. Annice was in a chair too, now, in a dingy old wrapper, and was crying so loud it gave you a headache. You see, the poor stupid creature had finally got it through her skull that she'd done something wrong, and she was trying to put things right by wailing. Women generally do, I've noticed.

They were in the process of "extracting a confession," to use my brother Blaine's words.

"Take a strap to her," said my Uncle Allen. "Remove a foot or two of hide." He was a great believer in direct action, and disliked to fritter away time.

"None of our people are whipped," said my father wearily. "You, Annice, be quiet. You're in trouble. You realize you're in bad trouble, don't you?"

She let up blubbering a little and nodded.

"Then you'd better tell exactly what happened here tonight. *This* villain"—gesturing toward McClintock—"claims he knows nothing about it. When we found him, he was setting out trot lines. In a cloudburst," my father added.

Well, by and by, they got it all sorted out, and then wrote it down, after which she signed it—made her mark. It went about as follows, only changed some from her way of talking:

"Four days before the commission of the act, McClintock told me there was a good deal of money in the room of my mistress and that I ought to kill her; that he would assist me; that we could get the money and with that we could go to California; and that I would be his wife and be free. On Sunday night, the night of the commission of the crime, he came to the kitchen where I was sleeping, waked me up and we proceeded to the house. McClintock hoisted the window and got in the house and pulled me through the window after him. He approached the bed, found my mistress asleep, and said to me, 'She lays right.' I took the axe which belonged to McClintock and made the lick. McClintock had the axe in his hand when I took hold. My mistess made a noise and we both ran out of the house; he went to his house a few hundred yards off and I went back to the kitchen and laid down on the bed."

There it was. An outrage like this was bound to cause a commotion, and it did. My father sent to Liberty for the Sheriff, but he'd gone down to St. Louis on a steamer—joyriding on the taxpayers again—so they hustled out a deputy, a fool, drunk at that, who made everybody mad by snooping around for "clues."

Well, there wasn't much sense looking for clues when they had a signed confession, nailed down with a perfectly clear "X," as one of my uncles remarked pretty brisk, so in the end McClintock and Annice were lodged in the Clay County Jail, though in different cells, of course. My uncles went in with the deputy to see it done, not being satisfied he wouldn't stop off in a tavern and let them both break free.

Well, sir, all the talk everywhere next day was about the crime Annice tried on my mother, and right off they ran into a snag: Missouri had a law where no slave testimony could be taken in court, and since McClintock declined to open his mouth (though several persons urged him to, with articles like harness belts and broom handles), where was their case?

The day after that, a whopper of a mass meeting was held; people rode in from every part of the county. In a nutshell, putting things in my brother Blaine's language, "It was decided to circumvent the law." Still and all, I don't mean to give the feeling that this was a reckless or hothead group. One of the neighboring papers said: "Annice was brought before the meeting assembled and, face to face with McClintock, firmly declared that he was the sole instigator of the attempted murder. No better class of men ever assembled to consider any matter and no men ever calmer and more deliberately considered any case than these citizens did this one."

As stated, they considered it calmly for a few hours and then voted to hang both McClintock and Annice as soon as convenient.

When we got home, my father and brother seemed unhappy. They had a talk with my mother, who was feeling better though shaken, and then with my uncles, who weren't entirely satisfied, either.

"Certainly justice must be done, despite the ruling out of slave testimony," said my father. "However, to hang McClintock's one matter and Annice is something else. It's—inhuman. She scarcely knows what's happened. Even in primitive societies, lunacy has always been given special protection. Frankly," he continued, "I don't mind at all in the case of McClintock. I always suspected him in the matter of the little pickaninny girl—Thelma's child?—we found mutilated in the fields. There's something evil about the man, something twisted—I've picked up other hints from the hands—but if we're to act on Annice, we'd better do it at once."

"Excuse the interruption," I spoke up, "but it wouldn't be any botheration to me to slip in there tonight with a hacksaw and saw her out. I'd enjoy it, in fact. You put a flannel cloth over the saw to drown out the noise. An infant could do it."

"It wouldn't be any botheration to me to lock him in his room, shackled to a bed-post, and saw down the tree outside," said my brother Blaine, in about as rude a suggestion as I ever heard.

"There's only one answer," said my father, ignoring us and getting up. "Blaine will ride in tomorrow and consult Alex Doniphan. You can go with him, Sam"—meaning me. "It won't do you any harm to hear some wisdom from a man of rising stature. No—don't break in again—you listen to *him*, don't *tell* him anything. And on the way back," he added, looking at Blaine, "you can stop by the Male and Female High School. Have a talk with Dr. Dewey Hutchins. Offer him extra tuition, if necessary, and a bonus at the end. I haven't done my duty by this boy—all my instincts tell me it's so. The time has come for outside discipline."

When I think back on that scene, it practically makes me laugh. What came out of our meeting with Doniphan was exactly what they weren't after—travel, soldiering, the bloodiest kind of fighting, adventures with foreigners in far-off lands—and I wouldn't swap it for a degree from every college in the universe.

II

Next morning they dressed me in bark janes pants and roundabout, and I went in to see my mother, mighty starchy and uncomfortable. She was all bandaged up like a mummy, and I sniffled a little to see her reduced so. But my sister Claudia said Dr. Ferguson was satisfied with her progress. She'd be up in about a week, he predicted, if complications didn't develop from the Jew David's Hebrew Plaster and kill her. So he claimed. I doubted it. If there ever was a case of professional jealousy, this was it.

Anyhow, my mother told me to put my "best foot forward" for Dr. Hutchins, at the school, and it kind of ruined the day. I'd forgot. Then Claudia said, "And be sure the foot has a shoe on it." The remark wasn't necessary; the girl had always been a smart aleck, and I made a note to look into her case when we got back from town.

We were aiming to cart home supplies, and Blaine had a wagon hitched around at the barn, near the rope walk. Like most people hereabouts, we raised mainly hemp, which the hands spun into cordage at the rope walk. In times past, we'd sold it raw; a ton of fair, unhackled, dew-rotted hemp brought nearly a hundred dollars, but there was more profit in spinning. We grew wheat, and corn, and tobacco, too, none of your "common Missouri," but the better species like Cavendish, Hain's Virginia Leaf, and Glasgow.

In all, we owned upwards of three thousand acres—rich bottom land, some rolly country, green fields, and beautiful thick woods. It was a proud plantation, laid out around a two-story brick-and-clapboard house that had four white colonnades in the center or brick part, along with an iron-railinged balcony and a kind of cupola above. There were broad stone chimneys at both ends of the house, and fireplaces inside that a person could stand up in, almost. Back behind was the kitchen, as well as a stone spring-house, the smokehouse, barn, and other outbuildings.

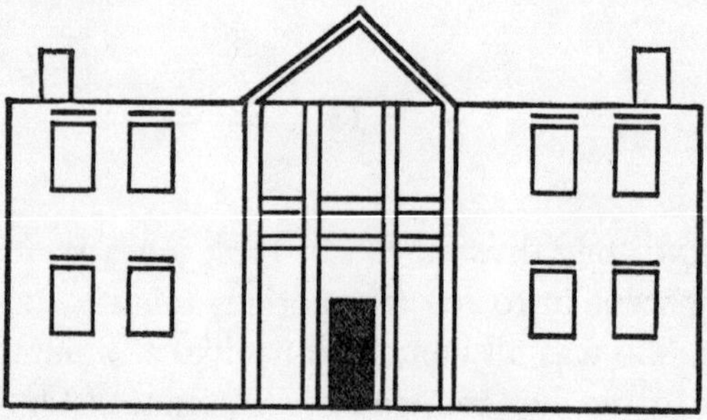

Farther south, it was said, balconies commonly ran clear across the house-fronts. I couldn't tell you; I'd never seen one, myself.

We climbed in the wagon and clomped off on toward Liberty. Blaine reading a book, as usual. He told me to drive, saying he didn't wish to be disturbed, but in about two miles, near the tree-arched entrance to the Hughes place, a girl came cantering toward us, astride in the saddle, careless-looking, entirely bare-headed—in the heat of the day, too—and it was Angelina Hughes. She had on tight-fitting riding pants, like a man, a floppy, low-necked silk blouse that wasn't so much like a man, and her blond hair drawn back into a knot. I might have known it. People said she'd had her cap set for Blaine since babyhood, and the truth is, she pestered him half to death. If he'd grabbed a log, pushed it out in the river, floated down fifty miles, and landed on a two-by-four sandbar, she'd been sitting there in a rocker, waiting.

Though handsome, she was a pretty tough proposition, and cared little for anything in Missouri except Blaine, even the dandified style of southern girls' conversation. What's more, she was always ragging.

"Well, I de*clare!*" (You see what I mean—more mocky than serious.)

"Oh, hello, Angelina," said Blaine, pulling up out of his book, slightly addled. "What are you doing around here?"

"Well, for one thing, I live here—you can see the sign, 'Crowfoot, Hughes.' My father's name isn't really Crowfoot Hughes; it's John. That's the plantation name. Mainly, though, I was just riding this nice old horse."

On the quiet, I slid the buggy whip over to where he could reach it, if he decided to fight back, but he said, "Mayhem? Wait till your father hears."

"Oh, I like a stallion, a real old honest-to-God *stud.* None of your mares and half-horses for me. A stallion knows what he wants."

"He'll kill you, Angelina. With a woman, there are times when; that is, you can't ride him all the—"

"That's *it!*" she said. "That must be what my mother was trying to explain." She rode up close beside us, and I could see where the sweat had made big half-moons of dark under her armpits. "Go on about stallions, but keep your voice low."

"No, thanks," said Blaine shortly. "We're due in Liberty."

"Why, that's perfect! I'll go with you. Sam can ride the horse." She started to get down.

"Not me," I spoke up. "I took a bad spill, and wrenched my back. I'm not supposed to ride. That's one of the things we're going in about."

"Liar," she said, laughing. "Listen, Blaine, I'm having a socially important barbecue—dozens and dozens of brilliant people—book readers, all—at the Landing a week from tonight. If you have an ounce of manhood, you'll pick me up about six."

"I don't know, I doubt it," he said, looking vague. "I may be in St. Louis, or sick."

"Perhaps you should understand something, Blaine; it's not a joking matter. You don't realize what you do to a girl with your impulsive vulgarity—all that loose talk about horses. I told Papa you'd probably be wanting to speak to him soon."

Then, "Don't worry—it isn't actually a party. We just eat the barbecue, and afterward go walk in the woods and so on."

"Get *up!*" I cried, and snapped the reins. I couldn't stood any more. Blaine half lifted his hat, as Angelina blew him a kiss, laughing, and we trotted on toward Liberty.

"That's one I owe you," he said, and came out with the only confidential man-to-man words he'd ever addressed to me in my life: "You know, I can't cope with that creature, I really can't. She's too much—too good-looking, too cocksure, too knowing, too forward, too—too sexual, even too quick-witted. I can think of things to say an hour after she's gone. Eventually, she may drive me out of here, possibly to Europe."

I felt sorry for him, and said, "Hang on a little longer. Something may occur to me. I've dealt with bullies before."

"Don't strain yourself," he said, then we were on the outskirts of town. They'd given us a list of things to buy—for family and darkies both—and we tackled the job one store at a time, before we called on Doniphan at eleven.

A good many of the purchases appeared to make Blaine mad. First off, we laid in some medicines at Garlichs & Hale's, including the celebrated Dr. Buchan's Hungarian Balsam of Life, which my mother used in the quarters for dosing pneumonia, croup, softening of the lungs, and tuberculosis decay. She once showed me an advertisement where it stated flatly that the Balsam was "the most infallible remedy known to the civilized world," being the only thing that stopped "incipient consumption," but Blaine, burning the paper later, said you might as well rub ground glass on your chest, for all the good it did.

Anyhow, we bought five bottles, at a dollar a throw, and got some of Reverend Bartholomew's Pink Expectorant Syrup, also for consumption—the medicine made you spit the disease right out, along with your tonsils and adenoids, if you weren't careful—as well as several bottles of Hyde's Nerve and Bone Liniment; Hull's Medicated Warm Lozenges—for children and dogs, you know; Judkins' Pile Ointment; Connel's Magical Pain Extractor, which was a favorite amongst the darkies, eighty-two per cent alcohol; and Garlichs' own Vegetable Ague Pills, cure guaranteed. Blaine said *that* one produced honest results, as least, for there wasn't any ague around here, and never had been. He said a person could easily package up some gumbo and hawk it to prevent leprosy, because the county was free of that disease, too. But he was a kind of sore-head about drug-store medicines; I never met a fellow so down on progress.

When we came out, there was a hullabaloo up by the Courthouse. Everybody was hurrying along to see the fun. Liberty, in 1846, was a tolerable town; there was something doing all the time, as there naturally would be with three taverns, eight stores, four tailors, three saddlers, three shoemakers, a carriagemaker, two wagonmakers, a tanyard, and a number of other concerns, including a Catholic church, a bag-and-rope factory, two milliners, an oil mill, a Baptist church made all out of stone—very cool to sit in on a summer day, crowded with the religiousest sort of loafers on hot Sundays; drunk, mainly—two private schools and a "Union Sunday School" with eighty scholars, an uncommonly pious group, it was said; of the eighty, none had ever been arrested. Over-all, there were people aplenty, with about six thousand whites and twenty-five hundred slaves in Clay County alone.

Anyway, a saphead named Applegate had fitted up a prairie wagon with mast and sails, exactly like a square-rigged ship, and stated that he intended to sail it across the prairie (which commenced near town) clear over to Fort Bent, in the Santa Fé territory.

He was dead serious, though having trouble with hecklers in the street, and was giving directions through a brass horn to his sons, aged ten and twelve. It was ridiculous. A man told Blaine that Applegate had found the prevailing winds to "lay perfect," and he meant to revolutionize trade along the Santa Fé trail. Ordinarily, wagon trains had to plough pretty heavy over those swelling, flower-strewn prairies. It was a mean trip, with either oxen or mules, and took a lot of time.

"How fast you calculate she'll travel, if a cyclone don't come along and roil the prairie?" a man sung out, and he answered, wholly undisturbed, "Fifteen mile an hour, friend. I and a full-fledged professor worked it out, using trigonometry and logyrithms, both."

"What! You don't mean Professor *Watkin?*" and they sort of washed back, laughing and doubling over, to reveal a tall, thin, red-faced young man with very frowzy yellow hair, standing in the doorway of a tavern, crying into a bandanna. He was practically the town drunk, but some said he had taught school in a college once, before he took to whisky.

"*Bon voyage* and God bless you, Applegate!" he bawled out, then crumpled back into the tavern. The sight was too much for him.

"*Hoist mainsail!*" Applegate cried to his boys, who cranked up a big-bellied sheet of canvas.

"*Break out jib!*" and they did so; then he kicked some blocks out from under the wheels and jumped aboard, grabbing his steering gear.

Nothing happened.

"You'll need a push, to overcome inertia. It's covered in the logarithms," Watkin called from the doorway, where he'd recovered. Several good-natured men clustered behind the wagon, which Applegate called a prairie schooner, and started her rolling down the street. Sure enough, the sails filled and the wagon begun ripping right along, picking up speed every minute. But there appeared to be something wrong with the steerage, because where they were supposed to round a curve and head out the prairie road, they went as straight as a string and sailed through the front window of T. J. Slaughter's Mercantile Company. The voyage couldn't have lasted over three or four minutes altogether.

The last thing I remember, because everybody was bent over, about to bust open, was Mr. T. J. Slaughter running out, shaking his fists, and Applegate hollering things like "Belay!" and "Heave anchor!" and "Luff to starboard!" which Blaine said he'd got out of a book, likely.

But he wasn't finished. When they unscrambled the wreckage, he allowed he'd rebuild the schooner and make the trip yet. And a man there that was a part-time poet hurried off to a tavern to write down the opening lines of a work he claimed would become a "frontier epic," whatever that meant. It seemed possible; he had several contributions in the Liberty *Tribune* to his credit, on such subjects as "Dreams," "A Farmer's Life," "To the Ladies," and a hard-hitting job about "Babies in Church," taking the negative side and stating that, as they were "wide awake as weasels," they should "either be stuffed full of gingerbread or kept home."

All in all, as Blaine said, Applegate's experiment was "lively but indecisive."

To the medicines we added a super moleskin hat, to make up to Hyacinth for being rabbit-trapped; some salt mackerel; several kinds of bonnets—Half Gypsy, Broad-arch Gimp, Diamond Straw, and Fluted Lawn—for fastidity darky women starting to work in the fields; a barrel of Cincinnati whisky; half a barrel of saleratus; several bolts of calico cloth, as well as alpaca, bombazine, casimere d'Ecosse, bobbinet, and Osnaberg; and a new Paris robe for my mother, to help her get well.

It made a considerable heft, but we evened it all up in the wagon, then studied some posters at the Courthouse, one advertising the coming of the Olympic Arena and United States Circus, and another announcing the opening of the Liberty Jockey Club, with all the regular horse races and feature matches between a mule and a pony, for a three-hundred-dollar grand prize. The entrance fee was only fifty dollars, but when I tried to borrow it off of Blaine, calculating to win the prize and take a trip around the world, he yanked me by the arm and said it was time to visit Doniphan.

III

Doniphan's office was on the south side of the square, near the Baltimore Cut-rate Cash Store of Schild and Siegal, a darkish sort of plain room with a big oak desk in the middle and red- and black-leather books jamming all the wall shelves, besides others piled helter-skelter on the floor, alongside a brass cuspidor. It was shiny clean, so I concluded it was for visitors. Mr. Doniphan himself was sitting with his feet on the desk, eating an apple. He had his coat off and his galluses slipped free of his shoulders.

Even sitting down, you could tell he was sizable—six feet four, it was said, (but maybe a little less, I think). A lot of people thought Doniphan looked like an Indian; he had blackish-hazel Indian eyes, high cheekbones, ears that lay flat to his head, a great deal of dark brown hair parted on the left, and a very odd, almost twisted mouth, what was called "humorous," or "quizzical." Watching him, you felt a sort of stillness, or quietness, as though there might be a volcano going on inside but it would remain under the tightest kind of control.

Like most Missourians, he'd come from Kentucky. His father was a pioneer there, a schoolteacher who had fought in the Continental Army; his best friend was Simon Kenton, the frontier scout, and Blaine said that some of that association must have traveled on down to the son. Long after this, when Doniphan was famous, and honored everywhere, I read that one of his main ancestors had been a Spanish knight—Don Alphonso something-or-other, a name that settled over the years into Doniphan. Anyhow, this Spaniard married an English lady, called Mott, and they finally wound up with Alexander Doniphan (though of course they'd been dead quite awhile by then).

The boy had an unusual upbringing, back in Kentucky. His father died early, and he was given over to be tutored by a "learned and eccentric" Irishman, as they said, a wild man named Richard Keene who was a graduate of Trinity College, in Dublin. In a book, it set forth that Keene was "ardent, enthusiastic, boiling with courage, entertaining the most romantic ideas of freedom"; commonly he conducted his classes for Doniphan in the forest, which seemed sensible, and taught him a good deal. Afterward, Doniphan enrolled in Augusta College, Bracken County, Kentucky, at the age of fourteen, and when he came out, still chipper and fresh, not at all damaged, he entered the law office of an Honorable Martin P. Marshall.

Right from the start, he was a bang-up orator, in demand for all occasions, but he had one flaw as a lawyer: he only *defended* people, the most of these underdogs, some trash amongst them. He got the reputation of being the "champion of the oppressed." Doniphan moved to Lexington, Missouri, and then to Liberty, in the 1830s, and right away got into a gaudy fracas involving the Mormons. What happened was, the Mormon's head prophet, a rackety fellow named Joseph Smith, a regular fire-eater, took to fighting all of his neighbors, who he called "Gentiles," right out and open, and Governor Boggs of Missouri placed Doniphan in charge of the State Militia, with the idea of "putting down the insurrections." As everybody predicted, he did it, in record time, and without spilling a drop of blood.

And then I'm a striped-bellied ape if he didn't turn around and *defend* Joseph Smith in court, got him a sentence of five minutes in custody, which everybody agreed amounted to an acquittal, particularly Smith. *That* old goat was cutting up rough again soon, amd moved out of the state bag and baggage, taking his herd along with him. With his disposition, he needed elbow room.

But Doniphan's popularity wasn't reduced any. People sort of idolized him in Clay County, and over the rest of Missouri, too.

He said, "Good morning, Blaine, good morning, son, take a chair," and stripped some more peel from the apple with his knife.

"Alex, we've come to see about Annice," said Blaine. "None of us want her hanged. She doesn't really know—"

"I figured it might be in your mind," said Mr. Doniphan, talking very slowly, and studying the apple. A person got the impression he'd never say what he didn't mean. "I spoke to Benton and the others, and they're willing to give her parole. If it's agreeable with you, she can be boarded with Abe and Sukey Woods, now freed and catching catfish for a living. The county will contribute five dollars a month for her keep. The Woods, with Annice's consent, have promised to lock her in her room at night for at least six months. Personally, I doubt if that's necessary, but the community temper is running pretty high—you may recall the slave fight last month in the public square: one man killed. It should be said that the co-defendant, McClintock, will hang as planned. I have no opinion on that, either legal or personal."

Mr. Doniphan paused and bit into the apple, then he stated, speaking in a kind of official way, "That represents, for the moment, the sum total of work done by this office in the cause of Clay County, or substitutes therefor, *vs.* Annice Shelby (last name to conform with that of owner) on a technical charge of attempted murder, with confession on file. The case presented no special difficulties," he added, looking up calmly. "There is a fee involving reimbursement, at client's leisure, for six drinks of bourbon whisky consumed during a conference."

Blaine sat back and laughed. "Tell me, Alex, did you ever *prosecute* anybody?"

Mr. Doniphan stopped to swallow, then he said, still in the style of addressing a court, "The policy of this office has been, and remains, that the jails are full enough. The taxpayers are sufficiently burdened already. We hold, further, that there exists, as someone has noted, good in everybody. On occasion, you may require a pickaxe to uncover it."

Then Mr. Doniphan tossed Blaine a copy of the Liberty *Tribune* and remarked, "No doubt you've read this."

"Mexico?" said Blaine, with a careless glance. "The fact is, I haven't paid much attention. We've been more absorbed in Oregon."

They had what was known as the "Oregon Question," on account of the dividing line up there between us and the British, as I got it. The Russians and Spaniards had stuck their noses in off and on, but now they were out, and good riddance. Anyhow, the British had occupied the land as a kind of hunting preserve, discouraging colonies, in their usual woolly-headed style, but the crowds of Americans traveling in since 1842 had set up a howl for "definition." They settled on 54° 40′ as a boundary (though you couldn't see it, of course), and made up the slogan of "Fifty-four Forty or Fight." My brother Blaine said the British would probably agree on that line, which might end the squabble and let people drum up another excuse for war. At least everybody hoped so.

But in this Liberty *Tribune,* Mexico crowded everything else off the front page. There was an article which said a formal declaration of war was coming any minute, to be made by President James K. Polk, a Tennessee man and a Locofoco at that; another saying General Taylor had won a big battle, been "Completely Victorious!!!", which seemed odd if we hadn't even declared war yet, and a third which announced that Governor Edwards of Missouri was about to raise a "mounted volunteer regiment of 1000 men."

The news was somehow exciting. I looked at Blaine, to see how he took it, and noticed that Mr. Doniphan (who had eaten all his apple and begun to whittle on a stick) was studying him with a shrewd glance now and then.

"You don't mean *me?*" said Blaine. "I'm not mad at the Mexicans. I don't even know any."

"They've been so indiscreet as to declare war on *us,*" said Mr. Doniphan. "That puts a different light on the matter, and comes under the heading of 'my country right or wrong.' I thought I might put things in order here—pick up the books and the shavings and the apple peelings—and enlist. I was going to mention it to Sarah and the children after lunch." Then he straightened up in his chair, looked at us perfectly direct and steady, and gave me a shock. It was as if his backbone had snapped into place like a steel rod. Beneath that calm and easy-jointed manner, he was about as loose and ambling and unorganized as a cougar. His dark Indian eyes hadn't any more give in them than a chief's. People said Doniphan was a born leader, and suddenly I believed it.

"They'll elect you colonel, Alex. It stands to reason."

"My plan was to go in as a private," replied Mr. Doniphan, settling back in his chair. Then he started in on the knife and stick again, and said, without looking up, "I understand Miss Hughes is entertaining next week."

Blaine's face sort of changed.

"It's a matter of regret to me," Mr. Doniphan went on, "that writing is not my first and principal mode of expression. Practically any fool can stand up among his fellows and exercise the vocal chords that nature has bestowed on us all. To transmit to paper one's ideas and observations is a higher art, the scholar's gift. If *I* were a writer, Missouri might eventually be the richer for a full and personal history of the Mex–"

"I see," said Blaine slowly. "No wonder your juries find themselves tied in knots. You had this worked out before we came, didn't you?"

"The duties of a family solicitor," said Mr. Doniphan, speaking officially once more, "are to maintain a constant alertness for the temporal welfare of his clients. He is bound by his professional ethics to pass along any suggestions for advantage that may occur to him." Taking out a big engraved gold watch, he snapped the lid open and said, "That concludes all the advice that this office had prepared corollary to the case of Clay County (Mo.) *vs.* Annice Shelby, colored. I hope it has proved to be of some slight benefit."

At McGinnis's Boarding House, we had what was advertised as a light lunch at a big table with a lot of traveling men–steamboat officers; a circuit preacher; two soldiers on their way to Fort Leavenworth; a doctor that they said was a phrenologist and felt the bumps on your head to see where you were sick; a trapper of a kind known as a "mountain man," that could have stood a bath; and two or three hawkers. They talked about the Mexican War some, but mostly they ate, with their coats off and tucking it in as if tomorrow wasn't apt to arrive.

It cost a quarter, but it was worth it, all you could eat—set down in big bowls and platters: fried ham, fried venison, fried pork, red gravy, a long boat of fried eggs, black-eyed peas, okra, green beans and bacon—cooked all morning in a black iron pot, so they had some flavor, blood-red tomato slices with thick white onion slabs on top, biscuits, corn bread, fresh-churned butter, boiled potatoes, hominy grits, coffee, tea, buttermilk, and apple pie. A number of men produced bottles before they begun, and passed them around making courteous little remarks like, "Up your leg, sir," "To the Queen—bottoms up," and one, by the mountain man, that didn't make much sense to me:

> "Coon-dog shinny up a sycamore tree,
> Pickaninny squatting at her Mammy's knee,
> Two of yours to one of mine,
> Up, over, down, around—
> Drink!"

Even so, he handed me his bottle, outgoing and generous, saying "Appeteezer, son?" but Blaine grabbed it before I got a drink.

After the toasts, one of the men, who they said was a State Senator, told of an experience he had that shook him up plenty. He was fuller of grievances than any man I ever met, but maybe a little tipsy along with it. Mostly, I don't aim to try and fetch the exact speech of all the people in this book, because Blaine says it's hard to read, but this fellow's is worth remembering, being what they say, typical. With his son and a darky, he'd been keelboating down the Missouri, and banged head-on into a sawyer, losing their cargo, which was salt, and turning over. This was only yesterday, and he had on a suit, supplied by somebody, that Blaine said hung about him loosely, "like the morals of a politician." A friendly woman waiting on table inquired if his son had been greatly alarmed.

"No, madam," he said, "I'm a real ring-tailed painter and feed all my children on rattlesnake hearts fried in painter's grease. There are a heap of people I wouldn't wear crepe for if they was to die before their time, but your husband, marm, I allow, had a heart as big as a *courthouse*. When we was floating, excuse it, arse uppermost (a bad situation for the people's representative) past Hardeman's garden, we raised the yell, like a whole team of bar dog on a wildcat's trail; and the black rascals on shore only grinned up the nearest saplin, as if a buck possum had treed. Now, madam, I wish God Almighty's *yearthquakes* would sink Hardeman's d-ned plantation—begging your pardon for swearing, madam, with my feet on your beautiful kiverlid here. Maybe you wouldn't like me to spit on this kiverlid you have spread on the floor to keep it clean; I'll go to the door—we don't mind putting anything on our puncheon floors. The river, marm, is no respecter of persons, for I was cast away with as little ceremony, notwithstanding I am the people's representative, as a stray bar dog would be turned out of a city church."

Well, when that bunch finished up eating, there wasn't enough left to feed an alley cat. The owner, a Mrs. McGinnis, a plump lady with powder on and more body behind than is common, came in to look at the remains and kind of staggered against a chair, seeming about to faint. She looked so mournful and put out, I was sorry I'd eaten three pieces of pie.

But the most of those hyenas, they only belched, patted their stomachs, thanked her politely, and remarked on how good the food was; then they apologized for not being hungrier. They disliked to offend her, you see, and the mountain man summed it up when he said, "I'm not a noon eater, myself, never was and ain't apt to start this late. In addition, I had a beefsteak for breakfast only an hour back; I shouldn't have done it, I realize that now, and beg your pardon for it." He was a wiry little rooster with a kind of squinted-up left eye and an expression so sober you might have thought he was joking.

Mrs. McGinnis merely stated that she had a second table to serve, and the blessed Lord Jesus only knew where she'd get the fodder. She said she'd likely have to go out of business, but Blaine told me, private, that she knew all of these men and went through this sort of thing every day.

The last visit on our trip to Liberty was to Dr. Hutchins, at the Male and Female High School, and it turned out better than I expected. The school occupied a big frame double house, needing some paint, half a mile out of town, and Dr. Hutchins received us in what his wife said was his "Sanctum Sanctorum," which made Blaine snort to start off with. Anyhow, it amounted to very little, being a little gloomy cubby of a room, all lined with books in different languages, a couple or three ratty imitation black-leather chairs, kind of cracked and dried out, an old yellowed globe, and a roll-top desk where Dr. Hutchins was sitting, with his hands together, fingertips touching, making a tent. You could have placed it all in one of the outhouses back home.

He didn't bother to get up when we entered, but waved us solemnly to seats. He was tall and gaunt, except for a little pointed pot belly, had on thick-lensed glasses and wore a gold key dangling on his watch chain. His collar was dirty and frayed around the edges and his teeth appeared stained, as if they might need a good brushing. There were black rims of dirt under his fingernails, and his white cotton socks were tumbled down around the tops of wrinkled black shoes. His nose was pretty fleshy, with dark red veins running here and there toward the end. Several long hairs were sticking out of his nose, and the knot of his necktie drooped down about an inch from his collar button. Still, his face had a very superior expression, sort of pinched and disdainful and tilted, on the order of a person smelling something that had died or gone to rot, and you could well believe what all the church women said, that he was unusually intellectual. They adored him, I heard my sister say; when it came to "foreign allusions," she claimed, he was in a class by himself.

I could tell that Blaine didn't take to Dr. Hutchins for some reason, especially when he began to speak. Even so, Blaine stated our case in perfectly even, accommodating tones, and said, "For several years the boy has been tutoring with me, studying Latin, the classics, a certain amount of mathematics—painfully—and, of course, writing. Frankly, I've tried, without pushing, to interest him in reading on his own. At Danville University, from which I have a degree, we—"

"No doubt, no doubt; to be sure," Dr. Hutchins interrupted in a deep, beautiful voice, "but a degree does not impute a trained pedagogue, especially a degree from Danville University. You may find that the present Male and Female High School requires more than minimal preparation. To dip into a tome is not to apprehend that tome. Of our curricula, what does the boy opt?"

"I beg your pardon?"

"We offer, *inter alia*—"

"Do you mean 'among other things'?" asked Blaine with an innocent look. I didn't know what they were talking about; it was over my head.

"One of the drawbacks of an eastern Doctorate in Philosophy," said Dr. Hutchins in a condescending but patient tone, "is an inability to descend to the common level. One forgets. I must beg your indulgence. We offer, among other things, Spelling, Reading, Writing, Mental Arithmetic and Geography, for beginners—at seven dollars the term. Also, General Geography and Arithmetic, English Grammar, History, and Watts on the Mind—at nine dollars. Also, Natural Philosophy, Chemistry, Geology, Botany, Geography of the Heavens—at twelve dollars. Finally, Languages, either alone or with any of the preceding branches—at fifteen dollars. Boarding can be arranged in private families at from one dollar to one dollar and a half per week. All factors considered, including the unquestioned *errata* involved in the tutoring, I should not hesitate to recommend the Beginners' Course."

"I see," said Blaine, but I could tell he wasn't finished. He had a kind of mule's head, once he got annoyed. "Do you find it necessary to teach all the courses yourself, or do you employ additional faculty members?"

"To answer your somewhat unusual question, the quality of learning absorbed at Male and Female is, shall I say, unilaterally derived. I perhaps should remark, *obiter dictum*—"

"'In passing'?"

"—in passing (from the Latin) that any enterprise worthy of note takes its flavor, extracts its *ton,* from the man at the top. We scarcely lay claim to a *kulturfest,* as such, but we follow a rubric *sui generis*—"

"'Unique, or of its own kind,' also from the Latin?"

"Mr., ah, I believe you said your name was Selby—?"

"Shelby, Blaine Shelby of Riverbend Plantation. This is my

half-brother Sam. My father, Wyatt Shelby, was one of the half-dozen who established the school we are now visiting."

I don't know when I'd ever heard Blaine speak so vulgar and rude. Dr. Hutchins sat up a little stiffly. "Your father's name is, of course, familiar to everyone in this region—an honored name, a man of progressive and liberal ideas. But your present examination, or docimasy, appears to have a subtly pejorative meaning. Without being repetitive, what further information may I supply you?"

"Surely you've misunderstood," said Blaine soothingly. "I intended no pejorative meaning whatever. I didn't even intend to be depreciative—put it down to awkwardness of speech. Now tell me, Doctor, for I myself am keenly interested in learning, what is your *method* in bringing home to the young minds the beauties of, say, Keats' poem, 'Saint Agnes' Eve'?"

Dr. Hutchins chuckled, and I was surprised. I hadn't any idea he was so humorous, though I didn't exactly understand what amused him.

"Without intending to cause offense, it might be simpler, sir, if you undertook the course yourself."

Blaine suddenly laughed very heartily, too much so, and I gave him a suspicious look.

"You were saying about the method, Doctor?"

"When dealing with this *genre*," said Dr. Hutchins slowly, his hands fixed in the tent again, "one must extrapolate from the many academic theses a central attack, or *caveat*, which, if it does not prove a paradigm of wisdom, yet avoids divisiveness in the immature mentality. It is necessary to identify, to fix in the memory. Seriatim, we begin with—"

"I was thinking of the actual discussion about 'Saint Agnes' Eve'."

I saw Dr. Hutchins' knuckles get a little whiter where he gripped the arms of his chair.

"Of supreme importance, which even the superficially educated will encompass, is to identify the form. What, if any, is the rhyme scheme? If in stanzas, how many lines does each contain? Then, how many feet to a line? Where are they accented? What nomenclature has the educator seen fit, in his superior critical judgment, to affix to this form? In essence, we must determine what's *wrong* with the work, where it strays outside our standards—"

"Excellent, excellent; and you would, of course, know. I'm getting a real feeling for the poem," cried Blaine, but he didn't look it. "Go on, pray do."

Dr. Hutchins relaxed his acid look slightly, letting his natural high-knowledgy expression return.

"Now, with some technical awareness of the, ah, work, we must, of course, list the figures of speech. That is important. Count the similes, sift out the metaphors, spot the personifications, pinpoint onomatopoeia—"

"I'm really dumfounded," broke in Blaine, shaking his head in wonderment. "I must repair straightaway home and read that poem again. I've missed almost everything of value in it."

The doctor chuckled again, in what they call a "benign" way; then he tapped out a little reproof on one chair arm.

"I feel it my duty to tell you, however, that, in my considered opinion—a view shared by many among the doctorate at my eastern university, as well as by critics of several learned publications—the versifying in question is almost wholly without merit. It comes perilously close to being a silly gallimaufry, of solecistic logic, monosyllabic syntax, and illiterate clarity."

"It should be more obscure?"

"You put it a trifle baldly," said Dr. Hutchins, "but speaking from the advantage of my superior erudition, it should. I might remark that Keats has always seemed so to *both* my wife and I."

What happened next more or less spoiled our visit, as far as I was concerned. It had appeared to be going very well, too, or as well as schoolteaching ever went in my case. That is, while the whole business was perfectly boneheaded, and unfriendly, without making any sense whatever, nobody had hit anybody yet, so that there was a pretty good chance of getting out before the police were called.

A bubbling up of laughter commenced deep inside Blaine, worked its way in stages to the surface, in spite of him trying to hold it down with a handkerchief, exploded in hopeless sobs, was got under control briefly, then broke out again worse than ever, causing him to stand up for air, bend over, straighten up, bend over, face beet-red, tears running down his cheeks, breath coming in racking gasps, and, finally, the seizure trickling away very slow, with a few bad outbursts on the way, like a thunderstorm that's passed over and disappeared behind a hill.

"You—really—must—excuse—me," he forced out, swiping at his face. "Nervous habit—all family have it—no accounting—good day, Doc, I mean—Doctor. Very kind—"

I remember Dr. Hutchins standing stiff as a poker, sour, too, in his doorway, and when we got down the street, I said, "That was fine, just fine. You've cooked my goose, as far as schooling's concerned. It's all right for some, but there's no sense in *me* trying to have all the advantages. I couldn't get back in that place with a set of burglar's tools. Many thanks."

I hadn't much wanted to go to the school before, but now that it looked impossible, I was anxious to get educated.

"Idiot! Pedant! The posturing, overbearing, patronizing *ignoramus*, with his silly, useless Latin and big words. '—Speaking from the advantage of my superior erudition, *it* should.' And, more hilarious, Keats 'has always seemed so to both my wife and *I*.' *I*, mind you." He turned to me so savage, I thought he was about to slap me. "Remember this, you young smart aleck, a man overstuffed with unevaluated erudition does *not* make an intellectual. Also, and maybe it's a small, personal point, if you *do* aspire to set up as intellectual, take the first baby step and learn grammar. It's no wonder people in this country come out of school speaking like bog-trotters. 'Saint Agnes' Eve' indeed! Five minutes with that counting-house bore and you'd hate the poem forever. *Doctor* Hutchins is no teacher. There *are* good teachers, even in our backward land, thank God, but *that* pompous eyesore isn't one of them. Do you understand?"

"Look here," I said hotly, "I didn't ask to be here. He's no relation of *mine*. Frankly, he struck me as smart. The man's got a real education; it's probably over the head of the ordinary book reader, if you know what I mean."

Blaine didn't hear me, as usual. "I understand that he's being replaced next year by a Dr. Cunningham, who comes highly recommended. This fool's finished in June, only he doesn't know it yet."

"I'll be mighty sorry to see him go," I said, and Blaine turned around to face me. "*No,* by George! I won't have it. I won't see all my tutoring go for nothing. As brainless as you are, I won't place you in that high cerebral zoo for even two months. The odds are a thousand to one against it, but you might, you just might, absorb something, and it'd be ruinous." He looked thoughtful, and said, "I wonder. It's an idea, the bare bleached skeleton of an idea."

"What is? If it's all the same to you, don't ring me in on anything else. I've had enough for one day."

"We'll take it up at home. Come on, my river-bottom Puck, we're now officially in a hurry. Great events may lie just around the corner."

IV

"As YOU SAY, there *is* the question of Dirk," said my father, with a musing look. "And yet, I'm certain he's dead. None of our inquiries at the time left room for hope."

"'Missing in action' is not proof of death," insisted Blaine, his face shiny and earnest in the firelight. "Nobody saw him fall, no burial detail indentified any such body. If it came to capture—"

"—then he's far better dead. I've heard stories enough of those swarthy ruffians. They hold life as cheap as dirt; atrocity piled on atrocity—"

"And I've heard some lively accounts of the Texans," said Blaine.

Dirk was Blaine's older brother, also my half-brother, a dark, broody, strange sort of fellow for our family, handsome enough though sharp-featured and straight as a slat. He'd gone off to the Texies war, ten years before, and hadn't been heard of again. My father traveled to the battlefields but found no trace of him, so they said.

Crouched where I was, with a very good view of the big oak-beamed living room—that is, outside, with the window propped up by a stick—I could see them all sitting around discussing the situation. Part of it was me, because I heard Blaine say, "My thought was, that Sam could go as drummer or some such—he *has* got a drum, I believe, unless he's traded it for a bomb—and keep a detailed journal as an exercise in English, instead of enrolling just now in the Male and Female High School. I'll look after him, of course. I see this as a kind of short, undangerous joke war, culturally broadening to the participant. The Texas Territory's one thing, the United States Army is quite another."

"But Sam's so *young!*" cried my mother, who was propped up on the couch, with bedclothes. "He would be coarsened by rough associations."

"He *is* young," said my sister Claudia, in a concerned sort of way, which made me feel warm inside. Ordinarily, I listed her among my worst enemies. "His emotional age could scarely be more than seven or eight. As to his being corrupted, my sympathies lie with the Army."

I knew it; she never missed a chance to stick her oar in where it wasn't any of her business.

It made me so mad my elbow slipped and knocked down the window on my hand, and I fetched a howl that brought them tumbling around in a hurry. They collared me and hauled me inside, then plopped me in the chimney corner and bawled me out in shifts, after saying I'd promised to go to bed. It was true, but I'd failed to mention that I planned to get up early.

"Alex Doniphan wants me to prepare a history of the Missouri campaign," said Blaine. "It's tempting; it may be the sort of thing I've always wanted to do.

My mother put her handkerchief to her mouth, and stopped whatever it was she'd started to say.

Then my father arose abruptly. "This is upsetting; we'll pursue it in the morning. I've already lost one son to Mexico; I'm not eager to lose two more. I cannot, of course, dictate to you at your age—but my decision about Sam will be final. *Sam stays here.*"

2

Fort Leavenworth, June 5: Troops are ganging in here from everywhere—"forming up," they call it—and Blaine's bunch are apt to be amongst them, so I figured I'd better start my Journal, else he'll shoo me home to Liberty.

A good deal has happened.

First off, to do this job right, I looked up the Post Library and checked out three famous Journals of history. But one was by a man named Samuel Pepys (called Peeps), a boozy old gossip who made a habit of dropping in on married women in the daytime, and the account got so raw in spots it was embarrassing. The old lady that let the book out came down to my rooming house and collected it back; said she'd made a mistake. It was on a shelf called "Unexpurgated," that was meant for Regular Army officers, and pretty hard-bitten ones at that. I couldn't stand the book myself, and it never got any better; the last chapter was as disgusting as the first. I went over it twice to be sure.

Anyhow, I studied up on all three Journals, and concluded that a simpleton could have written them. *That* part of my worry is *over*, thanks to goodness. I'll just rattle off the events as they occur, put in dates when I remember to, expand it into a book, pay a couple of reliable critics to praise it when I'm finished, and take my place alongside of Peeps, though maybe not so unexpurgated. According to the old lady, Peeps was the most unexpurgated case in the Library except a man named Cassanova, who was so unexpurgated a wife at the Fort took the book out and declined to bring it back.

To go back a little, I saw I had to escape, of course. I knew my father. When he'd issued a statement like that, it *stood*. So, there I was, practically enrolled with Dr. Hutchins, a barefaced pedagogue—I had Blaine's word for it—and about to miss all the fun. I realized what had to be done, and I did it.

Working fast, I said good night, went to my room, lit a candle, and tackled a Letter of Farewell. I copied it over three times, the last in large print, and when it was finished I couldn't help feeling proud. It struck just the right note, without being too mushy and sentimentalized, which was apt to make everybody cry, although I have to admit that my eyes got a little damp now and then; it *is* a hard thing to leave your family and loved ones, even Claudia.

To Whom It May Concern

This is to serve notice that the Undersigned, heeding his Country's Call, has taken his traps (including horse but not drum—it caved in while being sat on last March) and gone to the Mexican War. To put it mildly, it would be useless to follow me, *as I have removed the horseshoes off my horse and reversed them!* [Not wishing to appear conceited, the idea came out of a medy-evil book Blaine once read out loud where these marauding Barons got away as clean as a whistle.]

When the Undersigned arrives at my destination, he will post a letter telling further particulars. *But don't try to follow him me,* as ~~I~~ he would then be a Deserter, and Shot.

Hoping this finds you all in the best of health, I am

Your esteemed friend,
"Sam" Shelby

Naturally, I hadn't done any such jackass thing as turn my horseshoes around, but only said that to throw them off. To begin with, my paint horse, Chief, would have laid back his ears and balked, or maybe kicked me in the stomach, and that's no way to get to the Mexican War. He's a very good horse but occasionally has ideas of his own.

Well, I got into a pair of buckskin pants and a jacket, put on a cap and rough shoes, fetched out an extra pair of drawers, which I figured should be clothes enough to see me through the war, rolled up my case knife, toothbrush and comb in a blanket, tied it around with a leather strap, and borrowed half a ham out of the smokehouse.

I needed a gun pretty bad, but they were locked to the rack by a chain—it being the custom everywhere on account of Abolitionists—so I took down a cavalry sword of an ancestor with a crooked handle, then saddled up Chief.

As always he whinnied loud enough to wake the dead when he saw me, but nobody stirred, and I got him calmed down. He blew out his belly when I tightened up the band, hoping to shuck the saddle off later, and me with it, but I waited him out—I'd been there before—then led him frisky but silent down the dirt road. By and by, when it seemed safe, I climbed aboard, and we cantered along easy and slow toward town.

The night was clear, with a lovely smearing of stars all around and a moon as big and white as a paper balloon. A soft breeze blew in from the river, carrying the usual nice smell of dead fish and wet mud; and hoot owls tuned up here and there in the woods. You couldn't want pleasanter conditions for adventuring.

No lights at the Hughes place, none at the Morrisons, not a thing showing until Liberty, and I skirted around that, because I didn't have any real good reason why I was there. I'd heard everybody say Fort Leavenworth was where the Army would gather, including the Missouri Volunteers, and that was the road I took: forty miles, plus or minus a few.

Some time before dawn I got sleepy—cold, too—so I angled off the road into the woods, found a wide stream with a grassy patch and staked out Chief to fodder up. For me, I had a very enjoyable meal of ham, along with a drink from the stream, which tasted like weeds but not bad, and stretched out in my blanket. Then I said, that's pretty funny, because the moon's now *behind* me and this glow's dead ahead in the deepest part of the woods —a red center near the ground, with a kind of misty halo above. It wasn't a particle of my business, probably dangerous as well, but I was curious; I couldn't help it.

So, sliding the cavalry saber out of its scabbard, I tiptoed along the bank, being careful not to step on sticks, and holding back branches to keep them from whipping. After following the stream for about a hundred and fifty yards, I could see that the glow was a campfire, sure enough, built up against a half-rotted log, and with a figure stretched out on the ground.

I was scared, and stopped to take stock. I calculated as follows: people around here don't customarily sleep in the woods, not when there's a bed handy, and travelers stop at taverns. What if it's a Mexican? Nobody'd told me how far the war had spread, and I'd read books enough to know about spies and such. Well, it might be useful to capture a spy, the first Deed done by a Missourian, and collect a medal. *Then* wouldn't they sit up and take notice back home!—them and their drums.

I slipped out of my shoes and begun to move forward about an inch at a time, ready with the sword, hearing my heart thumpety-thumping away. But when I reached the rolled-up figure, I was puzzled about the official way to address it, as the only Mexican word I knew was *amigo,* which didn't fit the occasion, exactly. And an army command I remembered—"I hereby take possession of this fort in the name of the Continental Congress"—was downright silly.

Well, I realized I could cut off its head, him being asleep, but I wasn't convinced they would give me a medal for only half a Mexican; what's more, it didn't seem like good ethics. That's something Blaine was always preaching about. He had so many ethics he was kind of bogged down with them, like an overloaded pack mule in a swamp. And I felt pretty sure that one of his main ethics was not to cut off somebody's head while asleep.

Then the thought occurred, what if it *isn't* a Mexican? The only thing to do was find out, and I knew I could tell right off; I'd seen pictures enough for that—medium dark; black mustaches; pock-marked likely (for everybody has smallpox down there, so they say); greasy, coal-black hair; a dull but shifty expression; very frilly, sissified clothes; and considerable jewelry, especially on the men.

I leaned over and peeled the blanket back slow, and stood looking at a shirt stuffed full of grass, the rest being a human-sized log, though not particularly Mexican. The next thing I knew was when somebody behind me said, in a perfectly friendly drawl: "Help yourself to coffee, sonny—it's there on the fire under your nose."

I felt myself getting red—an idiot would have spotted that pot —and turned around, but not in a hurry, you can bet.

A medium-sized, lean, weathered, sandy-haired man of at least fifty, with a very peculiar color, something between yellowish and tan, dressed all in fringed (and stained) buckskins, stood looking me over in an entertained way out of deep-set gray eyes. He had a beaky nose, a high forehead, and skin stretched as tight as rawhide over his cheeks. About his eyes, though, were any number of little crow's-feet that fanned out like sunbursts. I had the notion he'd spent a lot of time searching far landscapes with those sharp eyes, probably in strong sunlight, to boot.

He said, "Odd place to hold a chivaree."

"Look here," I snapped, feeling my spunk come back, "I'm the one that's got a sword, so maybe you better watch out."

"Sit down, sit down, sonny, right there on the log. Careful, now —don't fall in the fire."

Confound him, I started to sit down without thinking, but when I caught myself and looked back, he was gone. Vanished lock, stock, and barrel, melted right into the trees. There not being much else to do, I sat down and waited, but I didn't feel comfortable. And all of a sudden, I swoll up with what they call homesick. That is, I wished I was back at Riverbend, safe in bed and dreaming up some new ways to get even with Hyacinth and Claudia. I hadn't reckoned on any troubles connected with the Mexican War. I thought you just signed up, rode off with the soldiers, having a high old time, saw some new country, killed a few Mexicans, rescued a beautiful damsel or two, as often as not riding on a milk-white palfrey, or locked up in a tower, and came back in a few months for a big celebration, with maybe a statue erected in the Courthouse Square.

Bending forward, I poked at the fire with a stick, expecting to get shot in the back, and when I straightened up—

"What's your name, bub? And where were you bound?"

By jings, the crazy fool was sitting beside me on the log, and I hadn't heard a sound.

I told him, told him the truth, too, for some reason, and he said, "You look like a pretty good boy, Sam, but a boy's only a boy after all. Don't you agree?"

There wasn't any reply to make to a donkey-headed statement like that, so I made it.

He said, "I heerd you ride in; I thought it was drovers with a herd of cattle for Leavenworth. On top of which, I smelt you when you cropt forward."

I interrupted to say something hot, but he continued on.

"A polecat wouldn't have announced hisself livelier." He laid a hand on my knee. "Now, Sam, I tell you what. You lay down here and snatch forty winks, after which we'll start you for home. It'd be a service to your pa, for Sam, take my word, you lack the cut of a mountain man."

"Mountains my granny. I'm headed for Mexico."

"The first night amongst Injuns, or, prefer it, Greasers, and they'll lift your hair. I been there some."

"Well, if you know so much, what'd I do wrong?"

"Man and boy, thirty-five year," he said, looking into the fire,

"I've took potluck in the woods, good times, bad times, click your heels, whoa there, risk it all, do-si-do, dance to the fiddler—broke and commence a new season, nor a Christian to say Howdy to month after month. And, as often as not, blood! Jostled, I've killed my share."

I hadn't any idea what he was talking about, he was babbling like a madman, then he sort of pulled himself together and said, in a different tone, "You're dead set; I can see it. I oncet had a bulldog with your disposition—he drounded while refusing to let go of a coon. Now, then, do you see this pelt of mine? What color do you make it?—speaking candid."

"Well," I said, hesitating a minute, "I have to admit, it's sort of—yellow, but not quite, either."

"Smoked, tanned and cured in the lodges of the Comanches! Captured early, married to Old Wolf's daughter, my partner ransomed for a jew's-harp, worship the sun morning and evening, brothers with the Arapahoe and Cheyenne, sworn enemy of the Sioux. And Sam, do you reckon there's much I've missed?"

I said no—I'd begun to believe it, too.

"We'll suppose—I haven't said positive—we'll suppose you're going to travel for awhile with Captain Gabriel Hobbs—"

"Captain of what?" I asked, still sore.

"Captain of scouts, when the humor's on. Along with Kit and Peg-leg Smith. Now supposing, again, that you spied a campfire and thought to sneak up on poor old Captain Hobbs, snoozing away in full view—what then?"

A little sullen, I said, "Circle and come up with the wind."

"Son, I can outsmell a fox; so can the Comanche. Remember it. A bubbling coffeepot means a man getting up ready for travel. An outdoor man has a saddle for his head; a dummy lays flat on the ground. There are two or three dozen more here, but we'll take them up later. Now you just plop yourself down, without further palaver [this struck me as pretty rich, for I couldn't shove in a word edgewise] and we'll move this expedition out after sunup."

We were back on the road about eight, Captain Hobbs riding a mean-looking buckskin named Limber Bill, that he'd trained to hide stock-still for hours in the woods, so he claimed. The horse had a slit in each ear, Comanche fashion, and a good Mexican saddle, of the kind all those Indians preferred. Captain Hobbs had been to St. Louis to sell furs and now was interested in the Mexican War, like me. He said we'd "sniff around Leavenworth and see what's bid." Well, I had to kill time till the Volunteers moved in, so I let him ramble on, not feeling talkative, being, in fact, curiously heavy about the throat. Trotting along, not hurrying, he surprised me by looking over sideways, quizzical, and saying, "I recollect pining for home at the start. Some say it wears off, but the better the home the longer it takes. In my case, it was almost immedjit. Watch out, now, this bridge is rotted; we'll slope down the draw and climb up. Bill's kind of notiony about busted shanks."

V

Well, we trotted into Fort Leavenworth about noon, and the first thing I noticed was that Captain Hobbs begun to sweat. As we passed groups of people—soldiers and humans—the sweat rolled down from under his skin cap and made his leathery face glisten in the sun.

He said, "It's beyond fixing—when they bunch up, I sweat, specially when corralled in, so to speak. Commonly, it wears off a mite."

I asked him if it had always been so, and he said, "Harken back to a wee toddler. Curious, too—I should have got used to it: they corked me up in a closet whenever they journeyed to town."

I didn't figure that would have got *me* used to anything, but I didn't say so, and we jogged on ahead. Soldiers were just everywhere, mounted, mostly, and there was considerable dust. This place—six thousand acres with five miles front on the west side of the Missouri—was set up in 1827, so I found out later, and named by the army colonel in charge; also, he had the good sense to name it after himself. When I heard it, I concluded that I'd pick out something handy in Mexico, like a lake or a mountain or a city that wanted a change, and name it after me. I'd noticed it was the fashion in history books; done everywhere; the maps were full of it.

The Fort was established mainly to protect the Santa Fé trade, and there were a good many heavy trader wagons being loaded from steamboats or moving out here and there. We noticed a few coming in, too—ox-drawn, for the most part, but some had mules, and all looked dead beat after the long trip.

I don't believe I ever saw a handsomer spot—the land sloping away to a green natural park from a high bluff along the river. The Fort itself was laid out with a row of log huts, stables, and a big stone wall on the south (to keep out the Delawares); quarters for the Regulars on the north; to the west a string of dwellings, a soldier station and a guardhouse—always full and overflowing, so they said. In fact, a very red-faced soldier sort of wobbled up to us, seeing us looking, and bawled out, "Swaller some advice and shove your reservation in ahead; they're booked up solid till Christmas"; then he said, "They've been knowed to make an exception in my case," took a couple of steps backwards and fell over a barrel, after which he got up, cussing, and knocking the dust out of his hat, but not very mad, either.

Anyhow, they had the colonel's quarters and a hospital on the east side—full of malaria patients right now, together with some loafers that had gone in groaning and limping and clutching their sides, and one or two asking permission to write "last letters," but only wanting a rest, you know—along with a battery, a two-story blockhouse that "commanded" the Fort, an army store plus a commission store, and, nearby, the road that ran down to the ferry. Most all the supplies that came to Fort Leavenworth—beef, bacon, vegetables, lard—were brought over, from settlements across the river, in flatboats made back home in Liberty. It gave me a nice feeling.

Well, sir, we hadn't been on hand long before various men began to hail Captain Hobbs, in the highest old humor but kind of respectful, as well. One grizzled-looking fellow, a sergeant or something like, cried, "Why, if it ain't old Gabe! How many you got this trip?" and a soldier alongside called out, "Hang onto your hair, boys—Cap'n Hobbs has branched out north."

I failed to understand them, and Captain Hobbs seemed more uncomfortable than ever, but he said, "I and Spiebuck only worked it as a sideline, times when game was sparse. It don't shame me." Then he explained that he had a Shawnee hunting partner named Spiebuck, who was as shy of settlements as he was, and they sometimes collected Apache scalps for the Governor of Chihuahua, at a bounty of fifty dollars a head. On the last haul out, they toted in forty scalps and collected two thousand dollars. Apaches hardly ever let up on the Mexican ranchers, Captain Hobbs claimed, but would swoop down and kill women and children and all, out of pure cussedness. They were the worst Indians anywhere that way, regular devils.

"Alongside of an Apache, it wouldn't strain me to trust a wolf." He squinted over sideways again. "And if you're searching for evidence, ask a mother right smack in the middle of Santa Fé. Take my word, a wolf trains easier." After a raid into Apache territory, to get even for some murdering and thieving, soldiers brought in some Apache girls and the gentlest was made into a nurse. But one afternoon, when the mother went into town, the Indian snatched both babies from their cribs and dashed out their brains against a wall.

"I've heard it said Apaches are human," remarked Captain Hobbs. "Me, I'd require further tests."

I couldn't help but run over Apache hunting in my mind, trying to puzzle out whether it would interfere with Blaine's ethics. They were annoysome; nearly everywhere I turned, I tripped over them. Still, I figured, you could hunt, or trap, say a hundred Apaches a season and wind up with a cool five thousand dollars, knocking off a trifle for expenses, such as salt for curing scalps. It was more than Senators got, and considerably cleaner work, taken all around. By buckling down and tending to business, upright and honorable, (because that's what my father always stressed to get ahead) I could retire before I was twenty. That is, if the supply held out. I was about to ask Captain Hobbs how many Apaches there were, when we came on a noisy hullabaloo of a rally, couple hundred people on hand, around a wooden stand that was being built for the Drum-and-Fife Corps.

An election was coming up across the river, and these fellows were hashing out the Mexican War. It was ridiculous, useless, too, but Blaine says I can keep this part in because it's "representative" of politics just then.

Well, there was a man up there talking, with side whiskers and a full frock coat as well as a stovepipe hat, that somebody said had been a Congressman once and hoped to again. He belonged to the Locofoco, or Democrat, Party, together with President Polk, who had declared the war, as stated previous. Sitting on a three-legged stool alongside him, making idiotic gestures, holding his nose, breaking into cackles of laughter, shaking his head and occasionally crying out, "Oh my God, what a lie!" was that same little rooster of a mountain man that had been eating at Mrs. McGinnis's Boarding House. He was wearing a coonskin cap now, and seemed happy. Standing beside *him* was an Indian with his arms folded, hair clubbed in two pigtails, no more expression than a side of mutton, and naked to the waist. The little man said the Indian was his "campaign manager—best political brain west of the Mississippi"—and hopped up to "confer" with him, dark and sober and mysterious, every two or three minutes. I never saw anything so absurd.

Before long, we found out that soldiers and other wags had arranged the whole business; it was a put-up job. That poor, addleheaded speaker *had* been a Congressman once, but he drunk himself out of his job and had less chance being re-elected than the late Judas. As to the rooster, he was the neighborhood joker, a trapper and trader, and only entered the election for a good time. A third candidate, a perfectly decent, serious man, had the whole thing sewed up. With none of the "formal" amusements available, these rough pioneer men often went a roundabout way to rig up sport. I saw it over and over, and Captain Hobbs was one of the worst. They had what Blaine called a "local school of humor."

Talking flowery, in a handsome, husky voice, Side Whiskers started to give the events leading up to the war, and said, "My friends—"

"Objection!" cried the rooster, leaping to his feet. "One more insult like that and I draw out. Hold up, I'll confer with Buffalo Hide." He whispered in the Indian's ear, not causing as much as an eyelid twitch, then turned and said, "That's all right. Correct parliamentary procedure. Continue."

"—the American Congress's rightful passage of the Resolutions of Annexation, incorporating the glorious new state of Texas into the Union, has been, of course, the prime cause of war. Nobody denies *that*."

"Exception! Strike it from the record!" said the rooster, jumping up again.

Side Whiskers seemed bewildered, and said, "Now see here, Mr. Briscoe, do you mean that *you* deny it?"

"Well, scarcely. Do I *look* like a fool?"

"Who, then?"

"The Mexicans."

The speech jerked on, but it lacked steam, somehow. There were so many interruptions that Side Whiskers kind of lost hold of himself and was talking, at one point, about the number of brewers in St. Louis, giving the total as seventeen. Then he straightened up and explained that the "immediate cause" of this struggle was the occupation by American forces of some disputed territory between the Rio Grande and Nueces rivers. This brought on the Mexican declaration, he said, and ours quickly followed, on May 13.

When he came out with this information, it offended Mr. Briscoe so much that he picked up his stool and moved it to the back of the stand, facing away from the crowd.

"Soon afterward," cried Side Whiskers in a ringing voice, appearing relieved at the change, "the villainous Mexicans crossed the Rio Grande in numbers even as blades of grass, headed by the notorious generals, Arista and Ampudia—"

"That ain't been proved!" cried Mr. Briscoe, without turning around.

"—and were repulsed with frightful carnage at Palo Alto and Resaca de la Palma by our gallant and courageous General Taylor—"

Mr. Briscoe quickly collared his Indian, and they got down and started off across the greensward, but some soldiers persuaded them to come back. I never saw a debate conducted in such a fashion.

"The war is *on!*" cried Side Whiskers. "Our beloved President ["Boo!" "Beloved by who?" "James K. Polecat" etc.] has called for fifty thousand volunteers to bolster the Regular Army. The cruel and inhuman butchery of Colonel Fanin and his men—all Americans; the repeated injustices perpetrated upon the persons and property of American citizens residing in northern Mexico; the wanton imprisonment of American merchants; the repeated insults offered our national flag; the contemptuous ill-treatment of our ministers—are these not sufficient? Or should we forbear until the catalogue of offenses is still deeper-dyed with infamous crimes, and until the blood of our brothers, friends, and consanguinity, like that of the murdered Abel, cries out to us from the ground?"

Some carpenters had arrived now to complete the bandstand, and Mr. Briscoe, jumping down, picked up a hammer and helped them. He made a racket that would have raised a corpse. The speech continued, but you couldn't hear anything; besides, a steamboat was coming in, so we moved on.

Well, the first thing I saw, when the passengers started unloading, was Angelina Hughes. She looked as perky and bold and brazen as ever, wearing a frock that emphasized her out in front, and carrying a small valise. Two women that I judged were army wives greeted her on the wharf, kissing and carrying on as falsey and gushy as if they were glad to see her. Me, I'd rather put up a rattlesnake.

I grabbed Captain Hobbs' arm and said, "I've got to get out of here. One of my enemies has lit ashore, and she'd peach on me sure."

He didn't argue; I'll say that for him. But when we led the horses up toward Headquarters, he said, "Sam, deep down you're hankering for home; I've noted it twicet." He pulled a string leather bag out of his shirt. "Yonder's a steamer, and here's passage money. How do you vote?"

Speaking as positive as I could, I said,

"I'm going to the Mexican War. If they steal my horse, I'll walk, and if they break my legs, I'll crawl. Here's where we part, with thanks."

He sighed. "As alike as two peas. Except I was flawed some, what with the sweat." Then he appeared to make a decision, squared up his shoulders and said, "I can't let you venture off alone yet; you'd be et alive." He allowed we'd call on the

"Sachem," whatever that was, find out when the Volunteers were due, and maybe apply for a job.

He meant the commanding officer of the Fort, but when we got there, it was so crowded we had to shove in by main strength. A war was on, you see, and things had briskened up. Orderlies were running back and forth, a sentinel stuck a rifle in front of us (which Captain Hobbs flipped back up), an officer inside was bawling something at a sergeant named Yerkes—though nothing complimentary—and finally we muscled clear in and faced a big black-mustachioed man wearing medals, sitting behind a desk, with a flag against the back wall.

He yelled, "Who in the blistering Hades?—Yerkes!" Then he had a good look at us and cried, "Hobbs! By God, I knew I'd catch up with you sooner or later. Guard! Guard!"

"Something amiss, Colonel?" inquired Captain Hobbs mildly.

"*Amiss!*" He stood up and walked around, so that their noses were all but touching. "Look here, Hobbs, you and your precious friends won me an official reprimand. Do you realize that?"

"Cut your salary any?" inquired Captain Hobbs.

"A joke's a joke, but Armijo was, and is, Governor of the State of New Mexico."

What happened was, Captain Hobbs and some cronies, on a mission from Leavenworth, arrived at Santa Fé and went to a big fandango, or informal ball. Well, around midnight, the Mexican men got sore about the attentions to their wives, but the Americans put them out of the hall and locked the door. The Mexicans returned later, with Governor Armijo and a bodyguard, and the Americans admitted the Governor, alone, with every courtesy, then got him drunk as an owl. After this they took care of him as considerate as they would one of their own, laying him out in a bedroom between two women, who'd also drifted off.

When Armijo's wife came and found him thus, there was a rip-roaring commotion. They said she created a disturbance that was heard in the outskirts of Mexico City, and tossed quite a few bottles through a window. She also tried to throw Governor Armijo out of the window, but couldn't lift him—dead weight. It was the principal scandal of the season in Santa Fé.

"What do you want, Hobbs?" said the colonel, quietened down

shrubs and weeds and so flat you seemed to be in the bottom of a bowl. I mean to say, you had the feeling you were looking up at the horizon, around the whole circle. Only gentle little rises, like ocean swells, broke the monotony now and then. No birds sang, and for a long time you never saw a tree. It was awesome. Once in a while, a puff of wind came along, rippling the grass forward in a line; it looked lovely.

I never noticed a landmark, and we had no compass; it was curious how Captain Hobbs made his way. Farther south lay the Santa Fé trail, he said, with faint wagon tracks for a sharp eye, but here not so much as an animal-run showed through the grasses. Once in a while he pulled up on a rise, sniffed at the air, listened, and darted his deep-sunk gray eyes all around, taking in everything, or maybe nothing.

Three times in the first day we walked the horses aside to miss rattlesnakes that lay coiled in the sun, and once, in a shaly, bare place—probably an old creek bed—we spied a whole tangle of them coiled up together, shiny and sluggish and wet-looking. One, alerted, lifted its head above the mass and forked out its tongue in little darting flickers—"tasting the air for danger," as Captain Hobbs said.

In later afternoon, Captain Hobbs stopped, sniffed again, and said, "Water's nigh." The air smelled exactly the same to me, clean and fresh and spicy with flower scent, and I wanted to bet on it, but a mile or so forward, we came on a beautiful clear deep green stream, so we made camp. I grazed and watered Chief, and tied him to a sage bush, but Captain Hobbs produced some iron stakes instead. He made me tether him by the leg, rather than the mouth, and said, "Come thunder or wolf-frights, you'll lose a horse, and a boy afoot here's a boy in a sorry mess."

It was warm even this late, with the sun sinking below the bowl, and we bathed in the stream. I noticed that Captain Hobbs' body, or pelt, as he preferred it, was mostly brown all over, from living like an Indian in the summer, and had a number of odd scars running here and there. "I been punctured some, by arrer, ball and blade," he said, as if in apology. Then he showed me where an arrow had gone in one side and come out the other.

They were different kinds of holes; the one behind had a high welt grown over.

I still had my ham, and Captain Hobbs carried what he called pemmican, which I took to be meat dried and reduced down, but he said we could "vittle handsome on fish." Then he produced some lines tied to bone hooks, about an inch long, and baited these with grasshoppers. It was easy enough here; grasshoppers went winding spring-legged through the weeds everyplace you looked, fat and green and dripping with tobacco juice, if you touched them.

Well, sir, I never got into fishing like that, even in the Missouri sloughs. Swing in a grasshopper, let him sink down, tug back a little, and smack!—you had a trout, brown and speckled and beautiful, coming in on the surface, looking like the whale that swallowed Jonah, mouth open seining water, twisting and churning behind.

When we caught eight, all of them over fifteen inches long, Captain Hobbs stopped and said, "Best leave some lay for the next man. I never yet see good come from hogging game." Then he added, as a sort of lesson—because he kept emphasizing that I was here as a pupil on my "whistle-wetter"—that you could also shoot trout with bow and arrow in water slightly shallower. And he concluded by saying that, in a season of bad famine, he'd taught the Comanches to scoop fish with buffalo hides sewed together and punched full of holes. "We garnered them wholesale—trout, bass and perch—and unwrinkled a power of shrunk bellies. I was a captured prisoner then; it was that got me Old Wolf's daughter. They seemed mortal relieved for the gorge."

We laid into those fish and made up for lost time. On the trail, Captain Hobbs ate mainly at night and in the morning, like an Indian. Among his traps, packed onto Limber Bill, were a skillet, a frying pan, a sheet-iron camp kettle, a coffeepot, a butcher knife, and two tin cups, one of which he'd bought in Leavenworth for me. He had some bacon for use as grease in frying fish, and things worked just fine. Laid out side by side in the pans, those trout sizzled along slow then fell apart, white and firm and moist, and we each of us ate four, though maybe mine were smaller. Besides, we had some greenery that looked like poke, picked by the river bank and boiled in the kettle with bacon. Altogether, it was a meal I'm not apt to forget, and I didn't mind not having bread. Indians don't eat bread; they eat meat almost entirely, but habits vary some from tribe to tribe.

Another article Captain Hobbs handed me was a new rubber poncho, along with an observation about "babes in the wood," but not unkind—nobody could be sarcastic with their stomach *that* full of trout—and we turned in. I was glad of the poncho. When the sun went down, the prairie turned a pinching cold, and then the wolves tuned up. I reckoned those fish would have a new lodging by morning, and was glad I'd enjoyed them earlier. You never heard such a yowling, and dismal? It sounded like a funeral chorus, closing in all the time. I stirred in my blanket, then reached out for my sword, but Captain Hobbs said, very low, "Lay quiet."

Well, in about ten minutes, I made out a circle of green eyes beyond the campfire, and concluded I'd start in on my prayers. I didn't count too strong on finishing—the list was too long for that—but all of a sudden an arm shot out, something flew into the fire, and a blue-green flash zoomed up like a bomb bursting. The smell was so biting and puckery my eyes streamed water, and I started off on a coughing spree. When I calmed down, the circle was gone, and with it the howling as well. "Funny, but I never see a wolf cotton to gunpowder," remarked Captain Hobbs. "They tend to disfavor the stink. That particular group's likely in Chihuahua by now." Then he said good night, so I sank back and went to sleep, drifting up into the stars.

When I awoke, at dawn, I was staring directly into the wide, studying eyes of an Indian as big as a giant. I sprang to my feet, casting around wild, and saw Captain Hobbs washing his face in the stream. The Indian continued to lie there, eyes still watchful, face motionless, but with the rest of him sort of shaking in his blanket.

"Spiebuck's laughing," said Captain Hobbs.

How he got there, I never found out. No matter; he didn't bother me any, but he seemed to think I was funny, confound his gizzard, so I let him alone. He had a horse, a mustang, or Indian range pony, very quick to wheel and turn, and purely tireless; he wasn't apt to slow us up any. He and Captain Hobbs appeared to know each other's minds, you might say, so they exchanged little conversation. What they did was sometimes in English, sometimes in Indian, crackling along, with hand signs to fill the gaps.

Now commenced some days of pretty hard and rapid travel. After two or three—I misrecollect which—we came to another river, with a fine cleared place, full of tidy farms, and this was Spiebuck's Shawnee village. The Shawnees had a reservation near Westport, Missouri, but most preferred to wander as they pleased.

An Indian put us across the river on a crude ferry, and attempted to charge us fifty cents, but Spiebuck laid *that* one to rest with a snort or two.

Well, the first thing we saw, across river, was a miserable, huddled group of darkies these people had captured—run off from slavery, I judged, but back in it now for sure. This particular bunch of Indians hadn't seen black men before, and it appeared to make the Chief mad. He was really sore.

"What kind people these?" he kept demanding of Captain Hobbs. "What black 'em for? What swinge hair for?"

Also, he kept rubbing on the shoulder of a frightened young girl, hoping the black would come off, like soot, but it never did. Finally he got so disgusted he went in his wigwam and sulked, one of the most outrageous old fools I ever encountered.

"I'd buy 'em out," said Captain Hobbs, speaking of the darkies, "but they wouldn't last a week on the trail. They'll settle in here, eventual, but they'll wish they was back home, first."

Before dark came, I wandered around some, and noticed a handsome lass pounding something with a mortar and pestle, sitting cross-legged under a tree. Attached by a deer-hide thong from a limb was a papoose in a bark swing; she reached up now and then and gave him a shove. Marked on the tree were some crazy figures in charcoal. She stared at me, but not friendly, so I said, "Nice weather we're having," trying to hit on something agreeable, when she got up and left. Frankly, I didn't care for the Shawnees, except for Spiebuck, and was happy to leave early the next morning.

In two days, we came out into different country, and in the

far distance, you could make out mountains with snow on the tops. They were new to me, though of course I'd seen pictures. We reined up, and Captain Hobbs drew a kind of sigh. Then he produced a buffalo-horn ring from out of his shirt and placed it on his marriage finger.

He said, "Home soon," Spiebuck grunted, and we jogged on. That night we arrived at a Comanche village which spread all over the valley and hillsides. There must have been twenty thousand people there, and different? Where the Shawnees seemed listless and dull, these Indians were as lively as crickets. Tall men, and likely-looking women, and all full of purpose and bustle.

Captain Hobbs said they were normally much sprightlier, but right now they were tired out from dancing for two months. It was in celebration of some Crow scalps they took, after a big fight in the Rockies. A party had lately got back from Mexico, too, where they'd helped General Taylor fight a battle, and on the way home they killed some Apaches, just to distribute their custom. These Comanches couldn't stand the Mexicans, but they cared about as little for Texans; I never found out why.

Well, we trotted on up a hillside to where a tall white skin lodge was standing apart from the others, with spidery decorations of skinny-legged deer and such on it, and a beautiful young woman, or girl, was tending a hard-baked clay kettle in front. Her skin was light tan, smooth and creamy, she had shiny black hair cut short to her shoulders, very silky eyelashes, a slender figure that sort of swelled out, like Angelina Hughes though not so saucy and bold, and a shy, kind look. She was dressed all in soft, fringed doeskin—clean, not grease-stained and ragged like some, a girdle caught tight around her waist, moccasins with polecat tails dragging behind on the ground, and leathern leggings. On one finger was a buffalo-horn ring identical to Captain Hobbs'.

It was hard to believe. She couldn't have been much over twenty; he must have married her when she was twelve, or maybe eight or nine. He said, "Hello, old girl," and gave her a stinging slap on the seat. Her face lit up, but she refrained from all that soupy business of white people hugging and kissing. About then, two small boys, say four and six, ran out and fastened onto Captain Hobbs' legs. He swung them up, one in each arm, and gave *them* a hug.

"Spotted Fawn," he told me, indicating his wife, and for the boys, "Jim Tom and Joe Fred—her choice; she wanted them outright white. They've got Comanche names as well, but it's a mouthful unless you're broke in and accustomed."

He took several yards of red silk from the pack for his wife, and gleaming new Barlow knives for the boys. They wriggled free and, when they found out how the blades opened, went to work on the lodge poles. I figured they'd have it down by nightfall. Nobody restrained them; the truth is, Indians seldom balk children. The grownups aren't troubled by nerves, and everything seems free and easy. It makes for interesting living. I was dozing one day when Joe Tom or Fred Jim or one of those combinations dropped a green mushmelon on my head from a tree limb. I jumped up and grabbed a skillet, planning to shake him down and fracture his skull, but everybody only laughed. They admired him for thinking it up.

When we arrived, I was on fire to tackle the contents of that pot, and so was Spiebuck, who stood six feet four and required considerable fodder to keep him in operation. But no, we had to attend the Chief, and report. It was their natural system, like the women kneeling to the sun at twilight and men doing the same in the morning.

It was nonsensical. We all sat around in a circle, as solemn as church, passing a smelly old pipe from hand to hand, while Captain Hobbs recounted his travels and mine. It was partly in English, but mainly in Comanche. In the English parts, Captain Hobbs permitted himself a few stretchers, for he never could stay serious *that* long, and said, "After selling the furs, I went to Washington by steamboat and called on the President. He requested my opinion about the war."

Every few sentences the Chief verified things from Spiebuck and then by me. It was their habit with all trips; each traveler spoke up to nail down accuracy.

We were on pretty thin ice about half of the time. Spiebuck only nodded, with what appeared to me like his laughing look, but I usually said, "Absolutely. He's hit it right on the nose. I'd take an affadavit."

Finally, I could see I was getting too frolicsome, for Captain Hobbs eased up on the lies. By and by, they let us go, so we went home and laid into supper.

We had a stew of turkey, grizzly bear, beaver tails and buffalo, all cooked tender in the clay pot. Captain Hobbs told me what each piece was, and said beaver tails were a great delicacy. Along with them, Mrs. Spotted Fawn Hobbs served us mush made out of acorns that the women gather each Fall and pulverize down to meal in a stone mortar. It was a ripping good meal, on top of our victuals of the trail, and afterwards, Spiebuck crawled into the wigwam and went to sleep. He was the easiest fellow to drift off that ever was, and the alertest when awake.

We all slept in the lodge; there was room enough for a dozen. What with all the robes and skins, and a small fire on a raised-earth box in the center, it was very comfortable. I kicked free of Jim Tom, who had commenced whittling on my right big toe, and cuffed Joe Fred on the sly when he brought a firebrand into bed to show me. After that, the night was peaceful, and you could see stars out of the hole at the top. Captain and Mrs. Hobbs slept under a monster buffalo robe, and seemed glad to see each other.

Next morning, four white trappers rode into camp, on the opposite side of the village. Some braves came and got us. Two of the men had been wounded in a fight with Sioux armed with rifles. One had a smashed upper arm, and the other's foot was turned around sort of backwards. He was delirious, and mortification had set in.

When we got there, the medicine men were preparing to amputate. It was the only thing to do; Captain Hobbs said so himself, but he acknowledged that the methods were "barbarious." He cut two short, thick sticks of very soft wood, for the victims' teeth to clamp down on, and the head surgeon set to work with a butcher knife and a snaggly-toothed saw made out of hoop-iron.

He tackled the smashed arm first, and sort of haggled it off. The trapper groaned and kicked some, but made no great fuss, either, considering his situation. At the end, the surgeon tossed the arm to a bunch of dogs that were sitting nearby, looking hopeful, and then sealed the stump with a white-hot iron. Afterwards, the squaws bound it up with a poultice made of pulverized bark from something like slippery elm.

They had a tougher nut with the foot case; that shinbone was stubborn. In the middle of everything, it was necessary to withdraw the saw and then sharpen and grease it. Altogether, this second operation took more than an hour, and would have been a grisly trial to the trapper, but they found out he was dead—died well toward the beginning, Captain Hobbs figured. A man named Bill.

Well, in two days, the other fellow was up and around, practically as chipper as ever. He was a hard nut, all bone and sinew, and weighed little more than a bobcat. These Indians had healing skills, all right, and had been feeding him deer livers to rebuild his blood.

All three came to supper that night, and naturally the talk turned to Bill.

"No man could ask a stauncher sidekick," said the fellow with the sawed-off arm, helping himself to more stew. "It's hard to think of him laying dead! With my own two eyes, I see him offer a rifle to a grizzly, to even up the odds."

"I've knowed Bill for twenty year," said another. "He was white clean through, inside and out, up, down and sideways. What's more, I'd repeat that in court."

The third fellow, shaking his head thoughtful and sad, said, "Bill handed me his last stick of tobaccer oncet, up toward the Dakoties." He thought a little more, and said, "His mouth had a running abscess sore in it. Chawing done that to him, always."

They ate a while, then one said, "As sweet-natered as he was, and he *was* noble—I'll fight the man that gainsays it—you'd best keep an eye on him with the Counting. I never met his match at outshuffling you with skins. It was his way, and I hope the blessed Almighty views it lenient, for I'll tell you candid and frank—I do. *I don't hold grudges!* I think you'll bear me out on that. Mose? Turk?"

They both did; they said he never held grudges, and one of

them asked, "Didn't Bill switch off and leave a young wife and daughter destitute and starving in Indianer?"

"He done it and bragged about it."

"Well, it's the first I heard," said the man that never bore grudges. "I'll own up being jarred, and it supports what I've always claimed—don't judge a man till the evidence is racked up complete."

"Oh, there's a good deal I could tell you about Bill."

"But none of it good, unless I ain't had my eyes open lately."

"A meaner hound never lived," said the man with the sawed-off arm, and they agreed that it was probably all for the best.

We ate more of the stew, and Captain Hobbs said, "How old was he, give or take a few years?"

"Why, if I was pinned down and shook, I'd make him in the neighborhood of forty."

"It seems odd he'd be so tough," said Captain Hobbs, spearing a hunk of meat with his knife. "There isn't hardly any fat on him at all."

"Wait a minute!" cried the man that didn't hold grudges, scrambling back from the fire.

"You mean—"

"By God, for two cents I'd—" and they all got out of there quick. I heard one of them hawking up what he thought was part of Bill, over by the trees, and another said something about a "dirty, low-down, Injun-loving squaw man."

Spiebuck was rolling around on the ground hanging onto his belly.

"No sir, if you're searching for true-blue companions of the trail, steadfast in fair weather or foul, there goes a bokay of roses," remarked Captain Hobbs, and we turned in for the night.

I thought we'd seen the last of those fellows, but the next afternoon, here they came, seeming a trifle sour, but after something, too. What it was, they'd noticed a tolerable group of dogs skulking about our place—dogs were everywhere you looked, over the whole Comanche camp—and they wished to acquire one.

"We lost ourn," said the man with the sawed-off arm, "in that tanglefoot with the Sioux, drat their durn red hides—begging your pardon, ma'am [this to Mrs. Spotted Fawn, very courtly and gracious]. We aped it and left him behind. It's useless to try and turn grizzlies without'n you have a bar dog. We thought you might offer one for purchase. Cheap."

Captain Hobbs thought a bit, frowning, then said, "Why, no, there's none here that I'd recommend—no, it wouldn't do—I couldn't bring myself to release him. Forget it."

"Which one was that?" asked the man that didn't hold grudges, glancing suspicious at our pack, and they *were* about the sickliest collection alive, skinny and low and disinclined to look you straight in the eye.

"I'd sooner peddle one of the boys," said Captain Hobbs. "Times past, I've watched him tuck into a grizzly and run it down to skin and bone. It's his only fault, if you're searching for bacon or oil. There simply ain't any left."

"I'd rather see it than hear you tell about it."

"Normally, I avoid to bring it up; I don't want him stole."

"Which one? What's it go by?"

"Grinder," said Captain Hobbs, and picked up a scrawny white mongrel from amongst the others.

"What! *Him?*"

"Stand back, get a little out of range. He'll have to be broke in slow, else you'll lose a hand for sure."

"See here, mister, I know a little something about bar dogs, and a bar dog's got a square stern. This specimen's as narrow as a schoolgirl."

Captain Hobbs chuckled. "Fool you, won't it? You see those two knobs hanging down betwixt his hind legs? Those are adjustable nuts. Right now, he's adjusted for rabbit."

Well, the man that didn't hold grudges threw down his coonskin cap and stamped on it, they all cussed considerable, and then they trooped off, pretty hot under the collar.

After this, they didn't come back.

VII

STARTING EARLY the next morning, we took a two-day trip to where thousands and thousands of buffalo grazed, moving slowly north. The countryside was covered with thick black smears for as far as the eye could see.

Captain Hobbs and Spiebuck taught me how to ride up close to a fat galloping bull and bring him down by touching the gun to his shoulder. Hit at random, from any distance, they seldom fall, with rifles of less than fifty caliber, but you can kill them even with pistols or bows and arrows up close. Also, shot directly in their shaggy heads, the ball only bounces harmlessly off.

We slaughtered as many as two dozen, then cut away their tongues and "fleeces"—large cakes from the back and sides—and toted these home on pack ponies. It seemed like an awful waste, but Captain Hobbs said other members of the tribe could come and gather the remainders, or what the wolves failed to get.

In the Fall, when the herds turned south, the Comanches laid for them near a high precipice of the Little Red River. On horseback, armed with bows and arrows, the Indians panicked the buffalo and drove hundreds over the cliff. Then everybody, squaws included, skinned them, cut up the meat in strips, and salted it with salt from natural salt springs of the neighborhood. They dried it in twists, with a streak of fat and lean stuck together, and bundled it into square bales for packing.

The women scraped the hides with an elk or deer rib-bone, and dressed them with buffalo brains. Commonly, a number of deer, elk and antelope sailed over the cliff in the drive, poor things, and both meat and skins from these were preserved in exactly the same way. The buckskin was prepared so clever for clothing that even wetting never stiffened it. It was as soft as thistledown, pleasing to the touch.

My clothes being ragged from getting brier-scratched, Mrs. Spotted Fawn Hobbs made me a suit of beautiful buckskins with a fringe—slapped it up overnight, almost—and gave me two pairs of moccasins beaded all around by shells picked from a stream bed. It was a handsome gift, and all I could offer in return was my sword, which she declined.

I'd changed appearance; they all said so, and even I could see it. I had slimmed and hardened down, and my face was the color of hickory. And eat? I don't remember not being hungry, any time of the day. I ate enough meat to keep a family of bears on the move.

In the following week, Captain Hobbs increased my lessons, because he said the time was near for the return to Leavenworth. It was along toward late May, now, of a bright, sunny season, the air dry and crisp here near the foothills of the Rockies. I thought about home some, and practically arranged to start a letter, to be carried by Indians headed for Bent's Fort, but I got sidetracked off into doing something else.

Comanches journeyed to the Fort to trade ponies, deer and other skins, and buffalo robes for tobacco, and beads, calico, flannel, knives, spoons, and jew's-harps. They were champion performers on the jew's-harp, confoundedest racket ever heard. It was enough to turn a person against music.

I learned so many things, my head begun to ache from the weight it was carrying. Dr. Hutchins' school would have been mild by comparison.

One day we were out near a ravine when a grizzly exploded out of cover and headed right at me, and me afoot at the time. I scuttled down into the gulch, but Spiebuck, nearby, whipped up his rifle and shot, and Captain Hobbs let out a yell to freeze your blood. He cried, "Get yore —— out of that draw!"

I scrabbled back up, and the grizzly swerved aside. He was hit, but not bad, and he kept biting at the wound as he humped on around a curve out of sight. Spiebuck's rifle had "flirted out of its stock," as they said.

It was the only time I ever saw Captain Hobbs mad. Or heard him use an oath. He bawled me out about as brisk as possible, and said, "Boy, don't never let a grizzly get you on the downhill side of a ravine. Keep to the rise of him, else he'll kill you sure. Truth to tell, I just about lost me a 'prentice." He was sweating again, so I reckoned it must have been close. I wasn't feeling particularly brash myself; my stomach appeared out of whack, and my legs wobbled kind of rubbery, so I sat down. And the rest of that day, I just listened, without adding any curlicues of my own.

Spiebuck gave me a bow and a buckskin quiver full of arrows, and taught me to shoot it, then Captain Hobbs persuaded the Chief to let me join the war games—for boys of fifteen and younger. I'd sooner been left out. It's one thing to play a game where you beat somebody once in a while, but I came out last every time. Those Indians had shot bows and arrows since the walking stage, and I'd been at it for only three days.

What happened was, they sewed two wolfskins together, very precise, to look like a man, and stretched them taut over a bush. Then you mounted up oh, say, three or four hundred yards back and galloped down on the figure at full speed. At the last second, veer off sharp, heave your body aside toward the skins, catching yourself with one heel against the rear flank of the saddle, and then shoot, bending low.

Sound easy? Well, on about every other run, I heaved right on out, missing with my heel, and lit in the middle of the skins. And those miserable Comanches had the rotten bad taste to complain about me "tearem up" their target. They took on even worse when I made a beautiful run, veered on schedule, heaved out but joggled the bow slightly and shot one of the judges named Trotting Elk in the thigh. I tried to soothe them down, apologized, and suggested that the judge could change his name to Limping Elk, but they howled me right out of business, looking ugly.

By and by, I improved some, but you take it all in all, I was left in worse shape than the wolfskins.

Captain Hobbs said the exercise was a wonderful toughener; he'd done it often when he was young, but now he'd grown past the learning phase, and he thanked God for it. A remark like that didn't deserve an answer, so I walked on off, but not easy.

Shortly before the tribe headed out for its meeting with the Arapahoes and Cheyennes, the braves practiced maneuvers with mirrors. Every man there had a piece of mirror attached to his shield. Mirrors were the main reason why this bunch was so successful in battle. Right now, they reflected sun glints into the eyes of buffaloes, finally causing a rouser of a stampede, and Captain Hobbs said they usually confused an enemy so bad he couldn't shoot straight. If the tribe had its say, they fought only on sunny days. A Comanche would trade a pony for a small piece of looking glass, but most mirrors were lifted out of frontier homes that these fellows raided in Mexico.

Well, sir, I thought I had ducked schooling, but Captain Hobbs took a set at me now on the subject of navigation. He practically wore me down to a nub. He produced an ignorant-looking map, with rivers and mountains and other objects on it, and made me memorize the whole tiresome lot. Then we worked on the position of the sun; not only now but at all seasons. And after that, we tackled the stars. This was the crusher. At one point, I drew out. I said, "I don't *want* to know where I am. I don't even care where I've been. And I'm *going* to Mexico with a troop of soldiers. Let *them* worry about it."

"Orion," said Captain Hobbs, pointing to several bodies that looked like all the rest, "comes useful when pinning down the line of northwest and southeast. You'll note that the three small stars inside the four main ones—Orion's Belt—"

"Certainly. There's nothing to it."

"—lie in the northwest-southeast direction. I'm glad you noted it, son, for it'll be a consolation to you later. Now, the one you'll tangle with most is the North Star, or Polaris—*not* down that way, my boy; that's south—right *there*. Got it? Good. And *how* did you get it, we'll ask. Why you drawed a bead on it from the two outside stars of the Dipper. They point it out perfectly—"

I let him moon on. He was kind of touched on the subject, and I have no idea where he learned it. He mentioned a number more, including Vega, which he claimed shone blue; Capella, that shone yellow; and Mars, that shone red, which I doubted, along with others. He mentioned an Irish star, important in navigation —Cassie O'Peia—which fixed a line to something or other; I wasn't paying attention very close. However, it did little harm to humor him, and I hadn't the least notion but what he meant well. So I nodded, and "um-hummed," and said it was mighty interesting all around.

After that, we passed on to other matters: how the moss grew on trees, what kind of growth was found in different spots of the map, which directions the streams flowed, the nature of soil, and even what sort of rocks were lying here and there. We covered everything, plus a little, including putting a stick upright in the ground, marking were the sun-shadow lay, then waiting half an hour and making another mark. That done, a line passed from one mark to the other was east and west. So they said.

I never met a fellow so hipped on geography. And him with so much to choose from. It was boring.

And then, all of a sudden, the Comanche camp came alive. It was the Spring "moving time." Down came the lodges, poles were strapped alongside horses (and even dogs) to make litters for dragging gear, the squaws hefted papoose baskets to be held on their backs by headbands, the braves took up a protecting file on either side, and a whole town of twenty thousand souls was emptied out in a twinkling. Nothing remained but a parade ground of trash.

I started to mount Chief, when we had all our plunder packed, and said, "Well, that does it as far as I can see. We're ready to tramp."

Captain Hobbs stuck out his paw.

"Now don't forget what you've learned, Sam. Above all, keep cool. You won't have a particle of trouble. It's all laid out on the map, and the stars will furnish directions."

"That's a pretty good joke. Now let's get along to meet the Arapahoes and the Cheyennes."

"I and Spiebuck will catch you up later, might be in Santa Fé.

Keep the stream on your left hand for the whole first day. You get a nice start thataway."

"You mean *me, alone,* to *Leavenworth?*" I was practically sputtering. I looked at Mrs. Spotted Fawn, who seemed concerned, but silent, after a glance at her husband, and then at Spiebuck, who wasn't laughing any more.

"Time comes when a bird has to wing-hop out of the nest," said Captain Hobbs, with his face as hard as flint. "Besides which, you was a master hand at the lessons, son. The best of luck to you."

He swung up on Limber Bill, pointed to the north, and cried, "Let her go! Fall in and don't straggle."

I stood staring, too choked up with rage to answer. I'd had a feeling all along there was something wrong with this fellow—I just remembered it—and now I knew: he was a monster.

But I hadn't any urge to shove in where I wasn't wanted, either. So I took stock and prepared to head out, calculating that I'd meet up with him again sometime and kill him.

Captain Hobbs had given me a spruce little rifle, short in the barrel but powerful, plus two hundred bullets; also, I had my bow and arrows, a copy of the map, my stout new suit of buckskins, with two pairs of moccasins, as well as a wolfskin cap I'd found hanging on a line. And that evening when I camped by the river, I discovered they'd added an extra sack of gunpowder, some cooking utensils, and other necessaries. I was tempted to throw them away, but refrained.

It was cold, not sleeping under a buffalo robe, but I made out all right, and no wolves called. Captain Hobbs had told me several ways to keep warm, sleeping, but I'd forgot them. Up early and off along the same trail, but before long the stream broke into five or six small branches, and I was stuck. I sat down to puzzle it out. Says I, the sun rises in the east and sets in the west; I remembered *that* much, but now it was directly overhead, so I had to wait. I could have thrust the stick down, to make things exact, but I couldn't call to mind how it worked.

By and by, the sun slid off a few notches, and I studied the map, then struck off southeast on Chief. Frankly, I was smiling inside. I couldn't think of anything more pleasurable than to show that old buzzard up. I could scarcely wait to ride into Leavenworth.

But two mornings later it was raining. No sun shone down to help me forward. Still, I was far from disturbed. The prairie country was close at hand, now, and I just *felt* the right direction. Instinct *is* a wonderful gift, worth more than forty lessons by know-it-alls like Hobbs.

So I followed my instinct and headed off through the rain toward Leavenworth. Thanks to my poncho, I stayed pretty dry, and my packs as well. No animals, few birds, not a thing to be seen except low trees and brush; a stream now and then; a shaley gully; a little brushy hillock; once, the tag ends of an old, old camp.

I kept on straight like that, using my instinct, and happy, when out of nowhere, in midafternoon or thereabouts, I hit some horse tracks. Fresh, too; there were smoky droppings to prove it. Well, sir, I was anything but scared, because I had my gun, there was no cover anywhere for hostiles to make ambush, and my instinct was working so well I was *glad* the sun stayed hid.

Out of curiosity, I dismounted, holding on tight to the bridle, and examined the tracks. I can't help but admit that I received a stunner. The left front shoe mark had a missing nailhead. Tightened up a little, I looked at Chief's feet, then leaned against the horse for a breather. Those tracks were our own; I'd been traveling in a wide circle, instinct or no instinct.

Nothing for it but to make camp, and dismal wet at that. I needed a fire but misrecollected that particular part of Captain Hobbs' lessons, drat him. I remembered him talking about rain and wet wood, but I was waylaid by something important at the time. So I fed Chief, adding two handfuls of grain to the crinkly grass hereabouts, and turned in. Captain Hobbs had mentioned an area of dry, crinkly grass, but he failed to make it clear.

Well, late in the night—it must have been two or three in the morning—I snapped awake. The rain had stopped, and the stars were shining. I knew my troubles were over now, on account of the navigation. But when I tried to sort things out, they got all swapped around. There were a number of names, including

Orion's Belt, which pointed out something or other, but the rest of the information was blurred.

If Captain Hobbs had been handy, I'd a shot him. A man that isn't any better teacher than what he was has no business sticking his nose in. Such people ought to be licensed, like steamboat pilots, to keep out the trash.

Total loss. I gave it up and went back to bed, and in the morning it was raining again. Within three or four hours, I came to a stream, thanks to goodness, so I studied the map. It was the first time I'd really seen it. The objects were very hard to make out, being hand-drawn, and what was the reason?—Captain Hobbs again. He should have had sense enough to explain it several times, and pound it in right down the line.

Still, all the streams appeared to run southeast, except one, so I prepared to cross. Because of the rain, this creek had swoll up considerable, and Chief began to sink, right out in the middle. Then I remembered: Captain Hobbs had talked about the "June freshets," and storms, and told how the streams have beds of quicksand in deep spots. You were supposed to take a stick and feel your way in high water. Or, better, put down stakes.

I splashed overboard in a jiffy, swam to the bank, holding the bridle, braced my feet, and commenced to pull. Nothing gave, not an inch. I needed stouter purchase; then I remembered a piece of rope, a *lazo*, used by Mexicans, that I'd tied around my pack.

Swim back, fumble under water for the rope, yank it off in a fit of impatience, because there *was* need to hurry—and then, by Jupiter, I knocked my rifle out of its scabbard and lost it. I almost took a dive for it, but Chief was still sinking, also neighing, now, very loud and pitiful, as well as thrashing around, which didn't help, so I tied the rope to his neck, struck out for shore again, and looped the other end around a bush. It pulled out, roots and all, and a blessed lot of mud I got in the face, so I tried another. This one held.

Now I had him stopped. But I couldn't gain any. I looped the rope round and round the bush, then knotted it tight, and swam back. Chief's head was out of water, and that was all. He looked at me very accusing out of panicked liquid eyes, with the veiny whites showing and his nostrils opening and closing, and I got behind him to push. You could have shoved a church down the street easier. Then I had an idea, and out with my knife. It sounds cruel, but I stabbed him sharp in the rump. He started, and jerked forward. I did it again: same result. I must have stabbed him as many as two dozen times before he fell on his knees in a rocky shallow; then we were free.

I lay down on my back—dead beat—and checked up again: rifle gone, fire-making ended, gunpowder ruined, pemmican soggy, blankets soaked, map coming to pieces, and horse injured. And still it rained; no sign of a pause.

We went on, me leading Chief till he got his strength back. By the next night, we'd entered the prairie, don't ask me how, and the sun shone off and on. But I was lightheaded, not really up to anything but plodding forward. The rain had long since stopped, the country was completely changed, and I begun to have trouble finding water. I recalled Captain Hobbs' warning about "water-scrapes," and what to do about it, including certain plants that stored water up, but the details were fuzzy in my mind.

The next night, totally parched, we stopped, and I tied Chief's bridle to a clump of brush, not bothering to get out the iron peg. I lay there panting for a drink, my mouth so dry it became a torture to swallow, while Chief kept up a complainy whinnying and stamping of his feet. I reckoned we'd both be dead by the following day, especially if the sun shone hot. Some time after dark, it came on to lightning and to blow, and I never saw a worse storm. The wind was screeching so loud I couldn't hear the horse any more. A howler of a gust tore my poncho off, and I legged after it, caught it, too, but before I got back, hailstones were falling as big as hen's eggs. Doubling up, I held my arms over my head, but Chief yanked his rope free and galloped across the prairie in a fright.

I felt too miserable to care. When the rain commenced to pour down—in buckets; the sky just emptied out—I stood with my head back, drinking it in, and when it stopped, I wrung out the leaves on bushes, holding my mouth underneath, I couldn't get enough, somehow.

No sun the next morning. For as far as you could see—nothing but prairie, the same bowl-like sea of high grass, flowers, and runty growth. I couldn't stand the sight of it. One direction looked exactly like another, and I hadn't got a horse any more.

In the first hour I had three rattlesnake scares. My blankets and poncho weighed heavy on my back, and I got hungrier and hungrier. When I got reduced low enough, I drank some muddy water out of a gully, then sat down to think. I was supposed to catch fish and shoot game, but I hadn't any hooks, now, nor a rifle or a bow.

Dim, way off in a distance, I remembered Captain Hobbs talking about roots and berries, and I found some berries and ate them, but they made me sick. I threw up over and over, till I had the dry heaves and nothing spewed out but green bile. And after that, nothing at all. I was too weak to walk, so I rolled up in the blankets and slept. In the night I felt hot and flushed, and once I thought I heard wolves. It was all right; they could have what was left. Then I had a lovely dream: a campfire blazed up within a few feet of my head, a bluish flash of gunpowder burst out, I smelled the nice, dry, puckery smell, and soon the wolves and my troubles all seemed to vanish, because Captain Hobbs had arrived to take things in hand. You could sleep with a dream like that, even in my situation.

I woke slowly, watching the fire. A green-twig spit straddled it, and a thick steak of red meat hung from the spit, dripping juice down and causing the flames to crackle and flare up. Spiebuck sat to one side, looking my way, neither laughing nor not laughing, and Captain Hobbs gazed at me as level and cool and deep-sunk and bumptious as always. Not far behind, Chief grazed, tethered by one foot to an iron peg.

"Morning, Sam," said Captain Hobbs. "It looks like it might come up prime, after all that rain."

I struggled up to sit, all muscles crying, but he said, "I wouldn't try to roust out just yet; slack up and take stock. I don't know a finer way of replacing the spunk than to chomp down on a slab of fresh-killed deer."

For a second, I had to fight off the tears, but I swallowed it and sat up farther.

"Was there something you wanted to say, son?"

I said, "Yes. Hand me a piece of that meat, and afterwards, if you don't mind, we'll get back down to brass tacks on Orion."

Captain Hobbs sighed. "I suppose that's why I took the trouble. As alike as two left shoes. All right, Sam. Your whistle-wetter's over."

VIII

"The Narrows," *July 3, 1846:* I begin my informal Journal here at the intersection of our route (that of General Kearny's Expeditionary Force to Mexico) with the merchant caravan trail from Independence to Santa Fé—the "Santa Fé Trail."

It has been agreed with Alex Doniphan that I keep a personal account of Missouri's part in this regrettable war, and, afterward, when official reports of possible battles may be completed, embark on a fuller and more austere history of the campaign.

To touch, first, on the least if most troublesome facet of Missouri's effort, I must mention that my scapegrace brother, Sam, has had his way, in general, and is presently attached to the Drum-and-Fife Corps. This represents a compromise. Certainly he did *not,* as he requested, obtain a commission (at the age of fourteen), his argument having been based on some dark and all-embracing tutelage received from a pair of conspicuously dubious-looking drifters, one of these an Indian. Indeed, the boy was very nearly sent home, at my suggestion, as a result of his delinquency during the past few weeks. To bring this odious subject quickly up to date, a county-wide search was instituted after his disappearance from our home of Riverbend, near Liberty. A so-called Letter of Farewell, found in his room, was dismissed by his father as being "the work of a lunatic"; the best brains concurred that he was probably hiding in the woods nearby, playing soldier.

It must be confessed that the child was grievously underestimated. *This had happened several times before.*

On June 6, when I reported in to Fort Leavenworth, ready to join my colleagues of the Missouri Volunteer Regiment (then forming), I found myself walking my horse across the close-cropped grass, near the blockhouse, when there fell into the range of my vision a slight figure in an offensively alien costume topped by a species of wolfskin cap, or wig. By his side was a stringy, middle-aged man of frontier mien, and beside *him* was something outsized in Indians. Altogether, the demeanor of this trio was furtive, if not conspiratorial.

"Go for a trader," I heard the white man say. "It's the next best thing, now they've cut off the bounty on Apaches. It's hard. Let a man build up a nice, good-paying business, and a war comes along and knocks it all down. The Governor of Chihuahua paid *cash.*"

Having uttered this intensely patriotic message, he lit a coal-black cigar.

I stepped forward and said, "All greetings to you, Sam. And from your mother and father as well."

He had the good grace to start and look sheepish. Then, recovering, he assumed his normally brassy manner.

"Well, now, I *thought* you'd be turning up. How's everybody at home? How's Ma?"

"Enjoying complete peace of mind, of course."

"They found my letter?"

"Masterly."

"A thing like that isn't easy to write. It *reads* easy, but try to do it sometime."

"I don't believe I've met your, er, associates."

He introduced the white man as "Captain" Hobbs, or Dobbs, and the Indian, mystifyingly, as one "Spewack." To the best of my knowledge, Spewack is a Jewish name, and I'd never heard of a tribe of Jewish Indians, at least in this locality.

"If Captain Dobbs and Mr. Spewack will excuse us, I think the time's come for a family conference."

"Spie*buck,*" the boy replied, and we retired to a couple of empty boxes, not far distant.

To summarize, my brother was residing, as paid lodger ($1.50 per week), at the home of a sergeant's widow, by orders of the post commander, a man of breeding and divination. The barracks were closed to all but sworn-in military personnel; Dobbs and Spewack camped—filthily, I imagined—outside of the southward wall.

In the next few days, despite my vigilance, the boy made himself available to the Drum-and-Fife Corps, which was scraping the bottom of the barrel for talent. He had obtained a child's drum from a peddler and ingratiated himself with a group of unmusical sentimentalists. They gave him a strong recommendation, on the ground that it might be "good luck to adopt a mascot so young and tender." The case of George Rogers Clark's drummer was recited in reference. I offer an objective guess that they will spend the rest of the war repenting their impetuous act.

In any case, after consultations with Doniphan, I consented to what was, after all, my original plan.

As to the excitement and bustle of enlistment, the eight companies of Missouri's Volunteer Regiment began to appear at Leavenworth on June 5, and were lettered in the order of their arrival. Over-all command of this "Army of the West" has fallen to Brigadier General Stephen W. Kearny, of the Regular Army's First Dragoons. His force, aside from the 850-odd men of the Volunteers, will include a battalion of light artillery, from St. Louis, whose field officer is Major M. Lewis Clark, son of the famous scout; a battalion of infantry; and the Laclede Rangers, attached to the First Dragoons. Thus General Kearny's total strength for his assault upon Santa Fé is 1658 men plus sixteen pieces of ordnance—twelve six-pounders and four twelve-pound howitzers.

This would seem to be a modest complement for what, at this moment, is intended as one of the three main thrusts of the northern war, the others being General Taylor's "Army of Occupation"—organized "to penetrate directly into the heart of the country"—and the column, under Brigadier General Wool, that is mustered to proceed against the city of Chihuahua.

Heavy or light in number, the men at Leavenworth are in high spirits. To use a phrase in good military standing, "they're full of beans and their tails are high."

The training of the Volunteers having been assigned to the First Dragoons, we were ordered out for drill twice a day (in the most gentlemanly and courteous style). It consisted of the march by fours, the saber manual, the charge, the rally, and other cavalry tactics. I should have said that, after careful study of the army's assignment, General Kearny elected to make the force, except for one battalion, a unit of mounted riflemen. Accordingly, our horses were evaluated, by a Captain Allen of the First Dragoons, at what many Missouri men regarded as a beggarly sum. There was much grumbling. My own stallion, Dancer, an expensive thoroughbred with blue-grass Kentucky blood lines, was accepted at a price of ten dollars. It makes little difference that I can see. *We have not gone to war for money.*

However, I should be journalistically remiss if I failed to relate that my brother Sam's mongrel pinto was set down as worth fifty cents, on the basis that such animals run wild for the taking on the plains, and that he lodged a formal protest, in triplicate, with General Ward, of Platte, the temporary commandant of the Fort. As far as I can determine, it was rejected out of hand.

Our training ensued for twenty days, the locale having been a prairie, at a short distance from the southward wall, which was named "Campus Martius" by the sufferers thereon. I can think of no better way to become acquainted with one's physical condition than to undergo an enforced and prolonged military drill. A good number among us, myself not excepted, were white-faced and panting in the early days, and there were casualties. The horses of two men were refused as being too clumsy for the wheel and charge; one man, a John Muller, angrily dropped out from exhaustion; another was dismissed for reasons of stature (he stood scarcely over five feet high); and a third was relieved because of a wretchedly aggravated hernia. The poor fellow was incapable even of walking, until Dobbs and Spewack, my kinsman's accomplices, trussed him up with a complicated (and perhaps, in the long run, injurious) system of buckskin pads and thongs. (The latter pair, by the way, have outfitted a wagon and will set out as traders, much as they've done before. They should bear watching. Sam, as might be expected, obtained his exemption from drill—he was "practicing" with the Drum-and-Fife Corps; two elderly whiskerandos, my brother, and a half-wit whilom fiddler. Musically, very little is expected by anybody from this graceless and incongruous unit.)

On the eighteenth of June, with all companies reported in, an election was held which resulted in the selection of Alexander William Doniphan, a private in the company from Clay County, as Colonel of the Regiment. Alex Doniphan's popularity in Missouri, his brilliance as a lawyer, his powers as orator, his all-around civic service, and, of prime importance, his military conduct of the 1838 Mormon uprising were such that he was virtually unopposed.

The election was of more importance than met the eye, it having been decided by General Kearny that, in the event of his death or disability, over-all command of the expedition should fall to the Volunteer Regiment's colonel.

As for me, I have steadfastly declined to take on the responsibilities of a commission. On the evening of Doniphan's election, he called me for conference into his makeshift "headquarters"—a rude room at one corner of the Fort, furnished with a hewn-oak table, two or three rickety chairs, a lamp, a spittoon, and the inevitable American flag (this one in a bad state of disrepair) hanging askew on the rear wall.

(Henceforward in these pages, I shall have a good deal to say about the informality of the First Regiment Missouri Mounted Volunteers. Indeed, its departures from military custom will, I suspect, become a conversational highlight of the Mexican War. Alex Doniphan's anxiety about protocol and Regular Army procedure amounts to, roughly, zero.)

I found him seated in a tilted-back chair, his feet on the table. His hat rested on the floor at his side. At the moment of my entrance, he was engaged in whittling his initials on the table rim. An orderly sprawled half asleep on the narrow porch outside.

"It gets lonesome around here," said the colonel, putting up his knife and waving me to a chair. "They tell me you don't want to be an officer."

"That is correct. For one thing, I have no great enthusiasm for this war. Or any war. For another, I don't fancy myself as a leader of men. I appear to lack that cornerstone of masculine success—the inflated ego."

"It may come later. Anything else?"

"Yes, I prefer to keep myself detached for the purpose of recording a Journal."

"With your education, you probably ought to be something," he mused, looking slightly worried. "They're bound to bring it up sooner or later. Would you consider achieving corporalhood?"

"What does it involve?"

"Potentially, the rank is a man-killer. If General Kearny should fall, and then me, and after that Lieutenant Colonel Ruff and Major Gilpin, along with"—picking up a paper—"company Captains Waldo, Walton, Moss, Reid, Stephenson, Parsons, Jackson, and Rodgers, as well as the Regular Army officers and some others, you would find yourself in full charge.

"Mainly, it would involve sewing corporal's bars on your left sleeve," he concluded briskly.

"All right."

"In one way, this leaves you in a position of advantage."

"How's that?"

"In the matter of laundresses. The regulations state that a certain number of laundresses will accompany the expedition. These are to be, in the main, the wives of non-commissioned officers. Confidentially, I understand that a few 'nominal' wives will be tolerated. Does this aspect of the struggle interest you?"

"I prefer laundering my own clothes to dragging along some shrewish Kate to make camp life even more miserable."

"Well, I thought I'd mention it. You may wish to change your mind."

"Never."

As equipment arrived by steamboat, we were issued similar saddles of Spanish design; they were skeletons only, consisting of a tree with girth and stirrup attached, the motive being to save wear and tear on one's horse. Each man was issued two Mackinaw blankets, to be used beneath the saddle on the march and for beds at night. A stout leathern waist belt that supported a butcher knife, a pistol, a saber (which latter proved a great annoyance to everyone), a carbine, a half-gallon India-rubber canteen, and saddlebags constituted the bulk of our gear. Our tents and cooking utensils were to be packed in government wagons that would accompany the troops in pairs, carrying eighteen days' supply of food. Larger commissary wagons in groups of twenty-five or thirty were to be started at intervals along the route. The drivers of these would be well armed, to account for themselves if they fell behind and were attacked.

The day of departure nearing, Fort Leavenworth quickened to a fiesta mood. The scene was one to stir the emotions, no matter how one felt about war. Members of the first families of several nearby counties began to arrive on the steamboats that were docking and leaving almost hourly. My own father, stepmother, and sister, with others from Clay County, disembarked from the *Missouri Mail*, and Mrs. Cunningham, the wife of our new schoolmaster, bore a cleverly wrought flag, with the motto: "The Love of Country Is the Love of God."

In a rousing ceremony of presentation, Mrs. Cunningham handed the flag to Clay County's Captain Moss, former Kentuckian and childhood companion of the writer, with the following bold address:

"The Ladies of Liberty and its vicinity have deputed me, as one of their number, to present this flag to the volunteers from Clay County, commanded by Captain Oliver Perry Moss, and I now, in their name, present it to you, as a token of their esteem for the manly and patriotic manner in which you have shown your willingness to sustain the honor of our common country, and to redress the indignities offered to its flag.

"In presenting to you this token of our regard and esteem, we wish you to remember that some of us have sons, some brothers, and all of us either friends or relatives among you, and that we would rather hear of your falling in honorable warfare, than to see you return sullied with crime, or disgraced by cowardice. We trust, then, that your conduct, in all circumstances, will be worthy of the noble, intelligent and patriotic nation whose cause you have so generously volunteered to defend: your deportment will be such as will secure to you the highest praise and the warmest gratitude of the American people—in a word—let your motto be: 'Death before Dishonor.' And to the gracious protection and guidance of Him who rules the destinies of nations, we fervently commend you."

After this rather ornate but well-meant panegyric—so generous in its disposal of other people's safety—we were occupied in greeting family and old friends. My stepmother, fully recovered, immediately expressed a desire to locate her youngest child (whose enterprise I had conveyed home by post), his sister Claudia now adding, "That is, of course, if he has the time."

The search involved no small amount of trouble. The boy was not to be found in any of his usual haunts, and he had been conspicuously absent from the public observation. At length, struck by an inspiration, I led his despairing mother, his stern-visaged father, and his sister, dripping with sarcasm, out of the Fort to the ratty Indian lodge of that unspeakable pair, Dobbs and Spewack (whose correct names are, I believe, Hobbs and Spiebuck, though it galls me to present them with accuracy).

Hobbs, Spiebuck, and Sam were seated on the ground at a campfire, forking objects out of a kettle. (These were subsequently identified as "chicken," but they may have been horse—several head had recently turned up missing—or even something worse: the reports of "desertions" may have been hastily drawn. I repeat: *I do not trust those two scoundrels!*)

In any case, the boy jumped up when we arrived, looking justifiably alarmed.

He said, "Hello, Pa—are you mad?"

Then his mother cried, "Sam! How could you?" and they embraced. He choked up, under the show of family affection, and submitted to a peck on the cheek from his sister, who sniffed the air with elaborate distaste.

"It's the mosquitoes, ma'am," explained the villain Hobbs. "They've blowed in from the river; I and Spiebuck were obliged to rub on some petrified bar grease. If you're troubled, I'll spare you a handful and welcome," and he started into the wigwam, but she spoke out crisply, "Thank you *so* much. I prefer the mosquitoes."

At this point in a most unpropitious reconciliation, the savage suddenly turned on us with his hand full of knives. Both my father and I braced to defend ourselves, but the fellow was, it seemed, offering food. To my amazement, my father bowed slightly, took a knife, and said, "Thank you. You are very kind."

With a sort of frontier politesse, Hobbs produced two buffalo robes and we sat down, my stepmother—patrician and gracious always—arranging herself as if she were attending a governor's banquet. Claudia's outlook may have been slightly less amused. The time approached midday, the air was crisp, we had expected to lunch aboard the *Mail,* and we were hungry.

In a word, the kettle, or clay pot, of this duo, contained perhaps the best stew I had ever eaten. It was rich with brown gravy, several meats and poultry—not chicken alone—and vegetables purchased, we learned, from farms across the river. I began to take an entirely different view of my brother's companions from what I had previously held.

For example, we were staggered when he brought out from the lodge a bottle of French red wine and handed it around in tin cups, making only the apology that he had been "laying in trade goods." (Later, I found that one trader wagon carried twenty cases of vintage champagne.) Drunk from the cups, the wine tasted slightly metallic, sharp, clean, and tannic—in short, it was splendid. I saw roses in my stepmother's cheeks for the first time since her mishap with Annice.

During the meal and for an hour afterward, this curious fellow entertained us with tales of his adventures among Indians, never vulgar or coarse, not monopolizing the conversation, quick to listen, addressing himself mainly to my father, with whom he appeared to have established a communion, and, toward the end, bending to Claudia's now unabashed entreaties to continue. All this in the most frightful grammar and idiom, which still seemed suited, somehow, to the subject matter at hand. He exercised a sort of hypnotic spell over us all, and I realize, now in retrospect, that it was done on purpose, as a form of reassurance to Sam's family.

When we left, shaking hands with Hobbs and with his silent partner, I said, as somebody who had suffered a vague and very mild yet unsettling rebuke, "Captain, I don't recall a meal of more general nourishment."

He regarded me steadily out of deep-sunk eyes, with a characteristic over-sober expression that gives the impression of concealing some private joke. He said, "In famine time, I oncet vittled successful with a wolf. We come to be good friends." Then he offered the inscrutable commentary that, "When I was younger, I knowed a heap less than I do now, but I expect to know more tomorrer."

On June 26, all was in readiness and the order given to march. The die was cast; we had committed our fortune to this martial adventure which some of us, at least, consider needless and foolhardy. Be that as it may, the pageantry was stirring, sufficient to the moment for smoothing away all doubts.

As far as one could see, the files of cavalry wound out into the undulating ocean of prairie. Banners fluttered, the sun flashed from a thousand polished sabers, the starchy stiff white of canvas-covered wagons rose up like sails.

No path leads from Fort Leavenworth to the Santa Fé trail; we steered southwest, and encountered many obstacles. The troops were staggered; each "detachment" (a company or two) functioned on its own responsibility. Soon those to front and rear were lost to view. Within a few hours, the forward groups were slowed by deep ravines and creeks with high and rugged banks. These banks must be cut down, the asperities leveled, bridges built, and roads constructed before our wagons could pass.

This called for patience. The heat was often stifling, the grass tall and rank—"horse-high"—and the earth in many places so soft that heavily loaded wagons sank over the felloes on level prairie. On such occasions, the mules (for mules had been selected as draft animals, for the most part) became refractory. Much harness was destroyed, and many wagons broke down completely. I began to understand that the planning for an army can never be perfect.

A word about our rations: Ordinarily each day (in the early stage) we received a small sour loaf of bread that was said by our sergeant to have been "kneaded by the foot of a Dutchman who warn't particular when he washed." I'm not certain what this meant, since the bread had a tolerable flavor, but let it stand. In addition, each man was daily handed about three eighths of a pound of pickled pork, plus strong coffee containing a few teasing grains of sugar. On especially arduous days a bit of low-grade beef was added, and half a pound of flour was doled out on three or four occasions. Most of the private soldiers converted this latter to dough fried in grease, the concoction called "slipjacks."

All in all, the food was bad, insufficient, and, to be sure, poorly cooked, every man acting as his own chef or combining with comrades at a common fire. Several officers—old friends—had taken along Negro body servants, and to the messes of these I was often invited, despite the difference in rank; but in the interest of appearances, I usually found an excuse to decline. It being understood that I was preparing a history, I was, I'm afraid, given special consideration.

Our beef, by the way, accompanies us on the hoof; that is, cattle are driven along with the troops; they live entirely off the land. At night, they are crowded into hasty corrals or tethered to iron stakes hammered deep into the ground. These patient, hard-pressed, lowing beasts are, and will be, slaughtered one by one by the detachment-wagon superintendent, then apportioned out with other provender.

In the beginning days, our horses were wild, fiery, and skittish, unused to military trappings in spite of our training. It was not uncommon, amidst the snapping of harness, the sounding of bugles, the rumble of artillery, and the clatter of sabers and cooking utensils, for horses to unseat their riders and scamper pell-mell across the grass, scattering arms, accouterments, saddles, and saddlebags in their wake. Curiously, no serious accidents took place from these mishaps. The horses were rounded up, they were calmed and repacked, and the march went on.

And what a scene each evening at the cry of "Make Camp!" Men disperse to find wood or dry brush; others pitch tents with some hope of order; others haul water for men, horses and cooking. At length, the flames leap up, the coffee is made, the meat is boiled, and the bread prepared according to taste. After supper, we stake out our horses in fresh grass, spread our blankets upon the earth, and gratefully fall heavily asleep, leaving our spies and guard to take care of the enemy.

On the twenty-eighth we arrived at Stranger Creek, where the detachment rested for twenty-four hours. We reclined at ease, read novelettes, and polished sabers. I bathed in the stream and tried, without success, to add fish to our diet. The Stranger is a branch of the Kansas, or Kaw, River, which latter we reached two days ago. The scene here improved greatly. The Kansas is a deep and beautiful ribbon of clear water, 350 yards wide, bordered by prosperous Shawnee farms. We were able to buy—but not at bargain prices—milk and butter, peas, corn, beans, potatoes, poultry, and fish.

As (I am told) at several other points of these rivers, ferries were operated by Indians, we were put across at Fish's Ferry, owned by one Paschal Fish, cousin to Tecumseh, whose two boatmen were dressed in bright-colored shirts and who toiled most agilely to accomplish a crossing in the swift currents.

Here at the Narrows, on July 3, we have joined (praise God) the Santa Fé trail, sixty-five miles out from Fort Leavenworth. We now follow a known route through this dull and limitless prairie, standing far less chance of becoming lost. Faint wagon tracks are to be seen in the fast-growing weeds, and our morale has brightened. The Drum-and-Fife Corps is somewhere in advance (unless surrendered to the enemy with a cash gratuity to prevent its return), Colonel Doniphan brings up the rear, and General Kearny with his staff was to have left Leavenworth three days behind us all.

Note: Of my fellows, I have thus far said little. From a colleague who intends to dispatch letters to a paper, I borrow a flattering quotation: "The Army of the West is perhaps composed of material as fine as any other body of troops in the field. The Volunteer corps consists almost entirely of young men, generally from the leading families of the State. Every calling and profession contributed its share. There might be seen under arms, in the ranks, the lawyer, the doctor, the professor, the student, the legislator, the farmer, the mechanic, and artisans of every description, all united as a band of brothers to defend the rights and honor of their country."

This is an exuberant but broadly accurate view of our corps. I have never sought vigorously after close friendships, but I find myself, now, the involuntary center of a madding and increasingly fragrant crowd. *Above all else one misses one's privacy.* It is awkward to remain at arm's length from a man with whom one has divided a broiled perch haggled from a dishonest Shawnee. I allude, first, to Sergeant O'Hara, who has made me his special concern of the expedition. (This entirely without any encouragement from the writer.)

It is perhaps not to my credit that, aside from Negroes, I have thus far never enjoyed any close connection with the laboring classes. Sergeant O'Hara is emphatically of the people. I have tried, without success, to settle on any single taste or experience that we have in common. Still he appears to admire me without stint; he is proud of my "eddication."

Physically, the man is a giant, far over six feet in height, broad, liberally sprinkled with a fine red down over his chest, shoulders, and stomach, his body in general being as tough as a piece of lean old beef that has soaked in brine for three or four months. His hair is thick, red, and uncombed, his eyebrows are darkish red and bushy, he is missing a pivotal tooth, the left upper molar, and his expression is offensively good-natured—resigned, I assume, to absorbing the ceaseless buffetings of his superiors. His laugh, reminiscent of the kind of force that cracked the bell in Philadelphia, makes wolves howl and small animals cower in their holes.

Sergeant O'Hara is comparatively new in Clay County. He was born, he tells me, in an unpronounceable hamlet in Ireland and emigrated, mind you, for the selfless and breast-stirring reason that a neighbor girl's father, carrying a shotgun, was seeking a conference with him on a domestic problem. After a number of moves, no doubt prompted by similar high-mindedness, he found himself a resident on the banks of our Fishing River. He soon went into business, that of seeking out, cutting down and robbing bee trees. Of all the poaching nuisances that face planters in our region, this felony is the most destructive. An incalculable amount of fine timber is annually lost to these predators. It is quite possible that I myself have chased off this same shameless thief with a rifle, in that dim, receding time before we took up arms as a hobby.

Sergeant O'Hara describes himself, in the mental way, as being "wobbly." "Bless you, sir," [he calls me "sir," an interesting address as from a sergeant to a lay corporal]. "Bless you, sir," he said, handing me the lion's share of the perch, "I've always been thick, right from the start. I can hear me sainted mither crying, many's the time, 'Oh, the darling boy—hung like a jackass and not a brain in 'is 'ed! 'Twould 'ave bin kinder to drown 'im at birth.'"

After this preposterous and vulgar utterance, O'Hara wiped his eyes and said, "I felt mortal sorry for her, always. Afflicted like that."

I have been curious why, considering his self-confessed vacancy of wit, O'Hara should have been mentioned for sergeant. I found out very shortly. He is one of those men, forever an enigma to me, who can perform any feat with their hands.

Does my tent have several missing parts and refuse to stay erect?

"Just rest yourself, sir—fine, so, your foot's wrapped up in the ropes, and she's upside down. Grand, grand, get right on with your litichure, sir. We'll cut a sapling, trim down, out with the thread and awl, bend grommets out of wire—there you are, sir; you've shaped it up neater than paint."

The confounded fellow does everything, and for some reason prefers that I get the credit. But his most pestiferous habit is sitting beside me in the evening, watching my work on the Journal. He himself can neither read nor write, it seems.

"Ah, see there, now. Scrabbledy-ass across, come back, slide across again, three little marks up, turn 'em over pointing down, a round one—that's 'o,' and bless me mither for teaching at least the one!—a wee tyke with a dot overhead, and a propped-up stick with a cross. It's a miracle straight out of heaven. Take a sip of coffee, sir, for your head must be buzzing with the strain of it."

The sentence I had written was, "Sergeant O'Hara is incomparably the most wearisome fool I ever met," but his patent good intentions made me so guilty that I rubbed it out.

The sergeant is athirst to fling himself into the fray, being an apostate Catholic and having a raging hostility against priests. In some misty, Neanderthal way, he appears to hold priests responsible for the war as a whole, neglecting the politician, the land-hungry Texans, the corruption of ruling Mexico, and other factors that might be mentioned. "They're devils, sir," he has confided to me. "Oh, you'd never believe the trickery, and me with the lass as ready as a plum for the picking. But what with their praying, and knee-buckling, and cross-kissing, and the dragging in of Jesus at every turn, they talked her out of her natural desires. And that but one case out of many—all me careful work gone for naught, not to mention the expense: ale and pigs' feet and horse fairs. No, you're correct, sir; the bloodletting can't start too soon for O'Hara."

Thus speaks my new friend; he sees the war in a broad, philosophical perspective.

And now my other burden, a stripling of no more than seventeen, I judge. This youth—a stranger to me heretofore—is the most curious mixture of diffidence (approaching hermitcy) and impudence I have ever encountered. In appearance he is slim and small-boned, a towhead whose hair is cropped close—untidily, as if done by some careless member of a poor farm family, though his hands bear no evidence of toil. He wears a forage cap pulled raffishly down over his forehead. This boy seems to have the greatest difficulty in keeping clean; his face is smudged almost to the point of non-recognition. Moreover, to complete the unattractive picture, his clothes might well have been bought for O'Hara: they hang loosely about his frame, with the trouser legs rolled up.

In fairness, I should say that his humor is sunny, he does his chores without complaint, and he is a master hand with horses. This last, indeed, may account for his having been accepted into the Volunteers. Seldom have I seen a person more deftly persuasive with an unwilling beast of burden.

The truth is that, because of shyness or some anti-social quirk, this inexplicable youth—Hugh Angel by name—actually prefers to billet himself among the animals rather than among the men. We are accustomed to it, and make no protest.

Now, despite his aloofness, Angel succeeds in adding his bit to O'Hara's in making camp life practically insupportable for the writer. A close examination of the American population could not conceivably ferret out a man less mechanically gifted than myself; in addition, my knowledge of things military is pretty well limited to Caesar's depredations in Gaul. Yet this damnable Angel insists on plaguing me with questions of the most technical nature. He prefers, either sincerely or in a spirit of careful mockery, to take the line that I am a career army man, and should know everything.

"Corporal Shelby, sir," he says in his husky voice (I suspect that it is only now "breaking"), "I wonder if you could give me some details about poliorcetics? So I'll know when the time comes."

"Polar cats?"

"Poliorcetics, sir."

"See here, Angel, you aren't required to call a non-commissioned officer 'sir.' In fact, I'd very much rather you didn't. I've told you so eight or nine times already."

"I'm sorry, Corporal Shelby. What about poliorcetics?"

"How the devil do I know? I'm not a real military person; I've told you that, too. Just what is, or are, poliorcetics, if anything?"

"The art of sandbagging, sir."

"Never mind, Angel. We don't need any sandbags here. The horses and wagons are having trouble enough with sand as it is."

"I only thought I'd ask my officer, sir. It's the only way I know to get information."

"Well, work up some other bore. Get on back to your tent. Come to think of it, there's a river down there, with a handsome lot of sand. Why don't you get a trowel and go dig?"

I'm ashamed to admit it, but it's impossible for me to be civil to that probing bumpkin.

IX

We've skipped along pretty well, though running into quicksand near a big river, so that they've had to double-team it to get the wagons through. Somebody said mules were selling at "thribble their usual price." I did some pushing but decided to refrain on account of possibly injuring my drumming.

Up here, forward, with Captain Reid of Saline County, we have to break the trail. The detachment wagons have straggled behind, as usual, and the rations are skimpy. There's a lot of grumbling, and it got so bad that Captain Reid rode back to Captain Waldo, of A Company, and got two jugs of whisky. Every man had a drink, or maybe five, and after that the grumbling slacked off. They wouldn't let me drink any, spite of a cold I was getting, but handed me a piece of stringy old beef, bought from Indians, one cent a pound.

We came on a cottonwood tree that had a dead Indian perched in a fork, trussed up in a buffalo robe. He was discomposed all over, except for his head, so they hauled him down and buried him, don't ask me why. He looked perfectly comfortable where he was.

Well, sir, the Drum-and-Fife Corps had an election, right after the whisky gave out, and they made me the leader. A person dislikes to brag about honors coming along so young, but I have to admit I felt good. Both of the fifers claimed they were too old to take the responsibility (and they *are* tolerably creaky) and the fiddler said he didn't want to get mixed up in it. He's a little mushy in the head; everybody says so, and says it's all right—it was the fiddle that did it.

Anyhow, I got him a drum from a Shawnee, paying out hard cash to the length of a dime, and held a rehearsal as soon as the fifers sobered up. On the Fourth of July, at Bluff Creek, we came out noble on "Yankee Doodle"; as many as a dozen said they would have recognized it right off, but these fellows are always joshing. The best compliment we had was from Captain Reid, who descends from a high Revolutionary War family and had a classical education at a place called La Porte, Indiana. He stood looking on as we marched and tootled, then shook his head and said, "Remarkable. Absolutely beyond belief." It's things like that that keep an artist going; I appreciated it, and thanked him.

There's nothing small about Captain Reid. The very next day he said the Drum-and-Fife Corps was "a boon to be shared," and he ordered us to stay behind, together with twenty-five or thirty men that he said were "equally sick," probably getting his words tangled, and after a couple of days of well-earned rest, here came Blaine with the company from Clay County. He was having some trouble with a Sergeant O'Hara, that looks like pictures of an orangutan, and a grimy-looking hayseed named Angel, but I offered to consider the situation, and he cheered right up.

We went on, from Bluff Creek to Council Grove, a champion place for what they call "rendevoo," being the last good timber around, so that broken wagons can be repaired and the like; then to Diamond Springs, which has water rushing in bright little streams just everywhere—mighty different from most places. Hot as blazes; everybody complaining about the heat.

Twenty-nine miles to Cottonwood Forks, through perfectly flat country covered with tall, rank grass having zigzag stripes through it, as if cyclones or lightning had ploughed it up once; on to Turkey Creek—plenty of grass and water, not so much as a twig of timber. The only thing to cook with was what they call "prairie fuel," or buffalo chips—leavings, you know—that makes a brisk fire and gives a sweetish but interesting taste to meat broiled over it. On the order of ammonia. They say buffalo hunters commonly smell like ammonia themselves, from eating food off of these fires all the time. They can recognize each other that way, and maybe go someplace else.

Before we fetched the little Arkansas River, a number of men took sick, because of having bad food or being soaked. A gusher of a rainstorm came down one night, with us comfortable under tents, but could they let it rest? No, siree. A Lieutenant Colonel Ruff said pull up stakes and march, so we did it, for practice and conditioning, you see. But he got criticized, and a Captain Jackson offered to knock his head off, but nothing came of it. As Blaine said, "A person's rank here is about as important as the size of his feet," and Sergeant O'Hara worked it out approximately the same, but there's no need to go into his version.

Well, around this time we got news that two detachments to the rear, directly under Doniphan, were starving, being cut off from provision wagons, so Lieutenant Colonel Ruff sent an "express," which was two men, to Pawnee Fork for supplies. But one of them, a fellow from across the county, a log-rafter, A. E. Hughes by name, drownded himself trying to swim the Pawnee River, which was swoll high by freshets. They fished him out and planted him, after firing off some guns to make it military, though what satisfaction it gave him or his relatives I couldn't say.

A good many men died in the next few marches, and lots of animals. An N. Carson died of what Surgeon Whorton called "reckless exposure," but others called it lack of medical attention. This Whorton was practically impossible to see, being taken up with a game called whist; what's more, he had the idea everybody was faking. If a man came in on one leg, having deposited the other with a grizzly, Whorton was just as apt to say, "Come now, my man, you cut that leg off to shirk duty—dismissed!" He also had a theory that all medical complaints were about the same: "Weak, tired, and nervous," and stated that he was weak, tired, and nervous himself. Nobody liked him, even the officers, and several men allowed they were planning to poison him, as soon as they got the chance. They said there was nothing personal or mean about it; it was research. They hoped to find out if he was doctor enough to cure himself, if he could get an appointment.

An Augustus Leslie, a young man of good education, from Cole County, died of a "chronic affection," something to do with his throat, and was given a handsome burial with a tombstone. Another man, named Redwine, died, probably, they said, from exhaustion and not enough to eat. Came across the grave of an R. T. Ross, written on a rough board. I didn't know him, myself. Four more men died of fatigue, and a lot of horses and mules have commenced to break legs in prairie dog holes; they're everyplace you look, villages of three miles or more around. And so many holes the ground sounds hollow when you ride over.

Several men shot prairie dogs and ate them, because these specimens are supposed to have a layer of fat that's sovereign for rheumatism. It's well known. You can eat the fat or apply it as an ointment, and with my own eyes I saw it rubbed on some saddle-galled horses, which cured right up, by jingo.

Blaine said it was poppycock, naturally, that the sores healed because the saddles were left off for awhile, but I noticed him putting some on his feet one night, after he'd walked his horse ten miles through soft sand.

There was also a belief that prairie dogs and rattlesnakes occupied the same holes, after the gopher built them; but we kept watch and it wasn't so: we saw three different snakes eating pups. The grown dogs move out as soon as a snake moves in, if he's lucky enough to gather up his traps and make it. The odd thing, though, is that prairie dogs often share their holes with owls. We saw it over and over.

Some mornings when the grass was especially wet, as many as twenty to thirty rattlers could be seen coming out to drink dew. Hereabouts, there was little else for refreshment, dry as a scoop of hot sand. That early, the snakes are so numb with cold you can easy kill them with a stick, and next month, in August, they'll be blind with their own venom, in the skin-shedding time. You have to watch out and be nimble, then, for they'll attack anything that moves.

July 16: The Arkansas River, and a good many changes, mainly for the worse. The river here is three or four hundred yards wide, sandy and unevenly shallow, with nice deep pools in between. Now I reckon I'd better get a shocker off of my chest, and forget about it. It's practically ruined the war for me, but things may get better by and by.

Most all the men, including Blaine and Sergeant O'Hara, peeled off and splashed into the water, which was just right for swimming. The banks are low bluff and the country almost handsome, with cottonwoods on both sides; yellow sandbars curving up in the shallows—sand that Blaine wrote down was "no less beautiful than the golden sands of the fabled Pactolus," whatever that meant (I judged it was somewhere along the Missouri); pumpkin vines thick in the prairies, and the river margins covered with tall grass, pea vines and rushes.

Well, it was an interesting sight—upwards of five hundred men, or all that had gathered so far, sporting about naked as a jay, scrubbing away the dust and grime and alkali, splashing each other and shouting, gaunt and haggard and bony, after no food and the hard marches.

Everybody whistled at Sergeant O'Hara, making jokes, and a body could hardly blame them. Most all his body was covered with red silky hair, and there was such a lot of him, that he didn't seem to fit into the human classification, somehow. He took it very civil, and said he had always been joked at, naked, except for a few dozen women here and there, and they'd been revived without trouble. It was his cross to bear; he was accustomed to it. He was uncommonly humble, for a man itching to get his hands on a priest.

Well, the water was so dirtied what with all the scrubbing, that I decided to go upstream and bathe by myself. But when I rounded a bend and started to undress, I spied that Hugh Angel, down below in a cottonwood clump, alone as usual.

I'd tried to talk to him once or twice, and Blaine was right; he was exasperating. There was a smart-alecky streak in this hick; you couldn't quite put your finger on it. What's more, he reminded me of somebody, I disremembered who.

All right, says I to myself, I'll just crouch here, and when you're in the water, I'll hide your clothes. *Then* we'll see what you can think up, caught out in the open for a change. So I leaned over and watched, and I don't expect to get another such jolt if I live to be a hundred. Angel threw off his forage cap, ran both hands in a funny way through his hair, shaking his head, wriggled out of his filthy old jacket and trousers, removed what appeared to be a kind of double hammock above and some cut-off underwear below—silk, too, by the look of it, with a fringe on the bottom—and he wasn't a man at all: it was Angelina Hughes. There appeared to be a good deal of her, or considerably more than there was to the fellow she'd left standing in the sand.

I gulped, but couldn't move to save me; neither could I make a sound. I was that taken aback.

Very cool, restored to her old style, she stepped into the water, bathed herself all over very careful with a piece of soap, washed her hair, washed out her underwear that she'd carried along, lay on her back, floating like a hussy whilst soaping between her toes and all, then wallowed on her stomach with her behind sticking out, and seemed to sigh and relax when she turned over to sit up, letting the river water trickle in little ripples around her waist.

All of a sudden, I felt sorry for her, alone amongst those roughnecks, working a double shift like a darky, too. Then I remembered how she'd plagued Blaine, and here she was, still at it, chasing him exactly as I predicted previous. So I crept down and gathered up her garments, hung them on some bushes out of sight, slipped on my drawers, and strolled out into the sunlight.

I said, "Enjoying yourself, Angelina?"

She whirled around, still sitting, then ducked under to her chin. She regarded me with her bold gray-green eyes, unscared as always, and said, "I rather expected to be caught by you. Quite evidently, you're to be my unlucky star. Now bring me my clothes."

"Not yet. We've got some things to settle first."

"Then I'll get them myself," and she stood up and walked forward, as brazen and bouncy as you please, swinging the underwear at her side, sort of whistling, so I scrambled out of there. I could have stayed if I'd wanted to.

"Not where I hid them, you won't," I yelled over my shoulder. "Just try. You're stuck, and so you'll find."

"Sam!"

When I turned back, she had the underwear draped over her shoulders, and was sitting down, facing away.

"Throw me my clothes." I did so, and she said, "I need a friend. I doubt if ever a volunteer cavalry girl more desperately needed a friend than I do at this moment in the Arkansas River, stark naked."

"Why don't you leave my brother Blaine alone? He isn't like you; he's quiet. You're crazy Everybody says so, and this proves it."

"In some ways," she said, sort of thoughtful, "your brother Blaine is a poor spiritless thing, a book-bound mole, but it happens that my fancy has settled on that man. I have a feeling he's convertible."

"To what?"

"To the better life."

"You'll never get away with this. They'll catch you sure. Anyhow, you ought to be ashamed, hanging around a thousand men, listening and gawking."

"Oh, bosh. Men! They all look alike, and they all sound alike. You forget I had brothers."

And then I'm a Hottentot if she didn't stand up in full view, before putting on her clothes, and kick high in the air with her right leg, knees straight, toes pointed, far up over her head, like a dance-hall girl, only worse. Still, there was something free and pretty about it, too.

"Nobody will ever understand how *bored* I get."

She put on her clothes and said, "Sit down and I'll elaborate, within the limits of your intelligence that is. Do you ever feel like exploding, with the pressure say at a thousand pounds to the inch, pressing from the inside out? By the way, do you have any idea what I'm talking about, you nosy young pest?"

I said no, but it was a lie.

"The awful, awful things I have to do, day after day. The Right things! I doubt if I've heard an entirely sincere utterance since I was ten years old. How *are* you? What does it mean? Another point: I'm pretty sick of pretending to be stupid. Also delicate. Also innocent. I could rip off profanity that would curl your hair. Interested in a sample?"

"Now look here," I said, starting to get up.

"Just one brief, sizzling obscenity? Be a sport. Well, let it go.

The chief thing I've learned in twenty-one years is that if one of my gushy friends—acquaintances, rather—says, 'I'm just *crazy* about that dress,' I'd better go check it in a mirror; the skirt may be missing. Now we'll take up the Seminary—"

"Let that one go," I said. "If it's school you mean, I'm with you on it. One hundred per cent waste of time."

She leaned over and pressed my hand. "Dear boy, there's more to you than I thought; we've become soul mates, right here on this sandbar. Anyway, men have all the fun: horse races, gun shooting, gambling, cockfights, travel, saloons, cursing at will, sex, fighting—would you believe, friend Sam, that the babbling crones of my family, including my mother—a half-wit, by the way—attempted to teach *me* to *faint*?"

"Sounds unlikely," I said, and meant it.

"'The men will adore it, so weak and feminine,' they said." She leaned over again. "I'm going to tell you a secret, Sam. Keep this under your hat. I don't give a tinker's damn what the men adore. I don't even care whether I belong to the upper classes or the lower. I despise the clothes I'm expected to wear, the customs, most of the people, their silly social life, the moonstruck, tongue-tied swains, my future, the thought of producing drooling babies at my age—everything. So does Blaine, but he doesn't know it yet."

"Just the same, they'll find you out. A female woman can't go to war dressed like a man."

"That's where you're wrong, darling Sam. I've done some research. Case histories abound. No doubt you're familiar with the saga of Emma Edwards, the wraith of the Revolution? Now an Irish biddy, peddling her cakes and comfits, now a quaint old darky *field hand,* slipping back and forth across the lines (an arresting footnote here is that she bought a wig of real Negro wool, in Washington), again a *stripling clerk in a country store,* gathering information. Shall I go on?"

"You probably will anyhow."

"In your probing, scholar's way, you've heard of the War of 1812?"

"I remember it mentioned a time or two."

"Fought between whom?"

Blast the girl, I figured she'd ask that; it was right on the tip of my tongue. "Between us and the Yiddish, if you have to know."

"Let me withdraw what I said about school. It wouldn't be *entirely* wasted, in your case. However, you were close; your keen ear almost picked it up. It was the British. Perhaps the name of Miss Eliza Alling strikes a chord?"

"I can't say I ever met her, myself."

"Known, from her own lively account, written after the contest, as 'The Female Volunteer.' Or 'The Life, Wonderful Adventures and Miraculous Escapes of Miss Eliza Alling, of Eastport, Maine.' Dressed in men's clothes, *she followed her lover,* one Billings, to the fray; wounded twice, in the shoulder, and arm; fought like a demon; found Billings (an undeserving clod); withheld identity; nursed him back to health (he had either hay fever or night sweats); took ship; shipwrecked, identity still secret; made port; went to hotel, revealed identity; reconciled and impregnated while still in uniform—a most extraordinary sight, I imagine; returned to parents, though not quite in the same shape. Curtain. Any comment?"

"Well, it's interesting."

"I've got to do this, Sam, and you're going to help me."

I sat thinking for awhile. The girl wasn't as bad as I figured. She had some sound ideas, and she was on the absolutely right track about school.

"There's one condition."

"How old did you say you were?"

"You're always ragging. Blaine doesn't like it; it puts him off. Can't you say something *normal* once in a while? What's the matter with you, anyway?"

She sighed. "Scarred. Very deeply scarred somewhere along the way."

"That's exactly what I mean—what you just said."

For once, she sounded sorry, and said, "I'll try to do better, I really will. Ragging of Blaine's over, finished. Depend on it."

I got up and said, "All right, then, I'll help you. But you better watch out. These people aren't as stupid as they look."

"Dear Sam."

"Never mind."

"Kiss?"

I went on up the bank and left. She wasn't apt to reform over night; *that* much was *sure*.

X

En route along the Arkansas River, having left the main Santa Fé trail for tactical reasons, and for water. *We shall soon find ourselves in enemy territory.* Occasional, flitting bands of Mexicans dressed like Indians bear testimony to this fact. They are ghost riders, eager to observe our strength and deployment.

General Kearny's detachment has overtaken Colonel Doniphan, and the leaders have been in consultation. At a wide and treacherous river crossing, the general verified his reputation for dispatch by ordering the felling of walnut, oak and elm trees that grow here, and supervising the construction of a bridge. Then, with the wagons emptied, their contents, together with the sick, were carried safely over across the trunks. Little equipment was lost. The animals, of course, were obliged to swim, and we floated the wagons across at the ends of ropes.

A flaw in the general arrangements is that the sick have been placed in the rough, unyielding baggage wagons. *Spring carriers should certainly have been made available to the medical department, thus saving many valuable lives.*

A path near the juncture of the Cimarron provides heavy going. The soil is often sandy and loose, with occasional stretches of friable, calcareous limestone; tangled wild pumpkin vines cover the ground, giving the illusion of cultivation; and serpents, horned toads, chameleons, land turtles, prairie lizards and (above all) grasshoppers are constantly underfoot. Horses, mules and cattle have been lost to the quick whirring strike of the startled rattler.

And yet, for the poet, who would find beauty on a burning plateau in Hell, the sweetest of flowers burst defiantly into bloom. The prairie pink—rich purple in color despite its name—may be seen waving its banners beside the dreariest of pumpkins; blue lilies, white poppies, mimic morning glories rise all around—for what? To live and die unseen.

We have passed a spot where Don Antonio José Chavez, a New Mexico trader, was robbed and murdered, in 1843, by a marauding party of fifteen men led by Captain John McDaniel, of Liberty, who pretended to hold a commission under the government of Texas. The unfortunate Chavez had five servants and gold bullion in the amount of $10,000. Giving at least a partial lie to stories of American lawlessness in New Mexico, the perpetrators of this bloody deed were promptly arrested and brought to justice. After court proceedings in St. Louis, McDaniel and a comrade were executed according to the decision of a jury.

The heat is withering, and the men are tortured by thirst, the more so when they consider that the Arkansas is only a few miles distant. Also, in this condition, we are confronted with that nemesis of the desert, the mirage. Conditions to evoke this apparition will be about as follows: the temperature stands at 95 degrees, the earth is baked to a crust, its grass crisped under the sun's pulsations, and the horizon stands off in limitless distance. Then, of a sudden, the horizon dissolves into green plains and pastures; a lake of shimmering silver appears in the foreground, with rivers leading into its corners. A shout goes up from a thousand parched throats, the men break ranks and ride—toward what? Magically the waters recede and disappear, the rivers dry up, the verdancy gives way to prairie or dry yellow desert, and all come trooping back. There is something shameful in this; the men are loath to look each other in the eye. Once again they have been tricked.

But we have compensations. When thirst and hunger gnaw at their fiercest, we breast a long rise and find, across the plains, buffalo blacking the land in uncountable numbers. The river lies beyond. This is no mirage. With wild cries (and no restraints from the officers), the men ride into the trampling, earth-shaking herds with guns, pistols, and even sabers drawn. Dozens upon dozens of the shaggy, panicked brutes are killed, deer and elk and antelope amongst them are killed, ripe grapes and plums are found by the river banks, and fish are caught from the deeper waters here. Then every man eats his fill, and nobody raises a voice to hurry. After all, what has the Army provided? Even a soldier has his limits of subservience to a fellow man.

Nearing Fort Bent (an adobe trading post owned by Charles and William Bent of St. Louis, on the north bank of the Arkansas, approximately six hundred miles west of Leavenworth) three Mexican prisoners, spies, were captured by the Dragoons. For some reason, each had a blank letter addressed to General Kearny, possibly to throw off suspicion by the American residents and traders at the Fort. In any case, General Kearny had the three courteously escorted through our lines; he pointed out the smart, professional demeanor of his Regulars, the grim-visaged faces of the Missouri Volunteers, and, at last, our artillery, dragged with such terrible exertion across the wilderness.

A note must be introduced about the Mexican character. These men, seized by their enemy, were wholly indifferent. Indeed, they assumed that they were dead already, and one, taking up a spade, inquired, "*Aquí?*" prepared to accept the usual penalty, in their land, of having to dig one's own grave in anticipation of the firing squad. During this palaver (none of the three spoke English), they begged "cigarritos," then began to puff away, laughing and chattering in what all thought were their last minutes on earth.

At length, it was conveyed that they would be freed, to return to Santa Fé bearing knowledge of what they had seen. It was impossible to decide whether they were impressed by our strength. One had the uneasy feeling that their chief reaction was contempt for our softness, or, perhaps, a conviction that the invading general was *loco,* an expression derived from the loco weed, or marijuana, a counterpart of the Turkish hashish, which is smoked for its euphoric effect by some of the lower classes.

The officers have kept the men clear of the Fort, with its drinking and revelry, but have ordered the unloading of many government wagons, returning these to Leavenworth for supplies. Also during the two-day rest, Lieutenant De Courcy and twenty men were dispatched to Taos, to learn the people's disposition and intent. His report to General Kearny is secret, but it is known that the New Mexicans, never having enjoyed protection from the Indians by their government, are eager to assume life under a responsible flag (to wit: ours). Now, as pretty Mexican and Indian girls wave enticements from the rooftops, we push forward from Fort Bent in the last long leg of our advance into Santa Fé. For awhile, we must travel through the Great American Desert, and our water kegs have been filled from barrels sunk in sand beside the river, in the interest of purification.

Here we encountered an open cache, probably looted by Indians—reminder of some luckless party long before. These pits, dug usually on an eminence near the water, were for stowing merchandise after the animals of a trading party perished. Our discovery was a large mossy hole in the ground, somewhat in the shape of a jug, and lined by grass and sticks to hold back seepage from the earth. Once, no doubt, it was sealed over against rain, even to the point of re-growing turf on the top. On occasion, I am informed, years passed before a party could raise more funds and return for the often valuable contents.

To cross this desert, the scene of numberless tragedies in the Santa Fé trade, we halted and made precautionary repairs to our wagon wheels. It is a curious fact that among the equipment of this large army—one of the principal American thrusts of the Mexican War—there is not to be found *a single portable forge.*

We have, then, been obliged to call upon custom, and upon the excellent O'Hara. Our wheels have become loose and "shackling," as they say, from the shrink of the wood. Many spokes reel in the tubs, so that it's necessary to brace them with "false spokes," firmly bound with "buffalo tug." Several times the wagon tires have become so loose upon the felloes as to tumble off while we travel.

The solution? O'Hara, and a crew working under him (often stopping their ears in anguish), have driven strips of hoop-iron around between the tire and felloe—frequently using simple wedges of wood in place of iron. All up and down the line, such a clitter-clatter of hammers nobody ever heard.

The march being properly resumed on August second, we are in the midst of one of the world's most desolate regions. The Sahara can surely be no more frightful and exhausting than this brooding American waste. Twenty-one men, desperately ill, have been sent back to Bent's with an escort. Animals are falling all along the way. Hot blasts of air pelt us in suffocating, mystifying waves, for there is not a breath of real wind blowing. It is as if these furnace drafts were fleeing like pellets from the sun, which hangs low and large and molten, glowing white, an enemy from which one cannot escape. There is no water, no grass, no living thing except an infrequent, lean and pathetic antelope or Mexican hare, hurrying fast to who knows what oasis.

To add to our troubles, the wind at last arises, and blows fine, stinging sand into the lungs of both man and beast. With bacon rind, the dried nostrils of these bellowing and suffering beasts are partially relieved of their pain, but it is really no use; they are dying by the dozens. Dreary, sultry, boundless solitude reigns for as far as the eye can reach. The Roman Army under Metellus never encountered more serious opposition from the elements than do our troops in their passage across the Great American Desert.

On the fifth, having made twenty-eight miles during the day, we passed out of the desert and camped on the southern bank of the Purgatoire, a lovely, rippling mountain stream. You may imagine with what zeal the men and animals propelled themselves into the lifesaving embrace of these waters. What does it matter that you bathe beside a filthy, bawling ox or mule?

All thoughts of fastidiousness are gone; at once we gulp great mouthfuls and bathe our sand-encrusted heads, oblivious of the brutes directly upstream. This sparkling branch is no less grateful to our detachment than was that stream to the Israelitish army which gushed from the rock when struck by the rod of the prophet.

On the sixth, to the base of Cimarron Peak, thence a tortuous climb several thousands of feet to the summit. The wagons are hauled up on ropes, and let down again in like manner. Several are smashed, and a Dragoon, one Withers, suffered a spoke driven clean through his chest. He died during the descent. Down below, a chasm, or pass, opens out to a vast, natural arena, perhaps sufficiently spacious to accommodate the whole human race. The amphitheater of Statilius Taurus, with its seventy thousand seats rising in circular tiers one above the other, would have been nothing in comparison.

Now, across the Cimarron ridge, we have wood, water and grass, but our rations have been cut to a third. And the final ignominy—we are obliged once more to assemble on level ground and drill!

There is great excitement. We have reached, by the fourteenth, the verge of the Mexican settlements. General Kearny has been caught up with, and a battle is said to impend. At "Las Bagas" (Las Vegas?), the first village on the road, our spies, W. Bent and Estis, report that two thousand Mexicans are entrenched six miles further, at a place called, simply, the *Cañon.*

General Kearny immediately formed the line of battle. The Dragoons, with the St. Louis mounted volunteers, were stationed in front; Major Clark and the battalion of mounted artillerymen were placed in the center, and Colonel Doniphan's Volunteers formed behind these. The two companies of volunteer infantry were deployed on each side, as flankers, and the baggage and merchant trains came next in order, with Captain Walton's mounted company as rear guard.

The cartridges were hastily distributed, the cannons swabbed and rigged, the post fires set burning, and every rifle charged. The advance was sounded by martial trumpet and horn. The banners streamed in every direction. All along the line the officers dashed, exhorting the men, and the general spirit brightened. It is a source of amazement to me why the prospect of wholesale bloodletting provokes such ecstasy in the human breast!

Upon entering Las Bagas, General Kearny assembled the *alcalde,* or magistrate, and the other leading men, then administered the oath of allegiance to the United States. He said, in part, "Mr. Alcalde, and people of New Mexico, I have come amongst you, by the orders of my Government, to take possession of your country, and extend over it the laws of the United States. We consider it, and have done so for some time, a part of the territory of the United States [I confess that this left me somewhat bewildered]. We come among you as friends—not as conquerors. [!] We come among you for your benefit—not for your injury.

"Henceforward, I absolve you from all allegiance to the Mexican Government, and from all obedience to General Manuel Armijo. *He is no longer your Governor.* [Great sensation, indeterminate in character.] *I* am your Governor. I shall not expect you to take up arms and follow me; but I now tell you, that those who remain peaceably at home, attending to their crops and their herds, shall be protected by me, in their property, in their persons, and in their religion; and not a pepper, not an onion, shall be disturbed or taken by my troops, without pay, or by the consent of the owner. But listen! he who promises to be quiet and is found in arms against me, I will hang!"

After delivering several more paragraphs, much of the material dwelling on how greatly he admired Catholicism, General Kearny gave the order to proceed on down the road against the enemy.

Alas! The Mexican "Army" had long since dispersed and retired helter-skelter toward Santa Fé.

This may have serious repercussions. After the weeks of hardship, the troops had high hopes of emotional relief in the form of a battle. They are now sullen and morose, given to recounting their woes. Petty grudges and spites, in usual circumstances alien to these volunteers, have been dragged into the open. Several fistfights have broken out, all, I believe, provoked by the St. Louisans, who make themselves obnoxious by referring to their county colleagues as "Grass-eaters," or "Doniphescans"—this last spoken in contempt because of the colonel's informal familiarity—and worse. I have an unhappy foreboding about all this. Rural Missouri was, in the main, settled by gentry, from Kentucky, southern Illinois and Tennessee. They are easy-going, slow-to-anger men who, when gratuitously offended, will nevertheless do murder without a grain of remorse. There is some justification for this. *It required a hard code to win and settle a hard land.*

XI

Well, Blaine's gone and done it. How a mild, milky-toast fellow like that, my brother to boot, can behave in such a fashion is considerably more than I know, but I heard Colonel Doniphan give an explanation, not seeming surprised.

After the battle failed to come about, we took up march, grumbling right along, and in a few days stopped early, for more repairs, at a place called Tecolate—nothing but adobe huts and the darkest-complected kind of Mexicans—and some of the St. Louisans commenced drifting back to chaff and make sport.

They took a set at Sergeant O'Hara, who drowned them out by pounding on a piece of hoop-iron with a mallet, and then at Hugh Angel, or Angelina, but she sprung on a horse and rode off to where the stock was grazing.

Well, sir, they spied Blaine sitting on a log, writing in his Journal, and that was what caused the trouble. They had a corporal with them, a long, lanky, bushy-haired giraffe, with very red eyelids, named Murdock, that they claimed was a butcher before the war, but he had such an ornery disposition, they had to let him out of jail to join. Always in trouble, for bullying and such, and as often as not for beating up his wife. So it was stated later. Nearly everything he said, even to his own men, had a sneer in it; he'd a been pee-rolled long since if he hadn't been so big. What I mean is, off at a distance he looked slim, but his forearms were all knotted up by muscles, from chopping meat maybe, or trying to saw out of a jail, and the veins stuck out like pipes. I never saw a man before with blood vessels that seemed to lie on *top* of the skin. They looked like snakes, and gave a person a squeamy feeling.

After some preliminary insults about Grass-eaters, and how much tougher the St. Louisans were, he spotted Blaine writing along, minding his own business, and says:

"It must be mighty nice, setting in the shade letting the men do all the work."

Sergeant O'Hara stopped pounding, and conversations let up here and there. All of these men liked Blaine, you understand, but they didn't know him very well, and I reckon they were curious.

Blaine went ahead writing, same pace as before, and finished the sentence he was on. Then he took his blotting paper and blotted it careful and slow, picking the book up to blow on it, then to wave it back and forth in the air.

"They tell me you've got a powerful hind-end suck with the officers, regular old smacking favorite," said Murdock, planting himself spraddle-legged with his arms folded, about two or three yards in front. "I never cared for rump-kissers myself."

This must have been the sixth or seventh time along the route that he'd made some lowering reference to Blaine working on the history. Up to now, it had been ignored.

You couldn't hear a sound, except for one fellow from Clay County who'd been polishing a saber and dropped it on a rock; in that stillness, it rang out like a gong. Murdock whirled around and kicked it about thirty feet, then said, "You're interrupting my remarks, and that ain't polite—seems like you clodhoppers can't do *nothing* without stumping your toe. No, don't pick it up. I'll let you know when."

I saw Sergeant O'Hara take a deep sigh and sort of tighten his grip on the mallet, but everybody else kept a bead on Blaine out of the corner of their eye.

Murdock says, "First I ever heard, fighting a war with a quill. There's something—well, I hate to put a name to it, because if there's one thing I ain't it's vulgar—but there's something womanish about it. I wonder if you'd just hitch down, now, and leave us make an examination?"

Blaine finally lifted his eyes (I calculated everybody figured it was about time) and said, in his normal voice, "What did you say your name was, my man?"

"'*What did you say your name was, my man?*'" Murdock gave a gritty kind of unpleasant laugh, that rubbed like sandpaper on a body's nerves, and said, "Why, I durn near forgot. They tell me you're an aristocrat, besides, one of them frilly-shirt bigwigs that's always sniveling on so lofty and pious and then grabbing a nigger wench down by the corn crib. It wouldn't surprise me none if the womenfolk had the same habit, oncet in a while. You take a big strapping buck, and a goody-goody white—"

Blaine's shoes had long ago wore out, so that he was wearing moccasins, like most of the men, and now he slipped one off, shook out the sand, stepped forward a pace, and whacked Murdock across the face so hard you could see a red welt rise up from the ear right across to his nose.

Twenty-five or more Clay County men rose softly to their feet, and not a single St. Louisan moved as much as a peg.

"Make a choice—rifle or pistol, at whatever distance you prefer," Blaine said, stepping back. "I had a thorough training in saber at college, so perhaps you'd better drop that one out."

I goggled like a fish out of water. *Was* this the same fellow I'd known all my life, reciting poety and reading books under the trees at Riverbend? Sergeant O'Hara restrained him by the arm, but Blaine snapped, very crisp, "Stay out of this!" and I saw Angelina Hughes staring as if she'd never seen him before this minute. Me, I was froze, too stunned to force out a word.

When Murdock got his breath back—he was practically paralyzed from astonishment—he bawled out, "You rich, yellow-bellied whippersnapper, I'll make you get down and *crawl* before you're through. You'll lick my boots and be glad of the chance."

He could have been heard half a mile, but there was something wrong with his face. He was trying, but the bluster had gone out of it.

"Rifle or pistol?"

Everybody waited, and it was a good long time, but he said,

"Pistol, by God! And you'd better get started on your prayers."

Well, I don't like to tell what happened, but they marched over to an arroyo, or dry gulch, and with two St. Louisans attending Murdock, whose legs were wobbly by now, and Sergeant O'Hara stepping along very reluctant with Blaine (not looking happy about it), they stood back to back—no sound, nothing stirring except three of those pink-eyed, wattle-necked black vultures that are *always* circling around, waiting, in Mexico—and then came the word like a gunshot: "Duel!" They'd had a discussion first, trying to patch it up, but Blaine brushed it aside.

They strode away, Blaine moving along with a regular rhythm and Murdock hurrying a little, then Murdock whirled on the count of nine, the miserable coward, and fired wild, way over Blaine's head, so they judged afterward. Blaine took a careful aim and shot Murdock in the chest—you could see the hole in his shirt before he clapped his hand on it—and he slumped forward, dead. He didn't twitch a muscle after he hit the ground—perfectly loose and heavy.

In the next minute, everything went pretty fast. Carrying their rifles, the Clay County men scrabbled up on one side of the arroyo, leaving the St. Louis volunteers looking worried and indecisive, trying to make up their minds, but just then Lieutenant Moss came riding up like a Comanche, and skidded to a stop. He'd jumped down and was running before he reined up the horse.

"In God's name, what's going on here?"

Behind him were Doniphan and the others, having just got the report. Standing there gazing down, Colonel Doniphan permitted himself a generality, as they say, but it was spoke so low not many but me heard it. He said, "Kentucky, and the dark streak of violence."

Two of the St. Louisans had peeled off Murdock's shirt and turned him over, then swabbed away the blood, but it wasn't any use; he was dead, all right, so they stuck a big tuft of cotton in the hole, leaving an inch or two of end protruding out. It was the main thing I remembered about the scene later.

"Well," said Colonel Doniphan, sounding as if he'd had trouble enough for one war, "I suppose you'd better come along to my tent."

I skedaddled at a good clip beside them, keeping to the brush, then crept up and eased my head under the rear tent flap. I was scared, and reckoned Blaine was about to be hung, but Doniphan sat down at a table and said, "No doubt you realize dueling is illegal in the Army?"

"I realize it now; I didn't think about it then. The fact is," said Blaine, seeming uncertain at last, "I don't quite know how this happened. The man was aggressively, obscenely, quite personally offensive, and then a kind of white, searing flash went through my brain. One minute I was sitting there, and the next I wasn't."

"Why didn't you pink him in the shoulder?"

"I'm afraid I meant to kill him."

Colonel Doniphan sat drumming on the table with a pencil, frowning. "The man was a scoundrel, virtually a monster, from all accounts. His men say they're glad to be rid of him. All the same, I have to take action. Worse, I'm a little worried about *you.*" He struck the table a smart blow. "Verdict of the summary court: self-defense, and justifiable homicide, with qualifications. Consider yourself under house arrest for forty-eight hours. Also, you're broken from corporal for awhile. I don't know," he went on, getting up, "Missourians don't appear to fit into army life. I might have shot the fellow myself."

"I'm damned sorry, Alex."

"*Colonel Doniphan,*" he said, then put on his hat and left.

XII

A FUNNY THING was, the duel set off an all-around outbreak of quarrels. And they weren't entirely amongst the men, either. In the next few days, a private named Robert Barnett drank a bottle of Mexican liquor call *aguardiente,* used mostly for removing whitewash from trees, so somebody said, and ran around on all fours howling like a coyote. Then he stabbed a bowie knife directly through the throat of Lieutenant R. A. Wells, of F Company, just below the ears. The end stuck out an inch or more, but practically no blood came, and he was only mildly inconvenienced; he said so himself. They called a doctor, while the victim stood looking in a mirror, mighty interested, and the doctor stated that, "No surgeon, however skillful, could put a knife through a man's neck at that particular point without death ensuing."

It was a handsome diagnosis, though unhelpful, so Lieutenant Wells pulled out the blade himself, and after that they patched him up. It missed the big vessel there, you see. Well, some Volunteers had tied Barnett to a tent-pole, but when he sobered up, he was sorry, and said so, as gracious as you please. Lieutenant Wells took off the bandage and showed him the holes (which was just the sort of thing that made him popular among the men—he didn't have to do it; it was done purely out of thoughtfulness and good breeding) and Barnett promised not to stab him in the throat any more.

During an alert, Colonel Doniphan found two sentries sleeping at their posts, but failed to invoke the death penalty, as General Kearny suggested. Instead, he gave them a brisk talking-to, then told them several jokes that more or less bore on the case, and said if they felt sleepy like that again, to come and shake him up; he'd stand watch in their place. He said he didn't have much to do anyway, only making the long-range plans, then carrying out the details, and almost always got to bed by midnight. I noticed those loafers slinking back to ranks, with their ears red, and from that time on, they were the reliablest sentries in the Army. Both laid into their work so hard they rose up to be sergeants, and later on transferred into spies, and were decorated.

But what caused the most talk was Captain Reid's ruckus with Kearny. That *did* jounce everybody around for awhile. We were drawing close to Santa Fé now, proceeding from one Mexican settlement to the next, administering the oath, buying supplies from those cheats, trying to keep from starving, and the men living in rags. None of the Volunteers had what you'd call a uniform any more, nor cared to make the effort.

Well, on the outskirts of a town named San Miguel—all crumbling red adobe and ratty vegetable patches, and sickly-looking goats, and *tortilla* ovens out in front, and dogs every place in sight—back comes General Kearny to Captain Reid's company for *inspection.*

Very smartly, Captain Reid drew his mounted men into ranks, what ones had horses left, and said, "D Company ready to be inspected, sir."

General Kearny and two aides rode stiffly along in front of those scarecrows, then he asked, "Captain, have your men no jackets?"

"Some have and some have not."

"Make your men put on their jackets or I will dismiss them from the service," said General Kearny.

"My men came to fight, not to dress," said Captain Reid. They sat stock-still for two or three minutes, each trying to stare down the other, stiff-necked and white-faced and angry, then General Kearny wheeled abruptly and rode back at a gallop. He understood well enough that the Regular Army hadn't provided any new clothes, nor any food to amount to, and not a dime so far in pay, so he wasn't in a position to holler very loud, if the truth was known.

Blaine said he figured the exchange would get into the history books, for as many as half a dozen Volunteers wrote it down word for word in their diaries.

The next day, we stopped early to noon, and decided to stay on for more overhauls, because the word was out that another battle was near. Well, *I* didn't need overhauling, and neither did any of the Drum-and-Fife Corps—all in tiptop shape, with the fiddler even learning to drum a little—so I stretched out in a tent for a rest. For once, the day was lovely and cool, and a breeze sifted in beneath the raised tent flaps; I was mighty comfortable, I tell you. I was having a nice dream about home, where I was carrying my rifle past an oak tree just jumping with squirrels, when somebody shook me by the shoulder, and it was Angelina.

"Wait a minute," I said, powerful sleepy, raising up and trying to reach for a gun. "What's going on here?"

"Shush. Keep your voice down. Come on; get up, quick!"

"What for?"

"This is an emergency. Wait till I've gone, and then follow me, but don't appear to—understand?"

I said, "Certainly not—" but she'd already left, so there was nothing for it but to draw on my boots and creep out. After my eyes got used to the sun, I saw her, the grimy, raggedy, slouched humbug, headed out toward the mesquite bushes and cactus, away from camp. I ambled along.

In five minutes I'd got pretty far into that dry, hard-baked, runty-growth country, and there she was, down in another of those arroyos. She was alone, thanks to goodness; for a second I figured maybe some St. Louisans had Blaine and were fixing to lynch him.

"*Now* what? I've got better things to do than prowl around in a desert looking for snakes. I was catching up on my—"

She took off her cap and shook out her hair, so that she looked more like a human, somehow. If she'd wiped off the smudges, she might have been good-looking, in a bold sort of way.

"You're acquainted with Pithecanthropus Erectus?"

"Acquainted with who?"

"O'Hara—the hairy ape. Patron saint of the Donegal House of Good Shepherd."

"Look here," I said, pretty hot, "you'd better start making sense, else I'm going—"

"O'Hara has raised the metaphysical point—*why can't I spit?* In brief, he's got a clue. The next thing you know, further suspicions will sprout. That slumbering brain might yet prove to be my undoing."

"Well, why *don't* you spit? Go ahead and spit, and maybe he'll leave you alone."

"Because I don't know how, you addlepated ninny. Nobody ever taught me."

"Oh, bilge. Everybody knows how to spit. A child of five can spit. It's something you're born with."

"Yes, *but not women.* I think it's handed down from male to male, like infidelity. I'll concede that in your world everybody does spit. My brother Kirk spits a beautiful stream. Anyhow," she said briskly, "quite aside from O'Hara, I'd like to learn. I wish they'd had it at the Seminary."

"You do it mostly with your tongue. But first you have to collect up some, right in the middle."

"Middle of what?"

"Your tongue. See here, you don't know *anything,* do you?"

"Sam, let's go at this thing calmly. Tackle it on a purely novice basis. I'll go to O'Hara later for the refinements. For one thing, I've noticed that he's deadly accurate up to about four yards, which is a very good working range for pests like cockroaches and lizards."

"If you could just shut up, I think we'd have a chance. You never stop talking. All right. Now. You've got some? Good. PUSH!"

I sat down and fanned myself with my cap. Perfectly hopeless case.

"You see? No farther than my chin. It happens that way every time. I hate to say this, Sam, but you're really a rotten teacher. Somehow you don't transmit that *will* to learn—so very, very important—from instructor to student. This may well illustrate that fine old adage: those who can, do; those who can't, teach."

"I resent that," I said, and meant it. "Watch here," and I let fly at a clump of organ cactus. I sliced off just a trifle to the right—it couldn't have been closer—but being worked up like that, I hadn't allowed for the wind.

"I'm sorry, Sam. That was splendid, an inspirational effort. Pound for pound, I believe you could spit with any of them. I mean that."

"Well, I don't like to brag, but I *have* rung up a few corkers along the way. Maybe not great, but—"

"No, honestly. You could be a tournament spitter, if you had the time. Right now, of course, we've got the Mexicans on our hands. All right, once again—*damn!*"

She wiped herself off, then I thought of something.

"I've got an idea, Angelina. There are two ways to hit this problem. You don't seem to snag onto the tongue-pusher—you fail to throw your lip muscles into it, to start with. Now—let's try the blow-out system. When it works, it's grand, sublime. It's in a class by itself—and talk about *range!*"

She was excited right off, I could tell. She says: "That's the *one*—I feel it. Lead on immediately; don't delay."

I rolled up a nice ball of spit, placed it toward the front of my tongue, sucked in my cheeks, then blew it out in a lovely long arch—not too high—and down about three feet *over* the organ cactus. It all hung together, and had a kind of professional look to it.

The girl broke down and gave me a hug; I reckon she couldn't help it, so I didn't complain. Also, and I may have imagined it, there appeared to be a touch of moisture in her eyes.

"Sam, that's *spitting!* Now let's go to work."

Well, sir, in about an hour's time, she was progressing fast enough to suit any teacher. On bursts of four and five, she was grouping a surprisingly close pattern. The girl had a natural knack for the method. I was proud of her, and told her so. She said she had never been much on organized sports, except for horses, but now she'd found one she liked, she meant to follow it right up.

A person ought to have something to do in later years, she said, and not just sit around the house in a rocker. You could go to pieces that way, and age before your time. She said she allowed she'd practice at least two hours a day and then do "a little off-the-hip spitting," as she called it, around O'Hara.

"I'll show *him,*" she said, and so we left it.

XIII

SANTA FÉ, *August, 1846:* After a march of nine hundred miles, we have entered the capital of New Mexico. This remarkable feat—the capture of an important enemy bastion easily capable of being defended—has been accomplished without the loss of a single man to combat! There is an element of hilarity here. Yesterday, at the Pass of the Galisteo, fifteen miles from the city, General Armijo and other high leaders, *with seven thousand men and artillery,* were all but impregnably disposed, awaiting battle at a narrow defile, a deep chasm or fissure through the ridge of mountains that divides the waters of the Pecos from those of the Rio del Norte.

Armijo had sent a curiously worded letter to General Kearny, stating that he would meet him that day in the Pass. Weeding through its over-politeness, its tricky phrasing, protestations of friendship, covert threats and other ambiguities, one could not be certain whether he meant to meet us in strife or parley.

In any case, we once again drew up our forces (less than two thousand men) and prepared to beard the scoundrel on terrain impossibly to our disadvantage. All of us were aware of the odds, yet we were keen. I must confess, for the first time, to emotional stirrings in my own bosom as the trumpets blared, happily drowning out the inconsequential twittering of the Drum-and-Fife Corps. On both musical and physical grounds, I would have sent

Sam back if I could; however, it was too late for that. In his juvenile ignorance (and swollen self-esteem) he alone, perhaps, failed to realize that we faced probable annihilation at the hands of an overwhelming force fighting with every tactical edge. Even the "laundresses" had a serious and thoughtful mien as this unequal contest neared.

Well, to sum up in terms as brief as the battle itself, we hurried at double time toward the Pass, General Kearny arranged our units, and we marched forth bravely, to find—what? For one thing, ample evidence that Armijo's men had been there very lately. An army of seven thousand leaves a disgusting wake of litter; every unsavory discard from the mechanics of human living lies strewn about to offend the eye, and the nose; (and with Mexicans, for some reason, this refuse strikes one as filthier than with the more fastidious races to the north). But what of the ravening legions? Alas as before, they had vanished. Now, on this second occasion of our trying to strike at ghosts, we produced an explanation, shortly after we arrived in Santa Fé. In my mind, it will remain the supreme example of the military, any military, selflessly at work.

As the hour approached to defend their country's honor (and soil), *Generals Armijo, Salazar, and others fell into a violent dispute over who held the supreme command!* In a word, they were unable to solve that vital problem. According to an eyewitness, they stood shouting and gesticulating, and waving their various orders and commissions, and nobody retreated an inch. Their demeanor, said the witness (a deserter filled with contempt), displayed valor far beyond the call of duty; each general was indifferent to all threats of the others to tattle to Santa Anna (the commander in chief) or to a court-martial, and remained doggedly demanding his rights. While this absurd charade continued, the soldiers lolled about, smoking, chatting, gambling, even sleeping at handy places in the shade.

At length, it appeared that none of the generals would give way, even if Mexico fell, and the order went out—probably uttered in concert—for the army to retire. So ended the second phase of our struggle against a fire-breathing foe bristling with bombast and threats. General Kearny, privately, conceded that he found it difficult to see how we could have forced an entry through the Pass of the Galisteo had the opposing regiments fought with any system at all.

As we jingled and clattered toward Santa Fé, the residents of every small settlement, or *rancho,* swarmed out to greet us, bringing (for sale) vegetables, bread, milk, eggs, cheese, fruits, peppers, chickens and other edibles, but our soldiers were restrained from trafficking during this critical forced march.

A few miles before we reached the city, the road emerged into an open plain; then, ascending a table ridge, we spied corn and wheat fields and what seemed to be piles of unburnt bricks lying here and there. Well, I supposed, we are nearing the suburbs, but no, these were *houses,* of crumbling, brownish-red adobe, some of them quite literally without roofs. One gained the impression that, during rains, the miserable occupants simply moved from one protected corner to another.

Entering the city proper, we marched in tattered array down the principal street to the Public Square, or Plaza, where the American flag was raised over the Palacio Grande—the mansion of ex-Governor Armijo—while Major Clark's two batteries of six-pounders fired a national salute of twenty-eight guns. Our American cavalry filled the streets, showing our colors, and I noted that many citizens cheered and waved from rooftops, quite openly welcoming a new regime, even if alien, that promised to stamp out corruption and defend New Mexico against bloody incursions by the Apaches, Navajos and Comanches.

The last day's march was so quick and fatiguing that our troops threw themselves down, where we quartered at last on a hillock out of town, and slept without eating. While General Kearny was busy establishing his headquarters in the Palacio Grande, no attention was given even to our animals; and many horses, without forage, died at their picket posts during the night. They were skin and bones before, and the last exertion proved fatal. To my sorrow, these included Dancer, my thoroughbred, who was never meant for the rigors of army travel; I was obliged to replace him, later, with the first of what will doubtless be a succession of tough mustangs. Alex Doniphan, tardily released from Santa Fé by his superiors, surveyed the pathetic scene with a countenance like a thundercloud, and many anticipated, at last, a showdown between the Regulars and Volunteers.

Today, the nineteenth, General Kearny assembled the citizens and read out a variant of the usual oath of allegiance, using the interpreter Robidoux. (He is one of three traveling with the Army, the others being Caldwell and Collins, all veterans of the Santa Fé trade.) *Surprisingly few Mexicans speak any English at all.* Kearny's theme equated the Catholic and Protestant religions and, in a few brief paragraphs, altered the nationality of his Spanish-speaking listeners: "You are no longer Mexican subjects; you are now become American citizens, subject only to the laws of the United States."

An interruption came in the form of successive waves of women from the lower classes, dressed in gay colors but covered with dark *rebozos,* who flung themselves prostrate in the street. An enquiry revealed that all had thought a proceeding was under way to brand them on the cheek with the initials "U.S." This misapprehension proved to be a seed implanted by the departed Armijo, a politician of withering resource. Reassured, the women arose, took a very curious and bold look at our men, and, I am told, issued invitations to a fandango, or informal dance, to be held in the evening. I do not expect anything very helpful will come of it.

After the ceremony, I was summoned to General Kearny's (and Doniphan's) headquarters, a large tiled upstairs chamber with a vaulted, much-decorated ceiling and arches that gave onto a broad balcony. The building's interior was a spacious, sun-drenched patio, with fountains, flowers, small trees, and iron benches artistically arranged—altogether a very sensible style of architecture, if one enjoys privacy. (This edifice, by the way, has the only glazed windows in Santa Fé; all others are simply empty holes.)

However, to return to the activity at hand, I arrived in the midst of a crisis. General Kearny, gaunt, gray, and exceedingly angry-looking, sat stiff-backed at an ornate mahogany desk, Doniphan lounged thoughtfully nearby, and before him stood a squat, darkish-sallow Mexican in respectable attire and wearing an expression of unctuous impertinence. Various others—officers and civilians—bustled about in the room.

"Ask the fellow to state his case again," said Kearny to Robidoux. There followed a rapid-fire exchange of Spanish, too fast for me to grasp, and Robidoux said, "He's the *alcalde,* General—the mayor—and he says you can't do any legal business without the payment for paper."

"What payment?"

"Well, the people have to pay eight dollars a page for any stamped paper in legal transactions."

"*All* the people? Including the ones residing in the roofless mud enclosures?"

"Unless they make an—arrangement. Things are mostly done by 'arrangements' in Mexico."

"What you intend to suggest is, by means of bribes?"

"Yes sir; for instance, in the Santa Fé trade, the *derechos de arancel*—the tariffs—were a hundred per cent on the contents of each wagon, but that was split three ways among the government, the tariff officers and the merchant. Then Governor Armijo added his *own* tariff of five hundred dollars a wagon, large or small, and—"

"Never mind," said General Kearny, and he scribbled something down on official stationery, then signed it with a flourish, blotted it, and handed it up. "Translate that to the villain." Robidoux read off, first in English and then in Spanish, "The use of the 'stamp paper' by the Government of New Mexico is hereby abolished. Done by the Governor, S. W. Kearny, Brig. Gen."

The news appeared to cause the *alcalde* great agitation. He twirled his hat around and expostulated in noisy bursts of rhetoric. As he did so, we caught sight of two prominent gold teeth that flashed in his dark, conniving face.

"Well?" said Kearny.

Robidoux seemed reluctant. "He's, ah, afraid you've misunderstood, General. He says you'll *get* your share, the same as Armijo did. He says we can all work together, you and he and the Church, and—"

"*Sentry!*" roared Kearny, "assist His Honor down the stairs—no, not by the arm; surely the United States Army can provide faster transportation than that—*excellent!* [as we heard the smack of a boot against solid meat]. That was well done, sentry. It may be irregular, but I intend to mention you in dispatches—the first satisfactory contact with the enemy."

The scene was reassuring, for I do not believe that any of us Volunteers had previously been given a glimpse of General Kearny the man. He appeared to be a cold, austere, grim-visaged, unlikeable martinet, and I feel that this episode can be nothing but beneficial. *Above all else, the Missourian loves a man capable of down-to-earth humor.*

As an attorney, Alex Doniphan had been assigned to draw up a Constitution, with new laws for the Territory, and he needed my editorial help, since he has limited Spanish. In a corner of the room stood a small hand press—found somewhere below and towed up by Dragoons—and we quickly stumbled onto the obstacle that the language has no "W." We agreed to solve this by juxtaposing two "V's," for the purpose of printing the material in double columns—Spanish and English—when there came another interruption.

"Corporal from the detail cleaning out the *calabozo,* sir!" cried the sentry, and a white-faced St. Louis Volunteer rushed in, saluted, and held up a pair of long rods upon which were impaled two-dozen dried human ears, *en brochette,* so to speak, or, as grisly as it sounds, strung like popcorn on pieces of twine for Christmas.

A quick investigation, that called in one of the principal priests of the town, a man of education and some integrity, disclosed that these trophies came from captured Texans whom General Salazar had executed *a lanzados;* that is, in the favorite Mexican style of stripping them, scourging them to the bare bones, and, finally, piercing their torsos leisurely with lances. Salazar, a thoughtful and generous man, had presented the ears to Governor Armijo as "souvenirs and evidence of my high friendship."

I could scarcely envy General Kearny as the job of taking over an enemy capital wore on. Our own troops, half-starved, unpaid, over-ready for dispute and deprived as yet of combat, provided much of the trouble. A Volunteer named Haskins (suffering from fatigue) went out of his wits and assaulted an officer; he was tried by court-martial and drummed out of the service. Lieutenant

James S. Oldham, of the Jackson County company (*a very good man*), was also court-martialed and dismissed "with a disability to serve in the Armies of United States for a period of twelve months." This for, if you please, disobeying an order from Lieutenant Colonel Ruff that forbade his starving men from buying provisions. At that moment, with the wagons *still* someplace back in the wilderness, we were on half-rations of very bad (previously sifted) flour, and less than half-portions of beef, from the thin, worn-out beasts that had accompanied us (and, in the end, been compelled to draw wagons). Though high-level policy received full attention in the Palacio, our common soldier had no pork or bacon, no coffee, no sugar, rice or molasses. At the height of this austerity, the patient and lowly O'Hara obtained some cheap Mexican liquor and ran amok, creating an incident that will not soon be forgotten.

Seizing up his pitiful handful of food, as well as mine and that of the sufficiently skinny Hugh Angel, he strode into town, red-faced and babbling a string of picturesque Celtic oaths; then he joined at last his quite private war. In the Plaza, an attractive area surrounded by four tiers of porticoed public buildings (which house the Palacio, the Customs, the barracks *cum calabozo*, the *Casa Consistorial* of the alcaldes, and the *Capilla de los Soldados*, or Military Chapel) he located, collared, and jammed into a corner—a priest!

In his intoxication, O'Hara had somehow managed to pin on the Catholic clergy the misfortune of our inadequate food. This is not surprising, in view of the fact that he blames everything on the Catholic clergy, including the war itself, the disappearance of the Holy Grail, his confrontations by the authorities (at home and abroad), the fall of the Holy Roman Empire, the collapse of London Bridge, and the untimely death of Cock Robin. On this occasion, he force-fed the priest, item by item, the rations he had conveyed into town, while a very fair-sized crowd collected to egg him on. The cleric in question is not popular, being the principal voice against the establishment of a local public school (which would collide, in his mind, with the fiercely selective Catholic ones and the six large, rich churches that run them).

Meanwhile, O'Hara kept up a running commentary, not necessarily calculated to aid digestion:

"I hope your Riverince will jine us. Try the beef; taste like strap leather? Bless you, sir, you've throwed flour all over your cassock. You're a pretty sight for a Lord's servant. I'm dogged if you don't look like a leper. Here, don't choke, now—it's irreligious. What's more, it's resistin' a sojer in the simple performance of his dooty," and picking up a stick, O'Hara dusted off the flour rather noisily.

Several times, persons in the crowd made gestures to restrain him, but his formidable bulk (plus his fever of the moment) proved an effective dissuader. At length a detachment of Dragoons, hastily dispatched, overpowered him, bound his arms, and picked up the priest, who was making signals that indicated an emergency interest in a lavatory. The fact is, I very much doubt whether he dines again for a week.

But to proceed to the core of the story, O'Hara was removed to camp and spread-eagled with thongs to a wagon wheel. The poor fellow being perfectly befuddled with drink, the spectacle angered the Volunteers who gathered here on Regular Army ground. There were cries of "Cut him down!", "We'll look after him," and the like.

Well, in a few minutes, Alex Doniphan appeared on the scene, riding up calmly, but wasting no time getting there, either.

"Do you have some trouble, Lieutenant?" he inquired of the haughty Dragoon in charge, and the reply was, "None that the *Army* can't handle."

"Well, you see, we're Army, too," said Alex, breaking into his slow, friendly smile, "so perhaps you'd better turn him over to us."

"Not without an order from General Kearny, I don't," replied the lieutenant, who was little more than a stripling, and exceedingly contemptuous of ragamuffin Volunteers. "This man's about to be flogged, according to Article 17, Section 22B. Get on with it, Sergeant"—this last to a roughneck standing by with a bullwhip.

The shortsighted fool; I was almost sorry for his failure to size up men. What happened next could scarcely have been covered in his training at West Point, and he had not the slenderest suggestion how to handle it. In fact, he was thunderstruck.

Doniphan's smile vanished, to be replaced by the startling flat glitter in his Indian-dark eyes.

"Get that man down from there and be damned quick about it!" He made a motion to dismount, all six feet four inches, but it was unnecessary. After only a second's hesitation, the officer said, "Yes, sir," and himself cut O'Hara free.

In a sentence remarkably lenient for a case involving the sensitive problem of religion, O'Hara has been confined to the guardhouse (the cleaned-up calabozo) for the duration of our stay in Santa Fé. His non-commissioned status has apparently remained intact, the feeling being, I think, that he might be provoked to resign, or desert, and that his mechanical skill as a trouble-solver is indispensable. In this general line, a number of desertions have already been logged, and there is official fear that the practice will become epidemic. Six Dragoons and two Volunteers were the first to be noted, and, making further dents in our ranks, others have been discharged as being no longer physically fit to serve.

The foremost question is, why in an area of abundance are we being permitted to go hungry? I must acknowledge that I myself am confused. Two separate answers are offered, neither doing credit to the Army. The first is that of economy, pure and simple; the second, even more angrily received, is that Kearny wishes the men to be starved down so as to be light in the saddle while on marches through the desert.

To date, the troops' billeting ground has been moved five times. With lackluster movements, they strike their tents, pack up their gear, and shuffle to another patchy stand of grass a mile or two distant. Now, at length, they have been emboldened to frame a petition to Colonel Doniphan. It is entitled "Camp of Starvation" and respectfully raises the points which I have mentioned above; in fact, it is precisely as respectful, and firm, as I could make it. Yes, a delegation of three Clay County Volunteers—all good lads—arrived and requested that I turn my bent to this assignment. With them was the impertinent Hugh Angel, who, I must say, had moderated his cheeky nagging of late.

"We thought you might put it into the proper form, sir," said one of the men. "Seeing as how you're writing up the expedition and all."

"Unless you feel so cozy with the officers that you'd rather not . . . *sir,*" added Angel, sounding, I thought, just a trifle sarcastic.

"Corporals are not addressed as 'sir.' I've stressed the point before, Angel."

"I beg your pardon, and besides, you aren't really a corporal any longer, are you? Not since the messy incident in the gulch."

I felt an unreasonable flush rise to my face. Aside from a certain temporary and mystifying coolness on the part of Sam, I believe I can say that my action in defending the rural Missourians has been viewed with deep and general admiration. Few of the men have said so—it is not a subject one cares to discuss—but I am not mistaken in their attitude.

I considered the unhappy condition of these starvelings, and made allowances.

"My corporalcy has been restored," I said, snapping shut my Journal. "More important, I'm just as hungry as you are. Let's see if we can jog a little common sense into this document-crazy Headquarters." Amidst the relieved exclamations, I saw Angel regarding me thoughtfully; then he turned and left, over-ready to retreat to his animals and his solitude, I fancied.

Two hours after a Volunteer had delivered our grievance to the Palacio, I was summoned to see Doniphan. He took me aside to the printing press—idle while he discharged legislative duties—and said, "Tell me, did you draw up this bill of complaints?"

"I drew it up."

"I thought it sounded like you. All true, fair, and in proportion?"

To be perfectly candid, I was feeling edgy about the abandoned plight of the men, and I said, as pertly as possible to this old friend and family solicitor, "Also relevant, competent, and material."

He gave me a quizzical glance, which took in, no doubt, my emaciated face, the frayed condition of my attire, and the fact of there being a substantial part of my right sleeve missing. Then he collected his hat from a table and stopped before the desk where General Kearny, at the moment, was interviewing the Pueblo chiefs.

"I'll have to be leaving for awhile, General," he said, lighting a cigar. "Some of my boys've sent up signals for a parley."

"I believe your assignment was to prepare a statement of intention toward the Pueblos," said General Kearny crisply.

"Well, the fact is"—Alex was having trouble getting the cigar started, and he struck another match—"their bellies appear to be empty, and the Pueblos can go to the devil till I get them filled up."

He clapped on his hat, and we left. But when we arrived in camp, we found the place boiling with excitement. A trooper named Perkins was in the custody of Lieutenant Colonel Ruff, on charges of stealing a goose from a Mexican. This was serious, for the first published declaration toward the local citizens centered on the absolute sanctity of their chattels.

"What's going on here, Colonel?" inquired Doniphan.

Ruff is a choleric man, given to flying off the handle and to petty and tyrannical impositions of duty—these in the interest of "discipline." Seldom does he wink at a trifle of bad conduct, and there has been intense feeling lately over his ordering three roll calls a day, drill on foot, and other unnecessary levies on starving men. He considers, in his words, that a soldier should be "kept in his place." Above all, he is appalled by Alex Doniphan's informal approach to command.

He replied: "This is an open and shut case, as I'm sure you'll agree. The prisoner, Perkins, stole a goose—snatched it out of a citizen's yard, flung it over a small creek, jumped across, picked it up, and ran. What's worse is that he brazenly admits it! I've ordered an immediate summary court-martial, but now that you're here—sir, [he had difficulty getting the word out] you will no doubt wish to take over."

Doniphan sat down on a log, took out his ever present penknife (to whittle) and stared judicially at the prisoner, who stood frightened but defiant.

"Well, all right, I suppose Court is now convened."

"You mean *here*, on this log?" asked Ruff in disbelief.

"I beg your pardon, Ruff. You can sit down, if you like. There's room enough for two."

"My intention was to hold a formal hearing—a military tribunal—in my tent. With the proper entries in the record, witnesses, and—"

"Oh, we've got witnesses enough," said Alex, indicating the throngs of silent, interested Volunteers. "As for the record, Corporal Shelby's got a good memory. He can scratch it up later."

"May I remind you, Colonel," said Ruff, "of General Kearny's orders—his first order upon arriving—concerning theft from the citizens, of the gravity with which he would view this proceeding?"

"I'm glad you did, Ruff. I'd hoped to tell General Kearny about it later, if I didn't forget it. Take a seat," he added, "and we'll get down to brass tacks."

"I prefer to stand," said Ruff stiffly. "I'd like the record to so show it."

Alex rapped on the log with his knife, then said, "Prisoner, step forward."

Perkins did so, but not very smartly. He was a youth of twenty or thereabouts. Sartorially speaking, he looked like a bundle of tattered brown pennants.

"Name?"

"William Perkins, sir."

"Outfit?"

"Saline County Missouri Mounted Volunteers, Company D, sir, Captain Reid commanding . . . I wish he was here."

"You do, do you? Why?"

Perkins was struggling to be respectful, but his gaze was fixed on Ruff.

"Because," he finally blurted out, "—he's considerable of a man."

"Well, now, I agree with you there," said Alex. "Offhand, I can hardly think of a better. Perkins, they tell me you stole a goose."

"Yes, I did, sir."

"Where is that goose?"

There was a stir among two or three of Ruff's non-coms, and a red-faced sergeant carried the creature forward. He handed it to Colonel Doniphan, as, for the first time, titters were heard in the back rows of spectators. Alex felt the fowl over carefully.

I thought of the many, many cases, the important and even celebrated trials at which he had starred as the defending attorney, and felt a glow of admiration for his poise in this squalid setting.

"Ruff," he said sharply, "why isn't this goose tagged?"

"Why, I don't under—"

"This is the prosecution's Exhibit A, and should be so marked. I'm surprised at you."

Ruff started to sputter, but the inquiry pressed on.

"Perkins, I hope you realize that you've stolen an unusually fat goose."

"I know something about geese, sir." He was commencing just slightly to thaw.

"Have that fellow there step up"—Alex pointed to the shabby, sombreroed owner of the bird—"and let Collins come with him. Now then, sir, what's *your* name?"

Collins bent to his work, then straightened up. "Says he's called Arnolfo Perez, and wonders if you have a spare cigarette, sir."

"Now I want you to tell him this: I'm going to ask a question, and if he doesn't give a truthful answer, he'll be shot. That question is, where did *he* get the goose?"

Breaking into incoherent protest, Ruff started forward, but Doniphan waved him back.

After a crackling exchange, Collins tried twice to report, but fell victim to laughter; then he paused to wipe his eyes. The Mexican, meanwhile, stood by grinning without embarrassment.

"He stole it from his brother-in-law, sir, but he says that was all right because the brother-in-law stole it from a farmer in an outlying settlement. He says his brother-in-law is not entirely honest."

Doniphan nodded, as if this outrageous utterance were perfectly reasonable. "Ask him how much the goose is worth in the market."

Another exchange, filled with vehemences and expostulation.

"On his mother's head, he swears that the goose is worth at least fifty cents, American. He'd drive nails through his feet before he'd take a centavo less. Saint Francis himself knows—"

Doniphan tossed a quarter to Perez, who burst into raptures of gratitude. He shook hands with everybody nearby, including Perkins, but was restrained from embracing Colonel Doniphan and kissing him on both cheeks.

Lieutenant Colonel Ruff said, "And now, sir, may I ask if you intend to render a verdict? Unless my knowledge of law fails me, we still have a prisoner to sentence."

"Your knowledge of law does you credit, Ruff," replied Alex, with unaccustomed irony. "The verdict, to be sure. The Court will now ponder its opinion." He arose and put away his knife, lit another cigar, and strolled back and forth. Twice he stopped and studied Perkins intently, and once he stooped over to reinspect the goose.

"Come, sir, have you reached a decision?" asked Ruff impatiently.

Alex disposed himself on the log and said slowly: "The Court has heard all the evidence and examined the witnesses for both sides. The case proved to be more complicated than appeared at first sight. It turned, if I may say so, on the unusual plumpness of the prosecution's Exhibit A. In the Court's mind, only one decision is possible. As the prisoner has gone to considerable trouble in stealing such a goose, the least the Court can do is help him eat it."

Ruff quite literally turned brick-red. When he recovered a degree of articulation, he screamed, "By God, have you gone clean out of your mind? When General Kearny hears—"

Alex turned very slowly to face him, as still as a statue. But there was a strong military question in his look, and Ruff caught the warning. Forcing the words, he stammered, "I—I beg your pardon, sir. You're in command here, to be sure." Then he wheeled around rigidly and left, followed, I'm afraid, by two or three catcalls and boos.

"Men," Alex called out, in a voice that carried over their heads, "there'll be no more stealing here. *None at all.* And if I can help it, no more hunger, either. I wish I had known earlier of the conditions in camp, but I've been detained"—he paused wryly—"to see that the town is fully documented. Now I'm appointing

Corporal Shelby to take a detail of four men into town, with fifty dollars from my pocket and fifty dollars from his, [he gave me a look as innocent as a baby's, causing me suddenly to realize that I'd been punished for my asperity] and start buying rations. We'll keep on buying them till the wagons arrive; you may consider that a personal promise." Then he added, "I expect we'll be reimbursed by and by, if they ever get word to Washington where we are."

XIV

Santa Fé: We've had a big whoop-jamboreehoo about the fandango, so I reckon I'd better write it up. Anyhow, Blaine jumped on me about keeping my Journal going, and we had a discussion about it. It may sound hard, but I told him the truth, said it was easy enough for *him*, because he hadn't aimed at any particular public, but I was writing a book, and a downright unexpurgated one at that.

He says, "A what?"

"Unexpurgated. All the best ones are, on the order of Peeps, and Casanova and Cellini."

"I see. And where did you learn about *those?*"

"Look here, Blaine," I said, halfway ashamed of him, "what *did* they teach you at college? Aside from the silly shenanigans pulled by the Latins and the Greeks?" (I knew well enough that both tribes were what they called "classical," and pretty high up on the ladder, but I was hoping to get him riled, and did so.)

"Never mind," he says. "I'd rather not go into it any further. I've only got a couple of hours to kill, in any case. *However,* I think I'd better take a look at your work before long. We may have got off on the wrong foot here."

"I wish you would," I says, "and I'll be glad to help you with yours. Sometimes two heads are better than one on these things. Any time at—"

He said "Goodbye!" seeming in a hurry, and I continued about my business. Among the first things I heard, not long after we hit town, was about Captain Hobbs being in the calabozo when they cleaned it out. You needed written permission to leave camp now, but I slid around it because one of my elderly fifers underwent a discharge as being "painfully unfit for duty," meaning drill, I reckoned, so I had to scrounge up another. It wasn't easy; fifers don't grow on bushes. I heard one of the officers say that the doctor in the case would go down in history as a patron of the arts alongside Lorenzo the Magnificent, but I didn't catch his drift. There wasn't any Lorenzo amongst the Missouri Volunteers, except a man from Van Buren named Sikes, a small-time pig farmer, and there was nothing Magnificent about *him;* filthiest fellow in camp; everybody said so.

Anyway, I went into town and found Captain Hobbs when they set him free. He and Spiebuck had bundled out of Leavenworth before the troops and sailed into Santa Fé with a wagonload of trade goods, same as always. Only General Armijo said there was a war on, which was true, so he seized the wagon and sold it and put the proprietors in jail. He said he planned to shoot them as soon as he'd defeated the gringos at Galisteo, but he'd come back and left for Chihuahua instead.

"I didn't in no wise figure he'd take the war so serious," said Captain Hobbs when I found him at headquarters. "We'd always got along tolerable well before, give or take allowances for him being a crook and a coyote."

He was practically a skeleton, being starved down to nothing for weeks, also spanceled to a cold stone wall by both wrists, but his face hadn't changed from its usual hawky-leather look. Spiebuck, when released, had gone scouting ahead of an expedition headed by Captain Reid, to persuade the Navajos to quit killing Mexicans and Pueblos and maybe develop some new interests. They were to ride toward a place called Albikirk, which some said means apricot, though it sounds unlikely.

The fandango had been postponed several times, but now they held it, in a "saloon" or interior court, and everybody came, and possibly several dozen too many. A good many Mexicans rode into the dance in *carretas*—what Captain Hobbs said were "bulger wagons"—homemade ox-drawn carts with giant wheels made out of cottonwood. Even the quality used these, bumping along on those irregular-hewed wheels with the most amazing lurches and skreeks. You'd a thought they might have jarred their livers loose. Mostly, though, a husband and wife of the poorer classes arrived together on one gray sickly-looking burro with half the nap rubbed off, the woman stowed forward, with a cudgel to keep him interested, and the man humped over in the stern, doing nothing but smoking, as usual. When they come to hand out prizes for laziness, Mexican men will waltz off with all honors. For instance, I noticed that they get up pretty early in the mornings, all ready to make the dust fly, but then they kindle a little bonfire out of sticks, outside, and stand over it all day long, talking and scratching for bugs. Wrapped around with a faded old poncho, or blanket, straw sombrero on, goatskin pantaloons unbuttoned down the sides, feet bare or sandaled, and a look of waiting in no hurry, as somebody put it, for the second arrival of Jesus.

To get back on the subject, they told us a fandango was a function that *everybody* joined in, rich and poor, while a *baile,* or ball, was of considerably higher grade. I hope so.

Our food had held up very well for days, but Colonel Doniphan was sent on a trip, so it caved in again. On this night, a number of soldiers and teamsters dined entirely off onion pie and a commodity called Taos whisky—pure alcohol, so it was stated. They were warmed up in wonderful shape for the fandango, and started the festivities by running in twenty-five hairless Chihuahua dogs with firecrackers tied to their tails. The dogs weren't damaged any, only scared, but they scampered round and round, barking at one end and firing off guns at the other, and a lot of the Mexicans got sore. For one reason or another, they stayed sore most of the evening.

I say evening, but the shindig started at nine o'clock, you understand, and was announced by church bells ringing. Then the women gathered in the saloon and got things ready. Compared to what people wore in Clay County (except Angelina, who didn't wear anything much) they were dressed frolicsome and gay, in only bright-colored skirts and shawls, or rebozos, over the top part. To give them credit, some women had on petticoats, ranging from one among the poor to four or five in the rich groups. This was a "mark of caste," somebody said. Later on, as these females whirled around faster, letting go all holds, a person could see most all of them, above and below, and a number of churchgoing Volunteers said it was wicked. We had three or four remarkably pious men amongst the Missourians—deacons and elders and worse—and these pressed up forward so as to get a better look and report everything accurate to the preachers back home. I reckoned they took it as their duty, and admired them for it, but Blaine said something on the order of "Piffle; religious fanatics are the most prurient people on earth." Then he mentioned a congregation named the Druids, on the order of Baptists, that upended big rocks and danced around naked in the moonlight. They held "orgies," which were like a communion service without clothes, as I got it, and must have been mighty uncomfortable in the winter. Anyhow, they worshiped so hard in the orgies that they worshiped themselves to death, and were now extinct, though not necessarily in Heaven. So he claimed. *I* never saw any Baptists dancing naked in the moonlight, or anyplace else, and the only rocks they fooled around with were ones that got in the way of ploughing. As I stated earlier, he was down on practically everything in good standing.

Well, the Mexican men begun to arrive, and soldiers and teamsters (what ones weren't sick and could get passes) and then we had the dogs, and after that things quietened down some. Everybody except the dancers sat in a circle on the floor. Off to one side were earthenware pots and bottles containing refreshment: pepper sauce, pepper soup, tortillas, and wine. These Mexicans grow a cactus plant called *maguey* and make several kinds of drinks from it—pulque, mescal and double-distilled mescal—which very few people drink at a fandango. One fellow was selling cheap brandy, but nobody bought any that I noticed. They drink wine, and precious little of that. The truth is, Mexicans aren't strong on drinking. I seldom saw a drunken Mexican on the streets here, which is considerably more than you could say for our soldiers.

Blaine claimed the style of dancing was a "swinging, gallopade waltz, like Byron's description of the Dutch waltz, taken to its extreme." He said it resembled the descent of a fellow named Aeneas to the Kingdom of Pluto. No matter what, it got hotter and hotter, and faster and faster, as the women practically forgot their rebozos altogether, along with the general scarcity of britches, and you could a heard the uproar in California. All the señoritas took to dancing with cigarritos in their mouths, and the high-class ones had little golden tongs, called *tenazitas de oro,* to handle them with. All in all, it was a gaudy old sight, I tell *you.* Twice, as women got whirled clear off of their feet, demonstrating how they could have used a good underwear shop, Blaine tried to send me home, but I wriggled free and joined Captain Hobbs. This ruckus was educational, and, if you come right down to it, unexpurgated.

Along about now the teamsters commenced to cause trouble, and dumped several liters of aguardiente into the wine. I'll say this: for awhile it briskened up the musicians three or four hundred per cent. They had a fat copper-colored man playing the fiddle and another plucking at a *bandolín* or *guitarra*—the size of a small skiff—and a Pueblo boy beating on a *tombé,* or little Indian drum. As a professional musician myself, I have to admit that they weren't bad for natives. What astonished us, though, was that this identical group played the next day in church, and played the exact same tunes!

They started off with a very slow dance called the *cuna,* the seated women singing and rocking back and forth, legs and skirts arranged any old way, and it sounded like a dead march. But when the musicians got hold of those cups, they took a new grip on life. Before you could wink, the whole room was full of people flinging themselves around, and the worst of all was the teamsters.

In several ways, these fellows were a nuisance to the Army. They were in it and yet remained separate. What I mean is, they were hired *as civilians,* with experience operating heavy wagons, and were assigned to officers, but they took orders only up to a point. If one of them felt in the humor, he could quit. They were about as rough and ready as anybody I ever met, and Captain Hobbs said the same. I introduced him to some teamsters and soldiers, and he made a big hit. They asked him considerable questions about the Comanches and he replied very civil, though generally making up a lie. He told about the tribe using only top-grade, sun-dried Apaches for pemmican, and mentioned the curious custom of baptizing new-born babes in buffalo urine. Then somebody coughed up a pretty raw inquiry about the Comanche women, but that squeaked by because another fellow, a big unshaved hulk of a teamster, with a breath to wither a jackass, said, "I heerd we're aimin' in the general direction of El Passer."

Captain Hobbs' ears pricked up right off, he was interested, and said, "That so?"

"I never been there myself, but I hear it spoken highly. Right down loose and unmoral," said the teamster with a leer.

Captain Hobbs chuckled. "I got a old friend down there, as true a friend as ever I've knowed. He's done right well."

The teamster only grunted, not really hearing, the way people don't when somebody else is talking, but he changed his tune when Captain Hobbs said, "Yes, he operates a cat-house, of the high-class type, *but it ain't expensive*. That's one of its better features."

I was surprised, because I'd never heard him talk blue before, but figured he was ruffled on account of his wife.

"Well, now, you don't tell us," said the teamster, and others chimed in. "What all does he go in fur? It might come in handy, seeing we're headed there."

"Folks in El Paso reckon it to be the best in town. He sold seventeen cats last month."

The teamster said, "Shucks!" and "Mighty amusing, to be sure," and after that they let the Comanches drift. But they were good sports, and clapped him on the back so hard his teeth rattled, then had a good laugh all around.

Their approach to the fandango was mainly over-serious-mocky, and would of set old Job to foaming at the mouth. When they had wore out all the women, barking their shins and spraining two or three ankles, they took to dancing with *each other*, one coming up as polite as whipped cream, imitating the Mexicans, and saying, "I wonder if you could honor me with the pleasure of this waltz, señorita, if you ain't too drunk to get up on your hind feet?" and then, after some ridiculous bowing and scraping, with maybe a few punches exchanged in the belly, off they went, as graceful as oxen on skates, bowling people over, knocking aside pots and bottles, and, usually, landing in a heap in some corner, lying there too collapsed from laughing to move.

The Army had fourteen guards on hand at the start, standing alongside one wall with muskets, but the teamsters got them drunk in about half an hour and took them to a side room where a woman was running a card game called monte. It was a curiosity to me, because the deck had four suits, clubs, swords, suns and cups, and only ten cards in a suit, running from one to seven and with a knave, a horse (instead of a queen), and a king. It was tough, but I figured I'd learn it and get back some of my money from Hyacinth, when I returned home. Usually, he had the dumb luck to beat me at seven-up; also he cheated.

If there was one thing these Mexicans liked to do better than loaf, it was gamble. They were always at it, even sitting on the curbstones of the streets, and if it wasn't cards it was roosters fighting.

The monte game was operated by what somebody called "an equivocal woman" (which is Blaine's spelling and probably wrong), formerly by the name of La Tule. She had an interesting history, coming from Taos, where she'd run into trouble making a living, because of the beautiful amateurs there, it was stated, and then moving to Santa Fé in about 1838. Well, she hung around doing odd jobs—so odd you could be jailed for it, one of the teamsters said—and took to playing monte. Right away everything changed. Her career advanced in amazing style. She was a natural monte player, being as crooked as a snake, which was necessary with Mexicans, and having a lot of luck besides. Anyhow, one night she hit a game for nine hundred American dollars; then she opened a bank of her own.

In 1842, she shipped ten thousand dollars to the United States, where it was turned into trade goods and multiplied several times. Before long she was rich, and found all the doors in Santa Fé flung open, the way they are when a person gets money and undergoes aristocracy. The two happen one right after the other.

According to Blaine, half the gentry in America were nothing but white trash before some member of the clan made a killing selling nuts and bolts, or hawking furs, or stealing bonds, or cheating Chinamen with a Boston sailboat. *His* ancestors had come to Jamestown, which was populated by natural-born gentlemen—entirely helpless, couldn't blow their nose without assistance, so fell easy prey to the Indians, which could—and so *he* was *all right,* and belonged in the best bracket.

La Tule was now known as Señora Doña Gertrudes Barcelló, and no longer had trouble with amateurs, being too old for it besides, and she still ran the monte game, right here at the fandango. She was received in the best circles of society, as they said, including the Palacio with the glazed windows, but her real fever was still gambling. Those fourteen soldiers didn't only lose all their pay, or, rather, vouchers for pay, but several men lost theirs up through Christmas, which was as far as she'd go, and two men went home without their muskets and trousers. A teamster that wandered in and tried to pawn off a mortgage on Fort Leavenworth was removed, though gently (on account of his size), so he came back to the fandango and worked up some different mischief.

By and by, a teamster insisted on climbing up and playing the guitar, having a merry old time of it, face thoughtful and sober and artistic, but he couldn't play music any better than a gorilla can, so they tried to waltz him out of there. He'd somehow got one foot through the hole in the sounding board, and was tangled up amongst the strings. He claimed it played better that way, but he was wrong.

Well, the fellow that owned it being practically in tears, they collected up a pot and paid him ten dollars—"insurance"—because an argument had developed whether this teamster could paddle the guitar across a canal. Here in Santa Fé they have three canals that run through the city, irrigating corn and wheat fields and others, as well as being useful for sewage and drinking (if you cared to spend the winter in a privy) and the biggest of the lot is the *acequía madre,* or mother ditch.

These sots went brawling down there, with a good-sized group following along behind, laughing and rowdying, but grumbling and threatening, too, among the Mexicans, and when he got ready to push off, with the other bank showing pretty and clear in the moonlight (but not close) I'm jiggered if he didn't hang fire and say the "cockpit" was too small. So they got a saw and sawed it out larger, shushing up the owner and assuring him it would do wonders for the instrument musically, and the teamster pushed off, using a musket butt for an oar. But as he'd forgot to uncock the oar, it went off and dropped into the water, after which he commenced to paddle with his hands. This didn't work either, because he only spun round and round like a wagon spoke, and the guitar filled up and sunk. It hadn't any calking or freeboard, and, as somebody pointed out, it wasn't really constructed for this work at all.

When that happened, you never heard such a sloshing around and bawling. He sounded like a sea calf that had lost its mother, so a group of good swimmers hauled him out and emptied him. And just in time, too; it was a mighty near thing.

Everybody trooped back to the fandango, but it appeared to have lost steam. The owner of the guitar skedaddled for home, taking his ten dollars with him, and nobody blamed him. They rounded up another guitar player, but his music came out fitful and jerky. The fellow seemed nervous, for some reason.

Around two o'clock, the teamsters fell into a discussion about how strong these adobe buildings were, and measured the thickness of the walls. Some claimed a small piece of artillery would knock the place apart; others felt not. When we entered town, General Kearny had captured six pieces of artillery that Armijo had left behind, being in a sweat to visit Chihuahua (where he had a lot of friends, they said), but only one cannon was any good—a little Texas piece taken by General Salazar from General McLeod in 1841 and inscribed with the name of General Lamar, the President of Texas. It fired copper slugs, instead of grape and canister like the big guns.

So, about a dozen of them fetched it, snaked it out from under the guards' noses, which were asleep, and rolled it down the street and into the fandango by a side door. Nobody paid them any attention, because the dancing was booming along fine again, and presently they loaded up and blew out the far wall of the building, where no people were gathered. No casualties; and most of the debris fell outside, of course, so the frolic could have gone on, once everybody had got used to the draft, but it didn't. When the wall collapsed, people took it as a signal that the dancing was over.

Moreover and in addition, a yowling hullabaloo was raised, with the alcalde jumping up and down, and several priests raising cain as well, and after that, finally, General Kearny himself was rousted out. Quite a number of Mexicans contended that no walls had ever been blown out of their fandangos before and they resented it.

Well, they arrested upwards of a dozen teamsters and placed them in the calabozo. But the next morning they were only fined fifty dollars apiece plus damages. They were badly needed by the Army, you see, so there wasn't any use getting worked up about a prank, after all. There were plenty of brickmasons around there, and the wall could easily be repaired. That was all of the fandangos for two or three weeks, though, and everybody agreed it was a pity. The entertainment was lively and various. You never knew *what* was going to happen.

PART TWO

XV

DOÑA ANA, *Nuevo Mexico, December 20:* Having received not one penny of pay since enlistment, and food so lean and scarce as barely to support life, our Missouri Volunteers are embarked on the second important leg of the campaign—to El Paso and, it is believed, to Chihuahua.

Late in September, General Kearny marched with the First Dragoons (numbering three hundred men) for California, leaving Alex Doniphan in charge of all the American forces in Nuevo Mexico. Then, with his usual disregard for the "Irregulars," Kearny sent us an express: "Proceed with the Regiment against the Navajos."

For nearly three months this order was discharged, as a kind of side or tune-up war, prosecuted often in bitter weather, high in the mountains, and, at last, resulting in universal admiration by our troops of the Navajo Indians. Future generations may tend to derogate these hardy aboriginals of the high plateaus, as "progress" will inevitably reduce them to the status of unpropertied prisoners, but your Missourians will remember them as an intelligent, cultured, brave, cleanly, and artistic people, having a program for survival that is based upon reason rather than sentiment —strict control of their population, a common-sense but not harsh view of the aged and infirm, and an unemotional look at slothful, inferior neighbors. The program may someday be widely copied if mankind is to endure (a premise that the writer declines to endorse).

It should be noted that, during the summer, a second Missouri regiment was formed, under the elective command of Colonel Sterling Price, of Chariton County, and it arrived in Santa Fé in time to relieve the First Regiment as the Army of Occupation.

In this unexpanded Journal, I do not intend to explore the labyrinthine pursuit of the Navajos, but a few high spots should be recorded before we proceed to the singular events of Doniphan's Mexican War.

Several columns led by the regimental commanders—Alex, Lieutenant Colonel Jackson, Major Gilpin (and, later, splinter groups under a number of the captains)—branched out into Navajo country, charged with a variety of missions. We were hungry, ill-clothed, and in resentful spirits, feeling that the fresh and idle troops left in Santa Fé might have been assigned this chore. Among our small boons was the fact of Lieutenant Colonel Ruff's having resigned his Volunteer commission, to take a lesser officerhood among the Regulars. It is pre-eminently where he belongs—a small-minded, inflexible martinet who yet may have certain qualities for the Regular Army.

Sergeant O'Hara, by the by, had been released from the calabozo some weeks in advance of the expedition. His parole was given on practical grounds: an expert was needed to carry out alterations in our harness, considered necessary for the changed and difficult terrain. (General Kearny, before departing for California, ordered his units' horses sent back to Leavenworth, to be replaced by mules. His attempt to impose this inspiration on the Volunteers met with protests so vehement that he gave it up.) I was present when O'Hara emerged from his durance, looking none the worse, possibly looking better, followed by an unidentified female of perhaps thirty-five—wonderfully buxom about the hips and bosom (which last was carelessly covered by a low-slung blouse), only slightly pocked, not a jot more than medium dirty, and supremely abandoned in all of her movements. Of her, more shortly.

O'Hara was dangling from his right hand what turned out to

be one of the spancel-rings with which he was supposed to be fettered in all but meal and exercise hours. When I asked about its use, he replied that he planned to "tidy up" the job he had begun on the priest. Failing to find him, he stated, he would crack a few clerical skulls at random, being out of practice and wishing to get back into the swing of things. "I'm right down rusty, sir. It's exercise that keeps a man honed, right enough, that and clean drawers." Quite naturally mystified by this utterance, I succeeded in dissuading him, after some difficulty, and he introduced the lady, with a leer.

"I hev the grandest honor to presint Señora—a widder by her own hand, and bless the spunk of her (it was a machete that turned the trick)—Mendoza. She come to me, like a angel in the night, seeking laundry—"

"Do I understand that Mrs. Mendoza has been with you in jail, O'Hara?" I asked sternly, despite my inferior rating.

"That she has, sir, and a comfort throughout. I'm as clean as a whistle; I'll sign an affy-davy."

"And what, if I may inquire, were our excellent prison guards doing in the meantime?"

"Why, sir, she done their drawers likewise—she ain't in no way perticular, as long as it's cash over vouchers. There ain't a particle of snob *in* Señora Mendoza, scalp to toenails. She'll launder till her back's broke—that or ourn," he added, again with a kind of lubricous chuckle.

It suddenly dawned on me that the poor, illiterate oaf had, in the whole of his life, never met a woman of any caste whatever, and that his amorous struggles were in extenuation of his condition. Like so many others, for a variety of pathetic reasons, he was trying to prove himself by trumpeting his most sensitive point.

"Then you intend to add this, ah, nemesis of grime to your responsibility as an official laundress?"

"The glory of it!—clean from stem to stern. Besides, I haven't exactly got the choice; I've lost it, when you add in and consider the machete—she's taken a downright fancy to my unmentionables. Meaning laundry," he said, his blue eyes as innocent as a babe's.

"You may live to regret this, O'Hara."

"Cleanliness is next to godliness, sir. I can hear me old mither crying it now, her that would have to be scraped down and hosed to make a positive identification."

The ignorant fellow was so blown up with this triumph—the expropriation of a middle-aged Mexican wanton who was available for anybody's peso—and enjoying himself so hugely, that I dismissed him from my mind as temporarily deranged. Later on, I hoped to relieve him from his dilemma.

As embarrassing as it is, the question of "laundresses" requires an amplification here. By the rules (this particular clause not appearing in print), non-commissioned officers have been permitted to bring along their wives, or a reasonable facsimile thereof (to my knowledge, no certificate of marriage is demanded). These women having been designated as laundresses, instead of the less formal terms employed in, say, the Mexican Army, often in fact carry out washing and mending chores not only for their husbands but for enlisted friends, in most cases for a modest fee.

It is also true, I fear, that the great majority render further services of a more personal nature. The Army hopes that husbands will not descend to renting out wives for the full assistance—"cleansing and polishing"—but the details of this remain purposely obscure. No "laundresses" will ever appear on the official rosters for future generations to wonder at. In any case, it is accepted that few of the women have trod the bridal path, at least with the non-coms to whom they are attached. As to their exact number, that figure, too, escapes me. A Mormon Volunteer unit that was formed in Leavenworth (and left directly for the California campaign) took with it twenty-seven such toilers. I have the information from a friend in Sterling Price's regiment, which is now in Santa Fé, as previously told.

The very names, or nicknames, of our dedicated appendages belie the matrimonial connection, for Missouri has never been regarded as a state wanting in gallantry. It is, however, a state rather strong on humor, and the reader may draw his own conclusions from such sentimental endearments as "Slats," "The Coffee Grinder," "Saber-Toothed Nell," "Old Bottle-Ass," "Titty Kitty," "The Wringer," and "Dry Gulch Maud."

(Note made on that day: Into this sorority of gentle militants, O'Hara must introduce his Latin discovery. I have no idea how congenial she may prove. The best guess is that the others will kill her. They take the attitude that they are fighting a war, and that a Mexican, any Mexican, is the enemy. In this respect they are fiercer than the men. Few of the women live in an openly connubial state with their "husbands"; they camp together, somewhat apart. Indeed, the entire operation is furtive, seldom officially mentioned, but carried out on a *sub rosa* basis, probably in deference to the church groups back home.

So, all in all, I await with keen interest the outcome of O'Hara's latest folly.)

We rode out in a pearly Santa Fé dawn, past the life-giving canals—motionless, now, except for ghostly wisps of rising vapor, past crumbling rust-red piles of adobe—"houses"—past the corn fields and pepper gardens and blue-green patches of maguey, toward the Rio del Norte. Thus far we followed General Kearny's route, and in the afternoon, we came on a memorable grave "stone"—left by the general himself.

HERE LIE THE BONES OF SANCHO PEDRO, THE ONLY DAMN DECENT GREASER I EVER KNEW

KILLED BY APACHE INDIANS, 1846

GEN. S. W. K., U.S.A.

The letters burned on a plank by, we found afterward, Kearny's own hand, done in genuine grief. Pedro, a half-breed, had served General Kearny as hostler for years, and probably had succeeded in establishing himself in that cold, strange man's affections as closely as anybody could. So said his associates after the war.

Generally speaking, the Navajo campaign remains in my mind a panorama of dizzying mountain scenery. Our group, not including Sam, O'Hara (with spouse) and the enigmatic Angel, was under the command of Captain Waldo, of Saline County, who is senior to Perry Moss.

We arrived at Albikirk, a depressing shamble of adobe, inferior even to Santa Fé; then we climbed by painful stages into the heart of Navajo country. Any news of the regiment's other thrusts was always sketchy, giving rise to the principal pursuit of the men: speculation and complaint about whatever it was we heard. At one point, it became known that a large merchant train, at Valverde, was in danger of attack from Mexicans, and that Doniphan had dispatched three companies to its aid. The rumor turned out to be false.

The Navajos range from the Rio Grande north to the Rio Colorado, and from New Mexico west to the California settlements, cannily maintaining strongholds of retreat high in the rugged and gorgeous Cordillera Mountains. They are of the Athabascan linguistic family, closely related to the Apaches. Like the Apaches, they have no fixed abode but in Tartar style follow their grazing herds—thousands upon thousands of horses, sheep and cattle (plus a few mules plucked from the New Mexicans, whom they detest with astonishing vigor). They are the lords of the mountains, challenged, really, by no one.

Through this fastness we moved deliberately, intent more on tracking down the principal chiefs—to "talk treaty"—than on fighting. Occasionally we came upon Pueblo ("Purbelo" in the local idiom) villages and listened to endless whines about Navajo depredations. Some of it must be true, for the Pueblos are hand in glove with the Mexicans, thus sharing the Navajo wrath.

In one compound, a middle-aged "brave" had been carried in on a litter. His bony mustang trailed along behind. Lying on his side, he was neatly, almost bloodlessly transfixed by a spear. The flint-tipped head, now stained black, protruded a foot or so from his shoulder; the rest was a limber wand dangling at his back. He seemed cheerful and uncomplaining. It was explained that the poor fellow had been minding his own business, on a "hunting" trip, and had been most capriciously attacked by a sizable band of the enemy.

At first we were inflamed and dismayed, but our present interpreter, one Caldwell, an Indian-wise old chawbacon of such cynical persuasion that he sets traps around his bed at night, began a line of shrewd questioning.

To sum up, our badly used brave was indeed hunting—he was hunting Navajo sheep. He had been about to bag some, he said, with excusable pride, but he had underestimated the Navajo pickets.

Worse, when we carried him into his wigwam, or hogan (these are curious dwellings of two stories, to the upper of which the occupants ascend by a movable ladder, for safety), one wall was embellished with three obviously juvenile hairpieces.

"Them's Navaher," said Caldwell, pointing.

"Ask the villain how they got there," demanded Waldo angrily.

"Says his squaw hung them up. She does all the decorating; he says he ain't handy about the house." (I assumed that the translation was embroidered; none of these mountain men seem able to stay serious for over fifteen minutes.)

"You know what I mean."

Caldwell buckled down again, quizzing several persons, and disclosed that the brave, some years before, had caught three children playing at a stream. He had knifed and scalped them immediately.

"He says they durn near dry-gulched him; it was a narrer squeak."

Waldo turned away, murmuring in disgust, and we continued halfheartedly on our mission. A Journal is, or should be, dispassionate, and I must record that Waldo left the medicine men to remove the spear. "They deserve each other," he said, and we concurred.

In the next few days, we picked up a seemingly friendly Navajo chief, one Sandoval, together with his twelve-year-old son. On his promise to guide us to the other principal chiefs—Sarcilla Largo, the tribe's foremost orator, and the patriarch Narbonah—we reluctantly took up the trail for further parts unknown.

Most of the men felt that we were being drawn into an ambush, because the terrain became wilder and loftier, with a limitless variety of concealment—in short, we were at the tactical mercy of a foe in any strength, and the Navajos number more than twelve thousand.

Even so, we plodded on, drawing sparingly on our meager stores and trying to keep warm. Some men strayed off the path to shoot animals—wolves, coyotes, foxes and deer, and fashioned articles of clothing from the skins. The reader may imagine how the ripe fragrance of these uncured garments added to our enjoyment of the chase. At night, always freezing, snowed upon often, I placed myself upwind from the main centers of pollution. Of cold comfort was the fact that predators, including the much feared grizzly, avoided our camp like the plague. Nobody felt snubbed.

Few Navajos speak Spanish, and we communicated with the impassive Sandoval through Caldwell. Apparently the grizzled old nuisance speaks all the Indian dialects in existence. Or pretends to. However, by now it would surprise me very little if he spoke court French.

"Where are we, Sandoval?" inquired Waldo abruptly, scraping clean the ground near a campfire.

With insolent deliberation, after Caldwell's offering of pig grunts, Sandoval drew a design on this nature's slate that could not have been deciphered by the wisest cartographer alive.

"We're here," said Caldwell, releasing his usual squirt of tobacco juice to one side. "We're headed there."

Neither point of reference had any connection with the outside world.

"Where's 'there'?"

"I bin there oncet, but I couldn't hardly say, exact. It's kind of over, and, of course up. I can tell you this much: on one side, the rivers skedaddle toward the Pacific; on t'other, they run toward the Atlantic. If you're searching for entertainment."

"You're immensely helpful, Caldwell," said Captain Waldo. "I wonder why you signed on as interpreter."

"I was always able to talk real good."

Our suspicions of Sandoval swelled and deepened, with good cause, as I shall soon make clear. We were fewer than a hundred men, daily straggling like a handful of sheep into a populous domain of wolves. Waldo would appear to have placed himself in a censurable situation, but he kept his own counsel, and there were no very vehement protests (not a usual attitude of Missouri Volunteers). At least not yet.

Soon after the above conversation, we arose to take the trail, and found Sandoval's son missing. The chief regarded us with what I took to be thinly concealed amusement. That is, his face was expressionless, as always, but his one-dimensional black eyes seemed triumphant.

"Where's the boy, Sandoval?" said Waldo.

He made a sweeping gesture with one arm, the Indian's over-dramatization, a unifying of himself with all the natural phenomena.

"He flies with the eagle" [according to Caldwell]. "He goes to prepare my people."

For a minute, I thought Waldo might draw his revolver, but he gained control of himself and retired (at last) for a conference with the under-officers. It was finally agreed that, since we had come this far, being now hopelessly deep in enemy terrain, we would trust the Navajo for a few more days.

Around a rocky bend, in mid-afternoon, we stopped, faced by a party of twenty or twenty-five horsemen. They sat like statues, painted with non-pacific looking black and red streaks across the cheekbones.

"Now we'll find out," said Waldo. "Look to your arms."

But they advanced slowly, with no show of hostility, and at length we accompanied them forward into a rocky remote valley where this part of the tribe kept secret "camps," for holing up in times of storm and stress. These were built mainly of stones, eight feet in diameter, four feet high, covered with poles and dirt.

During the rest of that afternoon, hundreds of additional Navajos streamed slowly, purposefully, down from the mountains and into the valley. Still no sign of belligerence, or of friendliness either, except to give us mutton and maize to eat and to point out a curious rock basin into which icy water gushed from some subterranean source.

Our first real contretemps occurred toward evening, when Indians suddenly appeared to seize our mounts.

"Drop those reins!" cried Waldo, swinging up a musket. "We'll thin this damned tribe out before you take a single horse."

The scoundrel Sandoval, unruffled, coolly appraising our strength, beckoned to Caldwell, who reported, "There ain't any grass here [it was true; no fodder except poor bunch grass was anywhere to be seen]—he says he's taking them across the ridge, to a pasture."

"If there's a pasture, why don't they live there?"

"Well, this here Sand-shovel [for an interpreter, Caldwell is conspicuously weak on names, or perhaps he prefers it so for some obscure whimsical reason]—Sand-shovel says they'd rather cross a pasture than live on it. He claims that contentment is a shiftable feast."

Waldo stood frowning, digesting this singular utterance; then we let the horses go and retired, each man sleeping with his firearms charged and ready. None of us expected to see the horses again.

Next morning after breakfast, a deputation of leaders arrived and requested to see our guns, all of our guns. They wished to "examine" them, carefully, in their own encampment. Navajo arms are limited to the lance, the cottonwood bow and arrow, and the *lazo*, or lasso. Even so, we viewed this demand as the last arrogant act in the reduction of our unit to impotence.

It was a tense moment, an impasse to which we could see no solution except battle. Standing white-faced in a circle, guns thrust outward, we arranged ourselves in defiance of perhaps seven hundred Navajos, awaiting the signal to fire.

At this critical point, another group came from the direction of the ridge—*leading our horses*. Well nourished, these were returned to camp without a word. If it was strategy, it was ably conceived, for Waldo barked out, "Count off to the right, starting with Smithers! Every odd man unload and hand over his weapon."

There was opposition, but we complied when it was pointed out that, probably, the Navajos had neither ammunition nor a working knowledge of guns.

Thus our captors (for that's what, in effect, they were) retired, and we waited for the next development. It came at about noon. Our guns were returned, and we were invited, said Caldwell, to a powwow involving the local chief (a wrinkled ancient), Sandoval, and others.

A dozen of us, led by Captain Waldo, joined the Indians in the time-honored but ridiculous squat-around-the-campfire, solemnly passing a noisome, long-stemmed pipe, nodding, prolonging the talk with all the ritual imaginable. At length, the chief (whose name I have forgotten) spoke through Caldwell:

He had seen many things, his eyes were sharper than the hawk's, his age shamed the owl and the tortoise. Many years ago his tribe had concluded a treaty with the palefaces. They were not skulking men like the Spaniards, nor were they Spaniards' cattle like the Purbelos—these were men of honesty and courage. By the treaty, the Navajos and the white men were brothers; neither would war upon the other; neither would ride in great numbers into the other's domain, especially armed with rifles. He (the chief) honored those men, he trusted them. He trusted all palefaces from the North, because he knew that their hearts were good. He saw no need for a new treaty. He hoped we enjoyed our stay in the Cordilleras. A fiesta and tribal dance would be held this same evening.

Well, there was no good answer to a stroke of diplomacy like that. Poor Waldo, I thought. He sat chewing on a weed, then he said, "The chief has spoken well. I believe him, and I would like to see that treaty."

With some ceremony, the chief and his acolytes produced from the largest hogan a thick sheaf of buckskins. This they began to unroll, skin after skin, until at last they came to an old, rotted blanket, which was reverently opened and laid out. Inside lay a yellowed paper.

"The treaty," said Caldwell.

Waldo held it up. On the printed side was a crudely drawn newspaper cut of a buffalo, all shaggy head and shoulders with disproportionate pipestem legs. Beneath this read the legend: "Hunters Hearken! Oil up your Sharp's. Top prices paid for prime pelts. Hard cash, or discount for trade goods. Dollar extry [sic] for animals unmarred by head shot. Stink no object. You deliver, we cure—Jorkins and Whistler, Wichita."

I caught Sandoval's gaze—a mixture of enjoyment and contempt—and confess that I was unable to meet his eye. With or without English, the Navajos had unquestionably known for years that this was a shoddy, worthless, dishonorable instrument. It was no wonder they placed a small value on our mission.

Waldo is a fearless sort of fellow, a natural leader, occasionally given to unexpected acts of bravado, and his facial expression has the boon of childlike candor. A mother wolf could meet him and turn over her cubs for safekeeping. With a quick gesture he tore the "treaty" in two, crumpled up the pieces, and tossed them aside. I believe that I came as near as possible to swallowing my tongue. Not a man among the Navajos moved.

"You have been tricked. Among all peoples there are bad men. These were very bad men, who mocked you. General Doniphan is making a good treaty. He sends to tell you that his messengers never lie. You must spread the word among your chiefs."

The statement was a departure for Waldo, whose bent is laconic. It was simple, Indian-like in its formality, and ringing throughout with truth, except, perhaps, for the spot promotion given Doniphan by his impeccable messenger. Waldo told me later that he'd thought it best to have all official dealings with Indians come from the highest-sounding source, saying, "Navajos respect that, and as a matter of fact, so do we. It was in my mind to say 'President Doniphan,' but I was afraid it might get back to Polk."

Whatever the means, it appeared to work, at least for the moment. The council was dispersed, and next morning we were escorted beyond the ridge by the entire tribe-in-hand. It was a tense procession that climbed up, up, up into craggy peaks and walls, around canyon ledges a foot wide—barren of handholds except gnarled and runty evergreens that twisted their way out of solid rock—beneath wispy clouds that drifted close overhead against the sea-blue. My head swam so that I was unable to look down into the shaded chasms below.

No matter how high we climbed, another ridge rose higher, and goats often scrambled up these, delicately selecting steps where none existed and loosing pebbles and dirt that trickled and bounded past, carrying, I thought, the threat of avalanche.

Two days went by, and we lapsed into a dull certainty that we were removed forever from the knowledge of civilized men. Our sullen guides remained plastered close to our sides. Though not yet treated to violence, we were prisoners. And their attitude now appeared over-bearing. At night in a high cleft, Waldo listened to protest and accusation—from enlisted men as well as the others, and gave us our plans.

"Tomorrow, at exactly noon, wheel—we'll have most of the tribe behind us—and begin firing at random. First platoon pick off the Navajos ahead. Then, those who remain will somehow get down out of these damned mountains and beat back. Remember, men," he said, "*we* have rifles—they don't."

Everybody was glad of the ultimatum, and a promise of action. The truth is that we were soldiers stale from months of waiting to fight. I, for one, slept better than for many nights past, and did so on a supper of unsifted flour and water, maybe three ounces in all. Try as we might, we never came within range of the goats; they were too quick, too galvanic for our guns.

At nine the following morning, our path took a downward slope, the footing grew easier—giving us the hope of a battle in something approaching our own element—and at eleven-thirty, as we surreptitiously looked to our guns, we crossed a ridge to stare down at a dazzling emerald-green valley! Flowing with bright-running streams, the banks bordered by cottonwoods and willows, quilted with cultivations of grain, and inhabited, at least temporarily, for as far as the eye could see.

"Is this when we fight?" said one of the sub-officers to Waldo.

"This isn't when we fight."

We looked down in silence, famished, weak and apprehensive, and truly, for the next few days, not a man of us knew a quiet moment. After months of hardship, hunger, thirst, filth, nakedness, exposure, struggles against prairie, desert, high plateau and mountains, of boredom, irritation, sickness, death, gloom, madness, homesickness, strife among ourselves, friction with alien peoples and loss of faith in our leaders, we had arrived at the rainbow's end. For awhile trouble took a holiday; nothing but merriment filled our minds. The Navajos, it seemed, had weeks ago decided *for* the treaty; now, having done so, they unbent to show the highest marks of their civilization.

The first feast (after our condition was observed): spitted mutton dripping grease; tender legs of young lamb, (one of which I ate by myself, clutching it in both hands, like the schoolbook picture of the eighth Henry); roast kid (a great delicacy); honey—pot upon pot of honey, with the comb packed tight inside; "hornets'-nest bread"; red beefsteaks two inches thick; grizzly-bear steaks burned in fat stored up for the winter; stews of hare whose white meat fell from the bone; mashed purple beans; dried apricots, apples and grapes; and tortillas, a savory borrowed from the Mexicans. These are made of Indian corn meal mixed with water, spread thin, then baked on large hot stones, the finished whole being flexible, bluish in color (from the peculiarity of the corn), the size of a dinner plate, and approximately the thickness of newsprint. What luxury to heap one up with meats and bean paste, double it over, and eat it as a sandwich!

My height is six feet, and my normal weight one hundred and seventy pounds. Our feast was ready by three in the afternoon; when I began, I weighed, I think, in the area of one hundred thirty-five. Probably to our shame we ate steadily until six o'clock. In the period I am convinced that I gained not less than five pounds. With a fellow glutton, I later fashioned a crude machine to gauge our progress: a tilted plank on a fulcrum—a species of seesaw—upon whose free end we dropped balancing stones as our bodies filled out. According to my best calculation, I added three pounds in each of the succeeding nine days (the ceremonial length of a Navajo fiesta).

But on the first, memorable occasion we defied the laws of caution. I had read that starving men can eat only lightly; there are ways to circumvent this. The Navajos drink a brew on the order of pulque, and we correctly judged that the more of this we swallowed, the more food we could manage. Nobody became intoxicated, there were no fights, nobody got sick. And before we finished, the unmarried girls had started up the dancing.

Most Mexican women I have seen are ugly, pock-marked, dirty, and bold, their flashing teeth and (sometimes) voluptuous figures being their only remarkable features. The female Indians of our expedition have been squat, lumpy, coarse-featured, very dark, sullen—in most ways subordinate to white standards. (Quite possibly, we looked as grotesque to them.)

Now I quote from the Journal of a friend in Waldo's company, a man slightly antipathetic to everybody except Missourians, and lukewarm about three quarters of those: "The Nebeho [!] women are very pretty, having small feet, but ankles whose size it is impossible to determine, as they bandage them with deerskins. This is of course done to render them attractive and beautiful. They wear brass rings upon their arms, the larger the better, and in following their fashions they may even exceed the most fashionable in our cities. They are of good stature, and fairer in complexion than any Indians I have seen. The women are treated as equals by the men; and altogether they are the most enlightened tribe of wild Indians presently inhabiting this continent."

I could have gone farther. Though starved below the level of sexual awareness, I became perceptive by stages. The phenomenon is worth scrutiny, and may prove of benefit to science (which is welcome, gratis, to call on these notes). When the feast began, I saw only a number of homogeneous tan people dressed in particolored attire. I ate a beefsteak and noticed that some of the group were wearing skirts while others had on trousers. Pondering this, I drank some pulque, ingested a small leg of lamb, and realized that the former individuals were women.

After a brief, gassy lull from which I made a strong recovery with two helpings of rabbit stew and a handful of apricots, I reassured myself that their hair was a rich, shiny black. This impression fading with my returning hunger, I ate—slowly, spacing it out over an hour—several ribs of kid, six tortillas, a potful of honey, two mutton chops, some apples and another small beefsteak. Then, feeling unaccountably sluggish, I sprawled against a log, resting. Upon several more applications of pulque, as a *digestif,* I felt a warmth spread out from my stomach down through the region of my lower limbs. Various important parts of my dulled anatomy began to return to life.

It was here that I faced up to the truth: these women, now whirling to the beat of an earthen jar covered with skin, had the earmarks of skilled laundresses, and one especially, a Venus-like creature with a posterior curve to delight Praxiteles, was matrimonial fodder. To this aberration, I admit without shame. Perhaps fortunately, my dream was interrupted by a need to retire to the willows. When I returned, twenty minutes later, I was faint with hunger. Quickly, lest the supply run out, I ate a section of fat-laden grizzly that Caldwell said was intact except for the head and claws. My maiden danced forward and beckoned, I seized her up in my arms, and joined in a revel that surged on through the night. Such is the madness of salvation.

"Ha ho, hi ho"—the lyric would appear to offer an unlikely spur to a dance that struck me as desperately romantic: an old man seated cross-legged before a ludicrous drum, made no more melodic by his habit of screeching like a panther at every third beat; a hundred campfires glowing like the furnaces of Hell all across the valley; and the whirling, stamping figures wrapped in scarlet blankets as the night chill deepened. I do not recollect what time I went to sleep. A feeling of unreality, an irritating insistence in the rhythm, a humming in my temples from pulque, and the feeling of plenty for the first time in weeks—above all else a disturbing memory of glossy thighs and warm breath against my cheek—blended at last to draw a purple, pleasant veil across my mind. My last clear thoughts were a shocking reappraisal of a lifetime's dubious values. What is happiness but an escape from anything fashioned by man?

When I awoke, I was covered with two wolfskins sewed together to make the snuggest of blankets. To my surprise, no complaint lingered from the most reckless overindulgence of my life. The sun was up, birds sang in this curiously temperate valley; I felt alert, strong, and cheerful. Perhaps a lesson had been learned from the Navajos—that unaccustomed excesses can be dissipated by dancing and sweating in somewhat uncivilized abandon. At a point in the stripping off of inhibitions, are the demons exorcised and the body set at rest? I made a note to lean on the remedy in the civilized years to come. Does one dweller-in-society in a million ever know an hour's pure freedom of spirit? We are all of us chained by our fears.

Our hosts were up and doing. The Navajo's superiority over other tribes (and peoples) may rest on a religion of combining work and play to fill in the idle hours. They had organized a mounted rabbit hunt, an excitement surpassing that of a steeple-chase. In the tall grass of a far section, a rabbit was started and five hundred riders came wildly on to fix it with a lance. There was competition but a complete lack of jealousy or mean spirit. The men are no more adept than the women. These horsemen must rank with the Arabs; I have never seen mounts handled with such sureness. As nomads, they live their lives in the saddle, but they seem never to tire of horsemanship as *sport.*

The Navajo woman's emancipation is astounding, when one considers the accepted notion of the lowly, broken, over-worked squaw. A Navajo regards his wife as a person with valid likes and dislikes, tastes and opinions, freedom of thought and action. The women manage their own business, trade for small articles as they see fit, saddle their own horses, and let the man saddle his. When the braves organize uncongenial sports, the wives collect to gamble and chat, playing a game resembling dice, called *Mug Wano,* which uses three bones thrown upon a flat rock. Around the rock's rim sit upwards of a hundred pebbles, to be used as counters. The women bet their beads, buckskins, rings, and other finery, and lose with no more show of regret than a ringing laugh. What they *need* they can replace; what in our case we only hoard is ferociously protected. Perhaps this rather than money is the root of all evil.

An impression:

A row of friendly women spinning, with a stick for a spindle, one end set in the ground. The stick is turned rapidly by hand, the wool spun out, the yarn twisted and wound upon spools. The spinners seem pleased by our interest.

Now, the same women weaving, apart, in secret, turning out the "common blanket," in stripes of blue, black and white, and fine blankets—"Navajo rugs," or ponchos, in gay and delightful colors.

"Madam, that rug hanging there, the one with the red and black figger—how much? Many tobaccos. My horse? By God, lady, I'm dead set on taking that blanket back to my old woman. *I'll give you a hundred dollars!*"

No reply. Indeed, for a change, black looks. He has insulted her; it is a point of tribal pride that Navajo women never part with the best of their creations. They are a miracle of manufacture, made by a process strictly guarded. Mysteriously, like their woven willow baskets, the blankets are as watertight as a birch canoe. I have seen women carrying water in them for hours without losing a drop.

No matter, we came away blanketless.

The full days passed, our other commanders came in with their troops, the treaty impended, I searched for my companion of the dance. To this moment, I have no idea what I planned to do if I found her. Perhaps after all she had been the phantom of a brain deranged by fatigue. But I had a double wolfskin blanket, an illusion of loveliness and first embrace, and a soft rustle that meant someone leaving in advance of the dawn.

Poor soldier. This strange new feeling over a will-o'-the-wisp who may never have existed at all. Long afterward—two years to be precise—a renegade Navajo scout told me that the chiefs forbid such "wrong" alliances to grow serious. They simply remove the maiden for awhile.

"Much miseries. White mans always leave sometimes, girl grief for many years."

"In my case, I mean to go back," I said, knowing it wasn't so.

The treaty was concluded on November 22. Winter approached and the tribe grew restless for its bastion on the Rio San Juan—a bustling place occupied all year by the old, worn-out warriors and women. Also, it serves as storehouse for the tribe's corn and trade articles; here, too, were the real headquarters of weaving.

With Doniphan came others of our column—O'Hara, Angel (a little filthier now, I believe), and, of course, Sam. It is probably a flaw of my character that I permit that child to get on my nerves. He has replaced the discharged and antiquated fifer with a half-caste Mexican who refers to him as *El Capitán!* This, I learned later, out of gratitude because the scoundrel was on the point of arrest for thievery; the Drum-and-Fife Corps rescued him just in time. In fact, there is some little discussion that Sam may be open to prosecution on the serious charge of harboring a criminal. Of extreme annoyance to me, he has assumed a proprietary air about the expedition and deals condescendingly with officers of high rank.

When he first spied me, near the council grounds, he clapped me on the shoulder in friendly fashion, and said, "Well, if it isn't old Quills and Blotters. What's new?"

I was about to reply that his conversion to total offensiveness was new, but he interrupted with some shouted instructions, in a hideous kind of pidgin, to Viesca, the Mexican mentioned above.

"*Holá!* Viesca. Vamoose—stew-pot; food for all hands. *Todos comida. Savee?*"

"*Sí, mi Capitán. Pronto. Muchas gracias.*"

Then, to me:

"New boy."

"He must be somewhat in excess of forty, at the least."

"A wonderful, wonderful performer on any kind of instrument. You name it, he'll play it."

"For a starter, how about 'Taps on a Wall Safe'?"

"Oh, people are always running him down because he's a half-breed. You know how it is."

"In point of fact, I don't. I assure you I'm quite white."

"See here, Blaine, you sound even crankier than usual. You sick or something?"

"I'm pretty sick of your pomposity, my boy, and I may wish to reduce it with a birching."

"Well, I've got to be going. Doniphan wants the Drum-and-Fife Corps to parade tomorrow at the treaty."

"*Colonel* Doniphan."

"That's right; it's the same man."

The treaty went off without much hitch, the central figures being Alex and the great Chief Narbonah, a lean, gray-haired, unsmiling, thoughtful-looking man in simple dress. Before a hard-and-fast agreement was reached, the orator, Sarcilla Largo, arose to make what struck me as a singularly penetrating speech. It was so apposite, and struck so straight at the heart of our usual lack of realism, that I reproduce it in full (as the interpreter relayed it sentence by sentence, stripped, I imagine, of much eloquent and picturesque rhetoric):

"Americans! You have a strange cause of war against the Navajos. We have fought the Mexicans long and hard. We have plundered their villages, killed many of their people, and made many prisoners. We had just cause for all this. For many years, before we grew strong, the Navajos were treated as dogs by the treacherous Mexicans. We suffered more than you know.

"*You* have lately commenced a war against the same people. You are powerful. You have great guns and many brave soldiers. You have therefore conquered the Northern Mexicans, the very thing we have been attempting to do for so many, many years. Now you are about to penetrate deep into their country. We would help you do this, but you tell us that we cannot. Indeed, you have turned upon us for trying to do what you now go ahead with yourselves.

"We cannot see why you have cause of quarrel with us for fighting the New Mexicans on the west, while you do the same thing on the east.

"Look how matters stand. This is *our war*. We have more right to complain of your interference than you have to quarrel with us for continuing what we had begun long before you came here. If you will act justly, you will allow us to settle our own differences!"

There can be no doubt that Alex Doniphan—that we all—agreed, but our orders, the Army's orders, came as always from the diplomatists! Has a more smug and unsuccessful breed ever evolved to snarl the affairs of nations? *I wonder if we shall ever abandon the folly of harassing our friends while giving strength and comfort to our enemies.*

XVI

El Paso, *December 30, 1846:* I've been reading over that stuff of Blaine's, and I really can't give it very much. He digs his nose too deep into the situation and fails to gallop. That was one thing you couldn't say about old Peeps. He shuffled right along, unless somebody's husband happened to be across town, and then he hung around quite a while. He was mighty sociable that way, and like to get shot for it.

If you ask me, nobody cares what a Navajo looks like except another Navajo, and even then, not very much. The tribe's got the big-head. Several came out as rude as you please, sniffing at the Drum-and-Fife Corps, and there wasn't a performer among them with the musical education of a gnat. "Ha ho, hi ho" was their only positive hit, and an elderly old man speaking English said they hadn't changed it in five or six hundred years. Didn't plan to, either.

What was worse, a group had the affrontery to come up one evening and offer to buy Viesca, said they'd pay five dollars cash. They were staging a feast and thought it might be nice to have the old-style entertainment of spread-eagling a Mexican over an anthill. They said it was best to preserve the ancient customs, so as to live a more graceful life. I haven't been as mad since we started on this expedition. If a commander of a unit like mine—artistic and sensitive to the core, especially when awake—can't be loyal to his men, then he'd better turn in his uniform and resign. They came up to ten, and after that to fifteen, if I'd throw in his horse and saddle, but I couldn't get them to twenty dollars no matter how hard I tried. Regular donkeys that way. (I wasn't really aiming to harm him, of course, only let him get chewed a little around the edges, because he *is* pretty lazy, as well as thieving right along—little things, mostly, to keep in practice—and I thought it might improve his military bearing, as the Army calls it.)

Well, I'll get on, because a lot has happened. At last we've had a battle with the Mexican Army, what's written down as a "major engagement," and we've had a lot of troubles, too, so I'll charge forward, like Peeps, only staying clear of the women.

When we left the Navajo country, with a fancy treaty signed —worth about two pecks of dried apricots, likely, and the Navajos know it—we straggled down toward Valverde in different columns and passed through a Zuñi pueblo where the chiefs took us to the ruins of a complete underground city. It was built on three levels down below, like a three-story house, and lay there in a surprising state of preservation—tables and gourds and such sitting around, not rotting at all in that dry air. Blaine said it was similar to a buried city he once saw in Europe, or Italy, I've forgotten which, where a mountain blew up on a place called Pompay. Said even the inhabitants were still on view there, caught lolling around doing this and that, along with going to the bathroom, but would the Italians hoist them out for a decent funeral? Not at all; they preferred to sell tickets to the tourists. Typical. Even Blaine said so.

Anyhow, the Zuñi medicine men had records to show that their underground city was more than a thousand years old. They were a very nice bunch, cheerful, and clean. Friends of the Navajos, more or less, so that people reckoned the underground city was given up about the time the Navajos became peaceful.

At a Mexican town named Pardeus, a Regular platoon from Santa Fé met us and paid out the first money we'd had—forty dollars each for uniform allowance. But everybody owed such a lot to the sutlers, not much was left after squaring up. A sutler is a kind of half-official wagon merchant that sells the soldiers tobacco and knickknacks and small articles of clothing and even whisky once in a while. They've got a concession from the Army, so to speak, and are more military than the teamsters, praise the Lord.

Which brings me to say that, sure enough, another monster fandango was held that night in Pardeus, what with all the money floating around, and you guessed it: the same thing happened. It broke up in the gaudiest ruckus ever seen in those parts. Several men are writing about it in Journals, so it will be recorded for Posterity, and besides, I've already described a fandango about as well as it can be done.

We went on to Valverde, picked up more teamsters' wagons, and pushed forward toward El Paso, or El Paso del Norte, as the Mexicans say. It's easy enough to translate, and means Pass of the North. What with the months in Santa Fé, plus some help from Viesca and a little from Señora Mendoza, I've picked up Spanish and am now fluid in both languages. Beginning, or *primer,* Spanish (which I've gone far beyond now) is so simple it's laughable—you add "o" to everything and point at what you're after. If that doesn't work, shrug and they'll go get a priest.

As we penetrated south, the country changed. The mountains were still near, but the plains broadened and the wispiest kind of vegetation grew. Things looked more *Mexican* somehow. Crosses stood on the mountain tops, and at the bottoms you saw piles of stones with flowers strewn across, because these people like to bury a person where he drops. Especially if the death was violent, and in this country, it's the main kind. People sometimes live to old age in the towns, but accidents happen when they go out with a burro after sticks. I mean accidents on the order of Indians or bandits. On these plateaus the nights are bitter, and sticks are worth more than gold. Often, marching, we saw what appeared to be big brushy thickets moving along a trail—the peasants load twigs so high on those poor, sway-back, undersized burros that the animal is scarcely visible; maybe the ears stick out. It's a wonder how the piles are balanced, and occasionally our men got mad and knocked them all off. They said it was unhumane.

I asked a few questions and made notes about the growth. In sparse patches we found mesquite and chaparral, or clusters of dwarfish acacia, with Spanish bayonet—green, green, green—on the low slopes, and now and then palmettos thirty feet tall. This last is used to build bridges which hold up a year or two before rotting apart, and then, like as not, the peasants go back to fording, exactly the same as before. The main thing they don't do is fight it.

In one village we encountered a funeral that gave everybody a turn. I never saw one quite like it. The corpse was a child who became dead by measles brought in by Mexican soldiers. Well, sir, here marched a procession that a person would have thought was celebrating the wedding of St. Peter. First off were two men dressed gay but holding spades covered round with flowers; next were musicians playing clarinets and violins—a very sprightly tune; and after that six children shouldering what Blaine called a bier, on which lay a pretty little girl in a starchy white frock. No coffin, no shroud, eyes wide open and arms lying down at her sides, one stiff hand clutching a cheap crucifix. She looked lovely and had flowers tossed just everywhere over the lower part of her body. You wanted to punch her to make sure she was dead. She did have a coffin, all right, but she wasn't in it; two children were carrying it in the procession just behind. It was black, with strips of white tape crossed all over. To keep off the Devil, I reckon; that is, if he wasn't already marching in the groups. You couldn't tell by looking; most disgusting sight I ever saw. Twenty to thirty grownups dressed fit to kill followed along after those poor, blank-faced children, and *this* bunch of Mexicans *was* drunk. Men carrying bottles of homemade brandy, singing, stopping to guzzle, several pinching women that appeared to belong to somebody else, but not minding, you know, and all hands having a grand old time. And dogs! Well, they were everyplace, yapping and scurrying and fetching up stiff-legged whilst sliding in the dust. It requires a special entertainment to make one of those skulking Mexican curs take notice, and this funeral was right in their line. But a very fat man in a straw sombrero decorated up with ribbons whacked one in the ribs with an empty bottle, and the pack drew off to consult. It was about all they ever got—kicks and abuse—the miserable starved creatures.

We loitered back and watched, curious. The procession wobbled into one of those off-balance churches, that had a high turret on just the one end—only decent building in town—and a ratty-looking priest in a brown habit paddle-footed out and held

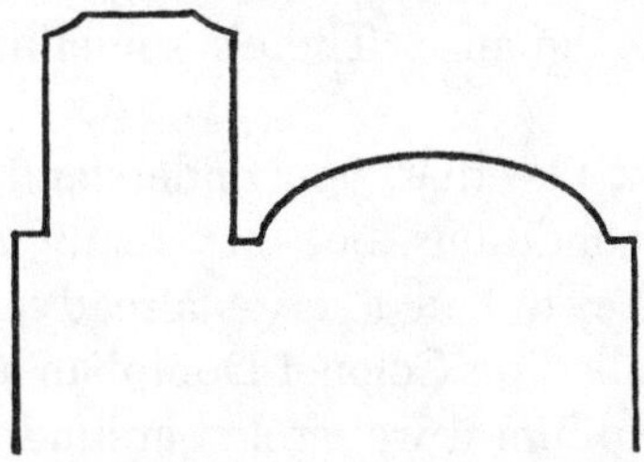

a brief service. He kind of hummed and waited, glancing up once in a while, with maybe a little frown or headshake, as if he had some fears that the girl wouldn't make it, so the family coughed up two pesos, (or all they could raise), looking not quite so festive for a change, and after that they all whooped and hollered out to the edge of town and buried her beside the road—just dumped the coffin into a hole. Then they piled up stones on top. Two or three other piles lay nearby, and the father stole a cross off the nearest, because he'd been too lazy to whittle one out himself. When they finally managed to thrust it down tight, everybody got considerably drunker and went home, probably hoping measles would come along again soon, and give them something to do.

A few days out from El Paso, we entered on the Jornada del Muerte, or, approximately, journey of death—where the road branches off from the river, a terrible dry stretch of soft sandy desert with no grass or fuel. I've noticed that peasants all through these parts, if asked how far to such-and-such, reply "three *jornadas*" (or four, or whatever it may be). Another way is to say, "so many water holes."

Well, these Volunteers were peculiar. A case-hardened Indian fighter, a man I met later, who was making a book, wrote, "I never saw such a set of men. There was nothing on the face of the earth, or in the depths below, that they wouldn't fight." But this Jornada gave them the jimjams; they didn't much mind being shot, as one of them acknowledged, saying, "It's proper, it's meet—we're accustomed and acclimatized to it. My pappy was shot several times and only mildly inconvenienced, aside from dragging his left leg, and they could have used my grandpaw for a sprinkling can. But I mislike to lay down my bones for the buzzards and the iguanas. There's something low-grade about it."

They could talk like that, you understand, joky and spry, under the worst of conditions, but they really *were* scared of dying in the desert. They'd had a taste already and didn't favor it, so a delegation called on Colonel Doniphan and asked if it would be just the same to him if we circled around to New Orleans and took a boat to Vera Cruz. Just as they suspected, it wasn't all right with him, so they came back and loaded up on aguardiente.

One man said, "By God, if I've got to suffer for three days, I'll take along old John Barleycorn for a companion; we'll do it together. I've never knowed him to fail me yet, the truest friend a man ever had," and he poured out the water in his canteen and replaced it with liquor.

It was the rottenest kind of judgment, because the Jornada *was* terrible, and before the first day passed, everybody was burning up, almost. The sun hung down like a wicked white eye, the kicked-up dust clogged your nose and throat, and the provision wagons fell way back miles out of sight. They were no use to anybody, as usual.

We hadn't any food, except for some men carrying bits and pieces in their pockets, and our water was rationed out careful between horses and men. But the ones with aguardiente were practically to the begging stage.

When night fell, the cold sunk down, down, down, and the men with water weren't so well off after all, because a lot of it froze solid in canteens.

Well, sir, the bunch with me would have froze along with it, but sometime after dark, a rider came galloping up alone, and it was my old friend Spiebuck. He was overjoyed to see me, though you couldn't tell it from his face, and gripped both of my arms hard. Captain Hobbs was back somewhere with their wagon, and had dispatched him ahead with instructions. It was a mighty good thing. Captain Hobbs looked on the Volunteers as babes in the wilderness, and treated them so.

So the Indian set me and some others to cutting a weed called, in the Spanish, *lechugrilla* (?) or *palmilla*, and in American, soapweed. They use it to make rope and sacks, along with a poor grade of soap. It's a plant that gets to be eight feet high and burns like tinder. That is, it makes a quick, exploding fire that flares up with a whoosh like gunpowder, lighting the sky with rolled-up smoke and flames, then dies down just as fast. Plenty of the weed grew around, and in a few minutes those Fourth of July fires were going everyplace in sight, throughout the darkness, anywhere you turned. It looked like the end of the world was come, and a man drinking aguardiente said he hoped so, said he'd had the feeling for several weeks now it had pretty well run its course. He was warming up for a few other remarks, even more ignorant, but about then he vomited, so they covered him over with a blanket.

No change for three days, exactly the same—men's faces blacking up and stripping off skin, horses weak-kneed and stumbling because in addition to the thirst there was nothing but tufts of skimpy bunch grass every few miles, and the commanders' expressions growing grimmer by the hour.

And then, suddenly, it was over. Dragging pretty heavy over a rise, expecting to find more empty, heat-parched, silent, desert ahead, we saw a pleasant valley on a long bending branch of the river. Well, everybody threw down their rifles and ran all a-clatter with sabers and tinware thrashing and struggling into the water. I let go my hold on Chief, let him forage for himself, then fell forward in a deep hole and sprawled there, gasping. The water was so cold it hurt your teeth. A town lay nearby, but we were above it, thanks to goodness, because a dozen or so women usually are squatting on the river bank, doing laundry while spitting in this direction or that, and naked children are romping in the water below *them*, so that things do get tolerably rank. Apart from that, I don't know what it is about Mexican rivers. They look pale green and lovely and winding, with white-sand or brown-pebble beaches and bright green trees thick along the banks, springing up alone in that desert like an oasis out of the Bible, but you wade in and take a good drink and you're apt to go to the bathroom for a week. Steady; no let-up.

Later on we walked the horses into town—Doña Ana—and bought forage as well as supplies for ourselves. Then we had a feast and slept up.

2

On Christmas Day, 1846, we were below the town, out of sight, and camped on a sprig of the river—a place called El Brazito, or "Little Arm." Half of the regiment was only now catching up, and the officers kept trying to stave off idle times. The Drum-and-Fife Corps played "Yankee Doodle," "Red White and Blue," and "Hail Columbia," doing it very well, too, and afterwards Captain Moss hauled out the musty old Articles of War and read *them* again. It made the thirteenth time this month; it had got so the troops kind of cackled the statements along with him, from memory.

He's a very good fellow, and popular, and he says, "Men, I'd like to relieve you of this tedium, but I'm only following orders. It's pretty thin material, as reading matter goes. For one thing, the plot's weak. I admit it, and wish we had something better on hand."

"Captain," sung out one of the men, "could you go over that part again about desertion? I ain't exactly got it through my head yet. You've read it so many times, I'm addled. What I'm coming at, is it legal or not? If so, I think I'll be drifting back after lunch, if it wouldn't put you out."

"You signed on for a year, Hardwick. If you desert, you'll be shot. That's what it says here, Article 11B, Section 27—'shot at dawn after recapture.'"

"Well now, Captain, that's pretty loose. It might be raining, and *then* where's your dawn?"

"It hasn't rained here in seven weeks," replied Captain Moss patiently, and another fellow observed that a billygoat could write a better document than that with its tail, after which we went over to watch the colored servants of some officers organize into a "platoon." There'd been several battle scares during the morning—bands of red-coated soldiers seen riding along fast at a distance—and the servants thought it was time they got ready to fight. There were twelve of them, and they went through a very civil and orderly procedure. Everybody was surprised, because not a single one had any military training, nor a particle of education, either.

They held an election and elected eleven officers and one "high private," a woolly-headed fellow that was a regular jackanapes—always chuckling and joking, not really officer material, as one of them said. *He* was satisfied, and said he'd only been a cook before, but now he was planning to knock off and enjoy himself, after he'd killed some Mexicans. But the lieutenant he belonged to had some other ideas, so he was back cooking again in a few minutes, new rank and all.

It was a peculiar Christmas. At home, a person got up early—in the dark, unless he was old or gouty or had drunk a lot of toddies while singing carols on Christmas Eve (like my brother Dirk). You tiptoed downstairs in your nightshirt to see what was lying under the tree, but you never opened anything, of course, unless it had become untied somehow, and the ribbon was loose. There was a red calico throw under the tree, with fresh-smelling pine cones strewn about and popcorn strings looped everywhere, along with ornaments that the darkies made out of stuffed velvet—imitation peaches and pears, with the nap kind of rubbed off from being used all those years—and tin stars and St. Nicks and candle-holders that clipped right onto the branches, but you had to be mighty careful; those spruces would go up like rockets.

On top, a handsome big angel with flowing robes and real yellow hair they'd got off a girl that died sometime previous—but it wasn't contagious, they said—and had a tin reflector on her back, for wings, and a candlestick sprouting out of her head—the ornament, I mean, not the deceased. It was a curiosity, and dismal if you thought about it; she looked like somebody had driven a spike in her skull. But you crept back upstairs and tossed and turned, waiting, maybe accidentally thumping on the floor now and then with a slingshot handle, or until some crabapple downstairs—my sister Claudia, likely—yelled, "Sam, you stop that, hear?" And after thirty or forty years you heard some nice noises of pots and pans banging and then the leather strap full of sleigh bells ringing—that was the signal—and you nipped down in a hurry, you bet, then hung on for a few more centuries while your father shaved. He was the slowest and cussedest shaver on record, and it appeared to come out especially draggy on Christmas. New Years had practically arrived before he finished, but it was worth it. Piles and piles of shiny new things like knives and skates and guns and sweaters, and the cold smell of snow on some big presents hauled in from outside (and couldn't wrap, you know). Then the darkies trooped in and I showed Hyacinth what I'd got, but he knew all about it, of course—the biggest know-it-all in seven states—and after that everybody knelt down on their knees and prayed for how they were about to treat their stomachs that day.

But here at Brazito things were different, and people missed it. I felt a bothersome big lump in my throat again, and kept trying not to look at Blaine. We had dried fruit and pumpkin for breakfast, and somebody said we ought to at least shoot off a few guns, in celebration, but the way the day turned out, it wasn't needed. Toward three o'clock, two Mexicans on beautiful mounts skidded up within hailing distance, and we went along for the fun. They shouted several things that the interpreter said were foreign to him, being probably "ornate" Mexican curses, involving articles like dogs and even meaner animals along with our sisters' honor, and then they spotted Viesca, who had on his goatskin pants—it was either that or scamper around barerump—and called him a "*Chivo!*"

Well, he was the maddest a Mexican can possibly be, because that's the most insulting curse against a male, and means he-goat. It wouldn't bother me any. I've been called considerably worse, especially by Blaine, times when he was teaching me about a man named Hannibal, which appeared to be a kind of early elephant trainer that worked mainly in the snow.

Here in the Drum-and-Fife Corps, a man has to be pretty witty to keep up his end, and Viesca called them he-goats right back. At this, one whipped up his gun and fired, missing everything in sight, then wheeled around to run. Our sentries let drive with their special rifle-yagers, bringing the rear rider off his horse with a thump. But he bounced directly up, and hotfooted it for more than a hundred yards, wigwagging his hat in one hand; I seldom saw a man run so. Then, all of a sudden, he crumpled like a straw doll going to pieces—knees and legs bent every which way, head flopped over, not a muscle twitching after he fell.

It was odd; we went with Surgeon Morton to look him over. "This fellow was shot cleanly through the heart," said Morton, bending down, pompous as usual. "He was dead before he left his horse. And yet he ran a very considerable distance on foot. It's a wonderment to me, and a case for the medical journals," and he jotted down some remarks in his notebook. Nobody paid any attention; this was the *busy* doctor, too busy to see anybody but high officers, and one man said, "Well, he got an appointment, and I expect it's a consolation to him."

Morton started to take the trooper's name, but right here the enemy made their first move, when three Mexicans rode forward behind an officer that carried a crude black flag like a pirate's, with *two* death's heads on it, plus the inscription, *Libertad o Muerte* (Liberty or Death).

I reckon it'll get into the history books, so I might as well say that Colonel Doniphan was, at the time, in his tent playing the card game of loo, with several other officers.

"They say we must surrender or all be killed, sir," reported Lieutenant Colonel Mitchell of the St. Louis Company. "What message shall I give?"

As nearly as I could see, Doniphan didn't look up, but said, "Oh, just tell them to go to Hell and bring on their forces."

The Mexicans were massed behind a low bank of hills about a thousand yards away. In the forefront, they had Dragoons, in gorgeous scarlet coats and high helmets, and behind them a swarming horde of what turned out to be volunteers rounded up in El Paso.

And now they started to come on.

Finally, when they'd closed up half the distance, Colonel Doniphan exploded. I knew he would; I suspicioned he was only sitting there hatching plans, to keep everybody fooled. A soldier's mind is never far from the field of battle.

And yes, sir, he slammed down his cards, and cried, "By God, boys, I had an invincible hand, but I'm damned if we don't have to get up and fight right away!"

Several heard him, and one or two laughed, but it was no time to be frolicking. Riding along our line, the colonel ordered most of our horses stripped and picketed, and kept calling out, "Lie flat, boys, and keep cool. Don't fire till you get the signal. Just lie flat and keep cool." He was chewing a plug of tobacco he had borrowed, and seemed perfectly composed, now and then staring off at the oncoming enemy, shading his eyes from the sun.

I commenced to get worried. When the Mexicans were no farther than four hundred yards, they begun to fire a ten-pound howitzer loaded with copper slugs. These plopped down here and there but did no damage except one that smacked into a wagon and knocked off a wheel.

Then, blam!—their first volley, and still no action from us. Over to one side, I spotted that wild ram, Captain Reid, hatless and mounted, hair every which way, charged up for the command to go, his horse backing and sidling with excitement, looking crazy in the eyes, and blam!—their second volley.

There was some muttering along our line, but Colonel Doniphan was whistling, while riding back and forth, and took no notice. Nobody had been hit yet, but you could hear the bullets hiss overhead like hail. They were shooting very high, which we learned later is easy to do when you're mounted, moving, and aiming at targets lower down.

"Let her go, boys! Take picks and *fire!*" There followed a howl of welcome and a thunderstorm that partially deafened me. I grabbed my ears with both hands; I couldn't help it. Those Missouri rifles make a racket, and they're dead accurate in the bargain. I saw Mexicans falling every few yards along their ranks. One Dragoon, a handsome young fellow, bad hit, crawled toward us like a spider, as fast as he could scramble; then he fired off his carbine feebly in the air when two other balls struck him with a splunk. He was a brave man, and no matter how much our troops reviled the Mexicans, those Dragoons were good soldiers. With any kind of leader, they might have fought well.

But it was practically finished. Captain Reid let out a war whoop to shrivel a grizzly, then led twenty of his men in a flying, hoof-pounding, rampaging charge at their lancers, on the left flank. Seeing it, the whole Mexican line stopped, wavered, and, at our second volley, broke helter-skelter into retreat. They didn't hesitate, but threw aside everything they owned. The entire field was knee-deep in lances, helmets, carbines, provisions, wine bottles, trumpets, sabers, camp stools, dead men, horses, and wounded men crying for water.

It was a jumbled-up scene, with bitter-smelling gun-smoke hanging over it all, and made my head spin a little. We hadn't undergone a single bad casualty, as I'll explain in a minute, and when Colonel Doniphan heard that, he collected his other card players and finished the game of loo. The pot had been a handsome white stallion, but during the battle the horse pulled up stakes and shifted, so there wasn't much sense in playing the hand out, it seemed to me.

At the Mexican camp, we found heaps more of articles on the order of wine kegs, surgical instruments, and ammunition, along with the usual refuse; also a petticoat and a rebozo. Then one of Lieutenant Reid's cavalrymen stated that the two people working the Mexican cannon were women. He had identified them, positive, through his field glasses. Nobody doubted it; Mexican men will shovel off onto women every job they can, and somebody said he was surprised that any men turned out at all.

Well, by questioning prisoners, we learned that the Mexican commander was a Captain Ponce de León, converted into a "temporary general" for the occasion. They didn't say who ordered it, and it wasn't good judgment. The Mexicans had no rear guard out, for instance, and when the Army—what was left of four hundred Dragoons and eight hundred volunteers—aped it toward El Paso (thirty miles away), a big bunch of Indians swooped down from a hill where they'd been watching, and killed thirty more, mostly to get hold of those red coats. That made about seventy killed altogether, and maybe twice that many wounded.

The young chap that scuttled toward us like a spider lived on for more than an hour. Two rifle balls had passed clear through his stomach, front to rear, and his left elbow was smashed. O'Hara propped him against some boxes and gave him a cigarrito, but it only made him sick. He was a very cheerful young man and spoke English; said he'd been to school in Europe. He said, "Please tell my moth–" and sort of slumped down inside his jacket, very still and looking smaller all of a sudden. O'Hara went white as a sheet, then slammed his hat on the ground and stamped on it, and after that he looked around for a priest to whip, but there wasn't any, of course.

When the battle commenced, our Volunteers had no more than four hundred men on hand. The rest were scattered around behind the lines, searching for firewood. In addition, some *still* hadn't caught up from the Jornada.

What made the Mexicans retreat all the way, said the prisoners, was a whopping big dust cloud rolling up to our rear. They thought it was an additional army of reinforcements; what it was, though, was a herd of seven thousand sheep that Colonel Doniphan had bought in Doña Ana.

No Mexicans returned, with the customary flag of truce, to gather up wounded and bury their dead. They left them sprawled on the field, so we dug a big hole and dumped in the bodies, including two or three Indians. But by the next morning wolves had dug the hole up and polished the Indians off; bloody-looking bones were lying around everywhere. On the other hand, the Mexicans had scarcely been touched. It sounds gruesome, but a dead Mexican is stuffed so full of red pepper that wolves won't eat him. So we had to bury the bodies all over again. The men on the shovel detail were sore about it, and uncorked some of their usual peeves against the Mexicans, saying it was typical and thoughtless to eat that kind of food, knowing how wolves felt, also being aware it was dead certain to cause extra work.

On our side, we had two Volunteers wounded, and one of these was Hugh Angel–Angelina. A ball had creased her shoulder. It was awkward; I couldn't figure any way out of it. But what I hadn't reckoned on was her brass. She *was* coolheaded, and no mistake. What's more, the business of getting wounded acted on her like catnip. Maybe she figured the jig was up, but she didn't appear to make any sense whatever.

When the surgeon got around to her case—and he took an aggravating long time about it, being busy, as somebody said, treating a major with hangnails—she peeled off her shirt and had *another* shirt, without sleeves, on underneath. It was a mighty tight squeeze, and embarrassing, if you knew the truth.

"What's this?" said Dr. Morton.

"I'm wearing a mustard plaster, sir. The undershirt holds it down."

"I see. And what is the mustard plaster *for?*"

"I'm expecting a cold."

He stared at her as if she was a lunatic, and I didn't blame him.

"You're *expecting* a cold! See here, young man, I don't quite follow that. Why would you be expecting a cold?"

"I fell in the river yesterday, sir."

"How on earth did you do that?"

"I was preparing the mustard plaster to put on, and my foot slipped on a rock."

The truth is, this Morton came within an ace of being feeble-minded, else he might have reared up and taken notice. Pulling down one corner of the shift—almost too far, by the way—he swabbed out the cut and coated it over with carbolic.

As he did so, he kept up a running fire of what you might call professional comment, to the effect that, "Let's see, now, what have we here? We've got a little blood, yes, yes, but we've been very, very lucky—rubbed, just rubbed; that's all we have. We'll be all right again in half a tick."

But Angelina picked her ears right up, naturally, and said, "They got you, too, did they, Doc? Does it hurt?"

But he was humming along, and barely heard her. He gave her a fatherly pat, then bandaged her up and commented, "Young man, that's the bulkiest mustard plaster I ever saw in the whole of my professional career. I'd like to examine it when you get it exposed."

Angelina said, "I'll certainly remember that, sir. I think you'd be interested. I really do."

I left, disgusted. The girl hadn't any more morals than an alley cat. There are things to joke about, and other things, and this wasn't one of them, if you know what I mean.

The injury sort of gave her the freedom of the camp, you might say. She'd got by without being discovered, so she loosened up even more and looked for somebody to jump on, and sure enough, it turned out to be Blaine. So there was another promise gone sour.

Frankly, I wasn't entirely happy about him myself. Toward the end of the battle, he'd jumped up, saddled his horse, and taken off like a Comanche, yelling and waving his saber. I didn't see him again for half an hour. It made me think back to that miserable "duel" in the gulch. And him the mildest, easiest, bookiest fellow on earth, before all this started. It had me worried.

After the hubbub died down, he'd gone birddogging around amongst the loot left on the field and came back with four beautiful bottles of wine. What I'm saying is, they weren't the ordinary run of stuff the others found. *That* was generally wine in kegs, or cheap-looking bottles that hadn't been put up very long. El Paso, we came to learn, was in a valley famous for its grapes, and some of those big estates turned out uncommonly high-grade liquids. I heard it said, and believe it.

Anyway, when dusk fell, various groups of our people began to organize into parties, with campfires going everyplace you looked and plenty to eat and drink for a change. The laughter and battle talk rose over the popping of piñon logs, and if it hadn't been for a number of dead horses and such lying around, the scene would have warmed your heart.

So Sergeant O'Hara got Señora Mendoza to knock off laundering back in the rear ranks, where he said she'd done some wonderful work, and we had a gathering of our own. Not stirred up by aguardiente, Mrs. Mendoza was a very nice person, spite two or three gold teeth and a kind of hearty manner that might take the form of knocking a person flat on his back in the middle of a joke, and she made a purple mash out of Mexican beans and cooked a steak in a style she called *Tampiqueña,* or some such.

But first we had the wine. To give Blaine credit, he *did* know wines, and always bought them for the cellar back in Missouri. He'd been on the Grand Tour, you see, and it had more or less gone to his stomach. But he was practically cracked on the subject, and it was funny, because he hated nearly every other kind of pompousy humbug you could name. People get that way about wine; I've noticed it in others.

He held up one of the bottles, which was old and cobwebby and had a cork sunk deep down—drove in, likely, by a maul—and says:

"Officers' wine, none of your common tub mash. Eighteen thirty-nine—a very good year on these slopes, I'm informed."

I've already said that Angelina was feeling her oats, so of course she couldn't let that slide.

"It was a good year on *all* slopes—everywhere, or so *I'm* informed."

"I beg your pardon, Angel?"

"But a very, very bad year on the flats. Nothing went well on the flats. People with any sense moved up to the slopes."

Blaine hesitated a second, frowning. "You're a queer sort of fellow, Angel. To tell you the truth, you're something of a mystery to me."

"You might call me an Angel in disguise."

"What's that?"

"Oh nothing, nothing. Go ahead and open the bottle—sir. I need a pull of that. I'm wounded, and may be turning gangrenous."

"Wine isn't 'pulled,' Angel. It's supposed to be savored."

"Well, let's savor a couple of bottles. There's too much voodoo about it; you act like a nervous witch doctor."

They gave me a teaspoonful in a tin cup of water, and it didn't ruin the water at all—only made it taste rusty, as if somebody had left a piece of rotting old iron in the bottom.

O'Hara tossed off his cup in one backward lurch, but Señora Mendoza, busy at the cooking pot, scarcely touched hers at all. She was so loose and good-humored and happy, she was practically drunk when sober, you might say. She was shy of Blaine, though, and kept in the background.

He rolled a mouthful around on his tongue, still standing and holding the bottle up for inspection, then said, like a professor:

"It's a light, airy wine, not presumptuous but undeniably assertive. Its character, actually, is reticent but basically self-confident, with elfin overtones, overtones of mischief—'Come dance with me, *but don't say I didn't warn you!*' it could be saying, if one may strike a fanciful note." He caught himself and gave a self-conscious little laugh.

Angelina drank off about half a cup, then spewed some out on the ground. "Stuff tastes toxic—probably made out of citric acid and water. That *is* presumptuous." She grabbed the bottle and gurgled down a pretty good deal. Then she nodded her head. "I thought so."

"Thought what, Angel?" said Blaine, looking pained.

"They squashed these grapes up with their feet. What you thought was elfin was *feet.* Don't try to fool me about wine. I'll take a blindfold test."

"For your information, Angel, the evolution of wine might well be equated with the refining of civilization itself. It could be said to symbolize the introduction of manners, and restraint, during the ingestion of food. It was a long step forward. Stone-age man probably fell on his meal like a hyena. There *are* graces, you know, that lift humanity above the animals. O'Hara, you're a sane and sensible fellow, if rough—a man, I think, with instinctive appreciation of the good. How do *you* stand on this vintage?"

"Why, I'm feeling it a-ready, sir. It's worked right down inside and knocked against the slats. Like you said, sir, it was dancing a tune on my bum-gut in the time it took to swaller. A straight shot down, then she bounced."

"I was referring to the taste, or aroma, or, if you will, bouquet, O'Hara."

"You couldn't beat it, could you, sir? There ain't a man in the Army that could tell it from the finest vinegar out of a keg. Why, this wine's got bokay all over it. And me not a wine man, particular. A pint of beer, black as a nigger's tit, was what *I* favored, and me old mither the same. I can hear her say it now—'Take me shift if you must, but leave the swipes.' She was that partial."

I could see Blaine kind of studying, as though he might decide to go over someplace else and drink his wine, but Angelina spoke up on another subject.

"Sir, I was wondering if you'd care to put me in for a medal.

Something in gold, preferably, with a brief inscription mentioning gallantry. After all, I *was* wounded."

"I'm sorry to say that I'm not familiar with the details of your feat, Angel," said Blaine coldly.

"Well, it was like this, and I can get verification from a witness, if need be. At first, I was lying almost directly in front of a very fat man named Boomer. Then, when I realized they were using real bullets, I quickly got up, leaving my rifle, and took a position *behind* him. As I did so, I heard him exclaim, 'Why, you slippery little bastard!'—I'll get that from him in writing, tomorrow. It was while crouched, half standing, that they hit me. I'll know better next time, of course."

"Your explanation does you no credit, Angel," said Blaine in about the frostiest tones you can imagine. "What I *will* put you in for is an official reprimand—something on government stationery, with a mention of cowardice."

Then he continued, his face lighting up very curious, but maybe it came from the wine:

"You must remember we are fighting a just and righteous war against a tyrannical and despicable foe, whose aggressions can no longer be tolerated—"

I didn't know too much about this fuss, but that wasn't quite the way I'd worked it out in my mind. Anyhow, he mooned on some more, not sounding like my brother at all.

"—and I don't mind admitting this: when I swung up on my horse, ready for the pursuit with sword in hand, I felt a singing in the blood! It's a grand thing to know that *you*, personally, have the power to right great wrongs by the simple, manly act of eliminating some very dirty scoundrels from the world. Moreover, there's an excitement here that can't be matched in any other way. To a hunter—and we're all hunters—man is of course the most dangerous and last logical game. To strengthen the breed, it becomes our duty to eliminate the curs. War may well be the sublimest of the human experiences. I've always considered it so."

I practically gasped out loud, and Angelina spoke up in what was near about her own natural voice, without the silly gruffness she tried to put on. I saw O'Hara give her a very odd and calculating look. He was by far the soberest of the three, and not quite as stupid as he generally appeared from his speech.

"What utter and exquisite rot! You've always considered nothing of the kind. Just the opposite, in fact. What's *happened* to you, anyhow?"

There was a little shocked silence, while Blaine tried to collect his wits. He seemed overtired, and befuddled—he was swaying slightly, now, and his eyes didn't quite focus—so I reckoned he would come to his senses in the morning.

"How do *you* know anything about *me,* Angel, if it isn't too much trouble to take the trouble to give a civil answer to a perfectly civil question?"

"Why, from how you used to talk in the early weeks—*sir,*" she said, sweetly, but she certainly didn't look it.

"O'Hara!" said Blaine, swinging around fiercely, with his eyes following a second later. "Tell the truth, speak right up, bold as an eagle. *Hasn't it been a glorious old day?"*

O'Hara sat staring off at the other campfires for awhile. "A young man like that, as well-favored and gentle-spoke as you please; black—black and curly like an Irisher; sitting there with the blood seeping out, him with a whole life ahead, or ort to be, and trying to give a message to thim back home. I bin trying to think on him as a scoundrel, but it don't come right. He was more like one of us, and he crumpled over against my shoulder without a peep. *Not* like a cur, not him. Why, he wasn't much more than a baby! No, sir, I can't agree it's bin a glorious day. I shouldn't say it, as hasn't the eddication of a hop-toad, but I do say it, and proud."

"Thank you, O'Hara," said Angelina. "You have been very gravely underestimated."

"Well, now, *there's* a soldier heard from! A fire-breathing, fast-slogging, rough, tough patriot of the front rank. And what about *you,* Sam? Are you among those who feel a little squeamish on this triumphal occasion?"

"Look here," I said hotly, "I don't have to talk to you. I don't have to listen, either. I'm going to bed."

Out in the dark fields the dead horses were filling up with gas and making funny hissing noises, and I had trouble getting off to sleep. It was hard not to think about home; once or twice I had to swab at my eyes with my sleeve. Altogether it was an unsatisfactory sort of Christmas.

XVII

(NOTE: THIS *Journal* will of necessity become more personal, as the writer has been victimized by a member of the local population. Beauty is, of course, no excuse for presumption, but it is my regrettable failing that I seem incapable of standing up against smart, handsome, *self-reliant* women of breeding. It was so in Missouri; it is doubly true now. My present involvement is, in truth, perhaps the most deplorable to which a literary corporal has ever been subjected.)

El Paso, January 30, 1847: The Army moved into this city on December twenty-seventh, without further opposition, though we had news of the usual gusty threats. At the edge of town, however, a cringing and subservient delegation greeted us, bearing a white flag of truce. The members were, it seemed, anxious to preserve their property. One of Alex Doniphan's first acts was to liberate from the calabozo three Americans—Messrs. Hudson, Pollard and Hutchinson—who had been immured in a dank, unwholesome grotto for five months and a day. They had been forced to subsist on next to no food.

Their crime? Why, they, as traders, had engaged a plausible Scotsman, one Graham, to guide them up the Del Norte across the Sierra Madre to San Diego. Upon receiving their advance payment, the hardy rascal promptly informed the authorities that they were Texan spies, and departed.

Captain Reid, seeing their condition, was moved to make a retaliatory gesture. He had five prisoners, who had twice attempted to escape and who, in doing so, had stabbed a young guard named Wilkins. Reid being desirous of making these villains talk—hoping to get information about enemy strength farther south toward Chihuahua—he examined our pitiful released Americans and then, lighting a cigar and seating himself in a chair, had all five Mexicans strung up to trees. Beneath each was a Volunteer at the end of a rope. The procedure went thus (through Caldwell, the interpreter):

"Wish to talk?"

"He says he spits in the eye of all dirty Protestant gringos."

"Hoist him up. Good, good. Getting a little purple? Wind cut off? *Not* dead? Then drop him down."

(Followed a hiatus while the man was revived.)

"All right, splendid. Ready again? Prisoner wish to talk?"

"He says his tongue feels powerful loose, Captain. He's got a downright old gabby outlook, to be sure."

"Take him to one side. Next man."

"This one expects to watch your mother bred to a stallion and hopes your sisters give birth to tiger cats with forty-five claws on each paw."

"Very poetic. Hoist him up, and let's sharpen the muse."

And so on. Eventually, all five prisoners—Regulars from Vera Cruz, Chihuahua, and Zacatecas—divulged intelligence that could be of great benefit to us in the coming battle for Chihuahua.

Reid is not a cruel man, but his patience has been tried by the frightful treatment of our citizens by the Mexicans. It might be said, too, that the El Paso populace were much braced by the exhibition. The ordeal by hemp took place in a small, sycamore-filled park—a kind of expanded urinal, if one's sense of smell is any judge—and the manners of the onlookers were greatly improved toward the end. A number of men took off their hats and began addressing us as "Señor" and "Capitán" and other comparative endearments.

Our first camping place was on a bare spot of earth south of the Plaza, but this proved so exposed to sandstorms that we were shortly quartered at private homes in the city.

El Paso is a fruitful area, enriched by numberless farms, large and small, many of them growing excellent grapes. The city and all the plantations are watered by ditches, called *sakos,* smaller than the canals of Santa Fé. These are, of course, supplied by the Rio Grande and are under the control of an *alcalde de sakos.* As a rule, each farmer is allotted one day's run of his *sako* per week.

On the morning of the twenty-eighth, three commissioners representing the city government called on Doniphan to inquire about the terms of possession. He in turn summoned me, and together we drafted a statement that read much as the one in Santa Fé: "We have not come to plunder and ravage, but to offer you liberty. The lives and property of such as remain peaceable, during the existence of the war, will be fully and amply protected; but such as neglect their industrial pursuits, and instigate other peaceable citizens to take up arms against the Americans, will be punished as their crimes deserve."

The tone of this was in refreshing contrast to a proclamation of Angel Trias, Governor of Chihuahua, which fell into our hands. Indeed, being deeper in enemy country, we began in general to suffer from what might be called "Manifesto-itis." These documents, incomparably florid, inconsistent, bombastic, and, usually, prosy to the point of non-comprehension, were being fired off by the Mexican leaders, including Santa Anna, at the rate of one every few minutes. Trias led off with, "Soldiers:—The sacrilegious invaders of Mexico are approaching the city of El Paso, an important part of the State, where the enemy intend establishing their winter quarters, and even pretend that they will advance further into our territory. It is entirely necessary that you go forward—you defenders of the honor and glory of the Republic, that you give a lesson to these Pirates."

Having alerted the soldiers in El Paso, he displayed marvelous tact by going on to insult the town's citizens:

"The State depended much upon the aid that would be given by the valiant and war-worn citizens of the Pass. But traitors there have sown distrust, and the patriotic people, because of a disgraceful mutiny, were forced to retreat at thirty leagues distance from a tiny force, under General Kearny, when they might have taken him and his group prisoners at discretion. Subordination and discipline were wanting."

I have noticed that a Mexican, preparing a Manifesto, is compelled at once to praise and revile, with undercurrents of physical reprisal, the very persons whom he is addressing. This strain runs through the stacks of these curious broadsides that I am gathering together.

After flaying the El Paso residents in offensive terms, having called them "treasonous and disgraceful," Trias made it clear that he trusted them absolutely: "I confide in your courage and only recommend to you obedience to your commanders and the most perfect discipline."

I was indeed struck by his reliance upon their possible "obedience to your commanders." When one considers that, before Santa Fé, a battle involving several important Mexican generals dissolved because they could not agree on the priority of command, and when one adds that the sainted Santa Anna, prime leader and symbol of the enemy war effort, shamefully fled south from Santa Fé in the face of our arrival, and, finally, when one adds further that "General" Ponce de León, at Brazito, was in that temporary designation only, having neatly skipped four ranks to make it*—why then the chance of a wholly sane Mexican placing confidence in any of his commanders whatever appears most unlikely.

However, Trias concluded by expressing the heretofore admirably restrained rage of the Chihuahuans to help. The reader's bosom was, possibly, stirred to find that "All Chihuahuans burn with the desire to go with you, because they are *Mexicans,* possessed of the warmest enthusiasm and the purest patriotism. They will march to join you! At the first signal that the circumstances of war demand reinforcements, they shall be forwarded, let it cost the State what it may. To the people of Chihuahua no sacrifice is reckoned when the honor of the Republic is at stake!"

It occurred to me, for one, that a signal had in fact been given:

*Note: We have lately learned that Captain Ponce de León was jammed into the breach because one General Cuilta had been leveled with a painful case of gastritis. From the accounts, he made a full recovery soon after the battle.

we were in El Paso and the Chihuahuans were still in Chihuahua. Further to draw upon Trias' excellent words, we were being greeted with the warmest enthusiasm on all sides. El Paso has been called "The Garden Spot" of Mexico, and her citizens are relaxed, friendly, rich, a shade less indolent than their countrymen, and, above all, realistic. They voiced the purest patriotism in stating that they were delighted to find a stable and incorrupt government now installed in this valley. In the future, it was felt, they would be protected by bullets, not Manifestoes, against raids by the Apaches and other predators. Lastly, it is my own opinion that all were greatly relieved finally to avoid the skull-cracking boredom of reading Manifestoes. That sort of punishment, prolonged, might tend to subvert the staunchest partisans.

After much deliberation by Alex Doniphan—for what purpose I cannot say—I was billeted (alone among the officers and non-coms) at the *hacienda* of one Don Diego Rojas y las Cruces, an enormously rich and plausible man, of about fifty-five years of age, with the princeliest kind of manners. He stands tall for a Mexican, very erect, has graying, well-brushed hair, nearly expressionless black eyes, a smile that turns off like a water spigot —ascending no higher than his prominent aquiline nose—a soft, modulated voice, no beard but long sideburns that would seem ridiculous in a personage of lesser bearing. His evening costumes tend toward dark colors, are heavily brocaded, beautifully edged, fit without a wrinkle, and are varied from night to night; there seems to be no end to them. In the daytime, he is apt to wear riding trousers of a cut that I suspect to be European, with silver rowel spurs, jangly and cruel; and he has, hanging on a peg at the stables, a pair of sheepskin "chaps" for use against thick brush when he rides, as he does almost daily, over his incalculable thousands of acres. Although a reasonable claimant to the description of inscrutable, Rojas has a telltale symptom of agitation. When disturbed, by sloth on the part of his Indians or *mestizos* (the product of a Spaniard and an Indian), or by annoyance from his family, his veins at the temples engorge and lie as visible as glowworms. It is, to me, a marvelous but no doubt costly and even dangerous sample of self-control.

In the hierarchy of this old, old land with its imposition of new culture from a conquering people, Rojas ranks as a *Gachupín,* or Spaniard from Europe. Thus, either he became wealthy from having been a favorite at court, or, most probably, he left home in modest circumstances to better himself in a new country where every advantage was given to his class. Socially, the *Gachupines* are exceeded in Mexico only by a few authentic noblemen whose titles no longer have great significance. Money is the real arbiter of distinction here, as it appears to be in all raw pioneer lands.

I am treated with perfect courtesy, yet I can never discard the feeling that I am a guest by imposition from the outside. An American acquaintance I made in the city, a man of culture and breeding, tells me that in nine years of business residence in El Paso, he and his very charming wife have not once been invited into a Mexican home of high caste. Oh, yes, he may have the most cordial dealings with these gentry during the day, but the arrival of nightfall brings with it an aloofness and formality as impregnable as the darkness itself.

I shan't forget the first evening of my own billeting-by-duress. I was met at the grim-looking gate of this spacious, white-painted hacienda (some six miles from town) by one León, the young "major-domo," whose racial designation is, I have learned, *castigo,* meaning the offspring of a Spaniard and a mestizo, and escorted with a sweeping bow toward a rather grand chamber on the east side of the rectangle. Like all important Mexican houses, this is built, mostly in one story, around a broad patio, containing gardens, small trees, a fountain, wrought-iron benches, and a circling driveway. On three sides are the formal living rooms and bedrooms; on the fourth are chambers for, I take it, numbers of house domestics.

The afternoon was warm, the time of the siesta was at hand, and my guide, who speaks good but amusingly stilted English, made a species of apology, saying, "Madame begs to convey that she rests, on account of the known precariousness of her health. She realizes that a gentleman will understand. Don Diego, as you comprehend, is in the city, by command of the invader"—this last spoken with an edge.

I was uncertain about the position of a major-domo—his attitude suggested that he considered himself at least a kind of illegitimate connection of the family—but I have had some experience of uppity servants and was in no mood to be patronized. After all, we *were* here by right of conquest, to the disruption of our own lives and affairs; moreover, I was in a sense the representative of our Army in this household.

"What others are there?"

"Señor?"

"I said, what other members of the Rojas family are about?"

He stood frowning, not able to decide on a course. Impertinence finally won out.

"Rojas *y las Cruces*. I am sure they will present themselves to our honored guest at such a time when persons of prominent society should do so in accordance with the customs of our land."

"I understand there's a son, named Cosmo. Is he on the premises?"

"Señor Cosmo is also resting. He was engaged at cards last night to a late hour."

The sons of Gachupines have taken unto themselves the motto of *Siempre alegre*—always lighthearted—and I assumed that we had here a prime example of this foppish, self-indulgent group.

"Get him up. By the customs of *my* land, I can't possibly settle in without announcing myself to the head of the house. I'll sit down here till he arrives."

At this moment, there were footsteps behind us, and a low and warm but authoritarian voice spoke out:

"Señor, you must forgive the members of this family their bad manners."

I turned to survey a stunningly flawless girl, as handsome as I have seen in any country. Women have not been a study of mine; I am a lame pen in matters of description, but the vision here was, in brief, that of a slender but mature creature with sleek black hair, an encrimsoned velvet bow of a mouth, startlingly clear green eyes—rare in this land of blacks and browns—and nearly transparent white skin that, curiously, was unprotected at the moment from the searching rays of a subtropical sun at high altitude.

Her beauty was such that her costume seemed careless, being,

I thought, a man's shirt at second hand, probably her brother's—sleeves rolled up—riding trousers of questionably close fit, with a man's silver-studded belt and dull expensive-looking boots that were far from clean.

It was in the matter of her mien that the onlooker read signs of trouble. In years of dealing with unbroken animals, I have never come across danger signals that said more plainly, "Don't tread on me." She was the incarnate spirit of revolt.

"But Señorita Carla—"

"Go away, León. We don't want you here."

Then she said, "My brother Cosmo is drunk: *borracho*. Sleeping it off, as I believe they call it. He will be fully revived about seven-thirty."

She led me to an elaborate if musty suite of rooms with a high, ornate bed and said, "This is yours. They should have prepared it, but I suppose you are accustomed to doing for yourself. My father's brother died here month before last." Having delivered this hospitable bit of news, she turned and said, "I think it only fair to say that we despise you."

I bowed, almost but not quite on the point of returning to El Paso and applying for other quarters. "I'm deeply grateful, señorita, for this improvement on your houseboy's manners." For a second, I thought she might cut me across the face with a riding crop she held in both hands, pressed sharply into her thighs. But we had instead a comical battle of looks, and she left.

Presumably, somebody thought better of my reception, for in half an hour's time, there arrived a pretty but shapeless Indian girl who announced herself as "my" maid, name of Carmen. She set to work arranging the bed, fetching (and pummeling savagely) fresh pillows, opening the broad shutters that gave way to the sunlit patio, and wrenching apart my kit, despite my best efforts to stop her, talking volubly and non-comprehensibly the while. When she examined the paltry array of soiled linen and poor personal effects, she gave a yelp of dismay, bundled it up in her arms, and made off, I was told, toward the "*ropa lavada*."

Shortly afterward, I had another visitor, announced by a soft scratching at the now wide-opened doorway. This proved to be León, much altered in demeanor—friendly, eager, fawning—who inquired in a whisper if I liked "señoritas." I made no answer, and he urged me not to settle for the common run of *"rameras"* in the city.

"It is to my good fortune to have as you say a stable of the much better class—*más elegante. Mucho más elegante."*

I was about to shoo him away when the Señorita Carla, striding along the patio at the moment, struck him briskly across the shoulders with her crop. "Stealthy little beast, always prying and snooping. Did he make a mention of 'señoritas'?"

"Something of the sort."

"Más elegante?"

I nodded.

"Well, they aren't más elegante. I've seen them. Depending, of course," she said, "on what one has previously encountered. We dine at nine. We assemble in *la sala* at seven-thirty. La Señora comes in briefly. But perhaps you'd rather not. I'm told that everyone has dinner at six o'clock in your land, and spits onto the floor."

"Quite true."

"Then no doubt you would prefer a tray." She directed a slow, insulting stare at my clothes, and said, "Yes, I'm sure it would be more suitable."

"On the contrary, I'll be there precisely on the hour."

In point of fact, still warm under the collar, I arrived at seven-twenty-five, in a broad, high-ceilinged, formal room of great richness, with a deep, pale green carpet; an ornate rosewood piano in one corner, all fretwork and filigree; a huge, multiprismed chandelier suspended from the exact center of the ceiling; a small dais in one corner for, I found, *mariachi* musicians; some spindly tables and chairs placed stiffly around the walls; full-length Venetian mirrors, rather candid and disconcerting in effect—it was virtually impossible to avoid staring at oneself from any point in the room, so that I constantly found myself feeling critical of what my image was doing—and, finally, the omnipresent León, now in a short white jacket, pouring modest portions of wine into fragile crystal glasses at a sideboard. He had a silver-tipped tray and seemed at ease.

The only member of the family on time was Don Diego himself, and he came forward with what appeared to be genuine cordiality, saying, "Ah, there you are, Captain. I am sure they have made you comfortable—"

"Corporal. I was greeted with every courtesy."

"Corporal, perhaps, *but a friend of Colonel Doniphan!*" He took me by one elbow, to propel me firmly around the room—something I especially loathe—and began a monologue, half humorous, half rueful, about the reduced state of his beloved Mexico.

"—But you, too, know what it is to be a patriot. We are a strange land with an even stranger population: four million Indians, a million whites, and two million of mixed white and Indian blood. Who, then, can say what a Mexican will do? He responds to conflicting racial instincts. It grieves me to say so, but even the pure Spaniard is a man of confusing origins. Doubtless you have raised your North American eyebrows at our lamentable inability to fight. But the Mexican, Captain Shelby [once again, I found myself promoted in the field] is not a coward. He is simply a man who has nothing to fight for. I say it—I, a landed proprietor who doubtless shouldn't. Our soldier has no faith in his leaders, and nothing to gain if he wins. It is common knowledge that the Mexican Army consists of twenty thousand soldiers and twenty-four thousand officers. Our hidalgo system of caste is so rigid that nothing could improve the lower orders short of a mass insurrection by the Indians. And they, thank God, are far too shiftless to care. A few tortillas, a handful of frijoles, a cigarrito to smoke and a woman to work and sleep with—that is the extent of their ambition. Why complicate life? *Mañana,* and so on. And who knows? He is right, maybe. Also, we are departmented, and land divided into separate states, almost, so that the people in El Paso do not care, really, what those of Vera Cruz are thinking. And yet, after all, we shall fight. From this point, you will not find your progress southward so easy, I predict."

During his discourse, which was, I thought, the over-candid and sophisticated utterance easily afforded by the man at the top, and meant to be presented so, others of the household drifted languidly in. To most of these, except for the brother, Cosmo, I was introduced with formal ceremony, being received with neither pleasure nor hostility; I was merely acknowledged. Cosmo was a different kettle of fish altogether. He was a vapidly handsome fellow of about thirty, with thinning black hair, rather hollow eyes, teeth of a striking whiteness (very much in evidence), splendid clothes that failed to conceal a figure thickening at the waist, and a manner that was frankly aimed to please. That is, he had no more motive in life, I concluded, than to stir those up around him to have a rollicking time. This took a faintly unpleasant form. His wife, a beautiful and very subdued young girl, was the butt of all his remarks. Her wedding night, I learned later, had proved to be a psychological horror, as shared with the self-centered Cosmo, and she had developed a morbid revulsion against the connubial couch. This unfortunate girl's problem was openly discussed in the household as an illness, on the order of brain fever, or consumption. "Poor Mariana" was the term most commonly used to describe her. "What a pity she's sick." No notice was taken of Cosmo's contribution to the impasse.

In consequence, as so often happens to the suffering, she had turned to religion. The time that normal young ladies devoted to dancing and fun, she generally spent on her knees. She was passionately fond of the small ikons of her cult, and was seldom seen without at least a rosary clenched in one hand. Her rooms, I gathered shortly, were a nightmare of theological bric-a-brac.

"Well, Cosmo, you've had a good day, or night, I trust," said Don Diego, with just the thinnest suggestion of a sneer.

"Unusually good, father. I got three crucifixes out from under our bed, removed a small, gilded Virgin from the medicine cabinet, and pulled down a quite hideous framed portrait of the infant Jesus, put up during my absence."

The parent eyed him with quiet distaste, and we moved on around the room. The gem of this exalted clan was Don Diego's wife, Alicia, a handsome and genuine *lady*, of middle age, going slightly to fat, the daughter of an authentic Spanish grandee, thus a social step above her husband. This was apparent in her assured lack of pretension. I liked her instantly. She welcomed me and said, in an accent more marked than the others', "I hope you will be happy here, señor. Veritably we are a terrible family."

With some difficulty, I overcame an urge to agree, and she informed me that, in the afternoon, she'd had no knowledge of my arrival. "My 'excuses' were invented by that regrettable, how?—yes, eavesdropper—León." (The subject of this praise was standing beside her at the moment, holding a tray and seeming flattered by her remarks.)

"We should be rid of him long ago, but, alas, he is deeply in everyone's intrigues. Some day he will go too far. That will be nice."

"You wish some wine, my lady?"

"No. Yes. Now go someplace, León. Over by the piano, out of hearing."

The Señorita Carla precipitated a contretemps that threatened to disrupt the evening, then we bumped on over that, and proceeded.

"I believe you have met El Capitán, no, Captain Shelby, a *close friend* of the Colonel Doniphan." Don Diego looked annoyed for a moment, and said, "I am forgetful in English; my daughter Carla makes it so—nerves." The veins in his forehead had engorged and were starting visibly to throb.

If possible, that wayward spirit was even more icily composed than before.

"My daughter Carla is preparing for her engagement, as I believe you call it. She will shortly make a journey to the South, even as yourself, Captain."

She said, "Your daughter Carla dislikes very much to travel in the winter. She is looking forward to thinking about her engagement in the Spring."

"You will do as you are ordered, Carla."

"In the matter of marrying, I will do as I am ordered in the Spring. Of an unnamable year."

I interposed with a complimentary remark about her costume, which was somehow more mannish than feminine, but she said, "It makes no difference at all to me what I wear."

There was a priest among the group, one Father Bernardo, a kindly, serious man who appeared to be in attendance on the unhappy Mariana, as a physician might have waited on an invalid; my host recovered his good humor by a course of determined and impious baiting.

"And how is your penitent this evening, Father Bernardo?"

"It is beautiful to see, Don Diego. She has turned full-face to our Lord in her time of need."

"But I believe she has turned full-back to her husband in *his* time of need."

"The ways of God are inscrutable, Don Diego."

"Just so. Tell me, Father, for I am always seeking the true doctrine, do you feel that God has complete faith in man, His creation?"

"To have less would be to suggest imperfections in the Creator, Don Diego."

"Then why, in the matter of cohabitation, did He think it necessary to provide a feeling of physical ecstasy at the climax? God's bribe, I call it. Surely a perfect creature would propagate the race out of duty."

The priest flushed, and muttered, in a low voice, "Perhaps we could better call it our Lord's reward. The position of the Church—"

"Ah, yes, *our* Church, yours and mine. The ruling is, I believe, that there must be *no* cohabitation *without* the intent to propagate. Now tell me, if you please, does this mean that we take the Lord's reward literally, or do we understand Him better than, let us say, the Mohammedans? You will recognize that these problems, which vex me, arise from the plight of your penitent, and, of course, her husband—my son."

There being no reasonable reply to this badgering, my host passed briefly to a larger analysis of the Church in Mexico, doubtless accurate but calculated, certainly, to offend: "You see, Captain Shelby, our Church is a house divided against itself. We have on the one hand the Gachupines, who naturally face toward Spain, whereas the parish priests, like our good Father Bernardo, are Creoles with Mexican sympathies. It would grieve you, señor, to learn that bishops and their kind have the income of princes, while monks and ordinary priests, again like Father Bernardo, have scarcely two picayunes to rub together. There exists no real connection between the two divisions, except, naturally, contempt on the one side and envy on the other—"

Father Bernardo tried to interrupt, wishing, I think, to disclaim envy (and I believed him), but Don Diego pushed on, excited, I gathered, by one of his favorite cynicisms:

"*Most* lamentable are the ignorance and immorality of these sainted brethren—have mercy, Father! I exclude all in this hacienda, of course. Would you believe it, Captain, when I say that a very large number, even among the higher clergy, are incapable even of reading the Mass? Yes, it is quite true. As to immorality—ah! The Mexican, you must understand, lives in the senses, differing only in the gratification sought, and our priests offer the people a sensuous worship. I have stood revolted in a darkened church to watch men crazed like animals with superstitious fears. Together with their women, they stripped themselves naked and scourged one another till every blow fell with a splash.

"At the best, these poor, benighted sheep, with the best part of their intelligence locked away fast, kneel at the Mass, gazing dumbly upon the appetizing display of gold and silver, rich vestments, beautifully worked images and carved and gilded woodwork; they breathe the sweet smoke of incense as it winds slowly up from golden censers, listen to sonorous incantations described as prayers, and confess to some fat priest well qualified to sympathize with their every earthly desire."

"Surely," exclaimed Father Bernardo, much agitated, "you overlook the great progress and reform of the twenty years past!"

"To be sure," said Don Diego, quickly penitent. "We have in truth abolished the Inquisition. That is most admirable; men's bones are no longer cracked by machines in the public square. There is talk, too, of barring ecclesiastics from legislative bodies. One at last hears, as now, philosophizing on clerical subjects; what is more, I, personally, have heard Protestants mentioned without rancor on three separate occasions. *However*, our clergy are still exempt by *fuero* from the jurisdiction of the civil courts, they are the unchallenged authority of the schools, and they continue as sole keeper of confessional secrets and family skeletons, sole dispensers of organized charity—"

His ranting was, happily, interrupted by the formal arrival of the matriach, "La Señora," a stately, thin, elderly woman dressed all in somber black, with a high comb and a black lace mantilla, now lifted. I, for one, welcomed her with relief. Don Diego's telltale veins had become prominent once again, and I was apprehensive that he might generate enough rage, given this rare listener from outside, to do himself an injury.

The old lady, as dry and brittle and luminous as parchment, took up a regal stand near the dais and received each family member in turn. Though composed with a kind of inner stillness, far beyond mortal distractions, she was intensely alive. Her few words, uncompromisingly spoken in Spanish, crackled with irony.

To me, she inclined her head perhaps an eighth of an inch, no more, and said, only, "*Bienvenido,*" meaning nothing and wishing me to realize it. To her son, after a glance at his forehead, "The Church again, Diego?" To Cosmo, "What a depressing sight you are." To Mariana, "My grandson has married a girl sick with nerves and religion." For Alicia, a kiss on the cheek. For Carla, a searching look and the observation, "All the family force has come out in the female side, if indeed you are female. That can be dangerous."

She disappeared to her chambers for dinner, which went off pacifically enough, the conversation being largely an added, tiresome monologue by Cosmo on the subject of his ecclesiastically cluttered rooms. His wife ate little or nothing, her head bowed, her lips occasionally moving in prayer, and Don Diego seemed exhausted by his exercise in la sala. He sat as a man in a trance.

As I ate, I aimlessly pondered the words of a well-educated but stiff-necked fellow officer who had written to his wife of the classes ruled by these people: "Gold is the God of the Mexicans. They have no motives but those of profit; no springs of action but those of self-love; no desires but those of gain; and no restraints but those of force. The eternal jingle of cash is music to their ears. Virtue, honesty, honor, piety, religion, patriotism, generosity, and reputation are to them pompous and unmeaning terms; and he whose conduct is shaped by principles of fair dealing is regarded as incomparably stupid. Vice, fraud, deceit, treachery, theft, plunder, murder and assassination stalk abroad in open daylight, and set order, law and justice at defiance. The virtue of females is bought and sold. Such is the moral and social system in Mexico in 1846."

In my present humor, I thought there was little to choose between them.

Altogether, I was relieved when, at the end, I was able to excuse myself and stroll out into the clean and refreshing patio. The night was as invigorating as it usually is in this climate and this season. The stars were smeared over the heavens and a cool breeze flowed down from the mountains. A strong scent of night-blooming flowers filled the air.

"Ah, I have found you at last, Capitán." I stopped, dismayed—the truth is, I had borne quite enough of this household for one day—and turned around, lowering my cigar.

Instead of León, as I expected, it was Cosmo, but his mission was identical.

"No doubt, sir, you have the true *caballero's* appetite for the señoritas. Shall you give me the honor to show you El Paso by night? We will visit La Gruta Deportiva. The most amusing postures—"

"Why, to be sure," I said recklessly. "I can't think of anything more delightful than a carriage ride into town. We'll be accompanied, of course, by Doña Mariana and Señorita Carla. Some fresh air might please them."

In the starlight, he had the look of a man stricken. "But you don't understand, señor. The suggestion was to go into the city *for amusement*."

"One does not have amusement with one's wife or sister?"

The notion was beyond him. He shrugged, murmured an excuse, and made off feebly toward the stables. And from that point forward, at this hacienda, he appeared to regard me as a person more than a little deranged.

Turning in, more exhausted than ever I'd been in the roughest passage of the trail, I drew only the lacelike curtains of my opening to the gardens. The apartment, sealed off by drapes or closed doors, was too funereal to endure. It was a minute or two after I had climbed gratefully into bed that a silhouette moved out of the shadows and slowly into the moonlight. I reached down to the carpet and slid my revolving pistol out of its holster, then the moonlight brightened, a figure emerged—all too plainly that of a well-developed young woman (Carla?)—and raised a hand to rap on the door frame. But she hesitated, thought better of her brashness, and left.

XVIII

NEXT DAY I rode into El Paso to take up my duties with Doniphan, who, as in Santa Fé, was housed with his staff in the local Palacio. For the first time, I found him depressed by the strain of his office.

"Have a look out there," he said, leading me to a window. Up and down the streets, everywhere within vision, our soldiers were seated at the curbs, gambling and drinking wine. The situation was out of hand, owing, oddly enough, to the unrestrained hospitality of the *Paseños* (for so they call themselves). Faro, chuck-a-luck, *vingt-et-un,* and monte were the principal games in progress, and as many señoritas as men mingled with our group.

Now and afterward during our forty-two day stay in El Paso, I noticed in these women a difference from those of Santa Fé. El Paso's people were in general a cut above Santa Fé's residents, but the women displayed sharper and, to us, more disturbing superiorities.

Las Paseñas were bolder in their behavior; they were better groomed; their forms, too, were fuller and more feminine, and the upper costumes, of these ladies in the streets, were entirely without lacings. Already, our soldiers were pairing off in attachments likely to cause trouble, and the Mexican men, surprisingly, seemed not to care. Wine flowed, silver and gold tinkled on the curbstones, laughter and merriment and boisterous amusement were the only concern, now, of an army intoxicated by easy victory.

"Draw up an official edict," said Alex, sounding for once more tired than tolerant. "From this hour on, gambling is forbidden in the open. It isn't that I'm a moralist," he added, stretching out in a chair; "I never much believed in *those* people, but by God, we do have to get back and forth through the streets."

I composed a sarcastic but firm statement, which was run off on a press and circulated through the town; then the congestion eased.

After that we went about requisitioning supplies. One of our largest windfalls came from a gentleman of the upper classes who now reposed in jail. He was, it was stated, a man of principle, something of a rarity hereabouts. His political views and the Government's diverging, he had been placed in confinement, though in circumstances appropriate to his station, with a valet, furniture from his own mansion, well-catered meals from the town, and two "maids" of rather dramatic domestic gifts. His wife remained at home.

From this amiable fellow, who lived in the hope of a momentary *coup d'état*, we bought a quantity of red beans and excellent *chile colorado*, or powdered red pepper. He gave us a draft on the storehouses of his ranch. Then he informed us, candidly, that he was one of the richest men in the state, with high-placed friends who soon would succeed to the management of Chihuahua. "Meanwhile, *amigos* from los Estados Unidos, I do not suffer. Clearly it would be foolish of the alcalde, for once I was freed, I would treat him likewise."

Alex Doniphan, in organizing the occupation government, never moved without having the alcalde at his side. All accomplishments through this charlatan were eased by a series of trifling bribes. He professed to have terrible difficulty with English, and if the bribe seemed insufficient, our interpreter's Spanish also struck him as baffling. A dollar—two at the most—would evoke intelligence of value.

"You wish, I am understanding, many bushels of—the word avoids me, señores. One's English! *Aha! muchas gracias.* I have successfully remembered: wheat! Where is? But I am desolate."

"Give the beggar another dollar."

"At the Falls, there are gristmills, señores. Now it comes back. Very much quantities of *wheat* stored there. *Sí*. Aha! Oh yes, unbolted flour in sacks, previously ground, for our glorious Army."

In all, we bought several hundred thousand *fanegas* (two and a quarter bushels each) of both wheat and corn, as well as a vast amount of fodder for the horses and mules. Alex scrupulously insisted on paying for everything. Most of our merchants and sutlers had hired showrooms in the city and were selling goods mainly to the inhabitants. To be fair, I must observe that some of these commercially-minded men had advanced large sums to Doniphan, for soldiers' supplies, taking in exchange checks on the United States Treasury.

It is a pleasure to watch the absolute indifference to reprisal with which Alex Doniphan proceeds. He has approximately as much legal right to draw checks on the national Government as the King of Abyssinia, but he goes ahead casually doing what seems needful in the interest of common sense.

In one particular we are balked. The citizens of El Paso have and eat little meat. The centers of cattle grazing lie to the north and to the south, at this stage in Mexico's development. And in any case, the few cattle grown are usually run off by the Apaches, together with whatever girls and boys they can scoop up for conversion into slaves. We suffer only slightly from the lack of meat, but I heard a soldier exclaim yesterday in the street, "By the living Jesus, I'd admire to get my hooks on a mess of bacon and collards!" The fellow was eating a dried apricot at the time, and seemed dissatisfied.

In the matter of fruits, the region is a cornucopia. We bought the finest of melons, apples, peaches, pears, quinces, oranges and grapes, as well as dried concentrates of several. The prevalent price of dried fruit (which goes a long way in providing nourishment) is about a dollar a bushel. The currency here is chiefly small copper pieces the size of our half-penny. Each is worth about three and a half cents, American. I am told that they were put into circulation to pay the Mexican soldiers. El Paso is, as stated, a very rich area; the markets overflow with produce, and the Missouri Volunteers are, for a change, reeling with satiety.

Pulque, mescal and aguardiente are so cheap that the occupation government has forbidden their sale to soldiers; still, nearly all somehow find means of getting drunk.

Other edicts, after a series of disastrous mishaps, banned the fandango and horse-and-mule races. The trouble lies not in frictions arising between the two peoples but in a rapport that threatens to destroy all military discipline. Our arrival here has no doubt marked the first time within memory that El Paso has been entirely free from anxieties about Indians and other marauders. I dislike to be vulgar, but the local population have welcomed our men with more than open arms; it would be impossible even to guess how many Volunteers have paired off to set up housekeeping with the eager señoritas.

Alex is doing his best, but he will be glad, he tells me, when we can continue our southward march into regions that might perhaps generate some hostility. "I shut up my office to fight, not to dance the fandango," he said, after some forty of our men were "rescued" from a species of bacchanal in a woods, "but I'm blessed if it hasn't turned into a Roman holiday. The Paseños are defeating us with kindness. I can't imagine what Sarah would say."

Meanwhile, we have apprehended large quantities of enemy guns, ammunition and artillery. Specifically, we took more than twenty thousand pounds of powder, lead, musket cartridge, common cartridge, and grape and canister shot; five hundred stands of small arms; four hundred lances; four pieces of cannon; a number of swivels and culverins, and several stands of colors. On the morning of January first, nearly everybody, including some dozens of Volunteers made groggy by wine and women, applauded the seizure, for it was reported in alarm that a counterattack was mounted and headed en masse toward El Paso from Chihuahua. Our picket guards dashed in, white-faced and shouting: immense rolling clouds of dust had been seen only a few miles from the city!

Alas, it was the old story, seen so often in the battles of antiquity. While the victorious American Army celebrated in disorganization, the enemy, apparently, had prepared to strike at our worst moment of weakness. Assembly was blown by the bugler, our soldiers ran (or staggered) to their arms in wild haste, the officers paraded their commands. We broke out the standards and formed in line of battle at an advantageous spot just south of town. Alex himself dashed up on foot, swinging his holster pistols across his left arm and carrying his drawn sword clutched in the other hand. It was a tense and chilling scene.

And then they came on—an impressive *atajo* of pack mules and file of Mexican carretas, hurrying in to trade. The good news of the well-supplied gringo had spread to the outlying villages, and everybody wanted in on the fun. If possible, the several hundred newcomers were warmer-hearted than the resident Paseños. I don't believe I ever saw Alex look more depressed. Back at headquarters in the Plaza, he sat down wearily, threw aside his weapons, started in on an apple, and said, "I don't know; it might be a good idea to surrender. We could work up some contempt that way, unless they insisted on immediate interbreeding, and contempt is a first cousin to hate. Then we could reorganize the Army in jail, and fight our way out. That is, of course, if we weren't felled by another wave of good feeling. Right now it looks like our only chance."

2

Once settled in, and with Doniphan's government beginning to roll, I went about the business of searching out Sam. It wasn't easy. The confusion, the lack of day-to-day records, and the boy's mulishness itself, served to make the task very difficult. I am reluctant to state in a Journal that may sometime be publicly scrutinized that our situation in El Paso, at this early juncture, was on a catch-as-catch-can basis. The soldiers had taken their lives in their hands; later, some order was restored. Sam's (and my own) captain—Perry Moss—had lost track of the boy, since he was forever claiming immunity to discipline on the flimsy ground of his musicianship.

To make this brief, I found him, by accident, on a Friday evening in one of the lesser parks. With no results, I had spent the afternoon checking the homes of Mexicans known to have accepted Volunteers for housing. Needing a breath of fresh air, after the stifling, adobe-trapped stench of spicy food cooking, dogs, and undiapered children, I strolled through the neighborhoods. Suddenly I became aware of music, recognizably un-Mexican, and I pushed forward.

Sam and his absurd crew (the Drum-and-Fife Corps) were established on a bandstand, playing Yankee tunes, while Sergeant O'Hara, carrying a rifle, passed through the crowd with a hat. I noticed that whenever one of the incredulous onlookers quite understandably tried to slip away, O'Hara collared him in the most genial manner and led him back, extracting some small coin or other in the process.

I put a stop to this instantly, but Sam was undaunted.

"How much did we take in?" he asked O'Hara.

"Why, allowing for the exchange, with the cheating and all, and subtractin' three brass buttons—oh, the thieving rogues!—I'd make it fourteen dollars and eighty cents, Sammy me boy."

"That's not bad on a day when there's a mule race going besides. Here's two for you and two for the others. I've spotted a better park for tomorrow; we'll step things up."

"Isn't it beautiful, sir? What a forward young head for finance! And look how easy he done it—two apiece for us and four-eighty for him. Sharks ain't the name. Why, there's genius in it. I wish to Jesus the boy was me own flesh and blood. There wouldn't be no worry about old age for Sergeant O'Hara."

"Well, it was my idea. You'd better go back and check Mrs. Mendoza. She may need your help."

"Hold on," I said. "What *about* Mrs. Mendoza?"

I was all but forced to shake it out of him, and then I was sorry I had. It seems that, in addition to her tireless gifts as a laundress, Señora Mendoza boasts a talent for gambling. Off and on, in Santa Fé and in other centers from which she was encouraged to move elsewhere, she helped operate games of chance. I use the word loosely. There was virtually no doubt about the outcome of any gambling enterprise in which Mrs. Mendoza dealt the cards. Sometimes they came from the top of the deck, more often from the bottom; there were even occasions, I gathered, when they flipped out of the middle.

Her specialty was monte, and this juvenile monster, my

younger brother, had her set up in a shack and going full blast. As partial recreation, he said, to keep her hand in, she did some laundering on the side. I think he took this literally. At any rate, I *like* to think so.

Filled with indignation, I marched them to the den in question, and the average person would have described the scene as a miniature preview of Hell. From the street, (as usual), you entered the *casa* by a dismal door, and then came out into an open square. Around this were several mean apartments, and, characteristic of these poorer dwellings in the city, a smaller square arose in the center of the first, surrounded by a mud wall three or four feet high, the interior planted thickly with evergreens, fig trees, and shrubs.

In the largest of the apartments, Señora Mendoza sat at a table, or bar, on which was piled a variety of money, most of it filthy. The room was deafening with laughter, exclamations in two languages, curses, and the clinking of coins; the air was blue with cigar smoke, and the floor was slick with spittle. There were no other furnishings, but on the walls hung garish pictures in the religious motif: bilious-looking Madonnas, Christ on the cross, wattled cherubs suspended over a manger that appeared to be on fire. Women as well as men contributed to the hubbub, but romance was not an ingredient of the evening's entertainment, at least not in the apartment at hand. Attention was focused on the cards.

"I'm glad to see this place is building; it got a slow start," said Sam, rubbing his hands. "It points up the value of advertising." The miscreant, prodded on by the hayseed Hobbs, had gone to the incredible length of sending three Mexicans—*léperos*, that is, low-caste beggars and thieves—around the city wearing sandwich signs. These had the gall to herald the "only 100 per cent honest" monte game in town. They were torn off and broken up by the competitors within a few hours, but apparently they did their work.

It particularly annoyed the writer of this Journal that the precise opposite of his message proved true. Señora Mendoza's monte game was, in fact, the only *completely* dishonest game in town, so far as I know.

Mexicans are quick to spot a trickster at cards, but they seem slow to suspect a woman. Not knowing Mrs. Mendoza's reputation, as either gambler or laundress, they had deposited large sums at her snare in the interval preceding the arrival of four troopers to close it down.

Before I restored Sam to the family that had consented to house him, as well as O'Hara and the ragamuffin Angel, I cut a switch and performed a long neglected duty, in an alley. It appeared to clear the air only briefly.

When I returned to headquarters, an uproar was in full cry. Overnight a bunch of Apaches had swooped down on an outlying settlement, killed two herdsmen, leveled their huts, and driven off thirty sheep and goats and two small boys.

Sam's friend Hobbs, with his Indian sidekick, were seated in chairs against one wall, Hobbs sweating, glancing about at the ceiling, and wearing an innocent quizzical expression.

Alex walked back and forth fulminating against the Indians, adding that we had neither the time nor the organization to prepare an offensive similar to that against the Navajos.

"Even so," he said, looking at Hobbs, "your suggestion is vile and preposterous."

"It warn't a suggestion, Colonel. You might call it a recital of history. Besides, me and Spiebuck's got a wagonload of truck to peddle. Or anyway half a wagon. I wouldn't in nowise admire to shift businesses in midstream. It ain't patriotic, and it ain't profitable. You take it all around and it's contrary to my commercial interests."

"Then what in thunder *are* you doing here?"

"Why, me and Spiebuck considered it our duty, open and clear, to tell you how the Governor of Chihuahua *used* to handle the problem. It sure would be a shame," he went on, "to let these here Paseñers lose confidence, just when they was getting so friendly and all. I heerd one man say in the Plaza, and he's a tolerable citizen, too—I've knowed him and cheated him for years—said, 'Well, the new government's as rump-sprung as the old one, and the Apaches can chaw up what they please.' Them were his very words, watered down a mite. You lose some in the translation, of course."

I thought Alex might explode. A man with his reputation—that of mildness and kindness and championship of the underdog—having to listen to this bloodthirsty pirate.

"The revolting notion of putting a bounty on the lives of fellow humans—"

"Why, it's right there that you throwed off the track. Apaches ain't human, Colonel; they're animals. They eat wolf meat—only Indians that do, and they ride down out of them Sierra de Mimbres, over toward Sonora, and commit atrocities that'd shock a vulture. With my own eyes, I've seed them cut a Mexican boy's tongue out, spang at the root, just for sport. Go down in the Plaza and inquire; you'll get all the news you need about Apaches."

Hobbs and his friend arose to amble toward the doorway. "I feel for you, Colonel. Take and you move in toward Chihuahua, things'll go directly to pot back here at El Passer. The Apaches'll see to *that.*"

Alex stood mulling it all over, then said, "Even the *financial* idiocy of shelling out fifty dollars each for actions like those. From start to finish, the whole concept—"

"Well, now, Colonel, I mislike to toss in a firecracker, but Apaches are getting dear. As a commodity, they've riz. What with the war, the risk of torture, and no greasers to help, I'd put hairpieces at a hundred dollars a throw, scaling down maybe to fifty for squaws and twenty-five for papooses—hold on a second; Spiebuck wants to break in—"

I myself hadn't seen the Indian twitch a muscle, but Hobbs bent over to confer.

"Yes, sir, I was right. Spiebuck's refreshed my memory—he often does that. The Governor of Chihuahua's paying a hundred dollars a scalp right this minute, and begging for the chance. You might say the price was fixed international, so to speak."

At this point, my brother Sam burst in, with a garbled explanation that he was late—late for what, I hadn't any idea—and Hobbs said, "We was just leaving, son."

Sam was carrying a rifle, and had a leather bag bulging at his belt.

"What's that?" I said, pointing. "You can tell me after you explain your presence here."

"Bag of salt. You dry out the scalps and salt them; otherwise you couldn't collect the bounty. Once it was ears, but they don't give a positive identification. After all, one ear's pretty much like another."

"You can go home now. And stay there till I come by for another chat, this time with a bigger switch. Don't leave under any conditions."

Upshot of this was Doniphan's final answer that, "Very well, if you wish to forage on you own, without a contract from *this* office, by heaven! on the assumption that somebody, in Mexico or the United States, will reward you for your efforts, go ahead. Mind you, I have no official knowledge of what you're doing; unofficially we'll furnish guns, ammunition, and supplies. Now for God's sake clear off before my conscience calls a halt."

"That's enough for me," cried Hobbs cheerily. "I know a trader when I see one. Now if it don't gall you, I'll ring in an old pard, Jim Kirker, a rank Irisher that can birddog Apaches better than any man alive. It's handsome to watch. I seen him in town this morning. When it comes to scalping, he's got a tal—"

"Hobbs!" roared Alex, ready to change his mind, I'm sure, but the rapacious pair were gone.

Retaliatory strikes against the Apaches grew into a greatly expanded operation, with Kirker and Hobbs in command of considerable Volunteers (plus Mexicans), but I'll omit the details here.

XIX

IN THE NEXT few weeks, my residence at the Rojas hacienda saw a crisis develop that finally involved me, much to my distaste.

We were at dinner, early in February, in the beginning a quiet, peaceful meal that had followed an equally subdued family rendezvous (for once) in la sala. Ordinarily, the gilded chamber was little more than an arena for acrimonious family disputation. From start to finish, I seldom heard a member address another in any but sarcastic terms. A stranger (to me) was present, an imposing, prematurely gray man from the South—from, I believe, the city of Puebla, near Santa Anna's headquarters. In some subtle way, it was made evident that, while his status as guest was acceptable, he was of a class below that of his hosts. He was, I should have said, an estate manager, or a confidential employee, an emissary of some kind. After the first stiffish bow of introduction he ignored me completely. I spent the pre-dinner hour listening to Cosmo's irritating gabble about women he had seduced or bought, horses and cards, all purposely within earshot of his melancholy wife and her comforter, Father Bernardo.

During the meal, my host and his guest talked in undertones at one end of the table, glancing often at Carla, whose expression was a study in indifference. Her color was high, though, and altogether the undercurrent of strain was so intense that I resolved to make my excuses shortly, even at the cost of violating one of their numerous, tiresome and stupid courtesies. Meanwhile, I sat eating *pollo* and blood sauce, to which I had finally become accustomed, with effort, and wondering about the curious Mexican custom of shunning all sorts of beverages at meals. A large cup of water always was set before each person, but nobody (except me) touched it until the repast was done.

On the evening of my arrival, I had drunk off half my water at the first course, which was peppery and hot, and Rojas had repeatedly inquired if I felt well; also, upon my picking up the cup, he had cried, "Hold, hold, there is more to come." Later, I found that all Mexicans, including this perversely sophisticated group, considered the drinking of liquids at meals to be dangerous. Occasionally, not always, wine was served at dinner, but it was drunk, even by Cosmo, before and after the courses.

In any case, an irruption now exploded with shocking violence. As Rojas' chat proceeded, I watched the veins in his temples swell, and suddenly he spoke out loudly:

"Well, then, Carla, you can commence packing your trousseau. You go to Puebla with Señor Ortega next week. Rosa accompanies you. For the protection."

(Carla had the usual *dueña,* or companion, or guardian that was provided an unmarried girl of the Mexican upper class, the purpose being to appease the anxiety of suitors when they appeared. The supreme affront to the "honor" of these sensitive gentry was a question, any doubt whatever, about the virtue of the bride-to-be. Even the technical existence of a circumstance wherein it would have been possible to raise a doubt was a matter of gravity, enough to jeopardize these heartless arranged marriages. I sometimes had the uneasy feeling that virtue itself, actually, was of less importance, in the eyes of the Mexican male, quivering with honor [and the fear of ridicule or insult] than the outward appearance of official respectability. The bridegroom himself could have wallowed in license for years—indeed, he was regarded as unmanly if he hadn't—but his lady, for his vanity, must be spotlessly above reproach. It should be said that Rosa, Carla's hopeful but exhausted companion, had fought an uphill battle. She had been outwitted, denounced, hidden from, outflanked, duped, lost, and generally left bewildered since taking on what proved to be a job beyond the hardiest woman's capacity. A platoon of especially alert Swiss guards might have turned the trick; a lone female was beyond her depth. Carla went where she pleased, often unattended, causing, in my presence, a number of merry rows.)

To get back, she merely replied, at first, "I have no trousseau, so I won't be traveling after all."

"Is this true?" Don Diego inquired of his wife.

If the gentle Alicia had a fault, it was procrastination. As a guest here for a month, I had seen numerous occasions when she was frankly open to censure. Whenever possible she left things to León. To make the smallest decision was, for her, torture, and she once told me, after a tumultuous scene in la sala, that her mother, and others, had for eighteen years relieved her of even the smallest functions of the human, down to arranging her hair, scenting herself, and choosing her attire, so that, as she said, with a helpless look, "Perhaps I wait for them."

She hesitated. "I thought there was sufficient time. Tomorrow, I–"

"It doesn't matter," said Carla coolly. "I've decided not to be married. Not in Puebla. Perhaps here in the town. I've formed an attachment."

I believed this to be a lie, but Don Diego arose at his chair and simply went to pieces. His face lost any semblance of protection and urbanity, his features were distorted, his mouth became constricted in an ugly, raging sneer, and he screamed curses, in Spanish, at both his wife and his daughter. He was really dreadful to look at. For some time, I had been aware that he despised his wife, besides hating both the loftier position she enjoyed and her unconcerned attitude toward it. Now I realized that he lived in this household without a jot of affection for any one of its members. His life, aside from discreet dissipations with friends in El Paso, was a stalemate of slow, soul-destroying contention. Little by little, he was being consumed by his hatreds, and under the system of religion to which he paid token obeisance, there was no way to escape it. Periodically, as his reason and his health sought relief, he simply dissolved into animalism. I began to understand his feeling about the Catholic Church.

Meanwhile, his wife sat white-faced, her eyes frightened and cast down, Mariana intoned her incessant and boring prayers (in which Father Bernardo now joined), Cosmo gulped down a glass of wine, spilling a good amount on the cloth, the servants disappeared, and the excellent Carla also arose.

"Yes, my passion has become incontrollable on the matter of José Gonzales, assistant in the *herrería.* Such shoulders! And the virility!"

"Carla, Carla—" murmured her mother.

Casting about in what had swelled to a lunatic frenzy, Don Diego seized up a wine cup to throw, but the girl glided contemptuously through the doorway, so he tore the tablecloth with all its dishes and silver crashing onto the floor.

Near midnight, pacing in my room, resolved to leave early in the morning and arrange normal quarters in town, I heard a scream from someplace toward the stable. It rose, was cut off abruptly, started again, then stopped for good.

I dressed, strapped on my pistol, and tiptoed out into the patio. The night was clear, but the moon was not yet up. The sky was starry and the shadows shifted as a sharp breeze stirred the foliage of this semi-tropical garden. The sweet, heavy smell of night-blooming jasmine, which I'd once thought exciting, had lost much of its romance.

The outside gate being locked, I bent over to inspect the mechanism; then straightened up, with a knife-blade at my neck.

"It is an impoliteness besides a stupidity to concern yourself with affairs which are not in the province of one's interest, señor. I am employed to guard the door. It is the foremost duty of which I am charged in my position of major-domo."

I said, "Take that down, you whippersnapper. Maybe you've forgotten who's in charge of El Paso."

"If the Señor Captain would consent to return to the Casa—with a thousand apologies. Otherwise—"

All of my life, I have been regarded as a mild, perhaps even a timorous man, but it may be that the lack of opportunity molded the temperament. Whatever the cause, I now felt a searing anger, an urge to violence, of the kind that led to my justifiable punishment of the St. Louisan, Murdock. Essentially, of course, I still considered warfare an evil of civilization, but I had learned that this particular war was both necessary and stirring.

My right hand eased the pistol from its case, then I whirled and struck the impudent beggar across the face. I heard some bones in his nose crack, he sighed, and went slack. And before I could catch him, his head thumped like a pumpkin on the tiles. In the circumstance, the sound was not unenjoyable.

His keys were in a pocket of his short jacket. I had them out and the door opened in a moment. Skirting the hacienda, I slipped around toward the stables, careful to make no noise. A few dogs came stretching up, and one gave a halfhearted bark, but they only sniffed, wagged their tails, said hello, and flopped back down, relieved.

Through the glazed window of the farthest stall a dim yellow light showed. I kicked off my boots and crept forward. The scene inside would have moved a vampire to pity.

The unfortunate dueña, Rosa, was suspended from a joist by a thong tied to her wrists. She was in a corner, entirely naked, gagged and dangling in such a posture that her face was turned away from the other persons in the room. In another corner, Carla sat on a stool, her arms tied behind her, Don Diego leaned against one wall, and Cosmo stood biting his fingernails. Waiting nearby was one of the establishment's *vaqueros,* a dark, mustachioed, vacant-faced, slightly cross-eyed fellow whom I had seen several times talking to Cosmo. He had a braided whip, and the woman's back was a patchwork of bleeding welts. At the moment he appeared to be resting. But the suspension of entertainment was for a different reason altogether. I heard Don Diego say to his son, in languid Spanish, "Get a bucket of water and restore the creature's wits."

"Where?"

"From where the water's kept, you fool. A horse trough. Anywhere."

"Take her down; she's done nothing."

"But my dear Carla, we must reaffirm your marriage to Don Narciso Noriega. Unless it's too late. As to this slatternly cow, it appears she was not of a sufficient seriousness—"

"I say it again—she did nothing. You're beastly and brutal. Whip me, if it's necessary to demonstrate your honor." Her voice rose a little. "The word makes me sick." She laughed. "The honorable Cosmo. And the comical rules. 'Never walk between a man and his drink.' I'd like to see *you*, my father, face down our provincial gringo guest, to start off the honor."

He stepped quickly across the room and slapped her as hard, I think, as he was able. Still expressionless, the vaquero rolled a cigarrito. I noticed a thin trickle of blood at one side of the girl's mouth.

"—in typical high Mexican style, you'd find some excuse why you *hadn't* been seriously insulted. And then, between gentlemen, a drink to seal your respect and friendship. And, of course, honor."

"If the witless he-goat of a gringo ever presumes to make one slighting remark—"

"I'll make it now," I said, stepping in and dragging Cosmo with me. I spun him across the room, where he drew up, hissing. The vaquero, at least, was a man of spirit, for he whirled round like a cat, unfurled his whip, and gave every indication of adding me to his other victim. My gun barrel, presented at his throat, changed his outlook wonderfully. He shrugged, and continued to puff away unruffled.

"Get some more water," I said to Cosmo. "Do it in a hurry, or I'll give you a thrashing with the butt of this gun." He stood for a second, nervously knitting and unknitting his brows; then he went out, taking the bucket he had dropped.

I cut down the dueña, who had begun to revive, removed her gag, and covered her with a saddle blanket. She sat on the floor, rocking back and forth and moaning. Then I released Carla's hands and addressed her father:

"Now, you, sir. I have suddenly had a sufficiency, as you say, of this house, its evil, all of its customs, most of its inhabitants, and particularly of you. It would require very little for me to horsewhip you as you've whipped this woman. Do you understand?"

"The gringo speaks to you, father. He has just insulted you. Challenge him to a duel, father. As between gentlemen."

It was amazing to watch his struggle for self-control. Before he succeeded, his color changed from red to unhealthy white, and his voice, when words came out, was choked up and shaky, so that he had to pause often for breath. Far too many years of self-indulgence and soft living had preceded this moment.

"You are meddling, señor, in this family's private affairs. The authorities in El Paso—"

"Don't worry about the authorities," I said. "I'm the authorities, and you're under house arrest. We'll see if we can't stop some of this feudal cruelty. You report to Colonel Doniphan's office at nine o'clock in the morning. And Rojas," I said, "don't be there at nine-ten. Make it at nine o'clock sharp. *Entendido?*"

I don't recall speaking like that before in my life, but I can't exaggerate my distaste for this family. Anyhow, nothing came of my complaints. Rojas, presumably recovered from his nerves of the previous evening, appeared in Doniphan's office at a quarter to eleven, accompanied by several friends, the chief alcalde, and two priests, and was dismissed after a soothing and diplomatic chat.

"We'd better not go too fast," said Alex, studying me reflectively. "And in a sense, he's right. Unofficially, I'll admit this much: it was a temptation to kick him down the stairs. But it *was* a family matter; we can't change Mexico's hierarchy overnight. Perhaps we don't want to. It's their land and will remain their land after the war's over. All except New Mexico, that is," he added with good cheer, putting his feet on a table and relaxing in his usual philosophical ease.

An occupation government being established at last, the order came for the First Missouri Volunteers to move toward Chihuahua at dawn of February eleventh. The march would be in excess of two hundred miles, over high plateau devoid of growth except mesquite, chaparral, cactus, and greasewood. Aside from some curious sand hills around Samatayuca, the area was said to be monotonous. It is the country of the harmless Tarahamara Indians, who since the Aztecs have been noted for their ability to run long distances without tiring. This in a region more than a mile high!

In the two days intervening, I was established in a modest home, whose family members I never properly met, since I dined, in this period of increased paper-work and confusion, at Alex Doniphan's mess. I had an entrance of my own and enjoyed, for the first time in months, a brief season of privacy.

Toward midnight of February tenth, all my gear assembled, polished and ready, this privacy was disturbed by a low knocking at my door. I opened it to find the tempestuous Carla, partially veiled. She came in without invitation.

"I have to see you on a subject of the gravest importance." She looked so serious, and, suddenly, so young that I almost burst into laughter. Instead I stammered something about the danger of her being on the streets unattended, as well as the impropriety of a visit alone to my rooms.

Then, starting to freeze as usual in the presence of women, I said stiffly, "Pray be seated," though there was nothing but a bed to sit on, and asked how she got here.

"Cosmo brought me. He's not at all a bad fellow. He's had no chance whatever. You see, my father—"

"I've met your father, and I misunderstood about Cosmo. Maybe you'll tell him I said so."

"It doesn't matter. He isn't anything positive of a man. But he's not a monster; that is very rare among the men in my family. My father's a monster of a common sort in ruling Mexico, but he's marrying me to a devil, Don Narciso Noriega of Puebla, a confidential friend of Santa Anna himself. It's a political triumph."

"You've met this man?"

"Last year at a formal baile in Puebla, where we go sometimes in the winter. He resembles a very tall snake, with shiny black hair and a beard that arrives finally at a sharp point."

"You were not immediately smitten?" I asked, mysteriously beginning to enjoy myself.

"Personally, I was made ill by his hands while dancing. Also, I am unpolitical in the matter of marriage. Aside from that of the snake."

"He was not as hypnotic as, let us say, the blacksmith's helper, José Gonzales?"

Suddenly she gave every indication of being near tears, and I said, "Never mind Gonzales. What did you come to see me about?"

"At certain levels in your Army you are permitted to take along women—laundresses?"

"An unnecessary provision, in my view."

She stepped to the door, made a signal, and Cosmo appeared like a frightened ghost out of the night, pale, shaking with nerves, and carrying an expensive leather valise. He glanced up and down the street, as though fearful of being attacked, which I myself thought likely in this neighborhood.

She said, "Put the valise in the corner and wait outside." When the door closed, she removed her shawl and sat down on the bed, with a determined air of expectancy. Her costume, which included a blouse cut lower than those of the loosest wantons in the cantinas, gave her a shocking look, possibly, I realized, because she seemed to wear it so naturally.

"Tell Cosmo he can go home. The matter is arranged to the satisfaction of both parties."

"If you're speaking of this party," I said, "nothing whatever has been arranged."

"My mind was fully made up last night. They can kill me before I consent to marry a person of such foulness."

I seated myself on the bed, eyes averted (with effort), tossed her the shawl, and said, "Put it on, then go home and reason with your father. He's bound to have some of the normal compassion of parenthood. I'm told that even the python protects its young."

"Do I understand that you refuse my services as laundress?"

"That is precisely and literally correct. In every detail."

She arose and took up the shawl. "Then the procedure is simple. I must establish myself in a *casa de mujeres*. Afterward, a marriage, any marriage, will be impossible."

"Hand me the serape," I said, with the familiar feeling of helplessness. "I'll make a pallet on the floor. Reveille's at six. As a soldier, I was prepared to practice certain austerities. This, of course, may prove a step too far."

Later, when Cosmo had been bidden goodbye and the light snuffed out, I heard a curiously small but brave voice from the bed: "Captain—"

"Corporal. Broken once to private and rating restored for reasons of administrative expediency."

"—you have not understood about those of the Rojas y las Cruces family. Despite the terribleness, there exists strong sporting blood. I am prepared to commence whatever it is that one expects of a laundress."

"Madame," I said, "or señorita, or doña, or even miss." I started over, "Look here, Carla, for more than a month, I've been a guest in your home, your parents accorded me a kind of nerve-jangling hospitality to which I flatter myself I stood up like a veteran; now you have placed me in the incredible position of taking you under my protection. You will indeed have duties in your new role. There exists a large duffel bag filled with soiled linen. Tomorrow night I expect it to be turned out in crisp, professional style. Should anything less occur, I'll be obliged to find a new laundress."

XX

Hidalgo del Parral: Well, I've run into some rough luck, along with Angelina, but I intend to continue making this book, no matter what they do. So far, it hasn't been bad; they've got me on the end of a chain, and in the little towns they show me off, like a monkey. Nobody acts mean, only interested, and in fact one woman at Ciudad Jiménez came up and felt my ribs, then gave me two tortillas. Not being in a specially good humor, I stepped forward, felt hers, then gave one back, and by George if somebody didn't kick me.

Angelina's in a wagon, or a carriage—a lot of these drove out from Chihuahua to see the battle—and I guess she's hard hit, so they're bound to find out she's a girl. I asked my keeper, his name's Pancho, how she stood the ride, but he shrugged as usual and said *"Quién sabe?"* That seems to be the better part of his education. He doesn't know. In that line, he's a real scholar, and has gone a long way: he doesn't know about the higher education as well as the lower. We talk once in a while—Spanish, mainly, in which I'm now fluid, as stated—and he lets me write in my Journal. He acts decent enough, and I've promised to send him a lot of money after Mexico's surrendered, but he doesn't much care; said the more money he has, the more time he appears to spend in jail.

Well, sir, my spirits are generally as high as the next person's, but I notice now that they droop a little, come evening. When I joined up, I hadn't planned to be captured, and I don't seem to get used to sleeping under a wagon, with my head stuck through a smelly old poncho and the end of my chain locked to a wheel.

Anyhow, I hope to swallow things as they are, try to see Angelina, and likewise run this Journal up to date.

(Note, put in later: I read that stuff of Blaine's over, same as before, and frankly, I'm not sure. As a writer, he's got a considerable distance to go, and the funny thing is, he won't accept help. Downright ungracious. If a person has a talent for something, he ought to pursue it, if you know what I mean. Otherwise he'd better lower his sights. Still, as Shakespeare said in the Bible, blood's thicker than water, even Mexican water, and I dislike to shake his confidence. So I decided to include it in the book and take a chance on the critics, who certainly know better—I'll agree to that—but sometimes make allowances for the persons that actually do the writing.

For one thing, Blaine has a habit of getting tangled up with women, the most of them about as troublesome and sassy as possible. Worst of all, he can't handle the situation. When the Missouri Volunteers moved out, Mrs. Mendoza and I split $700, subtracting $100 for Sergeant O'Hara's protection, which was able and needed [and got three more priests banged up pretty severe], all of it made fair and square from her monte dealing, and we never had a fuss from start to finish. We might have cleaned up a fortune if Blaine hadn't stuck his nose in and forced us out to a poorer location. I asked him if he was down on small business and he said no, but he'd always been biased against theft.)

Now to get on. The day before heading for Chihuahua, Colonel Doniphan learned about an insurrection schemed up by the curate of El Paso, a priest named Ortiz. But it was crushed before it got moving, so we rode out on schedule. A lot of men ranted and stormed about leaving, and a number took along the women they'd met in the city. During the forty-two days they had such a sociable good time, getting acquainted and all, that they decided to continue it on the trail, where there wasn't much else to do.

I almost forgot an incident that toned up the men and made them happy, directly before we left. Along with the Apaches, wolves galled the people terrible bad in the suburbs of El Paso. I say suburbs meaning the outlying farms and vineyards. Well, all of a sudden—nobody could explain it—wolves in the hundreds loped down on the sheep farms and begun raising the dismalest kind of havoc amongst the flocks. The farmers set up a howl, naturally enough—I've noticed that they're howling about something practically all the time anyhow—and Colonel Doniphan dispatched Volunteers to help.

I and Sergeant O'Hara went along to watch. These wolves had worked up a blood-lust, as an old teamster remarked, and were going it full tilt. Broad daylight, too, a very rare thing, as they customarily sneak down after dark, being more comfortable that way. Somebody said they'd jumped the corrals during the night and grew confused trying to get back out, but I'm not so sure.

Well, sir, our men had a picnic of a time, and not a shot fired. They dashed back and forth through those sheep killers—waded hock deep in wolf fur—and commenced lopping off heads with their sabers. They were rusty for action, of course, and tried to make it all up right here.

Looking on, I got a feeling that the men boiled up a blood-lust of their own. I never heard such a racket. "Over there! There goes three of the sons-of—!" and off a knot of men would gallop like mad, then haul in sharp, with a lot of skidding and dust, lean over, *swack!*, and, "By God, *there's* one that won't hamstring another ram!"

It bored into your bones. I found myself yelling like the rest, and Sergeant O'Hara he did the same, spite of the fact that he'd come out pretty strong lately against violence, excepting toward priests, which he said didn't count.

Altogether, the men went to six different places where wolves were tumbling over each other, snapping and throat-slitting in a frenzy, almost down on a level with humans in a war. And you needn't believe it, but the entire pack was killed, dozens and dozens and dozens, hacked to pieces while they tore around the corrals. It was awesome, but necessary, for there weren't any more wolf scares at El Paso for a year or more—somebody told us so later.

Another point was, our troops needed those sheep, though they were woeful small, sometimes weighing as little as fifteen pounds. I remember the quartermaster of Company F sending a big hulk of a man, Joseph Yount, to draw their dressed sheep for that day, and he came back carrying all eleven in his arms. Then, grieved and offended (because he'd been a fine farmer), he held one of those skinny carcasses up betwixt him and the sun and said, "A man could read the Lord's Prayer through this sheep."

To start off about leaving, I'll borrow from the Diary of another man that's aiming to write a book, though probably for the popular markets, not literary, which I don't mean to criticize, because he was only a country Judge back home, without too many advantages. He had a habit of leaving the Diary lying around any old place, so I reckoned he wouldn't mind if I helped him bring it to the public attention.

"On the 8th the whole Army, the merchant, commissary, hospital, sutler, and ammunition trains, and all the stragglers (women), amateurs, and gentlemen of leisure, under flying colors, presenting the most martial aspect (except the women) set out with buoyant hopes for the city of Chihuahua. There the soldiers expected to reap undying fame, to gain a glorious victory—or perish on the field of honor."

We were supposed to meet General Wool at Chihuahua, 240 miles from El Paso, but nothing had been heard from him, so were on our own, getting deeper and deeper into Mexico.

As the Judge said, in his over-blown way, "What then must have been the feelings of Colonel Doniphan and his men, when they saw the states of Chihuahua and Durango in arms to receive them, not the remotest prospect of succor from General Wool, and rocks and unpeopled deserts intervening, precluding the possibility of successful retreat? *Victory or death* were the alternatives. Yet there was no faltering, no pale face, no dismayed hearts. At this crisis, had Colonel Doniphan inquired of his men what was to be done, the response would have been unanimously given—LEAD US ON!"

It really was a risky business, because these Mexicans *would* fight, if ever they got lined up behind able leaders. Nobody doubted it.

From time to time, I've laid out some pretty raw criticisms of Mexicans, and they can be painful and shifty and worthless, but I've only told what our men said and how they felt. When you're making a book, you have to tell the truth, no matter if you prick a number of feelings. There was a considerable amount of good to be said, too, as I'll come to by and by. And Blaine once pointed out, in an unusual burst of common sense, that if you started a book about what's wrong with *our* country, it wouldn't turn out to be a book at all, but a library, and might require a faculty to assemble it.

For this march, which people claimed made military history (the men living entirely off the land, and without any pay, for all that time) we had less than a thousand Volunteers, including the artillery under Major Clark, (who somebody said was the son of a famous Indian scout) with 117 men and six pieces of cannon —four six-pounders and two twelve-pound howitzers. The artillery had been held up in Santa Fé, because Colonel Price was worried about an uprising there for awhile, particularly after a bunch of conspirators attacked Bent's Fort and killed Charles Bent.

Anyhow, here we are, back on the trail, not much different from the march to El Paso: dry, sparse, gray, dusty, low growth except for stream beds where the greenery blooms up into jungle on both banks. Aside from that, endless scrubby high plains, silent and lonely, and off in the distance walls of blurred purple mountains; nothing moving for hour after hour but those black soaring crooked-neck vultures keeping the death-watch high over-head; it gives a body the shivers; and then, when you'd bet your last penny that not a soul lived within a hundred miles from here, a raggedy little dark peasant wearing a straw sombrero and black-and-white poncho creeps out of the bushes by a hill and squats there studying us, staring without ever seeming to blink, maybe smoking a cigarrito, as quiet and still and unreadable as a man made out of stone. No dwelling nor even a sign of a dwelling as far as you can see, no water, no game, no livestock, no crops, nothing to support a person at all, yet here he is, appearing in good health, too, though maybe cross-eyed with a stump arm or club foot or something. You find a lot of that around, especially in the villages, and one of our doctors said it was caused by "home-grown delivery of babies."

Passed a big hot spring; it rose up out of the plain with enough force to turn a mill. Another four days later, but this one was enclosed with crumbly rocks. The Spaniards once used it as a bath, back when they were running the country. It seemed a waste; the water could have been better employed on the Mexicans.

After this, a series of jornadas—high, sandy desert, land entirely without water, always with a hot wind blowing.

For three long days we had a terrible water-scrape, maybe the worst of the expedition. Lots of livestock died of thirst and tiredness, and thirty-six yoke of oxen were turned free. Two wagons were abandoned in sand hills, and eight thousand pounds of flour and fifteen barrels of salt thrown on the ground. A lot of the sutlers threw away some of their heaviest commodities. Two American soldiers that had taken along brides deserted, with their women, and high-tailed it back to El Paso. And my good old Chief, starved down to a bundle of bones, finally gave up the ghost. I found him lying dead in the morning. I cried a little, then tried to collect my fifty cents, but they handed me a wind-blown old mustang instead.

When the whole expedition was about to bog down in despair, a cloudburst of a rainstorm broke loose, and the men ran around in it like animals, crazy with the feel of it, holding their mouths open, letting the water sluice over their faces and trying to catch some in hats, pans, skillets, and scabbards, even. And afterwards, of course, the streams rushed down from the mountains, making all the whooping and hollering unnecessary.

Back to dry, dry plains again, and then, taking the opposite tack, we let some campfires get out of hand and like to burned the place up.

We were camped two miles from the Laguna, a big lake twenty miles long. When the fire started, men were gathering a kind of alkali, such as the saleratus people used in cooking bread. But as the crispy dry grasses caught, everybody dropped all holds and lit out, you can bet. One or two company commanders tried making a stand to counter-fire, and Colonel Doniphan collected a group to ride back and forth, hoping to squash the flames, but two men got singed on the legs, and spoke up pretty high, so Mr. Doniphan eased off saying he'd rather burn the country than get shot in the back trying to save it. In the end, all the regiment nearby—men, horses, wagons, artillery, mules, livestock, everything—headed pell-mell for the Lagoon, drove out belly-deep and escaped by only a whisker. A few wagons actually did get caught, and viewed all around, it was a mighty narrow squeak. We spent the night sleeping on ground blackened like charcoal. There was one casualty: a Volunteer named W. Tolley, who it was stated had a young bride back home, drank so much water that he kind of swoll up and busted, spouting water out of this and that. I didn't see it myself, only the ceremony when they buried him near shore.

Next day we marched through a gorge, or cañon, sliced deep in basalt and puddingstone, according to Blaine, and afterwards hit a dark, iron-streaked volcano river, tumbled high with volcanic cinders, that snaked right across our path, a hundred yards or more wide. It was spooky, and must have brightened the country up beautiful when it happened, but all was cold, now; I stooped down and felt it.

Across that big lake, to the southwest, lay the rich hacienda of Don Angel Trias, the Governor of Chihuahua. He was the customer that had a weakness for issuing Proclamations then scampering out before somebody shot him for it. Well, he skedaddled again, just in time, because Captain Reid took a number of his Horse Guards, sneaked around the Laguna after dark, and surrounded the whole works. But the birds had flown—seven hundred Mexican soldiers inside the enclosure, plus hundreds of cattle and sheep. He rounded up a few sickly-looking cows—I reckon they were too decrepit to stir—but that was all.

However, one of our men climbed a hill early in the morning of February 28, and things busted loose all at once. He came scrambling back so rattled he couldn't talk straight. An enemy army, a real one—thousands of men—were within spy-glass sight, lined up on a rocky ridge between the Sacramento River and the "*Arroyo Seco,*" near their Sacramento Fort, eighteen miles out from Chihuahua.

Well, sir, you never heard such a hullabaloo of bugles blowing, horses neighing and stomping, wagons rattling into position at full speed, and commanders shouting orders. This promised to be a *battle,* and no mistake. It was what we had trudged and starved all these miles for, and everybody was practically frothing with excitement, and maybe a little nervousness, too. Because *this* army, when we got a good look, was none of your ragtag rabble. We must have been outnumbered four to one, and those deadly still, waiting redcoats looked able and businesslike.

Our four hundred wagons were thrown into parallel files, thirty feet apart, with the Artillery Battalion in the center; First and Second Battalions on the right and left; attack cavalry in front, Missouri Horse Guards on the right front, Missouri Dragoons on the left, and the "Chihuahua Rangers," under Captain Hudson, in the middle. That's the way the units, Volunteer and Regular, had come to be called by Colonel Doniphan, who rode along ahead, kind of slouched over and relaxed, but gazing here and there, perfectly alert, all the same.

The enemy had twenty-eight lines of redoubts and entrenchments, we learned later. They were dug in solid, and meant to hold the capital city secure. Not only that, but *this* time, they had some authentic professional leaders, headed by Major General José Herédia and aided by General Garcia Condé, the former Minister of War; General Mauricia Ugarte, Commander of Infantry; General Justiniani, Commander of Artillery; and, sure enough, Governor Trias, Brigadier General in charge of the Chihuahuan volunteers, who was likely writing proclamations as he rode.

Anyhow, we had a showdown here, and it didn't appear too cheerful, with our total of nine hundred Missouri riflemen. My mouth had dried up, and I noticed that Angelina, nearby in our Clay County Company, didn't seem so very sprightly for a change. I glanced around for Blaine and Sergeant O'Hara, but failed to spot them in the confusion.

Some men with glasses said the hills behind the Mexican troops were peppered with horses-and-carriages. The gentry from Chihuahua had packed fancy lunches, with bottles of wine and aguardiente, and driven out to see the gringo finally get his comeuppance. For them, it looked to be one of the best days in Mexican history so far.

That was the way they sized it up, and maybe some of us did too, but there wasn't time to moon about it because General Condé with twelve hundred cavalrymen dashed down yelling from a fortified height to commence the engagement.

Then Colonel Doniphan, raising a hand, deflected our whole regiment very rapidly to the right, galloped across the Arroyo, and gained the plateau beyond, leaving us on a highland as well. It was the best possible maneuver; everybody will probably say so when the battle comes to be written up in the books. For a peace-loving man who'd far rather reason than fight, Colonel Doniphan is a born soldier.

At the moment when the enemy were a mile and a half away, he was sitting cross-legged on his saddle, whittling again, and as the Mexican cannon balls began barreling overhead, he remarked to his aides, "Well, they're giving us Hell now, boys."

That was not quite exact, for what the Mexicans had was irregular-shaped balls of copper ore, and these looped toward us in as silly a curve as anybody could imagine. Even keyed up the way we were, it got to be a joke; you could hear laughter ripple up and down the lines. First off, you'd see a rolling puff of white smoke, then, seconds later, hear a booming report—drifting along behindhand and lazy, as all those faraway sounds do—and presently you'd see a sun glint on the copper ball soaring through the air. Up in a high loop, strike the rock-hard ground fifty yards before us, then bounce on over our heads and, at the worst, maybe hit a horse or a wagon in the rear. (Our Company was dismounted, you understand, with every eighth man detailed to hold horses or mules.)

Flash, smoke, boom, and, "Here comes a ball, boys! Look sharp, now, and dodge!"

Any number of men, in the rear positions, *did* jump aside, with no more trouble than playing three-o'-cat, and saved serious casualties.

But it wasn't all so easy. Another scary-looking wave—Mexican cavalry—broke into a wild advance, wearing bags of cotton for chest protectors, the way General Jackson's troops did at New Orleans, but they hung up finally, scattered and confused, in the face of our rifle fire. These Missourians could shoot. Whenever they lifted a rifle, they meant to bring a man down, and mostly did so. On the other hand, two different times, I saw enemy cavalrymen, anxious to sift out of that mess, fire their guns straight up in the air.

Also, the fast action of our artillery appeared to throw them off balance. Major Clark and Captain Weightman had four pieces discharging five times a minute—grape and canister and chain—and howitzers tossing a perfect shower of bombs into the Mexican entrenchments. Accurate, too. It was enough to get anybody running around in a circle. This American artillery was manned by Regulars, and they knew what they were doing. Between them and the Missouri rifles, the Mexicans didn't know whether to puke or go blind.

Blaine says it's hard to explain what's meant by the "gage of battle." During the first scrimmages back and forth, we worried about being outnumbered and out-positioned so bad. And at the time of General Condé's charge, the commanders were thinking *defensive,* but all at once, as the ridiculous copper balls begun bouncing over our heads, we knew we could beat these four thousand Mexicans, no matter how dug-in they were.

After that, we only had one setback, and it was ridiculous, too, if you mulled it over. There went up a whale of a cry, "We're outflanked, boys—they've attacked us on the rear!" Then came a wild scurry and bustle, but what happened was, the Mexican commanders had emptied the Chihuahua prisons—a thousand men in all, made into *lanzados,* or mounted lancers—and told them that a grand stroke of cunning, aimed at the enemy, or us, would set them free for good.

Well, that shifty set of villains got just about as far as they'd progressed in civilian life. The truth is, they'd better stuck to throat-cutting. They succeeded in worming around to our rear, sure enough, and were positioned for their exploit, when our teamsters back there, very bored and resentful, organized into a fighting unit and made things hum, I can tell you. In fifteen minutes, the *lanzados* found themselves right back where they'd started—collared, and, totally unconcerned, they set up a howl for tobacco.

Anyhow, along about here, Captain Reid launched his famous charge, and that was the beginning of the end. Colonel Doniphan had ordered Captains Reid and Parsons and Hudson to "carry the main central battery," but in the noise and confusion, Reid jumped the gun, crying *"Will my men follow me?"* Then he rode straight up the slope, jumped the embankment, and scattered the battery like quail. He was a wild buck, bareheaded again, and got more enjoyment out of this than a child burning a schoolhouse.

After that, everybody let go. The other companies, some mounted, some dismounted, swarmed into the Mexican redoubts, and the place looked like a nightmare. And right in the middle, I saw Blaine, *also* bareheaded, waving his saber, yelling like a drunken Indian, and converted, all of a sudden, into a kind of madman. I stood staring, open-mouthed, and so did Angelina, and right there was where we made our mistake. But I'll return to that in a minute.

Our left wing, under Major Gilpin, cleared the last entrenchment, working terrible slaughter, and the rout became, as they said, general. Still, a good lot of those Mexicans fought as brave as you please, and had to be *gouged* out of their holes. I saw a number of artillerymen shot down in the act of touching off their cannon. They stood just that firm. Not only the men, but Generals Herédia and Condé tried over and over to rally their forces —all useless.

Everywhere on the plateau, all you could see, aside from the smoke and the wounded, was units of shouting Missourians chasing Mexicans like bloodhounds. It resembled the wolf-killing back in El Paso.

It stirred you up, but it was a sickening, too, because men, or parts of men, were falling everywhere, crawling over the ground, trying to cower behind downed horses, cursing, praying, yelling for help, or water, and all the rest.

I've made this battle sound like the work of ten minutes, but it lasted three hours and a half, before the last troops were chased limping and creaky back to Chihuahua, to disappear into the hills toward Durango.

There isn't room here to mention *all* individual bravery, but everybody performed like a hero, Colonel Doniphan said so himself, and a Mexican priest named Rodriguez, arriving later in El Paso, said, "They fought like lions and tigers; it was more than humans could stand."

(You understand me, I put in much of this later, because I didn't see it right then. I'll get around to the reason by and by.)

Well, sir, we lost one man killed, a Major Sam Owens, a fine fellow, but a report leaked out afterward that he'd been drinking, from having family troubles: he just threw his life away—jumped his horse over an entrenchment directly into a cannon blast. It knocked him off, of course, but were the Mexicans satisfied at that? Not on your life. A whole swarm leaped out of their holes and stuck him with lances and sabers. They made a very good job of it, and left him more like a sieve than a man.

Still and all, aside from Major Owens, they hadn't so much to crow about. Their losses, when reckoned up accurate, were 304 killed on the field, about five hundred wounded and left behind, and seventy prisoners, including General Cuilta. Also six thousand dollars in gold, heaps and heaps of provisions—enough to run Chihuahua for weeks; mainly beans and *pinole*—fifty thousand head of sheep, fifteen hundred head of cattle, a hundred mules, twenty wagons, thirty carretas, twenty-five thousand pounds of ammunition, ten pieces of cannon, six culverins (or wall pieces), one hundred stand of small arms, seven fine carriages (some of those Chihuahuan sightseers neglected to bother about their rigs, but jumped down and took off on foot like antelope), the head general's escrutoire, and a great many other things. That was the main haul, and not bad, either.

It must have been a shock to the Mexicans, for they had the victory all tucked away beforehand. The prisoners we took carried rawhide lariats which they said were for tying us up with after the battle was over.

Well, it didn't work out that way, I learned afterward, because it was the Mexicans that got tied up, with their own lariats, and many of our men, polite and thoughtful like most Missourians, thanked them for having the foresight to bring the ropes along.

When the wreckage was cleared and the surgeons buckled down—saws and knives sharpened and tar-pots bubbling—our troops heaped up a pile, almost a mountain, of cut-off arms and legs and such, a whole detail was sent out to collect them from the field and from the surgeons' tents, both. The pile was too much to bury that day, of course, so the wolves pranced in, same as El Brazito, and picnicked here and there. But again, they declined to touch the ones that had fed on red pepper, except a bite or two to test the flavor, but turned up their noses delicate and disdainful, as if they were accustomed to dine on higher-class materials.

Now to get back, and it grieves me to write it. I had this war moving along very well, Drum-and-Fife Corps organized so's hardly anybody insulted it any more; Mrs. Mendoza suspending her laundering and making us good money dealing monte in the cities; and a good chance of getting a medal sooner or later, particularly if some of the officers had a bad streak at monte; and then—everything caved in.

During the briskest Mexican charge, Angelina and I were left behind when our dismounted Company scattered—shooting, kneeling, and the like—and I recall being about to lift up a rifle when Angelina cried, "Oh, *my!*" and clutched my shoulder, nearly falling. I tried to yell in her ear, but the confusion and dust and hoofbeats and shouts and gunfire and sabers clashing drowned it out. The truth is, I don't remember exactly what happened, but the next thing I knew, a fat grinning Mexican with a sombrero hanging at his neck by a string rode down, and instead of throwing his lance, swooped low over the saddle—they really *can* ride—and whisked Angelina up behind. And then, a second or two later, another did the same thing to me.

It hadn't a thing to do with mercy. They wanted to be among the first when it came to looting the prisoners. Anyhow, these two were powerful disappointed, because the battle went against their side so fast we never stopped. The whole "Army of Central Mexico" broke into the wildest kind of retreat, we became separated, and I have a blurred picture of people whipping up carriages and wagons, the gentry and their ladies looking scared and dismayed, officers striking fleeing men with swords, wounded men falling off and getting trampled, and everybody half mad to get out of there in a rush. An army turned into a panicked mob is the ugliest sight I know; there's scarcely anything too low-down for a man if he's trying to save his skin.

But the exceptions stick out in your mind. I remember a slim, handsome young lieutenant trying to make a stand against the tide, sword drawn but not being used, his face shamed and pleading, eyes red with dust, gorgeous hat missing, and the poor fellow shouting orders that not a soul heeded. We swept on past at full gallop, leaving him braced as if he might launch a counter-charge all alone. He seemed just that dutiful.

We fell back toward Chihuahua, me hanging on for dear life, to keep from being crushed under horses and wagon wheels; otherwise, I'd slid off and taken my chances—then we entered the city but didn't tarry. "*Doniphan viene!* He comes!" The cry rang out high above all the hubbub.

Even so, I got a glimpse of the Plaza (now filled with running, screaming people) and in its center a high marble structure with four spouts of water that played into a stone basin upwards of thirty feet across. The water was piped in beneath the city from an aqueduct outside, someone stated, but I reckoned it was the general run of Mexican water and would set a person to sprinting if he drunk any. Commonly you boiled it, but even then the poisons gave up hard; you needed a hot fire. Oddly, though, the Mexicans appeared to thrive on it. *They* weren't sent on any hike to the bathroom. According to one of our doctors, a very sour old fellow with a wavy beard that hated Mexico, their natural body poisons rose up and hammered the water poisons down, killed them before they attacked. "Medically speaking, a greaser can swaller carbolic acid and spit lemonade," he said, and claimed he had conducted the experiment "with full analysis," but it appeared extreme to me.

In the hurly-burly, I remember the Cathedral, with hundred-foot-high steeples in front, some fanciful-carved columns, and a number of life-sized statues representing Jesus and the twelve apostles. I was busy right then, but it did seem that the bunch looked uncommonly Mexican, all thirteen, and that wasn't the way I recalled it from the Bible. We were rattling along so fast I may have jumbled things up; anyhow, there *wasn't* a woman sitting to one side patting tortillas for the Supper; I checked that out later. Going lickety-split, the Mexican that captured me jerked a thumb in the direction of the church, bragging, but I swiveled around and pretended not to notice. Then I kicked his legs a few times when he tried to spur the horse, but he glared back so ugly I gave up.

Past the *Plaza de Toros* or Bull Ring; past an old ruin of a church—an unfinished Jesuit Cathedral called San Francisco, now made into a prison; past any number of odd-appearing houses, two stories high and adobe except for a front of hewn stone; then, leaving the city, saw the six-mile-long system of columns and arches that support the aqueduct in from the river. Lying across the town, it really was a sight, an elaborate water supply like that smiling down over plains, fields, and houses; it gave me a better feeling about Mexico.

Then we were on the road, headed toward Durango, and the time ran together till we camped, well on toward midnight. My keeper—he was a volunteer, and a threadbare one at that—chained me by the neck to a wagon wheel, after giving me half a pint of red pepper and three tortillas, same as the Mexican soldiers got. I ate it, Mexican style, using the tortillas for bread as well as fork and spoon, and was refreshed to know that the wolves wouldn't devour me during the night, unless one took off a foot or something as a sample.

The Army was in a rout, you understand, and it was days before any order could be restored. In that time, we fell back to a town called Las Cruezas, where the generals grabbed some food and fodder from a rich rancher, spite there being some jawing about it, so that in the end he was paid; then on to Santa Rosalía, alongside the Conchos River; and then to a big town called Parral.

Camped by a ranch making mescal from the blue-green maguey plant, biggest ones I'd ever seen, thirty or forty feet high and four feet across. The Mexicans here eat the stalk, boiled and raw; manufacture mescal and two or three kinds of liquors from it, including pulque, which resembles beer; and make summer hats and rope and bagging from the leaf. It's on the order of an E. Pluribus Unum plant, I heard a man say once, for they also use the stalk for cart bodies and build fences (from the whole vegetable) that the toughest robber couldn't snake through, unless he preferred to come out looking like a porcupine. And at last, after the mescal is done, they convert the remainders into sugar and food for stock.

So you see, a farmer with maguey is in business in nine or ten different directions. But mostly they distill the liquors, then sit up against a sunny wall somewhere and hope to get around to the others tomorrow.

We were getting along down South, now, and I saw some rare old sights. Today passed a corn field that was "unproductive," so a priest carried a miniature Virgin Mary up and down the rows, accompanied by a gold-toothed dunce holding a red umbrella. Another priest sprinkled Holy Water around (though an unholy gusher from the irrigation ditch would have served better) and two fiddlers made the air blue just behind. Bringing up the rear, a man kept shooting off a rusty old fowling piece bound up with copper wire. Taken together, it was calculated to make the corn grow, don't ask me why.

I couldn't figure it out. If the priests *really* had a toehold on Heaven, the man in the rear was wasting good buckshot, not to mention the fiddlers; likewise, if firing a ratty old shotgun made corn grow, why weren't the priests back in town collecting up money for another Cathedral? If you want my opinion, it was an odd combination of influences, and I'd like to place a bet that the corn wasn't affected in any way except bad; why, the fiddling alone would have wilted your average crop. They could have sent in a cart full of manure, and avoided the ruckus entirely. But you couldn't tell them a thing; I tried and got cuffed on the ear for it. Besides, the priests had the upper hand, always. If they stated, official, that the Church had a franchise on crop-growing (and threw a little side business to two fiddlers and a shooter), that's the way it was done. You saw it so all over Mexico, one line after another.

Here at Parral the Army received word that Doniphan was holed up in Chihuahua, so we slacked off on our pace. The generals were arguing about where to flee to, and finally they hit on Durango, which was still in Mexican hands, besides being off the main route down, so there was little chance we'd be kicked out again soon. Still, some units went off in other directions, and large numbers of men disappeared into the empty little villages.

Well, about this time they came to fetch me, said General Herédia wanted to quiz me on "Intelligence." I didn't mind, because I considered myself as intelligent as a Mexican, and was anxious to prove it. But when I got there—to a big tent with goatskin patches on top and a flap out in front for an awning—I discovered they were trying to turn me into a spy.

General Herédia, a medium-sized man a shade or two lighter than coffee, with black mustachios and a hat on, was sitting in a camp chair under the flap, and some others were lounging nearby. One, in another chair off to the side, had a notebook and pencil.

This Herédia didn't appear so fierce, but smiled and nodded, then said over his shoulder, in Spanish, "Where's O'Higgins? Bring up the interpreter."

"*No es necesario,*" I broke in, perfectly fluid, as mentioned. "*Yo hablo todas las linguages*—the works, A to Z." (I spread it on a little thick, but I was representing Missouri here, as well as the United States on the side, and didn't aim to hide my light under a bushel.)

Well, sir, never tell me a Mexican can't be insulting. They all burst into a loud hee-haw, and some doubled over and folded up. They seemed more informal than is usual among generals, but it failed to get my goat. I just eyed them, calm as old Doniphan himself.

General Herédia lit a coal-black cigar and said, in pretty low-down English, "What is it—thees 'works'?"

I figured he was joshing, with talk like that (knowing I was fluid in Spanish), so I answered up the same way.

"I speaking all languages. Heap much education up Norte—*mucho más* than Mehicano. Very great teachings. Savvy? What! No savvy? *Interpreter!*"

The next thing I got was a disappointment. Without changing expression—smiling and good-humored—General Herédia spoke to one of his aides and the fellow slapped me head over heels. This *did* give them a laugh; I thought they'd never quiet down.

Then the general held up one hand and said, even milder than before, "We are here seriously. Is serious, war. Savvy?"

I didn't say anything, but rubbed my chin and waited.

"Now, my boy (*hijo mio*), how old are you?"

"Thirty-two. I smoke a good deal."

I might have known; they hauled in the aide again. I picked myself up, not much hurt but not feeling helpful, either.

"Let us begins once more. You see this map—*carta*—map?"

"I'm sorry," I said. "I'll have to wait till my head clears up. I'll be over under my wagon."

"Lieutenant, you will kindly clear up this prisoner's head?"

"Never mind, it's all right now. I'm coming out of it fine. It was just for a second."

"So—this dot and circle. Chihuahua, no?"

I studied it for two or three minutes, then said, "Frankly, I can't be sure. I wouldn't have recognized it. I wasn't there for only—"

Whack!

I got up again, while General Herédia smoked, in no hurry. Confound them, you couldn't tell *what* these Mexicans were apt to do. They were as changeable as monkeys.

"Now, Chihuahua. Colonel Doniphan he is there—how many men?"

I swallowed my natural instinct and told the truth; I said "About nine hundred, give or take a few." I knew perfectly well I was obliged by the Articles (they'd been read out loud often enough) to tell only my name and number, but I had plans to cover the situation.

He nodded, pleased. "I see you learn the lesson. We estimate so ourselves. The same."

"Yes," I went on, "the Advance Guard was approximately nine hundred. That was the 'boob-squad,' the ones that needed training, that hadn't any knowledge of fighting whatever. Those and the cowards. The main Army's strung out behind, and to save my soul, I couldn't tell you the number. All right, go ahead and beat me up; I still can't help you. There's too many. President Polk may know; I doubt if anybody else does."

For the first time General Herédia seemed interested, but not happy.

"Is true? If not, Sergeant Pascal pull out your fingernails, one by one. Better yet," he said, warming up, "you be shot for being capture in civilian clothes. As a spy."

"Wait a minute," I said, just as hot. "What do you mean, *civilian* clothes? This is a uniform, all the uniform I've got, and I'll ask—"

His gaze was traveling up and down so offensive that I couldn't help having a look myself. It was the first time I'd taken stock in two or three months. To be fair, there was room for doubt. Captain Hobbs' Comanche wife had sewed the shirt; it was deer hide, with a few holes here and there and kind of ripe with sweat. As to my original pants, they'd wore out and been replaced by a pair fashioned from goatskin, property of an El Paso citizen that thought he could play monte before he met Mrs. Mendoza. I'd haggled them off even with a saw, but they hung down frazzled in back, scraping the ground. I'd meant to trim them up, but forgot. They had a pretty powerful stench, too, on the order of uncured goat, with some Mexican mixed in, which mostly drowned out the goat. For shoes, I had on a nice pair of huaraches I'd picked off a corpse at El Brazito—they were my best article—and over one shoulder I carried a poncho that might have stood laundering, after being fumigated, but whenever I mentioned laundering to Señora Mendoza, she laughed fit to kill, shaking all over and showing her gold teeth. For a high-minded person of character, she had a surprising lazy streak.

"Well," I said, staring back, "it's as close to a uniform as any we've got. You can't shoot me for that, and what's more, I never saw any civilian clothes along these lines in Missouri. Or even close."

It was true, and a very good point. That's one thing I learned from Colonel Doniphan: get hold of the legal side and stick to it, even if it's a lie. It's the way all lawyers proceed, just as long as there's any money left in the case. They're a mighty smart breed.

"We see about Colonel Doniphan's command numbers," said General Herédia, with a look of confidence. "Many cunning spies working for Mexican Army; they find out exact. No such spies in anyplace else. *Verdad.* I tell you." His English appeared to come and go, and occasionally it went all to pieces.

"I agree with you there; you're certainly right," I said, determined to talk careful and easy so's I could continue to think clear. "I got to know several after we rounded them up. As fine a body of men as I ever met. Everybody was admiring about how much they knew. Wonderful talkers, none of your shy, hangdog, bottled-up violets, and when it came to fighting! Colonel Doniphan himself decorated as many as a dozen on the field at El Brazito—switched sides without batting an eye."

For a second I thought I'd overdone it. General Herédia studied me with his black eyes glittering, his cigar dead between his lips; and finally he said, "So far, we are much patient, *hijo.* Now I means business, as your most comical speech go. *Where* are your armies headed? How many each unit, what place ordered for? Now—one false slip and—boom! Bring the shovels."

It was thin ice, but I hadn't any choice. I *did* make a last attempt to slide out, saying, "My name is Sam Shelby, and I've forgot my number. Now those are the rules, General, and you know it."

He took out a fancy gold watch with a lid, snapped it open, so you could hear it ticking in Jericho, near about, and placed it on a table. "Take your time, son; you have a minute, and then, very regrettable, but civilian clothes leaves me no choice. Commence, or be shot."

I took a deep breath, smoothed out the map, and said, "Very well, but I feel like the lowest dog on earth. What's more, I'll never be able to go home again. There isn't any meaner hound than a traitor—"

"Commence," said General Herédia, checking on his watch.

"Well, first off, you're lucky because Colonel Doniphan always had me in on his councils. He said, and he repeated it over and over, 'Let's get Sam Shelby in here—if there's a flaw in the plans, he'll spot it. The boy's got an instinct like a fox—'"

"Son," said General Herédia, with an ugly threat in his voice.

"All right, all right, I'm coming to it. The biggest bunch, the *main* body, maybe eight or nine thousand men, now hidden near El Paso, are ordered to proceed right down here"—I pointed on the map—"to, yes, Sombrerete, that's the name, making night marches only and carrying all their food, quiet as mice. Once there, they split up in two columns, one to strike at and destroy Durango—did I mention that they've got thirty-two siege guns? —and the other to head for the sea, meet the Navy, bottle up the ports—Tampico, Vera Cruz, etc.—*then* join what they've nicknamed the Allegheny Maddogs: Third and Fourth West Virginia, Second Pennsylvania, one or two others—say six thousand total—and capture Mexico City, tear down the buildings, especially the monuments and Cathedral, torture and kill all the inhabitants—"

General Herédia leaned back and held up one hand; then he said to an aide in Spanish:

"Does General Ugarte find himself improved? Yes? Good. Convey my compliments and ask him to come out briefly. This may complete his cure."

Then, when a pale, hatless man wrapped in a blanket took up a seat beside him, helped by non-coms, "Proceed."

"Well, sir," I said, run about dry but bound and determined to do my duty, "I dislike to tell the rest, because it sounds, well, uncivilized, and frankly, I was against it. I put up arguments, and I'd like you to remember it before you get out the firing squad. But they outvoted me. No matter what his other good qualities, Colonel Doniphan's a rip-roarer once he gets started. When the urge to kill gets on him, he'd make a weasel look like a vegetarian—"

"Is all right, *muchacho,*" said General Herédia in a kindly voice. "We bear your fine works in mind. Please to continue your narratives for General Ugarte. He have been *enfermo*—sick."

"Well, they've got five different corps—held back for the word to go—that are known in the Secret Files as The Exterminators—civilian killers, nothing to do with the Regular Army. They're to fan out down the country, from the Pacific to the Gulf of Mexico, plough up all crops, salt the ground, poison the rivers and wells, kill the children, and drive the young women up North. The plan is, and again it wasn't my idea, to leave Mexico so's it won't spring back again for two or three thousand years. Like Carthage in the history books—"

"Anything besides?" inquired General Herédia in a sort of dry voice. "Take a glass of pulque, don't strain—"

"Yes, sir. Now here's the worst. I promised not to tell this even if somebody cut my tongue out, but the war in California's finished, done, all Mexican troops wiped out. *Generals Kearny and Frémont are at this moment headed by ship for*, ah, *Acapulco!* Entire fleet. They'll come up to join General Taylor and General Scott from the South, and after that wipe out every last soldier in Mexico. That's the order—kill them all. Frankly, General, I hope you can get General Santa Anna to surrender before it's too late. I don't like to think about it."

Nothing else came to mind; I was worked out, and then some, so I quit. But I wasn't unsatisfied, generally speaking.

He stared for quite a while: I could see he was impressed. Then a low rumble begun way down inside, moved up, swelled a little, exploded on the outside, and was joined in by some other noises nearby. One man fell over backwards in his chair—he sprung his wrist, so they said later—and the sick man's face now had a hearty color to it, though he appeared to choke on something and they had to assist him back to his tent on a stretcher. A doctor said it would be about an hour before they could tell whether to give him nourishment or call in a priest.

General Herédia got himself under control in about five minutes. He'd been using a bandanna neckerchief for a swab and had removed his hat.

"Thank you, son. *Muchas gracias*, as we state in our ignorant style. War creates much, but only small amusements. *Orderly! Vea que este muchacho reciba ración doble de la comida de los oficiales*—officers' food, double ration. Such an imagination deserves very much. I doubt if it appear twice in a lifetime."

I didn't care much for the compliment, but I was happy to get the food. And somehow, in spite of the rude behavior of these fellows, particularly when I was doing my best to oblige, I got the notion that General Herédia was a sizable kind of man. This war wasn't over, not by a long shot.

XXI

I TRIED to see Angelina, but got put off because we were busy finding billets in town. My keeper, Pancho, knew a family that had a medium-sized house, so we moved in there.

Now we were past chasing (for spies *had* come back to report that Doniphan was stationed in Chihuahua), the Mexican generals tried to reorganize. But stragglers disappeared every day; they melted away into the empty plateaus and the mountains. Nobody took any action. I doubt if an accurate roster existed. And besides, most Mexicans look pretty much alike, it seems to me. Maybe their mothers can tell them apart; *I* can't.

Well, we stayed with a family named Dominguez, or along that line, and there isn't much to tell.

The dwellings in Parral were better than the red mud pies in Santa Fé. These were mud, too; that is, adobe—bricks about two feet long, a foot wide, and four inches thick, mixed with fine-cut straw, the whole dried hard under the glaring Mexican sun. But a difference down here was the roofs, which had a foot or so of earth on top of them, with bushy little trees growing all across! It gave you an odd sensation, seeing those wooded islands sticking up in the middle of town, but the trees kept the house cool in the hottest part of summer and, of course, tolerably warm in winter. It was a good thing, because heating systems were unknown. You couldn't have built a stick fire inside; the smoke would choke you in no time.

No glass in the windows—just holes, or slits, if it happened to be an area favored by Apaches. The floors were earthen, not a floor board anywhere, as far as I could tell; but most houses were whitewashed outside and in, the stuff made from bone-lime then laid on with a buckskin.

In the smaller places you'd have a crude seat, or bench, bordering the walls, and maybe a flimsy partition in the middle, so that ten or twelve could occupy a room together. No chairs, tables, knives, forks, spoons, plates or dishes, nothing of the kind. Your lap served as a table, and people generally sat on the mattress-blankets they slept on, folded three or four times. Often three generations of a family lived in the same house, sleeping on the floor, on dirty old sheepskins, or on blankets.

The children ran naked to the age of five, and after that put on a coarse-woven shift. No shoes; none but the men wore shoes (sandals) amongst the poor, and the women's feet were a study in grime. They worked and padded around the streets wearing practically nothing, unless it was cold, and commonly had a baby, maybe deformed or pocked, in a black mesh rebozo slung from their necks. Always smoking or begging tobacco or selling the dry shuck covering of Indian corn that they use in making cigarritos. For peddling, these are tied in a bundle, called "*hojas*," and I expect the country would collapse and go out of business if the crops ever failed.

Every Mexican I saw, men *and* women, had fixed to their girdle a bottle of powered tobacco, and the hands of most women were stained a yellowish brown. But down here towards the South, all women of family carried the small golden tongs, *tenazitas de oro,* to keep the yellow off of their fingers.

Bathrooms? No, a person simply stepped outside the house; and the younger they were the nearer they let fly. You had to be mighty careful where you stepped. This house of Dominguez had two stories, the bottom connected to the top by an inside ladder, and the roof, as suggested, reminded you of a runty evergreen forest growing out of a river-bed of mud. They had me upstairs, chained to a gun rack set in the wall, padlocked at both ends. Nearby was a window covered with an oilskin flap, the same material the men used for protecting their sombreros when the rains came, and the hole was big enough to crawl through. But I never tried it; I'd only of hung myself, of course, which was all right, they said, and would be satisfactory to the authorities. They left a three-legged stool handy in case I changed my mind.

Anyhow, to get back to bathrooms, the main system in this neighborhood was for everybody to pad down a slope that fell off behind to a rivulet of sickly-green water. Regular as clockwork. It was my main entertainment, like going to a dog-and-pony show. After breakfast, they dribbled down a ways, smoking, all but the infants in arms, and dropped aside at handy spots. Having no one else to talk to, I fell into a kind of commentary. "Well," I says aloud, "there goes old red-sash—behind a bush for a change." Then the two smart-aleck girls from next door, passing a cigarrito back and forth; Mrs. Tattooed Rump (with the rabbit [and very well drawn] disappearing into its lair); two men aiming to trade burros, having a business conference side by side; a bunch of children together; the one-eyed loud-mouth, standing up facing us, totally unconcerned, yelling up at his wife, who was cussing right back just as hard; the nice-looking young fellow and his girl—they had the decency to take opposite sides of a cactus, out of each other's view except for the top, flirting and then hugging and kissing against a tree; and pretty soon the Dominguez family, and afterwards, me. And all the while, first to last every morning, church bells tolled from all directions, every note in the scale, some round and pretty, others dull, harsh, cracked, muffled, or too loud—slam-bang, ding-dong, bong-ding, come to Mass, watch out, the priests'll get you, and several hundred dogs, resenting it and howling like the end of the world had arrived.

For my part, the sanitation placed quite a strain, because everybody strolled out to watch, being curious whether it worked the same way with gringos, but I grew accustomed to things soon. I've noticed that you generally do; a person adjusts himself to whatever's necessary to keep alive, even the prisoners that sat chained to the wet stone floor of a Durango jail for seven and a half years. I talked to one, a human skeleton with a few wisps of white hair on top, and he said, "I lived a spry old life in my dreams and imagination—I got so I could make up fancies as handsome as a book—and five times a day, not failing once, I tensed every muscle from toes right up to scalp, druv them hard within the limits of being motionless. I kept from shrinking down to nothing that way. Look here, son, my upper arm measures better than five inches around!"

But to move on, because I've been dawdling again, it was here that I commenced to think about escape. That lazy, good-for-nothing Pancho dragged me to the *herrería* one day to see about his mustang, which limped on three legs and was going lame on the fourth, and I noticed a file I could steal the next time around. Where he chained me now, it was two inches out of reach.

Well, the opportunity blew up, because we lost his horse on the way back, and I'll tell you how it happened. Clopping home through the Plaza, with the early morning breeze making things pleasant and nice, and a fresh-dew smell still on the flowers and elders and fig trees (also stepping around the old ladies beginning to set out eggs and goat's milk and piñones and watermelons), we ran into a knot of frolicsome, hard-looking loungers that moved in around us, blocking the way, chattering and laughing but not friendly.

One touched the mustang's flank, pointing. The others acted shocked, and a man took off his hat to pretend he was set back considerable, fanning himself, you know.

Pancho yanked at the horse's head, trying to push on, then broke into a screaming harangue when they stopped us with cries of "*No hay venta! no hay venta,*" or words to that effect. Then another set up a yowl for the alcalde, and a tramp with a shriveled hand scampered off in the direction of the Casa Municipal. It was annoysome even to me, and I didn't care whether Pancho lived or died. But as a general thing, if it came to a row between one Mexican and several, I tended to favor the one. The more I could oppose the better.

Well, presently up they trooped, a ridiculous-appearing fellow, so fat he could hardly waddle, dressed formal—that is, he had on a clean sombrero and a short dark jacket with a gusset in the back—and carrying his ignorant *bastón de justicia,* an ordinary walking cane with a black silk tassel on top. He was accompanied by the customary priest, in this case looking disgusted.

When they arrived, and listened to everybody's gabble, including Pancho's (which was so full of cusswords about animals and people's mothers and their sisters' virtue that it reduced his argument, it seemed to me), they begun a tedious inspection of the mustang, stem to stern, clucking, shaking their heads, taking notes, and acting mighty judicial and unpartial all around.

The trouble (and it was purely technical, the rawest grade of humbug) lay in the system of branding. Each time a mule or horse was sold, the owner marked it with an elaborate *fierro*—a "hieroglyphic stamp," in Blaine's words. Then, when it was sold again, the fools marked over the old sign with a *venta,* or sale brand. It made no difference how *often* an animal was sold, the rigmarole had to be performed all over. On an average, a ten-year-old mule resembled a road map of London. He didn't have any hide left that wasn't decorated.

Well, let a stranger ride into town and a bunch of loafers pounced down immediately. And if they spotted an *unvented* brand, they laid claim to the animal right off. It was simple, because a lot of peasants grew careless about ownership, and, of course, *estranjeros* were easy prey always; *they* hadn't any such idiotic system, and probably never heard of it.

The swindlers which made a practice of this kept any number of irons on hand, covering about all the known designs, so they'd piously step forward with something like the unvented mark, then walk off with the horse.

And that's exactly what they did here. A moon-faced fellow with a paralyzed grin disappeared and returned with a brand that was as similar to the mark as a shovel is to a hoe; but he nodded and jabbered, the same as if he was honest.

Pancho screamed, *"No es el mismo! Ladrones! Estafadores!"* calling them seven kinds of a thief, along with some other things, but the alcalde, shaking his tasseled stick, admonished him not to *impugnar* the honor of such leading, upright citizens, and said he'd have to impose a pretty stiff sentence unless he controlled his tongue.

"I *no impugno!* I call them thieves, carrion, vultures, *chivos,* lizards, cockroaches, illegitimate sons of *putas,* crawling with fleas, lice, mange, rot, pox, scabs, maggots, filth, pus, dung, and urine, and demand to be taken to the headquarters of El General Herédia. He is my father," he added as an afterthought, lighting a cigarrito.

Nobody believed the last, of course—Mexicans can tell a liar when they see one, as they see practically nothing else all day—but the request presented a poser. The country had three divisions of law, or *fueros.* What I mean is, one set of laws could scarcely cover everybody in a place where nobody was equal, or close to equal, so they came up with the *eclesiástico,* which provided that all priests were exempt from any laws except punishment by their holy accomplices farther up the ladder toward God; the *civil,* for ordinary people (usually meaning a decision on the spot by the alcalde); and the *militar,* which was for soldiers—officers and privates alike. In the case of people coming under the *civil,* the other two groups could charge *them,* but they couldn't charge back; they got it in the neck all around.

Well, the alcalde thought this over, then dispatched a clerk to "Headquarters," but everybody was off playing monte, and besides, the Army was breaking up to re-form farther south. In short, the *militar* had collapsed.

So—in the end they only took Pancho's horse, generously suspending all other counts. Afterward the alcalde congratulated him on not being shot, the new owners bought us a drink in a cantina, and we went home.

Nobody appeared to mind that he had called them thieves, carrion, vultures, *chivos,* cockroaches, illegitimate sons of *putas* crawling with fleas, lice, mange, rot, pox, scabs, maggots, filth, pus, dung, and urine at all.

Pancho himself seemed composed. He said he'd been put to a lot of trouble to steal that horse, from a farmer near El Paso, but he'd steal another before he left town. He stated that, by Our Lady of Guadalupe, he'd *venta* this one or saw off his left foot to make *carnitas.* He was fuller of oaths that way than any fool I ever met.

"Was not so good horse," he added, to close out the case. "I think she was much crippled in the breakage."

I believed him; the condition was generally true. You never saw such a people for mistreating animals. It was a rarity for a horse to survive a breaking intact.

Next day they sent for me and said I could see Angelina. She lay on a cot in a tent, better cared for than I'd hoped. Still and all, two other soldiers were there alongside her, one shot through the chest, which sounded like a busted melodeum when he breathed, and the other with a gangrened arm. The stench would have offended a polecat; it had a sort of physical quality, like being smacked in the face with a shovelful of manure.

There were no real doctors in upper Mexico, but the Army had a healer on the job, a former meat cutter that possessed what was called *oculto* powers—"*visibles solo para los que tienen visiōn espiritual*"—and he'd tackled the case with maggots. He had them squirming away at work, cleaning up the rot, all over the forearm from wrist to elbow. It was the standard treatment in such cases. It interested me. I tried to look it up later in a medical book, but the page had got tore out or something.

Angelina was a little too white to appear normal, and when she saw me, she commenced to cry. It must have been like breaking up a log-jam in the Yukon; she wasn't accustomed to it. Suddenly I felt homesick and low, and I begun to sniffle, too.

"That's all right," she said in a minute. "I'll stop. I don't like to see this in you, Sam. It isn't characteristic. It doesn't suit you at all."

Same old smart aleck; nothing changed, and I'd been thinking along identical lines about her!

"Well, how *are* you, anyway? Where'd you get hit?"

"*I? Me?* I could scarcely be better. Sam, I hate to sound whiny, but things are not entirely well with your old friend Angelina. I'm down here in Mexico, under arrest, with a hole in my shoulder, exposed as a fraud and sharing a tent with two dying *paisanos* and a bottle full of maggots. I'm not complaining, mind you, but it isn't perfect."

"I wonder why you have to talk so much. How bad hit *are* you?"

"I have this hole in my shoulder. They assure me it's healing nicely. He tells that to all the boys. I heard him tell it to a fellow who'd been dead all morning. Not the sharpest doctor on earth."

"Can I see it? You look sort of—chalky."

"On account of the blood. Most of my best blood ran right out on the ground. I miss it. But they're building it back with a concoction called, I believe, *tole*. Made from Indian meal, wheat flour, the meal of piñon nuts, bats' wings, eye of newt, and black mamba. I've heard it referred to, by half-wits, as *el café de los Mejicanos*. Poor devils."

"*Atole,*" said Pancho, chuckling. Sprawled against a tent-pole with the chain, he picked up a word now and then. "Much *agreables* for *salud.*"

"Is that something you're exhibiting? You'll make a fortune."

"It's the other way around."

I peeled down her shirt a few inches, lifted a filthy bandage, and had a look. Nothing but a purplish hole, surrounded by swollen and reddened flesh. It seemed clean, though warm to the touch. Then I remembered something, and fished in my pouch.

"It's healing bark—I got it from Captain Hobbs' wife." I put it under the bandage. "Take it off when they come, then slip it back. Soak it in a little water later. These Indian remedies work; I've been there and I know."

"I hope it's no worse than your bite."

"*Couldn't* you shut up, Angelina? If you tried hard? I suppose they know you're a woman."

"Girl. A young and innocent but brave girl. Yes, they lowered my shirt to my hips, whistled, clapped each other on the back, then admitted the troops one by one. I'm a topographic familiar to the Army of Central Mexico."

She started to rattle on, but a beautifully set-up young officer, kindly and intelligent-looking, wearing one of those gorgeous Regular Army uniforms, lifted the tent-flap and came in, followed by a clerky, middle-aged fellow with a sort of puzzled squint, as if he couldn't see well. He ran into a tent-pole and hurt his nose, then banged into Angelina's bed, drawing forth a surprising brisk statement from her, and after that the young man pushed him down on a cot.

"Stay there, Luis," he said in Spanish. "Don't move. If they can't replace your spectacles by tomorrow, I must send you home." Then he told him, "Assure the señorita that I hope I see her better."

"I hope you see me better than he does," said Angelina when she got the message.

I was disgusted.

"He's trying to be friendly. Can't anything stop up your impudent mouth?"

The young man appeared weary. The truth is, I don't believe I ever saw a person with a more concerned expression, and I think so still today. He was tall and slim but not skinny, with a straight back and a head held high; his hands and fingernails were as clean as if he had dressed up for a baile, and his tan face was taut and well-conditioned. His eyes were dark but hadn't any yellow mixed in the whites, like most Spanish-Mexicans. His black hair was trimmed close, like the *siempre alegres* in the city. Altogether, he had a proud look that had wore a little thin. I'm not describing him very well. What I mean is, he looked like *somebody,* but maybe felt that he'd straggled off on the wrong track.

He says to the interpreter: "Tell the señorita she was very foolish to disguise herself as a soldier."

"That goes for most Mexicans I've seen," she replied, and I got up to leave. There's a limit to how rude a person should be, even with the enemy, and *this* young man was trying to help.

He waved me back, not offended but looking more weary than ever. Then he addressed the interpreter again. "She is disarranged—*desarreglada,* upset. It is natural."

"For a person you can pour sand through, I'm remarkably at ease. Really, I never felt less *desarreglada;* take my word."

"Tell her I shall do what I can. It is very difficult. The Army's rough, and Mexico is not a—lawful country. Not yet."

He was making an effort to be loyal and honest at once; it wasn't easy.

"Tell him he's looking a little *desarreglada* himself," said Angelina. "Maybe he'd like to switch sides. That'd make three of us here for a starter. We could organize a Trojan horse."

"The lieutenant does not care for the war," volunteered the

interpreter. "He serves only to please his father. He dislikes the killing of people. He is also in opposition to the political—I tell you so in the strictest privacy."

"It sounds like somebody I used to know. I wonder what ever became of him."

I said, "He took a fancy for cavalry charges. He likes to yell and swing a saber. There's practically nothing that suits him better now than the killing of people."

For once, Angelina looked serious.

"It was all for nothing, wasn't it, Sam?"

I was pretty sore at Blaine, but he was still my brother, changed or not, so I didn't answer. But the interpreter took it on himself to pass along our conversation, and he put it about the way you'd expect; that is, he placed the lowest possible face on things, and added a few licks of his own.

"For several years, Don Ricardo, she has had a confident man, a lover, who has been transformed into something ferocious. He has beaten her so that she ran away, preferring to be shot."

I hadn't any intention of letting that slide by, so I broke in and cleared it up. For the first time, the officer smiled just slightly, and said, "Luis, tell the señorita that you are a gossipy old woman, with a mind of unbelievable foulness, and that I shall beat you with a stick when we leave."

The interpreter reeled it off, accurate and happy, not in the least embarrassed; it was plain he wasn't worried.

Before they left, the young man produced a package done up in Indian corn shucks, saying, "Here is a filet of beef, not of the sort one finds in France, or even in the Estados Unidos. It is tough, and not properly hung, but you must eat it for health." Then, to the healer, who'd slunk in and was eavesdropping around: "You will cook this for the señorita. Have a care to sear the outside, so that the juices are contained."

"But, señor, I am a doctor, not a cook! Consider my position."

"You are a butcher, and a very bad one. As to the meat, I should dislike to find it reduced in size." He flipped over a silver coin, and the man brightened right up and said, "It is true that I am a cook. It had avoided my mind for the moment. Among my powers, the cooking of meat has been a matter of the highest astonishment to thou—"

"Beyond doubt."

"I suppose I should thank you," said Angelina, in a voice a bit smaller than usual. I was glad to see her taken down a peg.

"It is not necessary. *Hasta mañana,* I shall see you tomorrow."

She stared at him a moment, nettled, as if she was mixed up a little, then said levelly, "Yes, I wish you would."

It struck me as going pretty far for her.

XXII

VERA CRUZ, *April 5, 1847:* From force of circumstance, I have neglected this Journal for awhile, and must now piece the events together from notes.

Briefly, Alex Doniphan's part of the war is ended, and with it, of course, my official duties as historian. But as my nuisance of a brother remains imprisoned by the enemy (unless he has been elevated to the Cabinet) and from other, nobler motives, I have been moved to join in the continuation of the struggle. (My searches for Sam, and for Dirk, have not turned up a scrap of hope to date.)

Perhaps more importantly, I am now able to see that this is a Holy Mission, and that, while warfare is not entirely purifying, it can be a powerful instrument for the good. Through it, the sapping fever of boredom is removed from one's life; Nature's balance of population is maintained; much of scientific value is learned in a hurry; rapacious ethnic groups (such as the Mexicans of different origins) are policed into compatibility with their neighbors; and, within one's own ranks, the weak and unfit are eliminated, leaving, to govern, the men of genius, strength, and enterprise.

We entered Chihuahua on March 1, 1847, while our band (somewhat refreshed under new management) played "Washington's March," "Yankee Doodle," and "Hail Columbia." We proceeded to the Plaza, Alex making this a triumphal occasion, with our colors broken out, the merchant caravans dressed in parade, and our *spolia opima* displayed for all to see. We found the population (forty thousand) polite but subdued. Only a few hours previously, owing to a false report that General Herédia had prevailed on the field, they had been dancing in the streets, ringing bells, and screaming, "The Gringos [corruption of greenhorn?] are gone, hurrah, hurrah!"

Feeling safe, they had also fallen viciously upon the thirty American residents and merchants in the city, crying their favorite anti-American epithets of "Texans! Yankees! Heretics! and Pirates!" then belaboring them with sticks, stones and knives. The Americans were told that, when Doniphan was dragged down in chains, the populace would be permitted to beat them to death in the Public Square.

The attitude upon our arrival was greatly improved. Despite a few laments (principally among the old) of "*Perdemos! Perdemos!* [We are lost, defeated, ruined]" the citizens recovered their shifty good humor with promptness. It is truly wonderful how adroitly these people can change to suit the occasion.

Scarcely a man lacked a friendly señorita (or señora!) to bring him coffee laced, here, with aguardiente instead of cream. The appearance of many women was startling; they have a local custom of encarmining their faces all over—a color of deep blood-red! Some, however, prefer to whitewash their complexions with thick paste, giving them a hobgoblin, Hallowe'en look; and still others mix the two effects, with red streaks about the eyes, down the noses, and across their chins, as well as daubing a bright red blossom on both cheeks. None of this is ever washed off; if the female alters her "style," proceeding for awhile undecorated, the paint must wear off, as all consider that water is abrasive to facial tissues.

Parts of the regiment were quartered in private homes, others in the Public Square and the remainder in the Plaza de Toros. Doniphan's administrative problems, as in Santa Fé and El Paso del Norte, began almost immediately.

While the Mexicans were eager to oblige, we ran into trouble with a haughty and supercilious Englishman, one Mr. Potts, who lays flimsy claim to being the British Consul to Chihuahua, though his papers have not to date been produced. In any case, he possessed, we were told, the keys to the (absconded) Governor's house, and Alex summoned him to Headquarters. He complied with ill grace.

"Well, Mr. Potts," said Alex affably, "we find ourselves obliged to ask you for the Governor's keys."

The fellow—lank, rather corvine of countenance, and ginger-haired, wearing a monocle that I believed to be ordinary uncurved glass, a piece of tweed vaguely shaped into a jacket, and an expression that appeared to place North Americans among the vulgarest of the earth's creatures—said in an affected drawl, "Ah, humm, yes, and I, in turn, representing Her Majesty as well as the *rightful* Government of Chihuahua, must indeed refuse, if you follow me."

It was with difficulty that we refrained from bursting into laughter. Alex was splendid, as always. His manners can be impeccable when the occasion demands; conversely, he can be the most irritating opponent on earth.

Instead of appearing ruffled, he placed his feet in their accustomed position, took an apple from a drawer, and peeled it carefully with his beloved penknife, leaving Mr. Potts standing in complete silence for several minutes. Then he said:

"Oh, I'm sorry, Mr. Botts; I was lost in other problems. Do I understand that you refuse to turn over—what was it? yes—the Governor's keys. What is your reasoning on that subject, sir?"

By now, though thick-headed and probably with a hide to match, Potts was beet-red, and would certainly have left, I am sure, but for the possible humiliation of being detained by the two burly sentries at the door.

"I don't feel called upon to examine my actions for a set of ragtag interlopers. You should be hurled back, sir, to your savage and uncouth property by force of arms, Britain combining with Mexico, if necessary."

Doniphan's feet hit the floor with a thump.

"Do I understand this to be a Declaration of War on the part of Great Britain?" To Lieutenant Colonel Mitchell, who was standing nearby, "This is serious, Dave. You'd better take it down. We'll want to instruct Washington—"

"Hold on, here, here—no such thing. I'll ask—"

"The keys, Mr. Potts."

In a word, the stubborn ass declined again, and Alex turned once more to Mitchell.

"Do you have a recommendation to cover this sensitive diplomatic case?"

Mitchell said, "Why, yes, I do, Colonel. Above all, of course, we'd better proceed carefully. I'd ask Captain Weightman to draw up a fieldpiece and blow down the door."

"Capital! We won't need the keys after all, Mr. Botts. You'd better come along and see the fun."

Potts only sneered in disbelief, but he followed outside after us, slightly more alerted to the occasion.

Very smartly, Captain Weightman and a squad of men rolled the gun up to the ornate mansion, charged and aimed it, lighted the port fires, then awaited the signal.

"Do you feel that you have selected the proper key, men?" inquired Alex.

"You might call this a skeleton key, Colonel," replied one of the squad, "because there ain't apt to be more than a skeleton of a house left after we let her rip."

"Very well, then. F—"

"Wait!" screamed Potts, and threw himself against the door. "Here they are, take them, and be damned! And be assured, you, you—*burglars,* that Her Britannic Majesty will hear about this."

"It wouldn't require anything additional to blow him right through with it, Colonel," volunteered the sergeant, trying to be helpful in his bluff Missouri style. "I wonder if you'd stand over a *leetle* further towards the center, Yore Majesty. Where you're at, I can't no more than clip off an arm."

"Hold it up, men," said Alex, and we took the keys, then ushered the sputtering Potts down the Plaza and out of sight and mind.

With a Lieutenant Kribbens, I commenced publication of the *Anglo-Saxon,* the first English-language newspaper in the history of the state. The *pièce de résistance* of our first issue was Alex's official proclamation to the citizens (printed in both English and Spanish) which went in part:

"The commander of the North American Forces in Chihuahua, informs the citizens of this State, that he has taken military possession of the Capital, and has the satisfaction to assure them that complete tranquility exists therein.

"He invites all the citizens to return to their houses and continue their ordinary occupations, under the security that their persons, religion and property shall be respected.

"He declares, likewise, in the name of his government, that having taken possession of the Capital, after conquering the forces of the State, he has equally taken possession of the State.

"He invites the citizens of all the towns and *ranchos* to continue their traffic, to come to this Capital to buy and sell as formerly, under the assurance they shall in no manner be molested or troubled, and as already said, their property shall be respected; for if the troops under his command shall stand in need of anything, a fair price shall be given for the value thereof with the utmost punctuality.

"He likewise declares, that the American troops will punish with promptitude any excess that may be committed, whether it be by the barbarous Indians or by any other individual.

"Lastly, we assure all good citizens, that we carry on war against the armies alone, and not against individual citizens who are unarmed.

"We, therefore, only exact, not that any Mexican shall assist us against his country, but that in the present war he remain neutral; for it cannot be expected, in a contrary event, that we shall respect the rights of those who take up arms against our lives."

I would be remiss if I failed to mention Alex Doniphan's (and most Missourians') growing distaste of this country, an outgrowth in part of fatigue. I obtained his permission to quote from a letter he wrote to a Major Ryland, of Lexington, Missouri, in which he said, "How often have I again and again determined to send you my hearty curses of everything Mexican? But then I knew that you had seen the sterile and miserable country, and its description would be, of course, no novelty. To give you, however, a brief outline of our movements, I have to say that we have marched, some of us, to Santa Fé, by Bent's Fort; thence through the country of the Navajo Indians almost to the waters of the

Pacific Ocean; down the San Juan River, the Rio Colorado and the Gila, back again to the Rio del Norte; across the Jornada del Muerto to Brazito, where we fought the battle of which you have doubtless seen the account; thence to the town of El Paso del Norte, which was taken by us; thence across two other Jornadas, and fought the Battle of Sacramento, and have sent you herewith a copy of my official report of the same. We are now in the beautiful city of Chihuahua, and myself in the palace of Governor Trias.

"My orders are to report to General Wool; but I now learn that, instead of taking the city of Chihuahua, he is shut up at Saltillo, by Santa Anna himself. Our position will be ticklish, if Santa Anna should compel Taylor and Wool even to fall back. All Durango, Zacatecas and Chihuahua will be down upon my little army. We are out of the reach of help, and it would be as unsafe to go backward as forward. High spirits and a bold front is perhaps the best and safest policy. My men are rough, ragged, and ready, having one more of the R's than General Taylor himself. We have been in service nine months, and my men, after marching two thousand miles over mountains and deserts have not received one dollar of regular pay, yet they stand it without mumuring. Half-rations, hard marches, and no clothes! but they are still game to the last and curse and praise their country by turns, but fight for her all the time.

"No troops could have behaved more gallantly than ours in the Battle of Sacramento. When we approached the enemy, their numbers and position would have deterred any troops, less brave and determined, but as I rode from rank to rank, I saw nothing but a resolve to conquer or die—there was no trepidation, and no pale faces. I cannot discriminate between companies or individuals; all have done their duty, and done it nobly."

So much for Alex's private summary of our situation. The truth is that, as usual with military commanders, especially amateur ones of good heart, the larger picture was too often obscured by the day-to-day trivia.

There occurred the matter of the baths. In Chihuahua, the Mexican aversion to water is at a minimum; on the contrary, there are numerous pools, for mixed swimming (in scanty costumes) and enclosed public bathhouses where the sexes splash merrily about, wearing absolutely nothing!

On the third day after our arrival, I was crossing the Plaza and encountered Sergeant O'Hara and five other men heading with suspicious haste in the general direction of the Cathedral. It occurred to the writer that O'Hara would visit a Catholic church, any Catholic church, only if there was some chance of inflicting mayhem on a priest. Accordingly, knowing how delicate was the business of keeping order in this important capital, I detained him, asking where he was bound. The day was warm—85 degrees Fahrenheit—yet the humidity was comfortably low, so I was puzzled to see that, besides sweating, O'Hara's expression seemed urgent, even excited.

"Why, sir, it's the—I can't rightly put a name on it, but it's the chance of a lifetime—"

"To get scrubbed up, he means," said one of his colleagues with a leer.

"That's *it!*" cried O'Hara, seizing gratefully on the explanation. "To git scrubbed up, and done handsome. None of your sponging and sprinkling. The way I am, it wouldn't cause no strain to grow a stand of corn on my belly. And last week—I'll take an oath, cross my heart, mire down in purgatory—I washed my feet and found two pairs of socks I swore I'd lost in Santa Fé. Me old mither—"

"Oh, the devil with your old mither!" said another of his group impatiently. "I'm kind of wore out hearing about your old mither. Most boring old buffalo ever crossed my path. Let's get on with it."

"O'Hara, this hasn't anything to do with priests?"

He blinked for a second, then stated, with the pawky humor he seems to be developing, "Not a bit of it, sir. Onless there's some in there a-swabbing their under-frillies."

Curious, I followed along, to a low, long, stone-fronted building with an access of air under the eaves. A babble of unidentifiable noises drifted out, and we drifted in. At first, the interior being semi-dark, I had difficulty seeing clearly, then it all came into focus.

Upwards of thirty Mexicans, some children included, were

splashing and wallowing in the water that was being heated at one end where a charcoal fire burned in a brazier and hot stones were periodically dropped into a partly enclosed basin.

On the surface, almost at my feet, a raven-haired señorita was floating on her back, stark nude, her tresses streaming out behind, her hands making little circles to maintain her equilibrium. Her face was free of paint and was, accordingly, rather carefully kept above the surface. Women of different ages and shapes sprawled elsewhere in the bath, some seated scrubbing themselves on the blue tile rim, and their menfolk soaked nearby, chattering with the crackling volubility peculiar to the race.

To the best of my belief, one of our group actually got completely out of his clothes before entering the water. He destroyed his shirt in the process, ripping it down one side. Another man, in trying to remove his trousers without first taking off his shoes, tripped and fell on top of an indignant Mexican family of four. They were uninjured, but he suffered minor damage to his groin. A third, with a piercing, libidinous cry that was later the subject of affidavits, took a short, sprinting start, still wearing his hat and saber, and landed near a girl in her teens, who was executing an eye-catching series of barrel rolls, turning over and over slowly, clasping her knees with her hands. However, it developed that he was unable to swim, and two Mexican youths retrieved him from the bottom then towed him to shore in time to effect resuscitation.

O'Hara, surveying what appeared to his single-track brain to be a species of marine saturnalia, groaned, muttered, "Hoisted aloft at last, and it was prayer that done it"; then, as his giant hulk spun loosely and toppled over like a man in a trance, he hit the water with a dull smash that rocked the establishment.

At this regrettable signal, most of the Mexicans clambered from the pool—the ones that hadn't been washed out—and the great majority covered themselves with clothes. I must take issue with a colleague who wrote in his Journal, of the baths, "These are constantly filled by the young and gay of both sexes, promiscuously splashing and swimming about, without one thought of modesty."

I dislike to be critical of a friend so intelligent and cultured, but the following additional passage from his memoirs (which he has let me copy, after some good-humored differences of opinion) perhaps shows that a long and arduous campaign may induce bias in one's observations:

"The people of Central Mexico are upon an average more enlightened and possess a higher degree of moral honesty than the inhabitants of the northern provinces, yet their complexion and language are much the same. The Mexicans generally, both men and women, are exceedingly vivacious, showy and facile, and at the same time shallow in conversation; extremely fond of dress and toys; hospitable when the humor prompts them; yet indolent and addicted to every extreme of vicious indulgence; cowardly and at the same time cruel; serving rather their appetites than following the admonitions of conscience; and possessing elastic and accommodating moral principles. Modest, chaste, virtuous, intelligent females are rarely to be met with, yet, notwithstanding they are few, there are some such. Many of the females are gifted with sprightly minds, have rare personal beauty, and most gentle and winning grace of manners. Their lustrous, dark, sparkling eyes, and tresses of glossy black hair, constitute a fair share of their charms."

In any event, it soon developed that we were indeed in a bathing house and not a *burdel.* Some spirited exchanges followed the first immersions of our group, notably when one fellow, having distributed some indiscriminate pinches and tweaks en route to the shallow end, essayed to teach the waltz, under water, to a full-blown but reluctant woman who turned out to be the alcalde's wife. A corporal's guard was summoned, the men were arrested, and the enclosed baths were declared off limits to the regiment.

On March third we buried Major Owens, in full funeral rig conducted by the Catholic Church, of which he was a member. As ceremony goes, this was the most ornate ever witnessed by the writer. At the Cathedral, three hundred candles were burning (like an ignited fence) in rows around the feretory where his corpse lay, and all morning bells tolled, processions of singing priests wound through the Plaza, accompanied by musicians playing instruments with which I was unfamiliar. In the church itself, services of prolonged and solemn ritual were performed. The local citizenry, who in a sense had caused Owens' death, seemed prostrate. Their lamentations all but threw the undersigned into tears, and I held no special love for the deceased. I scarcely knew him, but I feel that I knew him better than did a middle-aged woman who flung herself onto the floor by the altar and ripped loose the bodice of her blouse, neighing like a mare.

There is no explaining the singular conduct of Mexicans in the presence of birth and death. In sum (aside from galas such as the well-attended departure of Owens), it is a melancholy event when a child is born and a source of merriment if it dies. I witnessed the burial of two infants, at which the mothers were present. On both occasions, the holes were dug, the priests marked out a few cabalistic signs in the air, the infants were thrown in, almost without covering, and the mothers, in the highest spirits, took stones and pelted them with hilarity, treating those poor brief little lives with no more respect than if they had been dogs.

Again, I attended (out of simple curiosity) the burial of a Mexican who had been stabbed by a former friend. The corpse was quite stiff, and the grave was too short, so that his feet stuck up out of the earth. The situation was awkward. Making a game of it, two mourners took turns running and jumping on the upthrust extremities, finally bending (or breaking) them and forcing them beneath the surface.

I took pains to check the outlay for Owens' frilly send-off. As I'd imagined, it was not cheap. By good fortune, he had a sizable sum on him when he fell. The bill broke down as follows (from records presented to Doniphan's office):

Priests' services—$93.50. (I did not consider this exhorbitant, for, viewed as piecework, their fees came to about sixty-five cents per hour.)

Shroud—$33.50. (Rather expensive. In St. Louis, one can obtain a decent full suit for the sum, and Owens' costume, of course, lacked trousers.)

Candles:—$65.62. (Candles are somewhat dear in Mexico, where fat is at a premium. Probably no more than fifty per cent of this represented profit.)

Services of two servants—$7.00 (?)

Coffin, "including trimmings"—$70.00. (The trimmings—black and white bands of crepe, and tassels—seemed to me very inferior. Also, the wood itself [scrub pine] was of poor quality, and full of knots. One of these was adjacent to his left eye, which was open, and gave the observer a rather curious feeling. A swindle, but the central figure was in no position to object.)

Now we arrive, in this Journal, at the momentous point where Alex Doniphan and the First Missouri Volunteers ended their service to the nation. From the start, his informal custom had been to hold conferences with his top-echelon officers for all the graver decisions. Everyone was given a chance to speak, after which he weighed the remarks and delivered the order that appeared to him most sensible.

The official histories may or may not decide to quote here the preferences of individual officers, and I, except for Captain Reid's strong insistence on continuing south in combat, prefer to keep the remarks anonymous. They are no less accurate; indeed they are verbatim.

The commanders were seated at a long, heavy, carved-mahogany table on the second floor of Governor Trias' mansion, Doniphan at the head and seven others, besides myself (in the role of court reporter) filling the impressive, high-backed chairs. For men with the easy manners of Missourians, it was a sober occasion.

Reid led off with an impassioned plea that the present company, with all their men, re-enlist for another year and resume the fight until "an honorable peace is won and the foul, presumptuous and upstart enemy has been conquered."

Alex sat relaxed but carefully listening, his long, thick, Indian-like mane badly in need of trimming and his clothes in indifferent condition.

"Next."

Captain X, (an outstanding soldier and man though self-made and with little education): "Well, Colonel, our time's about up; you all know that. We did what we signed on to do, and maybe a little bit more besides. As far as the Regular Army's concerned, speaking personally, I'd ruther throw in my chances with the Swiss Navy. They told us General Wool would be on hand here to meet us, this representing the ass-end of our operation, so to speak. What I want to know is, where's he at? Again speaking personally, I haven't got a plugged nickel's use for a man that fails to keep his appointments."

Alex cocked a finger.

Major Y: "As you've pointed out yourself, Colonel, our position here is exceedingly embarrassing. Apparently, Generals Wool and Taylor are shut up at Saltillo. If they fall back to Scott in the South, we'll have to meet Santa Anna alone, and I hear he's got thirty thousand men. I don't figure how in conscience we can go forward *or* back; the men aren't fit for another two-thousand-mile march on half-rations. My vote is—hang on a while and see."

Captain Z: "I think I'm as patriotic as the next, but I put some store by promises, even if they're made by as low-down an agency as the Government. It's a small matter, but where's our pay? Not one dime have my men collected up to date. Forage? There hasn't been any. We've got a bare handful of horses left in all; most of the men have been afoot for weeks. Rations? Half-rations at the best, and mostly none. We've been obliged to live off the country, and a more miserable country to live off, I can't imagine. No clothes, hard marches, sickness without proper surgery, trifling little side duties like whipping the Navajo nations, and, for thanks, sneers from the Regular Army. *My* boys are worn to a frazzle; I venture to say there isn't a one in the company that weighs two thirds of what he started out carrying in June."

One officer recommended that, since we had fulfilled our orders to take Chihuahua (the orders were non-existent past that point) we make a cautious retreat to Santa Fé.

The majority, I recorded, favored a leisurely withdrawal to the coast by way of Monterrey. The army they faced, they felt, had been whipped, and whipped soundly. Altogether, though, it was a divided council. As I looked around the dimly lit room, I don't think I ever saw a more bedraggled and exhausted group of men. They bore only a superficial resemblance to the smart, eager Volunteers who had left Leavenworth nearly a year before.

Having heard from everybody (and twice from the boisterous Reid), Alex sat drumming with a pencil. Suddenly he straightened up, tossed the pencil aside, and smashed his right fist on the table.

"Gentlemen," he said, with a comfortable look of finality, *"I'm for going home to Sarah and the children!"*

"Well, the reader may imagine that this sentence ran through the regiment like a last-ditch hope of salvation. Far into the night and early morning, in the Plaza, in the parks, at the monte games, at fandangos, and at establishments of lesser repute, men banged each other on the backs with such greetings as,

"Well, if it ain't old Joe! Where *you* bound, Joe?"

"Why, dang my hide if I ain't *going home to Sarah and the children!"* Then a rough and tumble of exchanged blows in the stomach, rude but excited guffaws, bottles passed around, and, as likely as not, some small destruction of property to follow (with the usual piteous howls from the alcalde).

For the forgotten men of Missouri's First Volunteer Mounted Regiment, Doniphan's unstudied decision became the most memorable rallying cry of the war.

2

"You're quite sure this is what you want?"

"Any kind of orders would do—a letter to General Scott might be ideal. He could assign me to any unit that might be shorthanded after Vera Cruz."

"You mean as a historian, of course."

"No, I'd prefer to get into the more active phase, now, Alex. And you needn't worry—I'll undertake the formal account of our Missouri expedition the minute a peace is signed and I'm home."

"Well," he said slowly, "I'm going to detach you, Blaine. But first of all, I'd like your reasons, as nearly as you can give them."

"First and foremost is Sam—"

"Somehow I can't get very exercised about the safety of Sam."

"Yes, I know. He's down there, alone, or with that baffling and impudent hayseed, Angel, frightened, organizing crooked monte games, bilking paupers at 'concerts,' maybe blackbirding and starting a revolution as well—but he *is* my brother and I'd better look him up. I hate to think what our neighbors will say if I find him."

"And Dirk?"

"I've made inquiries from Santa Fé on down—nothing. But I'll keep trying." I stood up. "Well, Alex, it's been a fine war, so far. I never thought I'd enjoy it, but it stands out as the profoundest experience of my life."

He sat, musing. "I expect I'd better commission you. As a corporal, you'd never get past a Regular Army sentry. Even if you had a personal note from the President. The army mind isn't up to it."

"Yes, I wondered about that."

"Then you'd *rather* be commissioned?"

I said, "I feel it the duty of people like me, who've undeniably had certain advantages, to assume the responsibility of leadership. To shirk it is, well—it's cowardly."

After staring off into space for a minute, he sighed, stood up, humorously removed his saber from a hook on the wall, regarding it with less than respect, I thought, and laid it on my shoulder. "All right, I dub thee Second Lieutenant Shelby—I'll have both documents drawn up this afternoon."

"You couldn't make it Captain, could you, Alex?"

There followed a little pause, and he said, "Yes, I could."

"That's settled, then. And many thanks."

As I went through the door, he called out, "There's just the one thing that worries me."

I waited.

"What will I tell your father?"

I had a disagreeable duty to perform, and, bracing myself, I went to the modest home near the Plaza where I'd found quarters for Señorita Rojas y las Cruces. She had caused me surprisingly little trouble, and to tell the truth, I'd paid her virtually no attention, aside from providing her a tent and arranging for her sustenance. It would be misleading to say that I had avoided her company; I'd simply declined to pursue the unfair advantage of propinquity. Also, as my military chores grew, less important concerns had disappeared from my mind.

Happily, the welfare of this beautiful but headstrong girl had been taken in charge by Señora Mendoza. It was not a connection that, at first, I regarded as wholesome, but after several talks with

O'Hara and a personal inspection or two, I decided that she was in good hands.

Mrs. Mendoza, presumably with a soft spot for the upper classes, had appointed herself a dueña, or *ama*, of ferocious intolerance. She scarcely let Carla out of her sight. At the Battle of Sacramento, I am told, she crouched with the girl behind a clump of cactus, removed, then with a bull-whip and a lance shooed off three convicts before the lackluster and ridiculous attack on our rear collapsed of inertia.

I found Miss Rojas in a small, walled garden behind the house, standing beside two washtubs and a pile of soiled linen. The girl's impedimenta seemed incongruous as set against the wildly flowering nasturtiums that grew at the wall all around. To my disgust, a lighted cigarrito dangled negligently from her brightly crimsoned mouth.

For some reason, I felt nervous, and, like most nervous persons, behaved rudely.

"Well, I see you're picking up army habits."

"You mean the smoking."

"Young ladies, at least in Missouri, are not much addicted to tobacco. Either smoked or chewed. I can't recall that I ever saw one with"—and I glanced pointedly at her hands—"yellowed fingers."

"I've always smoked. In the beginnning it was necessary to climb a tree, to avoid Rosa. Now I can smoke quite openly."

"It must be a great comfort."

"Yes. Some take the smoke within to the lungs. I only—poof? But I am capable of holding it in my mouth for long periods . . . so."

"You are certainly very gifted," I said warmly. "I must remind myself to write your father and report on your progress."

She looked stricken.

"See here, Carla, I'm leaving Colonel Doniphan's command. I've obtained permission to travel to the coast and join the fighting in the South. I'm sorry, but I have no means of taking you along. When things quiet down, you can return home. I'm sure they'll listen to reason."

She stood with her head up straight and proud—you had to give her that—but her eyes were angry and flashing. I had the impression that the Rojas y las Cruces were unaccustomed to rejection.

"It makes little difference which of the soldiers I laundress. Or how many. One is remarkably like another; Señora Mendoza assures me. It is only significant not to be married in the city of Puebla."

I sat down on a bench and said, "Now listen—"

"My dear no-longer-so-pompous-and-frightened Corporal—"

"Captain," I said. "Promoted in the field."

"For what?"

"I requested it," I replied briefly. "Tell me, as I notice you take your job literally, do you *enjoy* washing that pile of shirts and underclothes? It hardly seems consistent with your background. In other words, wouldn't you *rather* be home?"

"It goes well. One must remain alerted for the buttons. In wearing clean clothes, I had never previously thought deeply about the buttons."

"I wonder why it is that I always wind up bullyragged by the same kind of woman."

"Eventually you will dominate; I sense it. As we sit here, I feel that there is much domination in you, though it is buried beneath the shyness and the duty. Right now, of course," she said matter-of-factly, "I dominate. It will be interesting to watch."

"Listen carefully," I said. "In *this* I *will* dominate: the next time I see you smoking a cigarrito, back you go. No arguments, no blackmail, nothing. It offends me. I assume that some day you hope to be married, despite the devilish trouble you're putting me to now. For what it's worth, no *norteamericano* of quality would stoop even to kiss a woman whose mouth stinks of tobacco. Remember it. I tell you it's important, and it is."

"*Ensaye, y el fumar no le incómoda.*"

I left, planning to translate her utterance, but it slipped out of my mind. Sergeant O'Hara and his multi-skilled companion of the tubs having obtained permission to accompany me, we set out, the four of us, early the next morning, with an armed wagon train of merchants who had declared a sufficiency of everything Mexican. Forgoing the heavy northern route, with its almost certain attacks by Apaches, they'd chosen the easiest means of leaving the country—that of proceeding to the city of Monterrey, to Reynosa, on the Rio Grande (Rio Bravo), thence by steamboat to the mouth of the river, and afterward by boat to (in their case) New Orleans. For our part, since our destination lay southward, we hoped to find passage on a provision ship bound for Vera Cruz, which, at the moment, was under siege by Major General Winfield Scott.

I do not intend to give the details of our journey, which was blessedly uneventful, as wartime Mexican travel of that period went, but I shall piece in here a brief summary (gained later) of Alex Doniphan's final acts before returning with the regiment to Missouri.

Word reached Chihuahua on March eighteenth of General Taylor's stunning victory at Buena Vista, where with five thousand men—Volunteers in the main—he had measured strength with Santa Anna and twenty-two thousand of Mexico's finest troops. It is inadequate to say that the outcome was triumphant; the result approached annihilation.

An express then sent by Doniphan thus reached General Wool, liberated at nearby Saltillo, and, after fifty-nine days of occupation, during which numerous Chihuahuans were whipped for stealing (and our troops became dulled by women, drinking, cockfighting, bull-baiting, and gaming) the Missouri Volunteers took up the tiresome march of 675 miles to Saltillo. The colonel, before leaving, was heard to remark, "Well, if the buzzard won't come to us, we'll have to swallow our pride and go to him."

As before, certain of the livelier Mexican girls, smitten by the Anglo-Saxons with "blue eyes and fair hair," preferred to join the forming units. For several hours before departure time, they were seen in the streets, gaily dashing to and fro on curveting steeds, dressed in the habit of Mexican youths, and without, it appeared, a care in the world. They accompanied their lovers to Saltillo, and bivouacked with them in the deserts.

The column passed through arid and desolate country, again losing men and animals to exhaustion, sickness and bad food. Their route was through Santa Cruz, Saucillo and Santa Rosalía. At this last, at the junction of the Conchos and Florida rivers, strong entrenchments thrown up by General Herédia were found; they were built before the Battle of Sacramento, and were meant, our men learned, to hold the public archives and munitions of war in case of defeat and withdrawal. The plans had seemingly been changed, after the disastrous rout.

On down to Guajuquilla, where the quartermaster providentially found (and bought) eggs, chickens, pigs, cheese, bread, wine and vegetables, then through a beautiful and fertile canal country to a long desert that extended to the Santa Bernada spring. The area was, from all accounts, the world's capital of lizards. The nights were made melodious by curses of "Damn the ——— ——— scorpions!" and "Don't fling your ——— ——— lizards over here." It was the practice, which became reflexive, for a soldier, upon finding a lizard in his bed, sleepily to seize it, throw it upward, and, shortly, to be cursed when it landed on the bed of another.

On May 6, the Army entered the State of Durango, advancing to the river Cerro Gordo, and on the ninth reached Mapimi, a mining town, and two days later arrived at San Lorenzo, near where, in thick chaparral, the bandit chieftain, Canales, lay in wait for an attack upon our provision train. It was frustrated by a sortie led by a Lieutenant Gordon; however, a straggling Volunteer foot soldier, a Mr. Mount, was pounced upon and slaughtered.

Approaching Parras, the Army paused at the splendid hacienda of Don Manuel Ybarro, a Mexican gentlemen of the highest character, educated in Bardstown, Kentucky, who received the regiment with every courtesy. He showed the officers around his fine houses and gardens with roses richly blooming, gave the Volunteers comfortable quarters for the night, supplied them with a number of mules and a guide through the mountains, then all but stripped his ranch to provide forage for the enfeebled and parched animals. It is such men, all agreed, that make the easy practice of generalizing about races a risky venture. The Mexican stock shot up for several days to come.

Shortly thereafter, at Parras, the regiment found the inhabitants in distress. A band of renegade Lipan Apaches had, overnight, swooped down from the mountains, killed ten citizens, carried off nineteen boys and girls, and driven away three hundred mules and two hundred horses.

I need hardly say that the indomitable Captain Reid volunteered to lead an expedition of succor. The savages, with loot and captives, were overtaken in a cañon, decoyed into the open, and engaged by Reid and his troop of thirty-five. In the skirmish of two hours' duration, Reid had the intense satisfaction of receiving two very severe facial wounds made by steel-pointed arrows; nobody on our side was killed. The Indians, however, lost seventeen men, left behind twenty-five badly wounded, including either the chief, or the sachem (there was a division of opinion here) and gave up their spoils—livestock *and* children.

Reid expressed himself as having enjoyed a rewarding afternoon's diversion; the sachem, thinking things over, remarked that the raid had perhaps been ill-advised.

On May 21, the regiment marched, or limped, into Encantada, near the battlefield of Buena Vista, and General Wool reviewed it in person the next afternoon. On this occasion, the First Missouri Volunteers *drew full rations for the first time since they had entered service!* Every skillet, kettle, and bag was filled; the men took all the articles dealt out except the soap. "Here, you fellows," a commissary officer cried after them, "you're leaving your soap; come back and get it." "Soap, hell," a private replied. "What do we want with soap when we haven't any clothes to wash?" I should add that the disbursement of food was viewed by our men as a most questionable bribe for them to re-enlist. It came a trifle late!

Other incidents enlivened the long-sought meeting. General Wool, a stiff-necked army man to whom Regulations were Holy Writ, insisted on a *formal* review. To lead off, he kept the exhausted and half-starved Volunteers waiting "on parade" for more than an hour. Now I borrow from the notes of a man who was there:

"[He] came out with his staff to see Colonel Doniphan. The troops were ordered in line to receive the general. It was an odd-looking line, for no two were dressed alike. Most of them were, at the best, in buck-skin hunting shirts and trousers, and many had their trouser legs torn. Some were mounted on donkeys, some on mustang ponies, and others were on mules; not a few were afoot. One officer on Colonel Doniphan's staff had on a cap ornamented with feathers and horns taken from an Indian chief. Colonel Doniphan himself had one sleeve missing from his coat, a fact of which he coolly took no notice.

"The Regiment's drill compared very favorably with its uniform—none had the least idea of precision in their movements or of the silence expected of regular troops. Offsetting some of this, General Wool and his staff were outfitted gorgeously . . ."

From another source, we learn that, as the general drew abreast of an elderly, disheveled, and especially undisciplined reprobate, the latter remarked with an impudent grin, "Well, old man, what do you think of *us*?"

Wool, reddening, turned his head away and passed on down the line. At length, mastering his distaste, he said, a little coldly, "Men, you have covered yourselves with glory." But this was not to be an altogether successful day for General Wool. A ragged private spoke up to observe in a friendly way, "Well, we surely to Jesus wasn't covered with nothing else." The general was said to have judged the review "unfavorably," but he sufficiently unbent to partake of refreshments in Alex Doniphan's tent. Midway in their conversation, an ear-splitting hullabaloo burst loose, and the general leaped to his feet, crying, "What in God's name is that?"

Doniphan said, "Why, I expect it's the boys up to some kind of foolery." The "foolery" proved to be nothing serious; a group was igniting and exploding several boxes of ball cartridges; they thought it a novelty to find so many in supply.

Later in the day, Wool's discursive chief engineer conducted a group of officers over the battlefield of Buena Vista, pointing out the spots where Colonel Yell of Arkansas had yielded up his life, and the ground "still crimsoned" by the blood of Colonel Hardin of Illinois and Colonels McKee and Clay of Kentucky. The engineer then marked out the positions where "Washington's, Bragg's, Sherman's, and O'Brien's batteries with thunderous roar mowed down the enemy's advancing columns; thereupon the chivalrous Kentuckians, the gallant Mississippians, the indomitable Illinoisans, the much-abused Indianians [?] and other equally courageous volunteer troops dashed into the Mexican lines." This speech was flowery and vainglorious enough, perhaps, but even the wily and deceitful Santa Anna wrote, in his official report, filed in the archives of the Government at Mexico City, "The ground was truly strewed with our dead, and the blood flowed in torrents."

Wool's engineer also kicked up, with one foot, several Mexican forty-two-pounder shells, split neatly in half, having failed to splinter as intended, because of inferior powder. It is through such failures—as a rule the bungling of venal politicians—that battles and wars are lost.

Having been bluntly told by Major Clark that the regiment had deteriorated too badly to re-enlist, General Wool proved the essential generosity of his spirit by drawing up a communiqué, or tribute—an official account—in which he said, "Missouri has acquitted herself most gloriously. Col. Doniphan has fought the most fortunate battle, and gained the most brilliant victory, which has been achieved during the war."

"Old Rough and Ready"—General Taylor, the Commander of the American Forces—presented himself to our men as a new species of Regular Army officer. He "reviewed" them from his camp at Walnut Springs, a little distance outside Monterrey. It was an informal bivouac distinguished by civilian-erected buildings bearing such names as "Rough and Ready Hotel" and "The Old Ranchero Arms," this first referring to the name by which the Mexican population called Taylor. Several men also visited the hotel of perhaps the most curious personage of the conflict, a strapping blond-haired woman with a splendid figure—correct name unknown—who went by the title of "The Great Western."

Hers was a success story, of a kind. Having drifted into Central Mexico from nowhere in particular, she interested herself in the war, with a passionate zeal for Yankees, and began at the bottom, as it were—as a laundress. Very quickly she laundered herself into a position of pre-eminence among camp followers, some reliable sources reporting that, at times, she sat in on the councils of the commanders. A scholar at the scene, describing her euphemistically as a *vivandière,* writes that "her fearless behavior during the Battle of Buena Vista was highly praised; she dressed many wounded soldiers on that day, and even carried them out of the thickest fight."

The regiment's introduction to the hero of Palo Alto, Buena Vista and Monterrey might pass for a catastrophe in another Regular Army camp. The Volunteers arrived at Walnut Springs in the morning, in characteristic disorder, and Old Rough and Ready had not put in an appearance by the afternoon.

Lem White, of Jackson County, seeing a nondescript, un-uniformed man whom he recognized as a typical army hanger-on, went up and said, "Pardner, where can a man get some good drinking whisky around here?"

The fellow pointed out the sutlers' quarters and said, "You can get it there, but you'd better not let General Taylor catch you; he might make trouble."

Lem thanked him warmly, bought a bottle of whisky and returned to his companions, asking, "Where's that fat old fellow that steered me to the sutler? This is mighty good whisky, and I'd like to give him a treat."

Since nobody knew, White decided instead to give Colonel Doniphan a "treat" and proceeded to the Headquarters tent. Trying to bulge his way past a guard, he looked in and cried, "Who's that fat old geezer sitting there?"

"That's General Taylor," the guard replied stiffly.

"The hell you say! Why, that's the very rascal that told me where to buy this whisky!" and White scrambled out in a hurry.

Another journalist on the field writes of this remarkable and much beloved soldier, "In the afternoon, we saw a common-looking man dressed in a checked shirt, trousers of poor stuff, brown Holland coat and large straw hat examining our pieces of Mexican cannon attentively. Somebody said, 'That's Taylor.' His face was far from handsome, with a simple, good and firm look and his figure was short, but when you heard him speak, you felt that a leader not of the common mold stood before you. He had on not one article that could be classed as uniform, yet his colored orderly, or servant, was caparisoned in all the finery of both the American and the Mexican armies. The contrast was ludicrous."

Taylor and Doniphan, the one from Tennessee and the other from Kentucky and Missouri, hit it off immediately. Sitting in chairs before Taylor's tent, provided with refreshment indigenous to their native states, General Taylor asked:

"By the by, Colonel, everyone is talking about your charge at Sacramento. I understand it was a brilliant affair. I wish you would give me a description of your maneuvers."

"Maneuvers be damned," said Alex. "I don't know anything about the charge except that my boys kept coming at me to let them go, but I wouldn't permit it; I was afraid they'd be cut to pieces. A last I saw a favorable moment and they were off like a shot. That's all I remember of it."

"But I'm told you were in the forefront of the battle," Taylor persisted.

"Yes, in the beginning, somebody sang out, 'Their cannon are overshooting; they're falling to our rear.' I got myself up forward in a hurry, and stayed there till it was over."

It was to be weeks before the Volunteers made their way northward to the Rio Grande and (sending their remaining animals back by an overland train, then destroying all cumbersome equipment on the beach) embarked for New Orleans. They were feted from there to St. Louis, and to their towns and villages throughout the state. In our home site of Clay County, the same celebrations greeted the adventurers that had sent them into the prairie from Fort Leavenworth. There were speeches, receptions, teas, balls, fireworks, ceremonies on the Courthouse steps, and an especially stirring address by that same Mrs. Cunningham who had been so offhand about flinging the men into the cannon's mouth before. While her remarks were perhaps dimmed by the fact that a number of them *had* come back, forgoing the supreme sacrifice, all agreed that she rose to lofty and selfless flights of oratory, somewhat beyond the call of duty.

So, now, we bid farewell to Alex Doniphan and his First Mounted Missouri Volunteers. By destroying and dispersing the Army of Central Mexico, they had freed our commanders for the final effort in the South. They had suffered, seen and done horrifying things, lost many of their friends, and grown curiously older. Yet their lives had been enriched by—comradeship, perhaps the best thing to come out of the war.

PART THREE

XXIII

Along about here, if he'd had my rotten luck, old Peeps would have stuck his quill back in the goose—called it off and looked around for another hobby, maybe a little more expurgated. But I haven't had a chance, as Yr. Correspondent will show in a minute.

Here's what happened: While Angelina healed up, the Army of Central Mexico kept breaking into little parts and fading out of the scene. Many of the regulars drifted South, which was now under siege, somebody said, and most of the volunteers disappeared into the hills, as mentioned. The situation was confused, and lawless, too, and the people's humor changed some. Pancho took to chaining me by myself more and more, and it was tiresome lying around like that, with nothing to do but watch people go to the bathroom.

Frankly, it's a recreation that wears out on you; there's no variety to it. And in this case the cast was always the same. Their performance got to be what's called "stylized"; they were a bore. A new family moved in about three doors down, and that helped some for awhile, but they settled into a rut by and by.

Well, this Pancho, which I thought I knew well enough, commenced hanging around the cantina too much, and he'd come home unpredictable. Some days he was in the jolliest old spirits, and gave me extra food—bread covered with *ranchero* cheese and *piloncillo,* which is a kind of coarse sugar, not bad if you're starving. Other times the least wrong word would send him into a frenzy, and he'd knock me around, calling me a "stinking damn gringo," and other names. It got so I was black-and-blue all over, and with some nasty welts, to boot. Then he had the idea of taking me along for "boy fights," in the saloon. It was a main entertainment, as satisfactory as the Plaza de Toros, and a good deal cheaper.

I was near onto sixteen now, and about as strong as the usual run of Missouri boys; maybe stronger, from rassling with the darkies at Riverbend. It was a regular exercise, and there came to be considerable skill in it. The darkies were quick and tough but gave up pretty fast when you got a good hold. Blaine said it was from being suppressed and downtrodden by white people for so long, and said they would snap out of it some day and go completely overboard in the other direction. Those were his exact words, but that was before he joined the war against the Mexicans and begun to foam at the mouth.

Anyhow, I was changing some myself, I guess. I was still homesick once in a while, but I was toughening up a little, and laying my plans for evening the score with Pancho, you bet. I don't know when I ever hated a person so.

The first fight they made me do was against a poor scarred-up, underfed half-wit they'd dosed with mescal and shoved out into the center of the room. He was stupid from the drink, and screaming a lot of over-blown brags, besides working his hands and feet around in the silliest fashion possible—which I think he took for a fighting style—and it was no trouble to throw him down, scramble onto his back, and put his head in chancery. He couldn't work loose, so the ruffians that bet on him gave him a hiding with a silver-studded belt. They said it was the first time he'd been beaten; and once had even gouged an eye out from a sick Indian nearly twice his weight. They gave him a peso for it, it was so entertaining, and put him in with a *puta,* the poor addled freak.

I didn't take much pleasure from the decision, and when Pancho gave me two *reales* from his winnings, I handed them to the boy, who was propped up in a corner, torn and bleeding, but he only cursed me and struck out feebly and said he would kill me next time. Then he threw up all over the front of himself, from the hard exertion on a stomachful of cheap liquor.

I won four fights that way, tying up the Mexicans so that nobody got hurt; then they put in a very nice-looking boy that only recently had got orphaned. He was handsomer than any I'd seen, with neat black hair, beautiful teeth and an unpocked complexion for a change. The uncle that took him—a no-good loafer who did no more work than was required to beat his wife into raising frijoles—stated, with a string of *sapristis* and *carrambas*, that the *mozo* could by Dios earn his keep or else beg in the Plaza, upright and willing, like his other nine children.

Well, this fight made me uneasy, for the boy was both scared and determined, and that can mean trouble. The uncle had been training him what to do. It was according to the code, or rules, that these courageous fellows had fixed up for boy-fighters (though they themselves were actually so mean and cowardly that the Apaches openly joked about using them for "herdsmen"): dig out my eyeballs, break the bones in my windpipe, smash my crotch, or tear my nose loose to one side or the other.

From the minute they yelled "*Vayan!*" I had to watch my step. The grownups—the "*bravos*"—were hoping to see a killing, of course. He was stronger than I thought, one of those wiry ones whose bones never accumulate fat during all their life, and as I say, he was very badly frightened. At the first whack, he jumped forward and aimed a kick at my middle, his body stretched out parallel to the floor (I say floor, but it was no more than ground, hard-packed), but I dodged, brushed his legs aside, and tried to climb onto his back. Missed, and whirled around, both of us standing again. Then I noticed that the boy was crying, out of anger and fright, along with misery, too, I reckoned, and I made up my mind not to hurt him, if possible.

But I didn't aim to *get* hurt, either, so when he quit rassling and struck me on the cheek, I begun to bridle just slightly. It raised a lump; I could tell without feeling. Well, I kept sawing around in a circle, looking for a chance to dart in and end this disgrace, but I couldn't quite connect. In the background, you could hear the *léperos* and others screaming for him to blind the dirty gringo, and could hear Pancho yelling some of his usual threats to *agotar* me if I lost. They were drinking mescal, or pulque, depending on their purse, and naturally this made them braver. And then, by golly, if he didn't knock me down! For just a second, I'd flickered my eye off to note the boy's uncle standing behind him with a piece of broken bottle, and he'd got in a good one.

I crouched on the floor, clearing my head, mad clear through. Back at Riverbend, as stated, I and the darkies had a sport of rassling, all right, and did it most every day, but there was another where you hang a tow-sack full of sand from a limb and try to knock it free. I was tolerable good at it. It depended on starting off from the right foot; you leant your body into it, not just your arm.

Well, sir, when I got up, I wasn't so interested in protecting him any more. He *was* a nice-looking boy, but one of us had to get hurt; we both knew that. On an ordinary day, they might have let it go with a tussle, but this was another of those dratted feasts of Guadalupe—there must have been six or seven hundred altogether—and people were over-excited. I now had a plum-sized bump beneath my left eye, and my chin-bone was numb, with blood trickling down my neck. What's more, I'd begun to breathe pretty fast; I could hear my heart blim-blamming along—*different* somehow, thick and heavy, all but choking me. I suddenly understood how Blaine felt when he was forced to shoot that pesky Murdock in the arroyo. I'd been as nearsighted as a bat before, hadn't been sympathetic at all. There were some things a person *had* to do; your people expected it, same as theirs had before them, and a body could get satisfaction out of it, once he overcame the squeamishness.

I tried another rassling hold, hoping to twist his neck back and break it, but he squirmed loose and *bit* me! His teeth sunk together in the flesh of my arm, and I sprung aside fast. And when he got up, I smacked him, roundhouse, full-weight, flush in the mouth. It was as hard a blow as I ever struck; I was perfectly balanced. When I drew my hand back, it was cut and bleeding, but there was a tooth stuck to the mess, too. Then I noticed that all the boy's upper front teeth were gone, broken off to their stumps at the gum.

He felt of his mouth, with a kind of horror, then ran to a piece of glass they had behind the smelly old bar—it was nothing but a rough length of pine—and examined himself; then he put down his head and cried, but not in the same way as before.

Those low-down bullies were yelling, "*'Riba! 'riba!* Go on—feenish! Big cry-baby coward, kill him!" but a man that had come in quiet during the middle—a traveler, or miner, from the look of his dusty clothes—said, "*Bastante!* Enough. The boy's had enough. Clean him up and let him go home."

This was a Mexican from a different level entirely, one of the class known as *meztanidos,* middle aristocrats who were trying to build the country into a real civilization.

"Hey, mister, who are you I wonder. You run this place? Maybe you want some like the same?"

He turned around very slow to the bartender, who was so fat his filthy apron bulged out like a jib-sail, placed a pair of saddlebags on the bar, and said, "I'll have a drink of mescal—no, not that bottle; the one you keep down below. That's it. Now rinse the glass out in fresh water." He tossed the drink off, and said, "Step out from behind."

"Hey, no, mister, I'm making a big joke. This is one friendly cantina. All friends—very fine fellows." Then, louder, "*Muchachos!* On the house—free drink for one damn fine fighter, you bet. You, too, mister. I like you fine."

I went over to the boy and said, "I'm sorry about your teeth." It made me feel guilty because, at that moment, I'd a knocked his eyes out with an equal lack of regard.

He shook his head, unable to speak.

"I really am sorry, but they made me—you saw how it was." I meant it this time. Seeing his disfigured face, with the handsome teeth gone for good, I felt low enough to walk under a snake.

Finally he said, "*Es nada.* I would have done the same." Then he said, in a tone so low and gritty and cold it made me shiver, "The worthless, thieving, murdering swine, I'll strike back some day. Gringo from the *Norte,* you hear me and remember it. This won't go on forever."

He sounded dead serious, but if I'd known then what he would later rise up to, and do for his country, I'd a stepped forward to shake his hand.

Then Pancho clapped on my chain, as rough and hurtful as ever, (being drunk), and off we paddled toward home, me sore and downcast, also resentful at the old women in the Plaza calling out their uncompliments about "Yankee invaders"—with some throwing stones in the bargain—till Pancho threatened to hit them with the chain, but happy to seem so important, all the same.

Well, he won so much money on the fight that he took me to see Angelina. She was sitting in a chair, fixed up like a woman, brazen and showy as ever—no underclothes, of course, and let you know it—and the young officer, name of Lieutenant Morales, arrived in a while with his bonehead interpreter. The man had on a pair of cheap-looking spectacles, now, and failed to bump anything important. He brought flowers—the officer, I mean. Then he commenced to talk about plans. Pancho went to sleep, leaning against a tent-pole, so it was all right. Nobody else was on hand. The fellow shot in the chest had died—of acute surgery, Angelina said—and the man with maggots on his arm rose up one day, stating that he was bored, particularly because Angelina declined to move her cot over beside his, and walked off. He hadn't come back, and on the way out, he said it was the poorest excuse of a hospital he'd ever heard of. He was some kind of high mucky-muck in his home province, so you couldn't blame him. But it caused a noisy commotion.

It was one of those cases where you have to see both sides. The surgeon was naturally in a temper over losing his best maggots, and tried to have the man arrested. He claimed that this was the primest crop he'd ever owned; he'd never seen fatter specimens, and had laid out considerable time and energy gathering them up from the officers' garbage dump. There was such a thing as ethics, he said, and when a patient skipped out with the doctor's costliest equipment, it might by God be brought to somebody's attention; it was poor ethics. He said it was a pity there wasn't a medical society around here, but Angelina said, yes, it was, and a few doctors to make up the membership, so that didn't help much. He was really sore. Another point was that he'd planned what he claimed would be a beautiful job on that arm. When the maggots got their fill, he aimed to take it off directly at the shoulder, and had borrowed a meat cleaver and a pruning saw for the purpose, greasing them up with pork rind. He'd even bought a bottle of aguardiente, out of his own pocket, as a pain-killer, and had a stocking full of sand standing by in case it didn't work.

Angelina needed to be whisked away from here fast, Lieutenant Morales said in a low voice. Already, during a feast, some officers had played monte for her, but the general changed his mind the next day. He said he was pondering the disposition of the prisoner, meaning he wanted her for himself, I reckon. Anyhow, Lieutenant Morales told us, looking sorrowful but proud, that he was in bad repute just now, and so was his father, because of their politics. His father had favored a real army career for him once, but nine or ten upsets of the government, each worse, had left him sucking hind tit, so to speak. They hadn't any influence any more, but he thought he might get detached to join the fighting below. His situation was so hopeless that—and here his eyes shone with defiance—he didn't at all mind stealing Angelina out of Parral and taking her south to his father's. If he got in trouble—well, one took risks. The big obstacle was that Central Mexico was in a state of riot and uproar; he doubted if he could get through by any of the direct routes. The roads and villages were filled by retreating army, deserters, and worse, and in a pretty scaly humor, too. Traveling south was dangerous, especially for a small group: there was no longer any way now even to keep the bandits down. But the chief threat was from the thousands of army men shaken loose from all discipline. "*Soldados!*" he said with a shrug, and that jackass of an interpreter repeated the word in English then gave precisely the same shrug.

As to me, there was nothing he could do; he had tried. But he slipped me (for Pancho was beginning to stir—from undigestion revolving around a pailful of peppers and four bottles of pulque) a paper with the name of his father, and the address, printed in the formal Spanish, with flourishes, underslung accents and all: DON ANTONIO MORALES, RANCHO CIÉNAGA GRANDE, CIUDAD MEXICO along with some additional directions and comments.

Then he leaned forward and said, "Tonight we shall leave for Durango, by an unimportant road that I know, then cross the mountains to Mazatlán, on the Gulf of Baja California. It will take many days. Do you understand?—*Mazatlán,*" and he spelled it out.

I told him I'd seen it on one of Blaine's maps.

"There will be no soldiers. I have friends who will see us to Mexico from there. Now, *muchacho,* you must escape. That is clear. *Travel by the same route to the place of my father. Entiende?*"

I said yes, but doubted it. Then came some protests from Angelina, a kind of argument, some tears, several impertinent hugs, and I was yanked back home. And then, three days later, I heard she was gone. In another day or so, somebody begun to put two and two together, but they couldn't prove anything, and besides, there were other problems more important.

I suddenly had all the trouble I could use, for one thing. Pancho's skull was so swoll up from winning that he staked all his money, every last real, against a boy which turned out to be more baboon than human. They carelessly gave out his age as seventeen, after counting his teeth, but I judged him to be about twenty-three, with a mind of around eight. Very tall for a Mexican, with coarse black hair growing low in front, deep-set eyes that had drifted over too close, a nose mashed flat, which may have improved it, and a mouth that hung ajar. I doubt if they could have closed it up with a vise. What's more, it looked *wet.*

His arms were very brawny excepting one that had a scar inside the elbow, where some flesh had been dug out by a knife, and he had an ugly hump on his back. I don't mean you would put him down as humpbacked; it was muscle, and lots of it. Somewhere in the scale, this fellow had wandered off the pattern, and I doubt if the smartest professor could tell you whether he'd come down from above or up from below. He *did* look like an ape; there wasn't any doubt of it.

They'd brought him in from a town named San Gregorio, which was glad to be rid of him, I judged.

Anyhow, from the minute they shoved us out, I knew I'd never handle him. That back was too strong; no matter what, it wouldn't bend. You get one like that once in a while.

Whilst I was darting around, trying to move him off his feet, he smacked me with the back of one hand. He made a wheeling motion, as if he was about to swing up into a tree, and I failed to see it coming. My left eye closed up, and this time I got mad. I hit him in the face with both hands, drove one fist up to my wrist in his stomach, hit him in the neck, which should have done the business, and then he knocked me down I had no idea where I was; the room whirled round and round and round. Dim, off in the background, I saw the bar, a row of bottles, crucifixes hanging on the walls, men's laughing faces, and the baboon grinning his wet grin.

When I got up, I smashed a copper spittoon into the area where his nose used to be. I shoved it as hard as I could, and hoped he would wear it as a permanent fixture, on the order of a second chin. He pried it off, slow and deliberate, still grinning, then knocked me down again. Altogether, I found out later, he knocked me down thirteen times. In the end, they poured a bucket of water over me, and I hadn't any recollection of stumbling home across the Plaza.

It was late afternoon before I came to, and I dislike to tell what happened. I was taking stock—all front teeth loose in their sockets, one eye closed and the other blacked, deep cuts on both cheek bones, bruises all over, my knuckles cut up bad, as many as two or three ribs cracked—I couldn't hardly move my arms, they hurt so—and, worst of all, my left ear bulged up red and wrinkly, like a cabbage. And then, at last, in lurched Pancho.

I never saw a man in such a rage, drunk or sober. His face was twisted like a lunatic's, spittle dribbled out of his mouth, and he screamed curses. Most of it concerned the loss of his *riqueza*—fortune!—which he said was in the nature of robbing his old mother and all of his children, including two, in Guanajuato, that were legitimate. I was too miserable to care, but he unlocked the chain at both ends, doubled it up and beat me to a pulp. I was really hurt. He'd a killed me, I reckon, if the people from below hadn't come up and calmed him. And the woman tiptoed up again, after dark, washed out my cuts with a rag, then daubed on some fluid that burned like the furies. She made a number of clucking noises, and murmured "*Pobre niño, pobre niño,*" sounding angry, but I was too sunk down to reply.

For two days I lay trying to recover some strength and assay what was busted; then Pancho showed up, jerked me up on my feet, and said we were going mining. Now that I'd *robbed* him of his inheritance, he said, it was necessary to accumulate some more property, to "keep the family together." This was hilarious because he'd once bragged that he had no idea who his father was but had narrowed it down, from his mother's conversation, to eight men, the most of them pickpockets, with one tailor, a jailer at the calabozo, a scissors grinder, a pimp, and a very successful practitioner that cured warts with a preparation made mainly from horse urine.

In any case, we headed out of town in mid-morning, him riding a burro, me walking, another burro trailing along with equipment. He'd borrowed or stole them, I supposed. The draft animal was piled so high with truck that it looked more like a giraffe than a donkey; it could hardly stagger. I was sick, besides being unable to walk without wobbling, and threw up several times in the first mile. Near Parral, as in most of high Mexico, gold could be found around any of the foothills. None of the big mines that scratched gold dust and earth, mixed, called *placeres,* or *placeres de oro,* were operating, but many of the poorer classes, known as *gambucinos,* worked small holdings on their own. The law was, that a man could open a *labor,* or pit, on any unoccupied ground ten paces away from another. As you might imagine, nobody took in very much—only enough dust to maintain life, with now and then a nugget to stir up their appetites and keep them on the job. The dust was virgin gold, worth $19.70 for the troy ounce, but the findings were so thin that, as a rule, people returned to town and cashed in every day. It was a shaky way to earn a living, but everybody agreed it was better than working, which seemed unsuited to the Mexican temperament.

Pancho said he knew a valley—*muy rico*—which nobody else had discovered, so we could gather up a fortune in about a week. Thinking it over, he said it might require ten days. When I sniffed, recognizing this for his usual rubbage, he tripped me up by yanking on the chain, then he dragged me along on my face through some cactus.

It was all right. As low as I felt, and I doubt if I had an inch free of bruises or cuts, I was lifted up, now, with a determination to escape and get even. This villain was fat, and out of condition, but a man can still lick a boy, so my only hope was to outwit him. However, I had an idea, so I bided my time. Except for a couple of ribs and the third knuckle of my right hand, nothing appeared to be broken; but that ear caused me concern. Instead of reducing, it kept getting bigger and redder and more wrinkled. It was embarrassing. Also, it itched. When I mentioned it to Pancho, he had a good laugh and said, "It stay like that all the time, I think. You sure one ugly son-of-a-bitch gringo."

We went to work mining, shoveling dirt from a ravine that led up to the mountains, then placing it in a *batea*, a round wooden bowl about eighteen inches in diameter. You dipped this in a pool of water then sloshed it around, after which the loose dirt floated off, letting the gold settle. Sometimes it took ten or twelve washings to arrive at the haul, and a bowlful generally coughed up twelve cents worth, on the average. No dignified man would have continued it over a few hours; he'd a taken up robbing banks, or murder, to get back his self-esteem.

Winter was the best time to mine, because the snows up above furnished water. Well, we worked three days, with me having trouble keeping food on my stomach, particularly Pancho's swill, and my ear itching more and more by the hour. If I stopped to scratch, or lay on a wet handkerchief, he gave it a playful cuff, to see me hop around and scream. He was a very humorous Mexican, and loved a good joke with the best of them. Commonly he supervised. That is, I did the digging, along with the filling up with water, and then the washing, as well as the heaving out of waste, fetching, carrying, cleansing of tools, and so on. During this, Pancho was never idle, but kept up a stream of critical oaths, speculation about my mother and sister, threats about what he meant to do with me eventually (since I didn't suit him as a miner), and emphasized his remarks by kicks, digs at my sore ribs, and mild little crowbar taps on my head.

On the third day, to Pancho's surprise, we encountered a horizontal shaft that ran twenty yards back into a foothill. In the tunnel were narrow wooden tracks and a rotted old cart they'd used to haul out the dirt. The roof was shored up with timbers. We entered and explored all around but found nothing of promise; whatever was there must have played out. But when noon came, with the sun hanging hot overhead, Pancho said we'd crawl into the cool for a siesta. He was kind of wore out from supervising. He said, besides, that there were no trees around here fit for a dog to lean on, and he was —— tired of laying asleep whilst sweating. He claimed it wasn't healthy, and said a sensitive person could catch consumption, or at least what he called "the snots" from breathing in the air from the snow patches. He was a main supporter of the siesta; he was higher on the practice than any Mexican I ever met, before or after. He said if he failed to get in two hours after his *almuerzo,* he was no good during the entire rest of the day. I agreed, and said he was of practically zero use in the mornings, too, but he whacked me on the ear with a leather dust pouch, so he had the last word as usual.

The tracks ran back to solid rock, where two iron rings were sunk into the wall, for pulleys, and he unlocked my chain from his wrist and fixed it to one of these. Then he arranged himself on some burlap, after taking a pull of mescal to settle his stomach, and fell immediately to snoring.

I waited ten minutes to be safe. He was smart enough to have that key tied around his neck by rawhide, rather than lying loose in his pocket, but I'd figured a step ahead. Back in Parral, after she doctored me, our landlady left a pair of scissors behind, and she forgot to return for them later. So—I waited.

Pretty soon the snores evened off, like a steamboat that's settled down for a long run—oiled up and steady, with a trifling amount of vibration—and I crept forward to even up the score. Now that the time had come, excitement had me sick again. My chest felt so tight, I knocked off breathing, to all intents and purposes. I remained black-and-blue, my front teeth were still loose (I reckoned they would fall out by and by), I had an ear that sent off heat waves in a rhythm, had a right hand as round as an India-rubber ball, and felt so sore in my sides, where the damaged ribs were, that it took several minutes to get me up on my feet.

One by one, careful and quiet, I snipped the two strands of rawhide. No movement; he was deep-down and had a kind of sweet little boy's smile on his face, as if he'd cracked somebody's shinbone with a maul. Now came the hard part, because these locks, being rusty, creaked like an old saggy iron gate that you see in an overgrown churchyard, where they've long ago filled up the space and moved to a new location. Finally I got the collar unhooked from my neck, covering it with my shirt to bottle up the sound. But it took half a dozen wobbly pokes to hit the hole with the key. I was shaking so, I was almost out of control.

Then—free! and I snapped the collar above his knee as fast as I could jump. One minute I was shackled tight, no better off than a slave, and the next he was a mole trapped in a run. The last part set up a racket like a boiler works, but the snoring only missed two or three licks, coughed, sputtered, backfired, then started off again in a smoother key. He was a champion sleeper; I admired him for it. His conscience was perfectly easy. If a thing bothered him, such as cutting somebody's throat in the dark and then finding out afterward it was his brother, he could always hunt up a priest and get it settled for fifty cents.

Anyhow, I looked him over, to be sure he hadn't any tools on him, slid his knife loose from his belt, picked up his hat, which might come in handy, took the tobacco, then carefully stepped off twelve paces—I must have measured it twenty or thirty times lately—and sat down on the cart. His machete and rickety old carbine were left outside by the burros, to keep me from grabbing them up on the sly. It was over, now, and I felt faint, so I held my head between my legs for awhile, till the blood restored my wits. I wanted to enjoy this. I'd worked for it, and didn't care to have anything spoil the occasion.

By and by, I picked up a pebble and tossed it at his stomach. Nothing doing. I tried one a size or so larger, with jagged edges; then, having a very satisfactory time, threw a chunk heavy enough to brain an elephant, just grazing his shoulder. The snoring was interrupted, and he reeled off a string of ordinary household oaths—nothing special; anybody could have done it—and made some motions to struggle up to the surface.

"Pancho," I called softly. "*Panchito mío.* I talking to you, *amigo.* You one damn dirty no-good lousy greaser. And you sure in one damn fine mess. What do you think, hey?"

He sat up, blinking. Then he shook his head like a dog, trying to throw off the sleep. He looked at the chain, running his gaze slowly up to the ring, let his mouth hang ajar, and after that put his hand to the snipped-off string. He had a lot of trouble taking in the situation.

Then he went absolutely insane. The fit he threw made his rage during the beating seem like a child's tantrum. I never saw a human being abuse himself so. He flung his body forward, wrenching to a stop three feet from my face, kicked out and missed, ran back and tried it again, nearly breaking his ankle, grabbed the ring and shook it, swung his weight from it, tried to bite it, scrabbled around in circles on the ground like a crab, yanked, jerked, tore the hide off his arm, screamed, cursed, babbled, and sobbed. I noticed that his face was blotchy and yellow; he was in no condition for this sort of thing. Then he tried the ring again, beating it with both fists until some soil trickled down from the ceiling.

The crazy fool scared me—for a second, I thought that ring *might* pull free—so I ran outside and returned with the carbine. Then I sat back down on the cart, all serene, and watched him sprawl in the dust, panting.

"You have a good time, *amigo?* You not give more beatings soon with chain, maybe. You one damn lousy stupid greaser. I say it again so you hear it good."

He sat staring for a long time, getting his wind back, and then, by Jupiter, I'm an Apache if he didn't begin to laugh. He wasn't putting on, either; he laughed till he held onto his sides. It was the curiousest race I ever struck. Under many conditions, they could be as cowardly as rats, but they faced death in the sunniest possible humor. From first to last, I never saw one cringe when his time came. This murderous old ruffian had studied me over and concluded that begging was useless. He knew exactly what he would do if things were reversed. So he shrugged and forgot it.

"You stinking gringo thief steal my tobacco."

I tossed him the pouch and the corn shucks. Against my better judgment, I filled a bowl with water, too, and shoved it forward with the gun.

"Well," I said, not too brash all of a sudden, "I've got to be going. You know how it is."

"You certainly one dirty son-of-a-bitch gringo," he called down the tunnel, laughing. But before I'd reached the mouth, he was cursing in earnest again.

XXIV

Working fast, I packed one burro and saddled the other. Throwing the mining tools in a gulch, I took along the gun, the machete, the sleeping ponchos, and the food, and that was about all. I needed Pancho's boots, but I wouldn't have gone back in that tunnel for a deed to Mexico City.

The day was clear and thin and silent, like most days on this mile-high plateau, and I struck out at the southerly slant over the low, gray, clumpy, dull, dry, twisted growth. Now and then you saw lizards, or iguanas, fat and scaly, but no small game, not even a rabbit, and you got used to the vultures soaring overhead. After an hour or so, I came to a stream and stopped to dirty my face with red mud; I rubbed it in hard and hoped it would stick. Under the wide sombrero, I could pass for anything, I reckoned; leastways, my hair was long enough, and my clothes were nothing but ragged skins, neither Mexican nor American.

I settled down to watch the sun, remembering Captain Hobbs' lessons, and thanking the good Lord for them, because I wanted to strike the back route to Durango near Talaca, well below Parral, and avoid getting nabbed again by the Army. I did it, too—came in four miles above the town, on a road that hadn't any traffic except an occasional burro piled eight feet high with sticks, with a ragged, stony-faced peasant slouching along behind, swinging a machete. I put on Pancho's smelly old poncho, and pulled my hat down, then called out "*Buenas tardes*" a few times, but attracted no more than hard looks, so I gave it up.

And in Talaca I grew downright uneasy. Maybe you know how it is in those backwater Mexican towns—whitewashed buildings crowding in on cobbled streets, a few open doors showing nothing inside but some religious posters on the walls, with maybe a girl or two sewing; donkeys and goats and dogs everyplace you step, peddlers selling *tacos* out of carts, women squatting in doorways patting tortillas, and others suckling brats slung in rebozos, men loafing around in clusters, talking and scratching and spitting; and then, as you move along, hoping not to get a knife in your back, the street opens up into a broad, pretty Plaza, built around a startling big church (with barefoot women standing in the doors, begging), nice flower beds, and iron benches beneath leafy fig trees (but full of birds, too, so that you'd better be careful where you sit). And always in the air, very strong, the sweetish-bitter mixture of tortillas baking, manure, peppers stewing in pots, urine, and red-petaled flowers blooming in the parks.

There were soldiers in the Plaza, so I passed on through, trying not to hurry and hiding my carbine under one trouser leg. They broke off talking and stared, and one said something that made the others laugh, but I failed to catch the humor of it. And then, sure enough, a group of swarthy roughnecks collected in a side street I entered. One held up a hand, to stop, and another cried, "*No venta!*" pointing at the burros.

Well, I'd been there before, so I made a quick decision and swung up the gun. I saw no profit in talking things over; there *may* have been some way to prove I owned those animals, but it didn't occur to me right off. Facing the gun, they looked as surprised as if the burros had spoken out like Balaam's ass.

"*Vamos!*" I said, and meant it. They washed back, shocked and hurt that somebody should take this illegal way of warding off a theft, but not anxious to get shot, either. Then one shouted a threat about fetching the alcalde, but I replied, cocking the gun, "The first he-goat that leaves gets a bullet in the back of his head. Right away, *muy pronto*. Now *vamos!*" and gestured down the street. They scrambled off in a hurry, and I laid into the forward burro with a stick. The penalty for horse stealing around here was the firing squad, as like as not, and I had any number of things I wanted to do.

No place to hide on the road near town, no abandoned hut, no grove or high patch of cane, so I humped along, darting glances back over my shoulder and feeling mighty exposed. And then, praise the Lord, if there didn't show up one of those blessed green rivers, with yellow sandbars sticking out and banks concealed by cottonwoods and willows. I clop-clopped over the usual rattletrap bridge and turned off sharp to the right, heading down the slope. Some women were winding up their laundry where the bar made out, but nobody saw me; I was in the clear. So I tethered the burros in the thicket by the water, then returned with a branch and smoothed out my hoofmarks. I did the job thorough, and no sooner finished than a squad of army horsemen came careening around the bend, riding sort of sidewise, pretty as a picture. With the prospect of an execution in sight, they seemed in the best of spirits, and were making lots of noise.

I crouched below the bridge till they passed, then crept on down to my burros. Later on, I heard them return, droopy and crestfallen, and one man said, while scratching underneath, "*Léperos* tell a damn big lie, I bet," and another, brightening up, suggested they could take turns beating them with sabers; it was better than no entertainment at all. I hoped so.

After dark, I gathered driftwood sticks and made a small fire, sheltering it with sand. I boiled some Indian meal and water and swallowed it, then boiled some more water to drink. I fed the burros, filled my canteen, slept a few hours, and got out on the road long before dawn, of a stinging cold morning.

When day came, I had a piece of luck. A few miles farther, at the crossing of another river, I encountered an *atajo,* or drove of pack mules, which had bogged down after an accident. One of the *arrieros*—muleteers—had waded out to get water and stepped into a pothole. He couldn't swim any more than a petrified goat can, so they fished him out, a hundred yards downstream, held him up by the heels, shook him, rolled him on a log, placed some lighted tapers to his feet, which failed to twitch, then poured a quantity of aguardiente down his throat. One of the men thought he'd detected signs of life before this, but the liquor finished it. He never moved a muscle afterwards; gave up completely.

Well, these men were friendly, and they needed a replacement. I told them my story as complete as I could, said I was headed for Durango to join my father, who sold mining equipment, having just delivered an order to Guadalupe. Nobody questioned it, though they knew perfectly well I was lying. Mud or no mud, I didn't bear inspection close up; my towhead looked about as Mexican as a Swede, and my story had a few general flaws, besides.

They were a rough and ready bunch, full of good humor, on the order of our Missouri teamsters, and maybe it was because they did a man's work. I've noticed that, broadly speaking, people who do hard things are five or six times the size of ones that don't bother. It takes out the scratchiness, somehow.

One says:

"This father of yours, *amigo*. How is he called?"

"Juan Madero," I spoke up promptly (I'd noticed it on a building front in Talaca).

"Small man with a scar on his left cheek, stout, with one leg shorter than the other? Has a funny way of talking, as if he'd swallowed a gourd?"

"Yes," I answered, not caring to elaborate on such a lunatic remark.

"We grew up together. We've been brothers. He is the godfather of my eleven children. Juan Madero," he said to the others.

"With the mining equipment?"

"I never go to Durango without calling at his store. Sometimes, if I'm sober, I go in twice. Juan Madero would cut off his right arm for me."

"If there was any justice, he would be President of Mexico today. Also, he could have risen high in the clergy."

One came up and shook my hand, saying,

"You have a very wonderful father, boy. Remember it, and act accordingly." He thought a second, then said, "He saved my life once."

Another remarked that, yes, in the forty years he'd known Juan

Madero, it was the only mean thing he'd ever done, so they veered off on that tack for awhile. It was all right with me; I'd as soon they let the subject drop.

They made me the *savanero,* which is the easiest job in the atajo, though you get little or no sleep. At night the mules were turned loose without tether or hopple, and I was supposed to keep track. In a region where good grass is so sparse you can't raise a cricket on ten acres, it wasn't easy; still and all, I had help, and good help, too. The *mulera,* or bell-mare, was on hand to keep them from straying. I couldn't make up my mind whether it was the bell or the mare that fetched them. Either way, it worked like a queen bee in a hive. No matter what kind of a disposition a mule has—sour, as a rule—it gets down in the mouth if the bell-mare wanders very far. I saw it happen once; the pack commenced to whinny and ramble off in every direction—rattled completely.

Well, this atajo was organized as tight as an army, and in the case of a Mexican Army, considerably tighter. The arrieros may have been frolicsome, but they knew their jobs. One man, called the *madre* for some reason, was cook of the expedition; he also led the mulera ahead during the day. It suited me fine. During the average night, I'd had enough of her to carry over for a week or more. Commonly I rode my burros and dozed, falling off now and then. At these times the muleteers would pick me up gravely, with comments about how dangerous such animals were, while making ridiculous jumps and feints to dodge the hoofs, which might have been nailed to the ground, for all they ever moved without flogging. Not one time did they indicate that I'd gone to sleep and taken a spill; no, they preferred to throw all the blame on the burros. They themselves were mounted on mustangs that went by the name of *caballos de sillas,* or, roughly, saddle horses, which were trained so expert you wouldn't believe it. They'd haul up dead still at the slightest check, charge against a wall without shrinking, and even attempt to clamber up its sides. I saw it with my own eyes.

Traveling over miserable country, we had our most trouble with the *aparejos*—pack saddles—which fell off as regular as breathing. There *wasn't* any way to keep them shipshape. A continuous battle went on between the mules and the arrieros. An aparejo is a big pad consisting of a leather case stuffed with hay, and covers the mule's back, extending halfway down on both sides. The men secure this with a sea-grass bandage, lacing it up so tight the mule's body is reduced down to about half its normal size. It sounds cruel, but when the *carga,* or load (in this case grain for the Army at Durango) is laid on, the bandages soon loosen up and require tightening again. In our case, a single mule carried three hundred pounds, but didn't seem happy about it. The interesting part was that when an aparejo tumbled off, the rest of the train continued right on. What's more, the arriero in that section replaced it while on the move. If he stopped, the mule lay down, then, customarily, arose when the notion seized it, though not necessarily the same day. You might hoist one back up with a bomb, but I doubt it.

Ordinarily our *jornada de recua,* or day's run, was fifteen miles, spread over a six-hour period without rest. You can't rest a mule, he goes directly out of whack and stays there. Well, sir, I begun to enjoy myself for the first time in weeks. It wasn't a bad life, and I doubt if those wild men would have chosen any other. Pulling up after a hitch, they removed the aparejos, stacked them in rows on the ground, covered them over with *mantas de guangoches,* which were weatherproof sheets of sea grass, then dug a ditch around the whole, in case it rained. They worked hard, and their skill was a marvel to all. They had a means of lifting the most astonishing loads, by leverage, using their knees and thighs and hips, often swinging a carga far up over their heads—one you couldn't budge from a dead lift. Half a dozen arrieros took care of forty to fifty mules, and none required more than five minutes to adjust a pack in the morning. As hard as they worked, they had a good time, telling lies and roughhousing around the campfire, and they slept like mummies. It was remarkable when you consider that they lived entirely off corn and frijoles, on a salary of less than two dollars a month.

Me, I wasn't sleeping very well. That Pancho was on my mind, and when a mule train hove in sight going the opposite direction, I drew off the leader for a chat. Then I gave him a packet containing the key and a letter I'd been composing off and on.

He promised to deliver it to Army Headquarters in Parral, and he refused to accept a peso I held out. I quit worrying, then. If he'd took it, I reckoned he'd a thrown the packet in a gully, muleteer or not.

The letter was smartly written, if I say so myself, and was spelled out in prime, top-quality Spanish. It told how the undersigned, Pedro Mateos, a reformed bandit, had stumbled across a wormy-looking Mexican soldier—a disgrace to his profession—and a handsome, intelligent boy of America del Norte whilst wandering around in the hills, and got in a fight when the soldier tried to pick his pocket. In the scuffle, a rifle went off and shot the boy, which was buried, so they could forget about *him*, but it made the undersigned so mad (wasting a promising young person like that) that he chained up the soldier in a tunnel. I gave the location as best I could, and told about our tools in the gulch. I hoped the Army would release the soldier, as worthless as he was, and then hang him on general principles.

It wasn't any bad letter. I was proud of it; it had a sincere, modest ring, though stretched some here and there, and it didn't do a thing for Pancho. After that my conscience was clear, and I got back to sleeping now and then. That is, I doubted if the Army would take the trouble, and even if they did it was likely too late, but I'd done *my* part, and that always makes a person feel good.

My injuries were mostly healed up now, except for my ear, and, less bothersome, my ribs, which had three lumps that I judged would remain on. The swelling in my hand went down; the knuckle wasn't broken after all. The chief arriero, whose name was Lopez, inspected the ear and said I had a very bad case of leprosy, but he said he knew an Indian family down the road that made a specialty of such diseases—they'd cured all the lepers in this area—and he'd get me treated when we arrived.

Well, the Indian woman made a poultice from materials I won't mention, and strapped it on with reeds. I figured the rest of my head would rot and drop off, but the ear was perfectly sound in three days. A puckery look remained, but I didn't mind that.

We sloped along toward Durango, over dull, straight, empty roads with a kind of purple shale on each side. But mainly it was desert, which gave way at last to fair grazing land, with horses galloping on open range. The adobe huts we encountered were tidier than before, and the men standing over the dry-stick fires had on better serapes. Often you saw windmills pumping water, ever so graceful, and far off, lavender mountains lay piled up dim and misty. Sooner or later, I judged, I'd have to come to grips with that ridge; it made a solid wall, sleepy and forbidding, all across the horizon.

The arrieros were fine fellows, easy and informal and enjoyable. They hadn't any nerves, and I saw one asleep toward dawn with a scorpion stretched over his face. This region near Durango stood knee-deep in scorpions. I woke a man up and pointed, but he only laughed, saying they made a perfect pair.

Clear into Durango they continued the monkeyshines about my father, speculating on how he'd got to be so superior, nights when we sat by the fire. To tell you the truth, it grew slightly boring; I wished I'd given out my name as Brannigan, or Spignoli, or Eisenblatz.

One said, "There was a General Madero with the great Cortez. Blood will tell."

And another chimed in, "He won all the important battles, though others tried to take the credit. The priests spoke often of it in my childhood."

"Yes, it was that which gained him the title—"

"The Duke of Madero," broke in Lopez, tearing off some ribs of roast kid, "became noted for his benefactions to the poor. He nearly expended all of a vast fortune, but his good sense won out in the end. One assumes," he said to me, "that you have witnessed the family statue before the Palacio in Mexico City."

"Many times," I said. "My father takes me to see it whenever things get slack in the mining-equipment business."

There was a murmur of approval all around, with expressions of, "To be sure; that's what he would do," and "How typical!" and, "Juan Madero would never deny his heritage." And that same busybody which stuck his nose in before said, pretty severe, "You have a good deal to live up to, boy. Some days I think you will, some I don't. My advice is—get a grip on your collar!"

I trotted out the bell-mare and went to see about the atajo. As much as I enjoyed these arrieros, there were times when I preferred mules.

All the same, that night, on the outskirts of the city, they produced some irons and vented both of my burros, saying they knew it was only an oversight and that my father would appreciate it, being as honest as the day was long, or words to that effect.

We went into Durango, and I told them goodbye. When Lopez paid me my wages—twelve reales, (adding another four as an afterthought)—he looked me over slow, a little different from before.

"Where do you go now, *muchacho?*"

"Why," I said, suddenly homesick, "to my father's. You remember—Juan Madero."

"And if you *didn't* go there, supposing there had been an accident in the family?"

"Well, Mazatlán."

He said, "Ah, so," and I wandered on down the street, leading my burros again. But not before he'd handed me a note made out to "Don Jorge," with an address, and told me, practically *ordered* me, to call on him at once. I nodded, seeming abstracted, and turned away. Maybe I'd been in Mexico too long, but I'd come to the point where I disliked to trust *anybody.*

This Durango was handsome, better than anything yet, though maybe it only seemed so, because of the friendly arrieros. The population—upwards of twenty thousand—lived on an irrigated level plain, with low mountains close at hand now. There were fine squares and churches, and open aqueducts ran alongside the streets. They came from big springs about a mile out of town. But the aqueducts were filthy from the offal that people threw in, so the inhabitants bought water from *aguadores,* who toted it in by donkeyback.

I was far enough south now that I commenced to see tropical fruits for sale in the markets—mangoes and papayas and bananas —and the maguey season was booming along at its peak. A hundred or more shanties were loaded with jugs and goblets of liquor that ranged from sweet-unfermented to stuff the strength of hard cider, and shopkeepers on all sides cried, *"Pulque! pulque dulce! pulque bueno! El mejor pulque aquí!"* You couldn't hardly hear yourself talk for the noise from the stalls. Still and all, you seldom saw a man drunk.

The scorpion season was also in good shape, and people had mosquito bars rigged in their houses, to keep from being bit. The pests resemble a big hairy spider, with a jointed, two-inch tail that carries a poisonous stinger at the end. Children often die from the bite, and adults can be made powerful sick.

The situation this year was so raw that a society had been formed to strike back. A *cuartillo* (three cents) was being paid to anybody bringing in a scorpion, known as an *alacrán*, and the idle boys of Durango—that is, the majority of the boys in town—were hard at it searching through garden beds and trash heaps. I could have accumulated considerable money if I'd had time.

The odd thing was, these scorpions lost their venom farther north, and became harmless even a few miles out of the city. It did appear to me that it might be Durango that was poisonous, but I refrained from saying so. Towns get mighty stiffish and prideful, I've noticed, organizing clubs and bodies that they feel outshine the clubs in other towns, and you can hurt their feelings before you know it.

I gave some thought to "Don Jorge," and concluded to look him up; it wouldn't cost anything, and I could examine him over before I spoke. Well, he turned out to be a free Negro from southern Illinois, with thick woolly hair and gaudy Mexican clothes, including a sword and a frilly satin vest, and a big bunch of chains jingling from his belt—the pompousest old blister I ever met—and he took me in hand as if he'd bought me at auction. I'd found him in his house (which seemed prosperous) sitting behind a rich mahogany desk. There were shelves full of papers sticking out, and memorandums, and notices stuck on spikes, and documents beneath glass weights on the desk—making him look busier than the King of Abyssinia. Oddly enough, he was the first darky I ever met that didn't belong to somebody as a slave.

On that subject, he said, "Where you from, where you live at when you ain't botherin Mexican gennelmun, white boy?"

I says, "Missouri, in Clay County."

"Yore pappy own slaves?"

I said yes, he had quite a few, the primest in the state.

"You get rid of them slaves, hear? If they ain't sot free, I'll know it."

I said I'd mention it the minute I got home. He had on ridiculous gold eyeglasses, which he couldn't see through, I judged, for he took them off then stared me over with an expression less painful. After this he read the note again. Then he put on a fancy sombrero and said, "You my responsibility, an what you need's a dawg, against them bandits up in the mountains. But that ain't *all* you need."

Well, sir, in the next hour, he took me to the customs house, burros and all, and browbeat a *guía,* or passport for merchandise, out of a clerk, endorsing it, according to law, as "Don Jorge," with several loops and flourishes, then got a number of extra *pases,* which required no endorsement, in case I wanted to "do some smuggling." And after that he conducted me to the elegant parlor of a house where the mistress, a beautiful woman of about thirty-five, received us very warm and hospitable, kissing Don Jorge on the mouth. She didn't appear to be in any hurry about it, either. To me she paid no attention whatever. He inquired about her husband, who she said was well, but absent, and gave him another kiss, this time trying to make up for the enthusiasm she slacked on the first round. Then her two daughters, which were more beautiful still, came downstairs, and *they* kissed him, one after the other. They threw themselves into it in a style that made the mistress seem stale and old-fashioned; even so, she looked on with the natural pride of a mother that's done a good job of bringing up two fine girls. For a minute, I thought they might cart him upstairs, then divide him amongst the three of them. I never saw such a house; my face was beet-red, but afterwards I found out that Negroes are very strong in demand among the ladies in this part of Mexico.

The mistress invited Don Jorge to sit down (only she called him "Señor Don Jorge") still making no mention of me, which appeared to embarrass him, so he said we'd come for a dog and we'd maybe better hike along with our business. He explained that I was an escaped murderer, and must slide out to Mazatlán ahead of the police, which they understood very well. Seeming sympathetic, they apologized for not buckling down right off.

Behind the house, in a walled-up pen with separate runs, they had ten or twelve giant hounds, mottled gray-and-white, and if noise was any consideration, a person would sooner take his chances with a boa constrictor. The entire pack showed its good nature by trying to get at my throat, and very nearly did—that wall could have used some more bricks, in my view.

"See here," I said to Don Jorge, "I'm not so sure I *want* a dog. And besides, there isn't any proof that these *are* dogs. I'd require a few documents. They look more like lions."

He paid no attention, so the mistress said to a boy lounging about, "Bring out Bollo," and he foolishly prepared to do so—an animal with a yellowish tinge, weighing in the neighborhood of a hundred and fifty pounds. The dog curled back its lips, showing terrible long fangs, then growled savage and low, and laid its ears flat to its head.

All right, I says to myself, if this is the way they feed their dogs, it's none of my business; a boy more or less won't make much difference around *here*, but there's no need for me to get mixed up in it. When I turned to leave, Don Jorge stuck his face down and says, "White boy, I tell you you need a dawg, you *need* a dawg. Bandits take and slit your gullet in de nighttime, else."

"Bring him out," I said, and figured I could get a wooden leg. Any number of people were using them in Mexico, and making out perfectly well. Well, sir, the boy snapped a chain to its collar without a hitch, and hauled it up within range.

"Pet de dawg," said the Negro, and the women nodded, happy and excited, like people toward the finish of a bullfight.

"No," I said, "I appreciate it, but there's no sense to bother. Just fetch out a saw. It'd be simpler to saw something off and hand it over. You could save all the preliminaries that way, and—"

"*Pet* de dawg!"

I gave a last look to my hand, which had been useful, and laid it on the dog's head. It quivered for a moment, then quit growling, uncurled its lips, and walked up to rub against my thigh. It nuzzled me, almost knocking me over, and wagged its tail.

"*Ain't* dat a relief!" cried Don Jorge. "Dawg tuk to you right off. It's a curious breed. An he *didn't* favor you, I spec he'd bit a big hole out of your stomick."

I tried to pay the woman's price, which was five dollars, but the Negro paid it himself, then complained about it all the way down the street. He said I'd imposed on him something awful, and said that, now he was a Mexican gentleman, he couldn't stand people from America del Norte, particularly white people, and especially smart-alecky boys. But when we got abreast of the main church, which stood back to our right toward the Mazatlán road, he wrinkled up his sooty forehead and acted perplexed.

"De point is, you ain't got no *bizness* travelin at road alone. It's abnormal and dangersome. It apt to lay on my conscience."

He said the family that freed him had a son about my age, or a little younger, and he never met a worse nuisance. The boy gave him nothing but trouble; he was glad to get shut of him. Then he says: "Yore pappy run a plantation—stylish, with quality folks cavortin aroun in fine clothes, the way they do?"

I told him yes, and it appeared to make him mad.

"*Ain't* you a sight!—nothin but rags. An one ear looking like it chawed by a bear." He said the lowest thing on earth was somebody that disgraced his family, and stated that it was none of his concern; that, in fact, he'd as lief I was captured by bandits, and eaten, except that Lopez had been pretty good to him, which was the only reason he'd bothered this far. Then he said, taking off his sombrero and wrinkling up his forehead some more, "Maybe you jes trot along back till de time come to 'scape. Dis *ain't* de time, an if it was I'd say so. It'll rub agin my grain to have white folks in de house of a Mexican gennelmun, but it ain't goin be for long, so don't argue."

I thanked him and shook his hand, and he gave me a kind of embrace (or maybe only cuffed my shoulder) then recovered in indignation but stood looking on as I led my burros and the dog off down the road. Presently I turned and waved, and he shouted, "You write me a letter soon as you gits in Mazatlán, hear?" And added, "That Lopez, he'll want to know."

He was a mighty nice man; you run into such now and then, and in the strangest places. Still, I was glad to walk free of the city, which was full of roistering soldiers, along with miners. This place was headquarters for prospectors headed up toward the hills, which were rich with gold, and some hard-faced characters loitered about in the parks, interested and bold. Too friendly, if you know what I mean. But Lopez had warned that strangers asking questions were apt to be bandits seeking information to rob you later, so I shrugged and kept moving when anybody tried to approach. Frankly, nobody seemed over-anxious to make the acquaintance of my dog Bollo, though he appeared willing to get to know *them*. He was a good companion; I was glad to have him along.

Well, when the road wound out of town, past the trees and the last houses, and started on a slow upgrade and rounded a curve into a lonely spot, some men stepped out from behind the bushes and stood waiting. I knew it; I had a feeling things were going too well.

One now moved forward, and it was Lopez. I wondered if they'd only put off murdering me, then felt guilty for being so suspicious. Still and all, I wasn't sure. But I told the dog to be quiet, then faced them with my heart thumping a little.

"*Amigo,* I wonder why you go to Mazatlán. These are very high Sierra Madre mountains, and the road is not so good, you know."

You could take it either way. I couldn't get the suspiciousness out of my bones, so I muttered something and hung on.

Lopez looked me over, and said, "You have one mule's head, *amigo,* but you'll need more than a poncho—very, very cold on the Sierra Madre mountains," and he handed me one of those thick Saltillo serapes, with blending rainbow colors. It wasn't new, but it was in good shape, even so.

I gulped, ready to sink down with shame, and another stepped forward with a packet of dried goat meat, saying, "Savaneros are not truly arrieros, my friend, but it is necessary to eat, all the same. Especially in the high altitudes."

A third had a flint-and-steel, in case my matches got wet; another turned over a spyglass with nothing but the copper dress bands missing—"to see the *bandidos* approaching at a great distance, and thus avoid them"; one gave me a new pair of huaraches—the exact right size, too; and others tied onto my pack burro a rubber sheet, several loads for my carbine, a curious present consisting of a ratty old book about Australian birds, written in English ("It is of much importance for a *Mexican* to improve the education"—the words issuing from a grave, serious face), and a bottled remedy for a bathroom ailment that the owner referred to as "Montezuma's vengeance."

After all this, instead of letting me thank them, these roughnecks went through an idiotic pretense that I was leaving because my father had died. They were cut up about it, and said so. The confounded fools came within an ace of affecting *me*—getting me sorrowful and downcast over somebody that hadn't ever existed in the first place. Drat the imbeciles, I'd taken that name off a store front.

"One presumes to grieve with you, *amigo*," said Lopez. "An unexpected tragedy, and, I think, *avoidable*. The question of foul play comes to mind."

Others shoved in their two cents' worth.

"A very great loss. And a sad, sad day for Durango," but a third corrected this, saying, "*All* of Mexico mourns. The type of death was loathsome. And one asks, who will arise to take his place? Juan Maderos scarcely grow on bushes, I imagine."

Then the saphead that was always advising me stepped up and delivered *his* crusher, first stating that it was a pity I'd miss the funeral, as it promised to be the most ornamental in the history of Durango. He said the Pope was going to attend, if he could get here on time. The dunce was wearing a black arm band.

"It's up to you to take his place, boy. You're the last of a long and charitable line. Can you do it? Does it place a strain? I haven't made up my mind yet. It takes a while; I'm slow to jump."

I said I'd try, and they shook my hand, solemn, every one. Then, a little way down the hill, they commenced to laugh, nearly busting themselves open, and, finally, so did I.

"*Hasta luego, muchacho!*" cried Lopez, waving his hat, and I stood there, too heavy again to think of anything clever.

The road begun to go up and up and up, winding around, and presently, looking back, I saw the town spread out far below in the afternoon sun, the roofs brown with tile or adobe, church turrets rising over everything, smoke curling up from wood fires, open spaces here and there like patches—where parks were, you know—and leafy green trees marching along the streets in soldier files, but seeming very small, like potted plants.

All growth played out as I pushed higher, and by and by nothing but shale was in sight anywhere you turned. I kept going till dark, riding and walking—resting the burros—then removed a distance to one side, ate a cold supper, fed and watered the animals, and turned in, tying the dog near my feet. Up early and started climbing again. It was wearisome; a person might think he'd *never* get to the top of those piled up ridges. Towards noon I passed a gray shingle shed, without signs of life, and shortly after this the grass came back, and after it nice thick bushes, and then, trees. The country begun to take on a pasturey look, rich and fertile.

A peasant crossed the road with upwards of a hundred goats, and later I encountered a dead burro lying by a gully. The remainders of its load—firewood, piled too high as usual—lay half scattered, and the animal was still warm. Dropped dead from exhaustion, likely; you saw it all over Mexico. I thought, Why not feed the dog? He can use it, and the burro won't miss it in the condition he's in. So I cut off a haunch, dripping with blood but lean, because of overwork, and Bollo tucked into it like a sailor saved from an island. Then I haggled off another and saved it for later. Though not cold in that thin, bright sunlight, the air was cool enough to keep it for awhile.

On the fifth day, nine thousand feet high, the country flattened out with solid green valleys and streams and giant trees on the order of beeches and handsome pines growing thick on the knolls. It was lovely but odd, because in most mountain places, the trees grow down *below*, with nothing but gray baldy rocks up above. No snow here, nor any sign of snow; we could have been in a deer park.

I was high enough for wispy white clouds to drift past directly against my face. Shut in like a fog bank, one minute, then everything open to show the sky deep blue and the sun lighting and warming and coloring the greenery beneath it. So far, I'd encountered one person, but like most peasants, he'd minded his own business—never even glanced my way—so I judged I *looked* like a Mexican by now, long as I kept on my hat. My face was burned brown, I wore Mexican clothes, I drove two sorry-looking burros, and made a practice of smoking a cigarrito now and then. It didn't appear to cause harm, and was a comfort to me all around. After the days with the arrieros, I could speak, and *understand,* the language, and realized I hadn't been quite so fluid, before.

Well, the scenery here was so lush, and the provender so ample—acres and acres of high grass for burros and icy clean water in the streams—that my spirits rose up the way they were back with Blaine and Colonel Doniphan. It seemed a long time ago. But I'd commenced to feel, now, that I really *would* get out of this mess, and wondered what nationality of ships put in at Mazatlán. So far, no signs of bandits, and I enjoyed a good laugh over the way those arrieros gave me such a fright.

That night, reaching what was called "The Devil's Backbone," which was the highest point—a steep, dizzy place that begun to look treacherous and craggy—I relaxed and made a fire. I mixed up some 'tole, baked three tortillas on a stone, and ate two ribs of dried kid, washing it down with water from a spring. I had a real feed, and needed it. Lying down to sleep, I felt happier than I'd been for weeks. But Lopez was right about the weather up here; without that Saltillo serape, I might not have made it at all. The cold was so fierce I added the rubber sheet to wrap up in all around.

Well, way off in the night sometime, dull and groggy with sleep, I heard Bollo growl; then a hullabaloo broke out that practically stopped my blood flowing. My campfire was burned down to embers, but I saw four fat, swarthy figures leap out from the trees, cartridge-filled bandoleers crossed over their breasts, carrying guns and showing knives at their belts, and charge down with a whoop to stir up a churchyard. They'd worked a surprise like a tiger that roars to paralyze a deer. It was almost successful; I couldn't of moved a muscle. But they'd made one mistake, and that was failing to see the dog, which was stretched out beside me. Then Bollo arose, all teeth showing and the short fur stiffened from head to foot, sprang forward, jerking out his peg, soared up off the ground, and snapped his jaws shut on the face of the fellow running in front. I heard the crunch of meat and bones, and closed my eyes for a second. He let out a scream, another started a sentence with "*Madre mía—*" and then I was up on my hands and knees. I shot the nearest man in the stomach—he dropped his gun to grab himself with both hands—and seized my machete. But the fight was over.

Yelling and cursing, they scrambled out, two helping the man with the crushed face, and the dog worrying them right on down the mountain. When he returned, half an hour or so later, he had a machete cut, deep and ugly, behind his right shoulder. I hugged him, and called him a lot of pet names, and he licked me pretty thorough on the face. Then I recalled that his mouth had just recently been crunching bandits, but I couldn't bring myself to care.

And now I had a disagreeable chore, so I turned to the man I'd shot. He was sitting against a tree, still holding his stomach. His hat was lying on the ground by his side. All the color had gone out of his face. I threw a stick on the fire, tied the dog, and walked over, queasy in my insides; scared as well.

"Water, *hermano.*"

I said, "You're not supposed to. Your friends will be back before long."

"Tobacco, then. Jesus Christ son-of-a-bitch if you're too stinking stingy for tobacco!"

I placed a cigarrito between his lips and lit it, and after that he pulled out a pistol and tried to shoot me, but the ball passed harmlessly up through the trees.

Call it cowardly, but I hadn't any wish to see him die—I felt poorly enough already—so I assembled my traps fast, held tight to Bollo, and pushed out of that pleasant little valley. His curses followed all the way; I heard them a long distance down the road, and sometimes I hear them yet.

Going down was the hard part. Climbing up had been gradual, almost in the nature of an outing. Now the green grass and shrubbery and trees gave way to gorges and chasms and tumbled-up rocks, shadowed and gloomy, covered with creepers and vines, and jagged cliffs that fell off for thousands of feet straight down. The road was narrow—hardly more than a goat's path—it made your head reel to walk it. I'd start a stone that bounced on over the edge, then seconds ticked by before it struck, the sound drifting up hollow and faint. I passed the Palisades, looking like castles of rock, awesome and sheer, and kept going down, down, down, steep and windey and tiresome. The trees thinned out to scrub, then, lower still, daisy-like yellow flowers appeared, and after that, on the low slopes, where a tropical feeling commenced, orange air plants grew like a carpet in the ravines. I saw a few deer, very tiny and sure-footed, and one afternoon, rounding a sharp turn, surprised a tiger-cat the size and design of a leopard. It lay sunning on a rock in the sun, then, startled and maybe a little peeved, bounded from rock to rock to the protection of growth far above. He needn't have bothered. I wouldn't have harmed him; I'd sooner picked a fuss with a cottonmouth, but I had to hold Bollo, just the same.

In the course of days, the road wound by a few dinky villages, El Salto, Saucito, Palmito, Presidio—perched high on dark-shaded ledges—but they appeared so poverty-struck I kept going. Also, they were just faintly hostile. The huts were no more than sticks laid against a rickety frame of limbs, with thatched roofs, and the men standing around gazed silent and hungry at my burros. The women—cooking outside or pounding laundry in a stream—seemed surlier than those on the plateaus. One made a gesture of spitting, slow and contemptuous, looking me over, but it failed to disturb me. I spit back, just as offensive. She called something shrill to her husband, but he only shrugged, pointing to the dog. It was funny; I would have swore he was one of the bandits. I stopped, staring deliberately, and he turned away. As primitive as it was, Mexico still had police, or anyway *rurales,* and they bore down rough on *bandidos.* Generally they shot them on suspicion, and worked up a case later on.

Often I encountered big gravelly holes in the earth, where people had searched for gold, but I never came upon miners, during the whole hundred and eighty miles. Toward the end, I figured

I never *would* reach Mazatlán. Likely, they'd done away with it, as being unhandy to civilization. Somebody'd said the name meant "place where the deer come down to water," but I reckoned that the deer had given up along with the humans.

Then, suddenly, I was down, at sea level after months of living a mile or more high—in the tropics, surrounded by sultry green growth violently blooming and everything changed for the better. I never got it through my head, and haven't to this day, why those ill-natured, half-starved mountain scum didn't climb down and live where food grew with little or no tending. Maybe their outlook was so sour, born and bred, that they preferred to gall themselves with the worst hardships available. I've known people like that; they're only comfortable when sunk in the dumps. The charitable thing is to let them stay so.

Well, now, here I was ankling along with a new outlook, entering Mazatlán across a cultivated plain, with the customary crumbled adobe houses on the fringe, and people standing and staring, of course. Past a log entrance sign at a lane, like the ones at big ranchos—  —that read "Campo Siete," and I inquired of a woman what it meant, but she flicked her thumb against her upper teeth and said it was disgusting. But when I pressed the point, being interested, she said it was an exhibition *muy grande* with both women and men as well as jackasses and dogs, and if her husband didn't stay away from there, she planned to doctor up his food. She knew some items, she stated, that would put him on the shelf for a month. I judged that the show was along the order of a county fair, and continued on. Women can be mighty petty sometimes; they get in a humor where they *never* want a man to have fun.

I breasted a rise, and, looking across the rooftops of the town, a mile or so off, saw an expanse of slate-gray that rolled on out to nowhere, and it was the ocean. I stood and gulped; it was the first time I'd seen it, and it did funny things to my insides. On through the town, which had buildings of different colors, cheerful and gay, and up to the public market, which was roofed over and buzzing with the racket of two or three hundred people bargaining, chattering and laughing. I gave a boy a cuartillo to watch my burros, then slipped another two cuartillos to keep an eye on the first one, then mentioned both to a priest and entered, just out of impulse. I tied Bollo's jaws and chained him up short to the saddle.

Commonly, I couldn't stand these clattery, strong-smelling markets, but this was better than most. They had sawdust on the floor, for the spitting, and it improved the general appearance, also made it less likely for a person to break a leg. But about the first thing I saw was a white naked pig's head on a counter, gazing at me mournful through empty sockets. It gave me the fantods; *I* wasn't responsible for his situation, and resented being accused. Its mouth was too pink, besides. Then an excited man tried to sell me a tiger-cat skin, but the curing had been so slipshod it was stiffer than a shingle. Moreover, I couldn't figure out right off how I could use it. On top of that, it gave off a stench like a gar that's been lying dead on a mudbank for two or three weeks.

He says, "Take it—do without something else. Take it for half the figure, and I'll go back to work hauling sand."

I pushed on, past stalls full of tomatoes, and peppers, and beans, and melons and fruits of all kinds, including a number unfamiliar to me—arranged neat and pretty, too—and women selling huaraches and straw hats, and beautiful imitation wooden fruit, and baskets, and cheap-looking serapes, besides mats and dreary, brownish pottery and religious crayons so gloomy they made a person wish he could find some cheerful studies of the Devil.

There were men with bloody aprons on, selling skinny little fowl plucked clean except for pinfeathers, and eggs that had got laid around Christmas, likely, dirty and spotted, and browned sides of kid, and sausage, but not much of that, because meat was scarce here, and long counters of shrimp and oysters and fine-looking fish from the ocean. I stopped to revive my spirits, because a fresh fish display *is* one of the wholesomest sights you can find; there's something clean about them, lying there in their bright sea colors.

A man was working the favorite game here for children—tossing up a wooden ball with holes and catching it on a peg—hitting the bull's eye every time. But when I bought one and tried it, it flew off at an angle, then came down and struck a very morose Indian woman on the head. She peeled off several observations commonly employed only by men, and ignorant ones at that, so I slid over to another part of the shed. They had booths where women made tortillas, and tacos—very crisp, hard sandwiches full of meat, maybe rabbit or cat—and sold roast kid and pork bones and sweet cakes that appeared to be favored by flies. It wasn't a bad market, but when I ate a few items, washing them down with liquid, I felt slightly peculiar in the stomach. So I went out and collected my burros. The boy hadn't stole anything important, only a frying pan and a sackful of flour, which he had divided with the others, so I thanked him and continued past the Cathedral down a cobbled lane toward the sea. All along the shore ran what they call the *Malecón,* or, sometimes, the *Paseo,* because young couples stroll there hand in hand in the evenings, spooning and such rot.

The sea air cleared out my system in a hurry. I don't know anything else that can do it quite as fast. Up close here, the water was deep blue and lively. Big rocks were piled up in front of the town, but a gorgeous sand beach stretched off ever so far to the right, while a nice little harbor lay over a hill to the left. Some sailboats bobbed and dipped out a ways in the chop—chasing sea gulls squalling over schools of rooster fish and mackerel—and half a mile offshore, two monstrous big rocks reared up with seals sunning themselves on the tops. I saw four wetly glistening, as clear as if perched on a plank in the market.

In the street by the Malecón, gentry took the air, in fine open carriages, and in the third that passed by, Angelina sat talking to the Mexican lieutenant and his addleheaded interpreter.

I tore off my hat, making a sorry spectacle—a sunburned ragamuffin with a man-eating dog and two burros—but she saw me and jumped out, coming mighty near to hurting herself on those cobbles.

"Sam! Oh, *Sam.*"

She felt warm, and soft, and, well, motherly, and I let down for the first time since I got captured.

XXV

NEARING PUEBLA: It is a matter of regret to the diarist that our overland journey to the coast, and southward voyage by steamer, prevented us from joining the siege of Vera Cruz, one of the sprightlier actions of the war. In some measure, this has been repaired, as I shall now relate.

Our wagon train of merchants made fast marches to Monterrey (being apprehensive of attack), thence to Reynosa on the Rio Grande (Rio Bravo, here), tarrying only once, toward the end, to witness the senseless execution of a Mexican guerrilla captured by Texas Rangers.

The fellow was a poised and brave *soldier*, and should, I think, have been treated as a soldier. His captors promised to spare him if he would reveal the hiding place of his comrades. His admirable reply, devoid of braggadocio, was, "I have killed many Americans and will kill many more if I am able, señores." Then he added, without dramatics: "My life is in the hands of my enemies, and I am prepared to yield it up. I ask only that I not be tied, and that I be allowed to face my executioners."

A priest there—of the kind that built this religion, I imagine—now stepped forward to intercede. He was a man of dignified, even noble bearing, a huge man of muscle and sinew, in whom strength and humility seemed to be at odds, as evidenced by his confused expression: a knotted-up forehead, signs of strain about the mouth, and mild, sad eyes that spoke of some troublesome inner fire. His tattered brown cassock proclaimed his unprivileged condition; he was of the Franciscan or Dominican order of monks, poor, dedicated, and, in this case, fearless.

"Brother," he said in slow, halting English to the Texan in command, "this man is a . . . *soldado,* soldier. He possesses a uniform; you see. True, he has fought. He admits attack on a . . . wagon train. But he is, soldier. Only . . . barbarians shoot a prisoner soldier. I put myself forth between him and thee . . . In Christian hope."

"Very interesting, Reverend," said the Texan, a loud and uncouth boor, obviously risen from the ranks and, unlike his captive, *out* of uniform. "How'd you like to put yourself alongside him at that wall? We got bullets and to spare."

The wrinkled forehead smoothed out, and the pale blue eyes gave a telltale glitter. I reflected that we had here a man of action jammed into a most unsuitable costume, and wondered how it had happened.

"Sir, you could doubtless . . . accomplish it, with your many . . . *Rangers*" [this last with ill-concealed contempt]. "But we plead in Christianity, that you show mercy to the—weak." (I was glad he had hesitated on the word.)

"One thieving, mackerel-snapping holy Joe's exactly like another, as far's we're concerned down here. The only good spic's a dead spic. Savvy—*brother?*"

"Sir," said the priest, with a terrible wrench of piety, "you have great . . . advantage. True. How simple if as between *hombres,* forgetting the war and my poor cloth, you must *put* me at the wall. Or, failing by God's will, be . . . generous." He laid aside a kind of shepherd's crook he was carrying and observed, "I have heard it said that one Texan is . . . worth ten Mexicans and that all are anxious to . . . prove it."

I blinked in amazement. Unless I misunderstood him, the priest had suggested that he and the Texan fight the matter out physically. Several Rangers tittered; I gathered that their commander was not popular.

"You flap-tongued bastard, I'll show *you!*" bawled the lieutenant from his horse; then he yelled to a squad of soldiers, "Lay hold of that snotty hex merchant. Grab him and hog-tie him in a tent."

I am not entirely clear about the next events, but the squad—four men in all—appeared to dissolve in a flurry of dust. They'd been suddenly bowled over, arms and legs badly tangled; they attempted to rise again, went down, hesitated, then gazed up in wonder as the priest placed one of their number in a sitting position on a low limb of a tree.

"Shoot him! Go ahead—shoot him down!" But the order was never carried out. The lieutenant raised his saber, then, surveying this very explosive arm of the clergy (now standing with bowed head, apparently in deep penance) he barked out, instead, a command to proceed with the execution.

O'Hara stirred angrily beside me, and I laid a hand on his shoulder.

The priest lit a cigarrito and placed it between the prisoner's lips, gave him the last offices, held him by both arms for a moment, and stepped back. The unfortunate—one of Urea's men—was smiling and smoking calmly when balls from the rifles of six Texans struck him in the forehead and breast. He remained upright for two or three seconds; then he collapsed in a heap, an empty sack of clothes. A group of women ran out and carried him off, and the lieutenant, nagged by doubts about his showing, said, to the priest, "If it wasn't for all the mush-bellied Yankee regulations, I'd ventilated your guts, too, you blow-hard, over-grown hypocrite. To tell the truth, I durn near clumb down and pee-rolled you myself, officer or no officer."

Regarding him serenely, the priest said, "Brother, I am . . . sorry that my . . . vows restrain me from calling you a dog and a coward and a murderer. I would like to do so. I very nearly—did. My vows are sometimes a very great strain."

"By God, I'll *still*—"

"Oh, slack off it, Bill," interrupted one of his men in disgust. "You had your chance. Speaking frankly, you didn't come out so shiny and bold. You had a kind of greenish hue in the region of the gills, as if you'd et a spoiled fish and needed a handy place to puke."

"Well, now, maybe *you'd* like to—"

"You git off from that horse," said the Ranger, spitting, "and lay aside your bars, and I'll undertake to kick your ass down to Yucatan and through Guatamaly and into Brazil as well as further points south. You never seen the day you could lick me, nor nobody else, for that matter. What you're best at's licking up to the colonel, so stick to it and stay healthy."

The trouble blew over, but the execution provoked heavy criticism from the members of our train, including the armed guard. And O'Hara never fully recovered in the time I knew him. By some dim, perhaps Celtic process of ratiocination, he transferred his animus from the Church to politicians. Politicians, he advised me later, were responsible for everything. Wasn't it a monstrous thing they had done, for example, in organizing the Spanish Inkersition? He became bitter to see the clergy so downtrodden, here in Mexico. Thenceforward he never missed a chance to seek out priests for conversation.

As to my own view, it was hard to take sides. During the Texan revolution, in 1836, in the town of Mier, an entire force of Texans was captured and dispatched to Mexico City; en route, when they attempted to escape, Santa Anna callously ordered every tenth man shot. He said he had decided to "decimate" the force, which was "unwieldy." Another time, a large detachment of Texans was cold-bloodedly slaughtered in a calabozo. Again, no quarter was shown the gallant defenders of the Alamo; they were destroyed to the last man. Not one Texan—no wounded, no prisoners—survived the battle, an outcome unique in modern, or civilized, warfare. There is no means of exaggerating the passionate mutual hatred of these two neighbor races. It will endure for generations.

From Camargo (after Monterrey) we proceeded down the Rio Grande to Reynosa, a small town where we first began to see steamboats. The stream at this point was six feet deep or more, having low sandy banks covered with chaparral—scrub evergreen oak.

The merchants finally deciding to drive their wagons (with wares) overland to the North, we pushed farther to Matamoros, where the river lay at a low stage, thence to Boca del Rio Grande, spying the ocean at last. The settlement here, built around some commissaries and private stores, was both dismal and rowdy, and "Bagdad" on the opposite bank was worse, so we ploughed ahead nine miles, through very heavy sand, to the favored anchorage of the region—Brazos Santiago. In the harbor rode all manner of craft, military and civilian, a fine, inspiring sight, but we were obliged to wait four days for passage to Vera Cruz.

Not much reluctant, after the exhaustions of the past months, we made camp in a solitary place and roamed the beach in pursuit of oysters (which lay thick and sweet in the tidal rivulets), crabs, sea fish and other delicacies. Also, as the sun blazed hot at midday, we took frequent sea baths, after some small acrimony as between Señora Mendoza on the one hand and Doña Carla on the other.

When first we prepared to swim, in a delightful cove that sloped easily off from white sand, our intractable charge strode out of her single petticoat and approached the water without as much as a scarf around her hips. There was no suggestion of exhibitionism, she was simply unaware that she had an audience.

The shriek that arose from Señora Mendoza shot sea gulls into the air for several hundred yards in both directions. Carrying a tent-like species of shift, she ran into the shallows and encumbered the girl in its folds, accompanying the action with a withering drumfire of rebuke. It now being impossible for Carla to swim (for her arms were pinioned in the cloth) she merely stood immersed and gently swaying, like a beautiful sea fern, glaring at her tormentor.

For herself, Mrs. Mendoza added two petticoats to the three that she habitually wore (as an admonition to Carla), and O'Hara commended her with sanctimony. It was enough to turn a person against the human race. O'Hara's self-acknowledged record of mendacity, false promises, seduction, defloration and rape was scarcely to be matched in literature or fact, and now he had set up as a model of deportment. In the beginning, too, he had lusted for combat in very manly style, excoriating the enemy (or Church) with oaths too hideous to list, but he had lately displayed an unnatural aversion to violence. It is always depressing to see a stable and worthwhile personality in process of deterioration.

"'Tis for the best, sir," he informed me with unction, pointing to the struggling miscreant. "Nudity can be arousing to the lower-down emotions, 'neath the belt, if you follow me. The Church has took note of it, and so has the Holy Father, and God bless them both, is what I say. I only wish me mither wuz here to see it"—removing his sombrero at this last absurdity, presumably in reverence of what I am sure was a sorely tried, if ghastly (and perhaps even non-existent) woman.

"You certainly ought to know, O'Hara," I replied coldly. "I doubt if anyone has been as villainous in that department as yourself. If I understood your many boring accounts, you could have been greatly improved by any competent veterinarian with an oversized pair of snippers."

"Ah, but that was before me Reformation, sir. I seen the light of blessed Jesus. Saved, to sum it up. It's been a-coming on, but I shoved it aside. The Devil's always a-skulking around, hauling and tugging and goosing. Watch him! Put him down. Don't hesitate to kick him in the crotch, sir. He'd serve you the same."

I snorted, and entered the water wearing only my underdrawers, as a gesture of independence. The ass O'Hara, following Mrs. Mendoza's example, wore on this occasion his full uniform, with sword and sombrero. He removed only his cartridge belt and a few knickknacks from his pockets, and apologized for doing so. I do not believe I ever saw a more ludicrous sight anywhere.

Hearing Carla hiss—the standard summons of all Mexicans—I paddled toward her, and she said, "If you please, disengage this fishnet in which I am trapped—it buttons in the back." In a fit of recklessness, and observing O'Hara and Mrs. Mendoza conversing apart—no doubt laying out a program of saintly Good Works—I did so, and she thanked me. Then, standing indecently close, she launched into a tirade of complaint. Mrs. Mendoza was as bad as Rosa; she was worse than ten Rosas. With Rosa one could hope to outwit; one *could* outwit. The unspeakable Mrs. Mendoza was plainly familiar with every human wile; one could *not* outwit. On mature reflection, unspeakable was too strong a term; one could become accustomed to her, even like her, *under different conditions*. But what a girl needed was freedom, a chance to breathe, to permit the flowering of her personality. In the case of herself (Carla) she might as well be married, and shackled, to Don Narciso Noriega, the monster of Puebla.

"Well," I said, overflowing with other people's problems, "we're headed in that direction, so we can manage it all right. I'll look him up as soon as we arrive."

As her expression changed to alarm, she swam forward until she held me in a shocking embrace of both arms and legs. Her body felt glassy at the surface, and then, as she pressed in tighter, surprisingly warm beneath. She gave me a scalding kiss—a slow, wanton's kiss—and pushed away, laughing in conceit. O'Hara was right; nudity has a tendency to arouse the lower emotions. I waited a while, thoughtful and annoyed, my mind briefly distracted from the all-important mission of the war, then walked out of the water.

By showing my orders, arguing, hinting darkly that President Polk was a close family connection, if not actually my father, then distributing some largesse, I arranged our passage on the sailing ship *Morillo,* pressed into service (at an outrageous fee) by our government as a vessel of general utility. The accommodations were sketchy, but our run down the Gulf was accomplished in smooth seas and (we are told) record time for this craft. The two women and I shared a large, bare, ill-smelling cabin, beneath the water line, which Mrs. Mendoza pointedly curtained off with a serape, while O'Hara slept on deck, as part of his biblical regimen of deprivation patterned after the early Christian martyrs. I regret to say, however, that it came on to rain pretty hard during the night, and the martyr, forsaking his bed of spikes, crept in to lie on the floor by my bunk. It should also be recorded that, as he wrung out his sea-stiffened jacket, he gave voice to a number of un-Christian oaths, spoken in a hoarse Irish whisper, without reference to his mither.

Before dawn we lay off the Isle of Lobos (near Vera Cruz) and when the sun rose, we saw the destruction done by our siege guns to the church spires, the whitewashed double-story buildings, and the "impregnable" Castle-Fortress of San Juan de Ulloa. Such part of the city as was visible from our berth, while we awaited clearance through the naval blockade, looked gaunt and skeletal, a shattered reminder that war is a costly game and that this phase of it was, to us of Doniphan's command, a wholly different experience.

We were put ashore in a launch, at a spot where, roughly, the sixty-seven surf boats had landed on March ninth, to begin carrying out General Scott's strategy for the capture of Vera Cruz. The troops built trenches that were soon filled with water, from a series of "northers," and conducted the siege in appalling conditions of hardship.

As a diversion, I must mention that I encountered an incredible Englishman, a critic of General Scott's "amateurish" operation, with whom I had a few brisk exchanges. The man in question, a writer, for he is preparing a history, was one George F. Ruxton, Esq. (whatever that appendage may mean in actual practice), who showed me, with condescending aplomb, the following crack-brained utterance in his book: "Since my visit, it [Vera Cruz] has also felt the force of American ire—and withstood a bombardment for several days, with what object it is impossible to divine, *since a couple of thousand men might have at any time taken it by assault.*"

The italics are mine. I met this omniscient gentleman in a *fonda,* or hotel-tavern, and, upon reading his insolence, asked about his military experience. With a dainty wave of the hand, he replied, "How typical! No American I've met is capable of carrying on an abstract discussion without the involvement of personalities. *My* military experience indeed!"

Farther on in his book, he referred to the bombardment as "an act of unnecessary cruelty," and I asked him, gripping my wineglass, if he had any direct knowledge of that fact. I inquired, rudely, for I was annoyed, "That is to say, sir, were you at any time within physical range or sight of the guns?"

Again the foppish wave, and the observation:

"And they call us *cousins!*"

"Let us say, instead, cousins twice removed—by force."

He finally sat up, alerted, and eyed me sourly, and when I came across the ultimate offense, *"The American can never be made a soldier!"* I said, "Sir, you are a liar and a fool and a nuisance to these shores. You had better be conveyed back to your shrinking domain, where you can do the least possible harm.

Now I hope you will resent these remarks, and insist on satisfaction."

He blinked several times rapidly, the most astonished Englishman in the raw New World.

"I say, you needn't blow me up like that. There's such a thing as free speech, you know. My word, how quickly you Yanks become angry!"

Then, apprehending I had been with Doniphan, he had the good grace to show me, in an "expanded version," his history's opinion that "there were no defenses round the city which could not have been carried, including the city itself, by a couple of battalions of Missouri Volunteers." (He was much in admiration of the Battle of Sacramento.)

I declined to be mollified. The insufferable fool shared the trait of most English I have met, that, smarting with failures and defeats, they are yet superior to everything American, and, further, wish to make a career of saying so.

In an earlier meeting, for example, Mr. Ruxton (Esq.) spoke bitterly, savagely for an Oxonian whose militancy was best expressed by the brandishment of a lace nose-rag, of our "inhuman institution of slavery." Even as a southerner, I submit that there is no moral justification for slavery, aside from the invalid fact that great numbers of blacks have been provided a quiet life and regular diet after centuries of remaining naked in their native bush, wholly static, no more capable of progress, in the aggregate, than the Australian aboriginal; *but,* it is the English themselves who have proved supremely heartless and cruel and self-interested in their maltreatment of colored colonials. However, they refuse to consider these shortcomings, preferring to concentrate on ours. No doubt it will always be so. In fairness to England, I should add that slavery got its start and blooms at its vilest among the dark races themselves. In that laggard section of the world, black owns captured black, young girls are sold like sheep, and torture is the daily coin of subjection. Odd, but the fact is seldom mentioned. Let us hope that Abolition, when it comes, is made universal, even at the cost of depriving several African gentlemen of some very valuable property.

As to General Scott and Vera Cruz, authorities agree that his campaign was superb. What seems equally important (in regard to the unimportant Mr. Ruxton) was Scott's overture preliminary to the siege. It was, as stated, on March ninth that our surf-boats landed the troops ashore. *No bombardment of the city was commenced until the twenty-second.* The delay was purposeful, in order (1) to call on the Governor to surrender and thus "spare your beautiful town"; and (2) to allow the escape from Vera Cruz of the "neutrals," meaning all women and children as well as the members of foreign consulates, etc.

When the shelling began, the enemy replied at the rate of about three shots for every one of ours. Both the city and the trenches were soon filled with smoke. Within a few hours, a large percentage of the Mexican guns were silenced, and it could be seen that most of the spires, domes and high houses had been knocked to ruins. This had been accomplished by ten 10-inch mortars, four 24-pound breaching guns, and two 64-pound howitzers, the bulk of our artillery not having arrived, whether lost at sea or driven to leeward was not then known. Helping out, off and on, were two small war steamers and five gunboats with heavy guns. These last, incidentally, ran so close and so dangerously in toward shore—within pistol shot, during the surf-boat landings—that the enemy's vedettes of cavalry (squadrons of lancers) withdrew from the beach. Commodore Perry at last gave an order for the reckless little craft to put back out of range.

When the Governor's order came for surrender, on March twenty-sixth, General Scott had to report only two officers and fewer than a dozen enlisted men dead, while the Mexicans counted depressing casualties besides delivering up five thousand prisoners, four hundred pieces of ordnance, five hundred stands of arms, and the shattered city with its not quite impregnable Fort. It is difficult to explain this disparity, except to say, again, that our commanders were trained and skillful men—not only Scott and his fellow professionals from West Point, such as Captain R. E. Lee, whose engineers did admirable work in placing batteries, digging trenches, and erecting fortifications—but the Volunteers who led troops of foolhardy spirit. The enemy, on the other hand, appeared once more to have fought in disorder.

A Lieutenant Barbour whom I met in town took O'Hara and

me to the Castillo of San Juan de Ulloa, which lies side by side to the city on an island of twelve acres. We were rowed by an extremely surly Mexican, whose pique, we found afterward, arose from the fact that he had been spying for both sides and been paid by neither. He was remarkably offensive. A brisk chop was going, and as he rowed he caught crabs with his right oar, grinning the while and knocking spray against the wind to soak the three of us seated in the stern. Barbour remonstrated mildly two or three times, but got no more response than oaths untranslatable (I surmised) by him, but which, to me, seemed dangerous.

"I wish you would bear off a trifle to port," said Barbour, who was one of the best-mannered and most courteous and forbearing young gentlemen I ever encountered. "And do please watch your oars; we're quite damp here." He had understated the case; we were drenched, while the Mexican, of course, remained bone-dry. The latter's reply was, roughly, "Go put a ram to your mother—I'll hold her legs."

Barbour broke off whistling in the blandest humor, picked up a boat hook, inspecting and hefting it as if it were a foreign curiosity, then fetched the rower a blow that came near to killing him. It caught him on the side of the neck, knocked him out of the boat, and left him in the water, struggling feebly.

"Would you be so very good as to take up the oars, Sergeant? There, a few feet more to the dock. Good, good; thanks *very* much"—this while he towed the baleful Mexican along with the hook caught up in his collar.

Whistling again, Barbour leaped nimbly out, made us fast to a bitt, and hauled the rower into the boat. Then, tucking both oars under one arm, he pointed toward the Castle.

"You'll note the iron rings set in the outer walls. That's for ships to moor to during northers. Dear me, I believe that fellow's bleeding," and he helped bind up a gash, as solicitous and interested as if it had been his own kin.

From first to last, he never suggested that anything untoward had happened during the passage.

Briefly (since a blow was coming on), we toured the Castle, escorted by a Lieutenant Colonel Wilson and a surgeon who was recovering from yellow jaundice. We were shown the various apartments, from the highest point where vessels far at sea were sighted, to the lowest arches were we saw moldering piles of lances and old English tower muskets. By special dispensation, we descended to the calabozo and looked at sixty long-term prisoners, men for whom Scott had not yet interceded, the basest species of criminals, guilty of acts all but unknown in northern countries. Poor animals, they were alabaster white, not having seen the sun in years. They flapped about slowly in their cells, like sad gaunt cranes, uncertain on their legs, hopeless, filthy with long hair and rags, only the embers of their sunken eyes betraying the life that was left.

The walls of San Juan de Ulloa were fifteen feet thick, constructed of white coral faced with hard stone. Despite this, they were full of shot-holes, and so, as we saw later in town, were most of the fine churches. The dome had been knocked from one cathedral by a large shell that had killed a number of women and children. I peered into the ruin, feeling uncomfortably alien at staring up into open sky, while a sad-faced beggar woman stared at me, and had a stab of wonder about the material benefits of war. It soon passed. On the walls of this church I noticed for the first time wax figurines, of the Savior in the color gradations of every race, from the pale skin of the European (accentuated somehow by the artificial pigment), to the darkest African tinge.

We were anxious to join the fighting toward Puebla—that is, *I* was—but found it necessary to get precise information about the route, as well as fresh animals, so I quartered us in an overcrowded fonda, then with O'Hara, sallied forth into the town. Vera Cruz had now a dilapidated look, a post-battle look, and the crowds were careless and bold. The streets surged with soldiers, sailors ("horse, foot and dragoons," as the catch saying went), wounded, drunken men, wagons, carts, artillery carriages, mules, donkeys, Mexicans, Indians, beggar boys, musicians, and every type of adventurer. It was amusing to read the signs and advertisements—Joneses and Smiths and Johnsons and Thompsons were interspersed among Crapauds and Ximénes and Garcías and Minas. Vera Cruz had become a Babel in miniature.

The city being walled, a lack of ventilation was apparent in the stale, tropical, breezeless, sea-level air and the sweetish-ripe stench that overhung the streets. The smell could be laid partly to the throngs of peasant women selling fruit: different here—"maumee" apples, alligator pears, and bananas, a luxury after the sparse rations of the North. Higher up, in the multi-storied dwellings of the rich, a sea wind stirred awnings and laundry, and for a moment I felt casteless and lost. It seemed impossible to find order in this chaos; even O'Hara's normally antlike wits were dulled. I stopped a private in the street, a middle-aged man with a peculiar gait and a hard glassy look, and said, "Direct us to Information Headquarters, soldier." He froze to attention, then brought up his arm in an ornate mockery of a salute, and toppled over backwards—out cold. Automatically, I touched a finger to my cap as he collapsed; the order had been issued: all officers were to be saluted, and to return salutes with a suitable gesture.

In Christian charity I directed O'Hara to fetch and pour water over the fellow. Unconscious, he would have been robbed and even stripped before he awoke. We sloshed him with three full buckets without effect, and a crowd began to collect, pressing in silently, until I drew my saber.

"More, sir?" O'Hara inquired.

I felt my face darken in anger. One's nerves are jangled by the Mexicans' way of standing close and staring, impassive, without self-consciousness, living far down in the odd stillness of their wonder. It suddenly occurred to me that I was performing my first military chore as a captain, and I bent to the work.

"Keep it up till the rascal revives. He's a disgrace to his uniform."

The buckets continued to come—seven, eight, nine; he lay now in a broad puddle—when an undersized Mexican holding his sombrero said, *"Señor, el hombre está muerto."*

"Stand back and keep out of this," I snapped. "Perhaps you've forgotten who won the city."

"Los ojos están abiertos."

I turned and said, "O'Hara"—at the same moment feeling the sweat break out on my forehead.

O'Hara was on his knees, in tears, holding one of the man's hands. He was babbling some kind of apology.

I made my way to the nearby fountain and sat down. Heat, exhaustion, too many years, and a great wound in his side that was indifferently covered with a bandage, had killed Private W. T. McGivern, fifty-five, of Massachusetts. These factors had been aided by the military attentions of Captain B. Shelby, thirty-five, of the First Missouri Mounted Volunteers.

For half an hour, while O'Hara (and, now, two members of the soldier's outfit) saw to his identification and removal, my thoughts turned homeward, for the first time in months. Something had happened along the way. The answer would come after a while, but not on this hot first day of my officerhood in Vera Cruz.

During the rest of the afternoon, O'Hara's manner was strained, and I felt empty and dejected. I felt, in fact, so wretched that, toward dusk, I steered us into a cantina for the very express purpose of having a *drink*. Strong drink. This proved to be an unnamable triple distillate of maguey (as I deduced from the German proprietor's incredible Spanish). It far exceeded mescal in authority. In a word, the liquor refreshed our spirits. O'Hara condescended to forgive me, on the ground that I meant well (only partially true) and I, in turn, made the acquaintance, this time, of an authentically intoxicated soldier at the next table, who, also wounded, had just returned from Cerro Gordo. He answered my questions civilly, the words finding a circuitous path around his tongue, which was anesthetized. They tumbled out at tardy and implausible moments, rather mutilated in the process. Then he showed me the inevitable Journal. If my experience is an indication, this may prove to be the best-annotated war in history. Approximately every third man appears on the battleground with a saber in one hand and a quill in the other. It would be difficult to assess which is doing the more damage.

My acquaintance being a picturesque person from one of the wilder parts of the nation—New York or New Jersey (a roughhewn poet, one might confess) I begged to quote the following etymological curiosity dealing with his colleagues:

"The nature of my comrades and the officers of the Brigade generally, were the subjects which occupied the large share of my attention that evening. In our company we had a captain from Virginia, a first lieutenant from New York, and two second lieutenants, one from Massachusetts and the other from Maine. There were some decided galoots in our regiment, and some 'toodles,' who had neither character nor stamina. We had officers who spoke to the men in thunder tones, and others who addressed the soldiers as though they were ladies. We had some who were 'slashers,' gay rollicking devils, who delighted in the idea of getting into a fight, and some who were too genteel almost to touch a musket. We had officers who were handsome, well dressed and emphatically 'ladies' men,' and others as rough and uncouth as Polar bears. We had a general who dreamed nightly of the music of four-and-twenty pounders, and colonels whose eyes gleamed with happiness when they thought of the red fields ahead. Lieutenant-colonels we had too, who could pound with heavy sabers like the clear ringing of anvils, and majors who drew their tall forms more erect when an enemy's bullet whistled near at hand. We had assistant surgeons who would kneel and worship at the shrine of human loveliness, 'and then dissect a Cytherean Venus to trace the course of an imaginary muscle.' We had commissaries who prated about the generosity of Uncle Sam, and at the same time gave us scant rations of moldy flour. They 'cribbed' us close and looked on in ghastly astonishment when they saw us stow their flinty crackers and dangerous beef. But why should I say more, my blanket was warm and clean, and the spirit of dream-land, with his dark and smoky plumage, was hovering over my couch."

Our route inland toward Mexico and the fighting posed no problem. Leaving Vera Cruz, one simply took the "National Highway" and followed the markers of dead bodies and animals, refuse, discarded guns, ammunition, clothing, harness, spoiled provisions, fragments of broken wagons. The road was a sequined testament to the disruptive glories of war, and my mood quickened. Only with difficulty did I remember what had seemed so depressing back in Vera Cruz.

Not so the rest of my unit. We had replaced four used-up burros and two lame mules with comparatively lively mustangs.

These were bought at larcenous prices from a Mexican trader who announced himself as "Mr. Edwards," then conducted the rest of the transaction in Spanish. Their jerkiness provoked comment. The day was scorching hot; beside the road, masses of emerald-green vegetation appeared to steam and breathe, consuming the air; and occasional bandaged soldiers, crippled and listless, drifted toward Vera Cruz from Cerro Gordo. I noticed a man, defeated by exhaustion, asleep with his head pillowed on the stomach of a dead Mexican dragoon; occasionally his hand twitched feebly at the flies. My companions complained steadily, directing their first feeble barbs at the horses, which were "malicious in their movements," then descending to Carla's absurd remark that the bright color of the foliage was "melodramatic."

"It's your country," I replied, and thought the point well conceived. "If you have a grievance, take it to Santa Anna." Rude, but I was uncomfortably warm, myself.

Twelve miles out, we came across El Presidente's modest "farm," thirty miles wide and fifty miles long, extending to Jalapa. Sixty thousand cattle are supposed to roam over its pastures. These chattels in addition to horses, sheep, goats, crops, and other enterprises. During his time in power, the tricky politician has profited brilliantly. When I mentioned this to O'Hara, forgetting the shift in his bias away from the sectarian, he blew up like an over-charged boiler. For a few seconds I had serious fears for his sanity, and indeed a touch of sunstroke may have influenced his conduct.

"Oh, the corruption of it!" he cried in a frenzy, sliding off his horse and whacking wildly at a row of weeds with his saber. "Oh, the vile, thieving slant-eyed heathen Chinee, goggling and hissing—"

(This was a phrase that O'Hara had picked up from an English-speaking priest, who meant only to indicate the religion farthest removed from the tenets of the Catholic Church. It had, unfortunately, stuck.)

"Oh, the low, idolatrous, opium-eating heathen, abusing his office to rob the poor—graven images, garlic, firecrackers, snakes—"

The man had begun to babble like a lunatic. "Get hold of yourself, O'Hara," I said sternly. "President Santa Anna is not by any stretch of the imagination a Chinaman. Also, as far as I know, he is a dedicated Catholic. In fact—"

"Where's his fence posts? I'll chaw 'em out with my teeth, if I have ter. This time tomorrer, there won't *be* no farm. Nor any Chinymen hereabouts neither. Drat the oily devils, gobbling up everything in sight. If there was one thing me old mith—"

"O'Hara!" I jumped down and took him by the arm, removing the saber with a quick wrench. "Get the other arm, you women—yes, you, too, Carla, damn your superior airs—do it *now!* All right, let's put him over against that tree."

I soaked a rag with water from my canteen, and we cooled his forehead, which was fiery red. He submitted meekly, trying to struggle up only once, to inquire of Mrs. Mendoza whether she had any Chinese blood; upon her indignant answer of "only on my mother's side," he sprawled back down. Meanwhile he continued to rant, the bulk of his observations being aimed at Santa Anna, stressing the fact of his Oriental birth and swearing vividly that no damned skulking, bamboo-eating, pigtailed Chinyman was going to own sixty thousand cattle, or as much as a sick porkypine, while he, O'Hara, was on the scene in Mexico. It was why he had come down here, to drive the Orientals out and restore freedom of religion to the natives.

I was surprised at the scope of his subconscious; he came forth with numerous facts, arranged unrealistically, of which I was sure he might be ignorant. Also, he provided Carla with a far deeper insight into the lower workings of profanity, a scholar's insight. Offhand, I could think of nothing he omitted (and I later jotted down several expletives whose derivation I meant to quiz him about in time). At length he went to sleep, and when he awoke, in an hour, he appeared rational, though, to me, he still wore an alert, calculating look that I divined would have serious repercussions for any stray Chinese who might wander down the road driving sixty thousand head of cattle.

As to Carla, she had somehow conceived the ruffled notion that I had bawled her out. She held her head high, and her manner was haughty.

"Is it permitted for a former member of the upper classes to have a drink before we continue this abomination of a journey?"

I drew her aside. "See here, my girl, in every military unit there must be a commander." I exhibited my rank. "I am a captain in the United States Army—that much is clear, to use your phrase. Until such time as you, or Mrs. Mendoza, or our Occidental friend over there comes up with a major's bars, I will command. Now have a drink. I'll put that in writing if necessary."

She looked overhead and said, "It is the hour of siesta. We can wait a few minutes longer. Come with me, down here—"

"The United States Army," I interrupted stiffly, "neither officially nor unofficially observes the 'siesta.' Perhaps," and I coughed, with significance, "perhaps that is why I am now following our troops to Mexico City."

"—down by the stream, away from the eagled-eyed Señora. Yes, here. Please seat yourself briefly on the log. I have some words to deliver."

I sat down, pulled out my watch, and said, "You have exactly five minutes; we'll call it a trooper's request for a personal interview. It's covered by the Regulations. Now, I hope this is in the nature of gratitude. Perhaps I should remind you of an old saying, 'He travels fastest who travels alone.'"

"Yes, closely in that line. You have taught me something of value."

"I'm glad," I said, and meant it. "Gratitude is possibly the emotion least natural to the average hu—"

"You have demonstrated, clearly and well, what a truly insupportable ass the best person can become with a little authority. Especially that of the military."

I sprang to my feet. "We're within fifty miles of Puebla. This may be the time to deliver you to Don Narciso."

"Yes, I would prefer that, if you please. My father is a fool and a tyrant, my sister responds only to the Church, La Señora belongs to the old ways—what I wish is of no importance in a marriage—and my brother's a weakling. Contrary to my thoughts, they're all I've got. This man of Puebla seems better every day. I like him. His personality begins to emerge."

"Damn it," I said, sitting down again and removing my hat—it really *was* most awfully hot—"you have me."

"A *captain!* Listen, my friend, Don Narciso Noriega, of Puebla, has served as a general in the Army of Mexico. Likewise he has been of the Cabinet. He may be yet. No, no, many thanks. Consider my position. It is a matter of simple military precedence."

Blast the fool, she had me so confused that, suddenly, I felt like O'Hara.

"Well, by *God,*" I shouted, springing back up and permitting my speech to get a trifle careless, "you're *here*. Deny *that!*"

"It is quite impossible. Surely you can see it—a *captain*. Don Narciso," she went on, musingly; "there was much strength in his hands. He has a passionate nature; I'd missed it before."

I slapped her; then took her by the shoulders, after which she fell forward, perhaps half conscious, and I found her hotly yielding.

"Wait—"

I barely heard her whisper, "Go ahead, without talking; the talking's stupid . . . and it's all right about the rank," then we heard the angry hiss and Mrs. Mendoza led her impetuous ward (no doubt deranged by hardship) off through the thick couch of greenery toward the road.

We reached the Puente Nacional—a remarkable formation of stone arches that support a long high bridge over a rapid mountain stream. A stone fort frowned down from above, and a town that surrounded this, on different levels, was entirely deserted. It gave one a strange feeling—the rows of startling white huts under a glaring sun, the rocks and crags making sharp-edged shadows all around, the streets empty and silent; not a sound except the ghostly echo of our horses' hooves on the cobbles.

Then, around a crooked bend, a man, in uniform, sat leaning against a wall. I called down, "*Soldado,* you there—" and touched his hat with my rifle, wishing information, but he rolled over on one side. The lower part of his jaw had been shot away, and his neck, jacket, and trousers were stained black. The wound itself had not necessarily been fatal, I thought, but the loss of blood and starvation that followed (since he had no means of taking food, nor of calling out for attention) had combined to let him die slowly, sitting as if asleep against the wall.

We looked on for a moment, O'Hara's face as grim as granite;

then we climbed ahead, winding in and out over the littered highway, my friends trying to ignore the reminders of Cerro Gordo, and descended a steep hill to a larger village—Plan de Río. Every hut, every shelter was filled with wounded, the dangerously wounded, not capable of walking, waiting their turn to be conveyed to Vera Cruz. The lamentations and stench of death were too much; we proceeded without addressing a soul, but a private, a surgeon's assistant, ran out and shouted, "Hey, watch out for guerrillas! Behind every rock. I'm telling you—"

Cerro Gordo, where the Mexicans some days before had suffered the bitterest defeat in their history, lay only four miles farther on, a natural retreat, a commanding eminence beyond a deep ravine where the river runs, surrounded by mountain walls. There being but one way for the Americans to pass, Santa Anna and his crack troops—eighteen thousand in all—occupied the ridges and slopes arising from this basin, waiting with artillery in fortified positions.

From talking to soldiers here, we made out a rough sketch of the battle, which, I feel, will prove to have been the turning point of the war. Here were no untrained, timorous, inexperienced, or amateurish Mexican leaders. On the hill known as El Telégrafo, the almost incomparably brave General Ciriaco Vasquez placed five heavy guns and arranged his Eleventh Regiment and General Canalizo's superb cavalry to back them up.

On the Sunday morning, as both sides gathered and dug in sober-faced for what everybody (except, it seems, Santa Anna himself) knew would be a terrible and desperate fight to the death, the red, white, and green Mexican flag fluttered and whipped in a sharp breeze atop El Telégrafo. I stood and looked up, as we rested below at the *venta,* or stopping place for travelers. It was heart-warming to see the Stars and Stripes now flown on the peak. In that spot, and from La Atalaya and other peaks nearby, Mexican trumpets had blared in all directions, preparing for the "barbarians from the North." The cockadoodle was excusable. Indeed, the situation did appear impossible. Two young officers, writing home, told how they felt when they viewed the task ahead. Lieutenant U. S. Grant, of Galena, Illinois, thought the redoubts on El Telégrafo "hopeless," and Captain R. E. Lee, of Virginia, described the slope as an "unscalable precipice." These qualms did not reflect faint heart; both officers, at Cerro Gordo, were outstanding, and, as professional West Pointers, will no doubt fight again for their country.

A case could be made that Lee, through brilliant reconnaissance, assisted by Engineers Beauregard and Tower, found the access to El Telégrafo that proved to be decisive. Scott himself had arrived on the scene on April fourteenth; a giant of a man wearing an old straw hat, which he doffed right and left to the soldiers. On his arrival, the rumor went round that El Telégrafo would be taken by siege rather than attack, and a great deal of tension went out of the troops. Then General Worth arrived with sixteen hundred hand-picked assault troops, and the opinion changed. Then the immensely profane and energetic Twiggs; Patterson, in whom all the men had confidence; Pillow, in whom they had little; Shields; Colonel Wynkoop, of the First Pennsylvania; Campbell, of the First Tennessee; Haskell, Second Tennessee; Roberts, Second Pennsylvania; and others. Eighty-five hundred Americans in all, with great guns staring down in their faces from what surely must be one of the world's best natural fortifications. Leonidas at Thermopylae could scarcely have found the terrain better suited to defense.

The word came on the morning of the nineteenth. Attack! A long siege had been ruled out. The bugles sounded, the men gave each other last messages—notes for home—slapped one another on the backs, and our several columns began the advance upward over rough trails thick with scrub oak, mesquite, chaparral and cactus. At an open spot, easily seen, in direct line of the enemy's guns, the indefatigable Lee hastily piled brush as a screen; then the shouting, screaming, cursing, bareheaded Twiggs found himself under attack. Instead of holding, he sent his mounted riflemen, deadly accurate—the "cursed riflemen," wrote the Mexicans in dispatches—at full gallop against La Atalaya. In the midst of this, a captain shouted to Twiggs, "How far shall we charge 'em, General?" "Charge them to Hell," Twiggs replied, his bull's voice ringing through the mountains, heard even by the Mexicans on El Telégrafo. After heavy fighting, La Atalaya was taken and its defenders killed or chased down to the chasms.

Against this feint, our Second Infantry and Fourth Artillery moved to Santa Anna's rear, to the Jalapa road and the summit trail discovered by Robert E. Lee. Colonel Riley ordered his men into position, and at seven o'clock the word came to attack "impossible" El Telégrafo. In the face of blistering grapeshot, showers of bullets and canister, the men clawed their way up the slope—"like a wave of fire in a burning prairie," as a private soldier would record. And a Mexican wrote, in astonishment, "They seemed to depise death!"

Just below the crest these men crouched, pausing for breath, their ranks mutilated, awaiting the order to retreat. Then Colonel Harney of the First Brigade unexpectedly stood up and began cheering. From all accounts he was an inspiring sight, unusually tall, athletic, red-haired, with steel-blue eyes, tempestuous by disposition, now waving a sword and beginning the cry of "Charge! Charge!" All up and down the lines, apparently, men fell into a kind of berserk humor and took up the wild yells, until, someone noted, "it seemed as if the trees themselves were cheering."

Harney was the first man to vault the breastworks, and in the hand-to-hand fighting that followed, the impassive Vasquez fell. Harney himself stopped to pull him out of the fire, into the shelter of a wall, and crossed his arms on his breast before continuing. Vasquez' troops, demoralized at this loss, were driven in panic from the summit. A Sergeant Henry of the Seventh Brigade leaped recklessly to the flagstaff, hauled down the red, white and green pennant and ran up the Stars and Stripes. Captain MacGruder seized the Mexican artillery, turned it on the enemy, and the flight became a full rout. A gallant Mexican, General Banereli, standing fast in the deadliest kind of fire, tried hard to rally his men, but it was too late. The pell-mell dash of soldiers and commanders down the hill amounted to what a historian will call "indescribable confusion." Santa Anna himself, hastily changing his attire, fled in only a shirt and underdrawers, leaving a soldier wearing his conspicuous uniform to be captured. Oddly enough, El Presidente had, shortly before, publicly taken a pious oath at an altar to "conquer or leave my body on the field." To the best of everyone's belief, he was the first Mexican fighting man to make the exit, and certainly his was the most ignominious.

But none of Cerro Gordo was a matter of levity. More than a hundred Mexicans flung themselves to death over a high precipice rather than be cut down by lead or steel. The sad, tattered, torn, bedraggled and humiliated remnants of their Army, fighting a chaotic retreating action toward and quickly past the excellent bastion of Jalapa, left dead and dying at, literally, every step of the way. Along the road, the cry of "All is lost at Cerro Gordo; all, all!" went from settlement to settlement, and much of the civilian population joined the Army in flight.

At the end, General Scott came among his victorious troops, embracing common soldier and officer alike, exchanging an especially fierce and emotional hug with the relentless Harney, with whom he had had serious differences in the past, saying to the men, "I am here not as your commander but as your brother-in-arms."

So ended Cerro Gordo. The Mexican losses—twelve hundred of their finest soldiers; the American—387 men and thirty officers. Four thousand stand of arms and forty cannon were destroyed, as being too old for service, and approximately five thousand prisoners were taken, of whom many escaped in the following days. Scott himself released three thousand "on parole," hoping to soften further Mexican sentiment for resistance. How grievously he underestimated the enemy I will show soon.

We moved on and up, we four, climbing to Jalapa, a pleasant and colorful resort that, in my fatigue, I thought might make an easeful resting spot for a few weeks after the war. Truly a beautiful city, built on the side of a hill, flowered and clean and smart, scented with gardenias by day and *huile de noche* after dark, festooned everywhere with white hanging lilies, gay with violet-red bougainvillaea blooming on its rooftops. High up, it smiled down on the groves and cultivated fields spread out below. Here was the dividing line, one might say, between the low tropics that stretched back to Vera Cruz and the high plateau of inland Mexico.

The citizens had returned to the town, mixing with our soldiers. They differed subtly from the ones we had known farther north; perhaps more cultured, a little more pleasing to the eye. I confess that I barely saw them, but a companion wrote of these women of Jalapa, Puebla, and Mexico City: "The higher class of ladies dress in the most captivating style, and follow closely the Parisian fashions, with the exception of the bonnet, which is unknown in Mexico. In its place they wear a long satin mantilla that is thrown over their heads while walking, and is fastened to the dark back hair by a large diamond or gold pin. Their dresses are made purposely rather short, that they may better display the faultless symmetry of their beautiful little feet. A Mexican lady in full dress is a dangerous object to meet with, and unless a man is very cautious, he is apt to see her walk away in a proud and stately manner, bearing with her his heart. They coquet with their Spanish fans in the most exquisite manner, peering over them with their large, dark, Juno-like eyes, their raven tresses falling in heavy masses over their noble foreheads. To use a friend's expression, 'It makes a fellow feel anguish to look at them.' They are magnificent creatures, and no man could help but do them homage. A little lower down the scale of womankind come the middle classes, who dress in fancy-colored petticoats, satin slippers and loose waists cut very low in the neck. They go bare-armed and wear a long shawl called a rebozo; these women, too, are polite and graceful in their manners, and very animated in conversation. Go where you will, they treat you as ladies should, and everything like vulgarity or low breeding is unknown among them. Their ideas of morality are certainly rather different from our own; but in politeness and high breeding they excel any people I ever saw. They smoke little paper cigarritos, and it is esteemed a mark of impoliteness not to take one if it is offered to you. The Peons or slaves, who are mostly of the Indian blood, are quiet and peaceful, and attend to the wants of their mistresses with much zeal. Every lady, in walking, has one of these slaves following her."

We stopped and made a cold lunch beside the fountain in the Plaza. We ate without talking, and, indeed, without looking at each other. I don't believe that, ever in my life, I had so wanted to wander off and be alone. A pretty girl in a blouse too careless for decency leaned over the fountain and tossed a gardenia in my lap; she made a gesture of raising one arm, with the other hand on its wrist. I glanced up dully, then noticed Carla's high color. Suddenly she and the girl exchanged a few sentences too rapid to understand, and both laughed.

Out of town again, we descended past green pastures with rich soil, and corn fields and barley fields, the whole rather similar to New England except for the absence of population. Near the foot of a rugged hill, we rode by a cotton factory with an indecipherable Indian name, and all along, the snowy-white cone of the Orizaba rose far up into the sunny blue sky at our left. Occasionally we heard cracklings and thunderings of other volcanos grumbling deep in the earth, threatening, quiescent for years, now.

Then into the rocks again, and a diversion, not unwelcome. At a lonely place, a wounded Mexican lay sprawled in the road directly across our path. Only his right hand moved, clutching and unclutching, making a fist. His hat had been knocked back from his head. I dismounted and walked forward, carrying my India-rubber canteen.

"*Amigo, soldado*—do you hear me?"

There being no answer, I tried again, bending over.

"*Sí, gringo*," he said, smiling and sitting up with a derringer pointed at my head. At the same time, a loud hazzah arose from the rocks ahead, and eight or nine tattered soldiers broke from concealment.

Without thinking, I kicked the pistol out of his hand, kicked him again—in the face—and cried to O'Hara: "Take cover! Draw and fire!" Vaguely, I saw him stop, look perplexed, then cross himself as if to yield, victim of his new, will-sapping piety.

"You fool!" I yelled, "it's them or us. Guerrillas! Bandits, O'Hara! Dismount and *move!*"

Then Mrs. Mendoza yanked his rifle out of its sheath, slapped him hard on the face—a crack like a pistol shot—and dragged Carla behind a boulder. Two balls knocked up dust beside me, and I scuttled back, crouching low. As I ran, more balls whined off stones nearby, one ricocheting far on up the slopes, plink, plink, plink, growing fainter, like a billiard ball completing its carom. The scoundrels really *were* the most appalling marksmen; we had seen it in all the fighting thus far.

No action for four or five minutes, then the kicked man, groaning, began to drag himself aside to join his comrades.

"He's hurt mortal bad, sir," said O'Hara, peering. "His front teeth is tore loose, ear to ear, the poor—" but Mrs. Mendoza, with an exclamation, raised his rifle, took careful aim, and shot the fellow in the back. He spun in a circle, kicking like a horse; then he lay still.

"*Chivo!*"

Where before I had been moody and depressed, I now felt first-rate, stimulated and happy.

Our situation was by no means hopeless. The villains were dug in behind low rocks on both sides; they were unable to climb higher without being seen; and we commanded all of the road from our protecting boulder. Further, we had better guns, plenty of ammunition, and accuracy unknown in this land.

"*Hombre,*" one sang out, easing up into view a bayonet fixed to a scrap of dirty white cloth. "*Tregua. Suspensión.* Flag of truce, we talk, smokes together. We like you fine."

"Kindly step out," I said, "and I'll arrange a hole through your skull. It's badly needed."

There followed a jabbered consultation in undertones; then diplomacy entered its second phase.

"*Hombre,* you not understoods. *No dinero;* we very rich mens. Deliver the girl, and all go out forward. I swear it by Guadalupe." A pause, and, "She is my long lost cousin, *el amor de mi corazón.*"

This produced some ribald laughter, then a curse or two followed by a sound of blows exchanged.

"Do you wish to join them?" I asked Carla. "They like you."

She took my revolver, cocked it, and sat waiting, badly frightened but determined, too, her nose a thin line and her lips bloodless.

"*Cabrones, hijos de putas,*" I called. "La Señorita spits in your faces. She has seen many dogs she prefers, and hopes to officiate at the removal of your *cojones.*"

Mrs. Mendoza gave me a slow, dumfounded look, but I

clapped her on the back in high spirits, and simultaneously our friends, stung into action, leaped howling out of their nooks and charged. Mrs. Mendoza stopped the leader, with a bullet in his shoulder, O'Hara, like a man in a trance, shot another with his revolver; at the same time Carla and I killed a third, the two balls striking him close together in the face and neck.

They slowed up, hung fire, looking chagrined and uncertain, then ran back to their holes like rabbits, dragging the two wounded.

"Now we kill you for sure, you son-of-a-bitch bastard *gringo del Norte*. We kill you slow, by *cuchillo,* with the thousand-slices. You one unfriendly son-of-a-bitch!"

A several-ton rock overhung the group on the right, delicately balanced on several small stones. I began very deliberately firing at these supports, making the splinters fly on each round. It occasioned hissing and angry comment below, but no further exposure to our guns. After half an hour, and a particularly efficacious shot, the boulder swayed, slid a little, and fell forward with a crash, to blood-curdling screams that welled up and up and up and were choked off abruptly.

Silence. Across the road, the survivors were too stunned to move. Then, all together, as at a signal, they scrambled up and tore down the road, their hats bobbing on strings at their backs.

We heard the sounds of horses switching and stamping and snorting; then the irregular flurry of hooves moving in a hurry. It was a complete and unquestioned victory, as pleasing in its way as Cerro Gordo.

"Well," I said, walking forward, "here's a pretty sight. Three men squashed like mushrooms. Look, here's a pair of heels; there's what's left of a head. And here's a surprise for you—the man had brains. Behold the proof! No burial detail for these, *amigos,*" I added, making a joke.

O'Hara stared at me with an expression I was unable to interpret, and the women seemed silent and reflective.

"Oh, come. Them today, tomorrow us. If I may remind you—'When the blast of war blows . . . imitate the action of the tiger: stiffen the sinews, summon up the blood.'"

XXVI

Rancho Ciénaga Grande: When I woke up, the second day in Mazatlán, I felt poorly—feverish and sick to my stomach, also mighty interested in the bathroom. They had some here, the first I'd seen in Mexico, and I mentioned it to Angelina, who floated in and out of my apartment, looking worried. I asked where we were, but she only said, "With friends. Don't talk—save your strength." I tried to, but it wasn't much use; I left most of it in the bathroom. In bed for say five minutes, stomach eased and empty, then cramps that began up high and worked down slow, becoming knotty and painful on the way. Totter up, then, and feel along the corridor again, barely making it, too, except once toward the beginning. It was absorbing; it took up time, but a person wouldn't care to do it very long.

Later, they said I was out of my head, what's called delirious. Everything appeared to swim around, especially the big colored picture on the wall of Jesus holding a fish. It gave me an odd notion of religion, because I got the idea He was operating a merry-go-round, with fish for tickets. "I handed mine over," I yelled once or twice, and Angelina ran in to promise I wouldn't be put off, after she heard the story. But she looked pitying, so I said, "Well, let Him pick on somebody else or get a new position," but she said to hush, that it was irreverent, or words to that effect.

After a week or so, when the room quietened down, we got to be good friends. I liked that picture. The fish was drawn as pretty as you please, and often made me hungry.

Then Angelina and the young lieutenant, with his interpreter (who appeared so uncommon similar to the fish it was uncomfortable) came in and quizzed me about what happened.

"Did you drink of the water at this place or that?" inquired the lieutenant.

I said, "No, and that's what I can't understand, because I *always* boiled anything from a stream. It's a mystery to me, and will remain so. I kept up my strength, too, and had a hearty meal directly before we met."

"Indeed? Where was this?"

"Why, there in the Market. I'd eaten light for days—'tole and bits of kid—and I seized the opportunity to stock up, without overdoing it, you know."

"What, ah, do you mean by not 'overdoing' it? That is, my question would be—what precisely did you eat?"

A lot of the past two weeks was fuzzy, but I remembered that Market as clear as yesterday.

I says, "Nothing important, or in the bulk. No *one* thing so much—"

"Kindly list the items that you recall."

Confound the fellow; he was a worse pry than Blaine. You'd a thought he was my uncle or something.

"Well, if it'll do you any good, there was a piece of sugar cane —not enough to hurt anybody, less than a foot long; and some boiled shrimps with lime squirted on top; I remember that much. And a glass of papaya juice which sticks in my mind because the man lifted a fly out on a straw then knocked the price down; and two *carnitas* and an orange and some *piloncillos*—the best I ever ate; and a mushmelon, then a dish of raw oysters, and afterwards a very small and harmless bottle of pulque, because I was thirsty again by that time; and in a little while (being careful not to squeeze things together) two tomatoes, a very nice-appearing taco, with a lemon to cut the grease, and after that a lump of chicle to chew on, produced right here; the woman said so herself. Now that was *all*, and if—"

"Just lie back in the bed and don't strain yourself," said the lieutenant. "We'll have Dr. Ventosa in again this evening. There may be something he missed, bound to be, as I think it over."

Well, I'd been poisoned, sure enough, and it must have been that chicle. The commodity was sugared and came from a grove of sapodilla trees just south of town—I inspected them later—but it had a stale, gummy taste that failed to strike what I'd hoped for. I remembered not being exactly at ease when I walked off. Something abnormal was going on inside. I figured I'd learned a good lesson, and was glad it happened.

The next time I went to the Market and ate sugar cane, boiled shrimps, papaya juice, two *carnitas,* an orange, *piloncillos,* a mushmelon, raw oysters, a bottle of pulque, two tomatoes, a taco and a lemon, I'd leave out the chicle. It's best to know when to stop.

After my rough weeks on the road, it was pleasant to laze about. I wrote letters home, and one to Don Jorge, read books, and snoozed. The room I had was big enough to raise a flock of goats in, with a very high ceiling having a number of painted-on pink fat infants sailing around playing gold harps. They looked like bumblebees, somehow, and the traffic was so thick it made you nervous about a collision. The house itself was a regular square double-storied mansion with high tropical trees growing in the patio and pretty blue tiles, with pictures, set just everyplace—on the balcony, in the bathrooms, around the fireplaces, in the floors, even around the doors, outside. My windows looked out to the sea, so they gave me a brass telescope to watch ships through. But I used it mainly for the seals. In the mornings, when the sun rose over the mountains behind us, the rocks and wet seals gleamed like blue ice.

One day when I was medium delirious, two handsome girls climbed down from the Malecón wall to the flat rocks below, stripped off (out of sight except for me, you see) and lay stretched out in the sun, flopping over now and then when the heat grew too brisk. They were as interesting as the seals, though different. But when I mentioned it, I was delirious again and got things mixed up, turned it all around, stating that naked women had been sunning on the seal rocks. The men said it was an outrage, sprawled on exhibit before the whole town that way. They said it was the wives or daughters of fishermen, likely, and it was their duty to report it. For two or three days they took turns with the telescope, glued to it, you might say; I hardly got any show at all. They gave up everything else to do their duty, but the girls never returned, of course, and it seemed to make the men sore. They said it was a waste of time handing over a high-powered telescope to a sick person, and a boy at that. What I wanted was some lead soldiers, or mud pies, any kind of gimcrack to keep the house from being tied up in knots. I wasn't disturbed much. Frankly, they didn't appear to have anything very pressing on their hands, war or no war. They could have sat gazing at a spider all day, and not slowed up the works two swings of a busted pendulum. The servants did it all.

By and by I improved so much, they said I could have my dog Bollo up in the room. They'd been keeping him at a farm. The dog had hardly been any trouble at all, killing two very small sheep that got out of a corral, as well as one of those nasty little hairless Chihuahuas that belonged to the overseer. He hadn't bit a single human, though he chased the overseer's wife up a tree one morning and kept her there all afternoon—sporting around the way he did, grinning, and frothing, and gnashing his teeth. A case could probably be made that he was a one-man dog. The overseer was peeved about the animals, even though it was his own fault, and the woman chipped in her two bits' worth, claiming she'd left the fire going and it had scorched the kitchen, so I gave them my burros, which calmed them down some.

I was glad to see the dog, and after I cleaned up the fragments of a vase he accidentally knocked off a table, he settled down as happy as a pig in swill. It was lucky about the vase; it wasn't even Mexican, but a piece of trash from China, so old I was surprised they still had it in the house—ming or sing, cheap pottery turned out by the barrelful by those poor, skinny, underpaid coolies. All in all, it was a good time, getting back my health there in Mazatlán, and a fine, cheery town it was in every way. When they released me outside, I hung around the harbor, watching fishermen unload boats, and strolled the long, deserted beaches above and below the city. Once in a while, as I walked along barefoot in the waves, a rough-looking customer or two crept out from the heavy fringe of palms and stood studying me over. But they seemed shy about the dog.

"*Muchacho,*" said one, a horrible sight, in rags, with a gold tooth and a black patch over one eye, "I think we can do some very good business." He had a sailfish carved out of bone and mounted on a board. Half the loafers in Mazatlán sold them, so I reckoned he'd followed me out, keeping pace under the palms. He kept licking his lips, and trying to grin, also glancing nervously over his shoulder, so that I finally spotted two other figures crouched back in the growth.

"Walk on up and let's talk about it," I said, happy to be taken for a fool. I'd had some dealing with Mexicans of this breed, and enjoyed getting even a little.

"That's one very big ugly dog, *muchacho*. I think you'd better tie up his jaws, then we do some business—if you know what good for you." I heard some laughter at this, but one of them shushed it.

"Why, no," I said, looking concerned, "I wouldn't care to do that. It's his feeding time"—I glanced up at the sun—"no, I was wrong; he's an hour past due, and I'm at fault. The way I figure it, you and those thieves under the palms should about make him a meal. I might have to throw in your mothers and sisters later, but you may just hold him. It's possible, as smelly and rank as you are. Anyhow, let's try," and I started undoing the chain.

I never saw a man take off so. He kept looking back, and when he saw he wasn't being followed, he slowed up to begin cursing. He was the maddest hombre I ever met, changed over in an instant from being oily-cringy-humble. There's no way to describe how fast their mood can shift, Mexicans like that.

The others straggled out from under the trees and commenced yelling and throwing rocks; but the man with the sailfish ran around in circles like a person demented. His hat had tumbled off, and his patch was slipped down, showing a red socket, and he couldn't find anything to improve his humor. In a kind of frenzy, he kicked out at a sand-rill, calling it an uncomplimentary name and promising to show it who was boss, but he hadn't any shoes on, so that didn't work, of course, and in fact like to killed him, so he lay down and hung onto his toes. Then he snatched up a palm frond and bit it. The others were obliged to grab him, finally, to keep him from having a seizure.

When I turned toward town, they followed along at the fringe, the man recovered now and calling out threats. He said they'd get me later, no matter where I hid, and would put me in a pit full of Gila monsters. "I've dug that pit," he shouted, "and collected the *culebras*. I'm glad I dug it, *muchacho*. The work was nothing."

I decided not to let matters rest, so I headed directly at them and said, "Don't shrink back, *cabrones*. The dog likes you; I can tell it. I only wanted to get a good description—for Don ——" (naming the people I lived with). "His vaqueros will find you very *pronto*. Maybe he will buy your sailfish, hey?"

Well, their attitude picked up in a twinkling. They didn't like the sound of this at all, but kept coming out to say, "*Hermano*, you realize we were making a little joke, between friends. Here" —placing it on the sand—"take the fish, as a favor."

I went on into town, glad to be rid of them. It wouldn't have disturbed their conscience any to have robbed me, cut off my head, and buried me there in the sand. It happened all the time.

There came the day for leaving, and I was almost sorry. Of all the places I'd seen in Mexico, Mazatlán was the sprightliest. It was tropical but not hot (being no farther south than Lower California); the people were generally friendly; the buildings clean and pretty; the beaches long and white and empty; the sea deep blue and handsome. They said the temperature stayed about sixty-seven in the winter and eighty-one in the summer. The waters right on shore were full of mackerel, rooster fish, dolphin, striped marlin, and sailfish, and you could hunt javelina and tiger-cats up in the mountains. On top of everything, the Market just bulged with good things to eat (excepting, maybe, chicle). I could have walked in there any day and loaded up for fifteen or twenty cents, but I never got around to it. If I strolled in that direction, my stomach appeared to steer me off somewhere else. It was curious.

I resolved I was coming back some day. On account of my

sickness, I hadn't got to know the people in our house very well. Even the religious young men that seized hold of the telescope talked in undertones, ignoring me, mostly. Neither did I eat with the others. It was decided that my nerves would recover better in my room. They were stand-offish people; Angelina said so herself. For some reason, this bunch had an attitude of superiority to Americans. Nobody had told them they were inferior, so they didn't know it yet. It doesn't sound likely, but it was true. Lieutenant Morales said we were the first foreigners who'd ever dined in the house, and the elderly old white-haired Don in charge would probably have to be shriven by the priests or he'd catch it later on when he died. I didn't know what it meant, but reckoned it had something to do with hair-cutting. It was a peculiar religion, here in Mexico, and embraced a barrelful of dodges and obligations. No ordinary person could sort it out.

For instance, I heard gunshots one day when in town, and, hurrying along, found the *azotea* of the parochial church occupied by armed men, who appeared to be firing at the people in the streets. At first it seemed unfriendly, but somebody explained it, I think, by saying that these bravos belonged to the Bishop's party, or that of the *Escocéses,* which opposed the "liberalists, anti-liberalists, or *Yorkinos,*" and were using this particular means of bringing it to the public attention. "If you value your ears, my friend," advised the man, "you will remain indoors till they pass to the next phase—that of Prayer." I thanked him, said it was all perfectly clear, being similar to the Baptists and Methodists back home, and scooted out of there. I was the last person on earth to buck up against a passel of saints when the worshipful fever was on them. I'd seen revivals in Missouri, and knew what to expect. Stomped was the least that could happen.

We boarded a boat, a vessel about ninety feet long with both sails and a steam engine that sounded as if somebody'd dropped an anvil inside, and got ready to sail down the coast. Directly after a noisy luncheon in the patio, many of the family came along to assist us. I was glad to see them. Off and on, I'd wondered what they looked like. I said goodbye to a number of people I'd never met, had two or three stranger women weep on my shoulder (and one burn a hole in my jacket), had one man hug me with emotion and say I'd been a veritable son to him (though he was nothing but a luncheon guest and hadn't laid eyes on half the family till then), and finally ducked out during the hullabaloo when Angelina slapped a harmless young fellow, standing in line, slightly drunk, who'd given her a real rouser of a farewell but turned out to be a member of the crew. She could skim the cream off a person's high spirits quicker than anybody I knew.

We were headed down the coast to a port called Acapulco—meaning pretty water, I believe. It was the easiest route, avoiding the worst mountains and traveling a fine old road, one of the oldest in Mexico, on the last hitch. The sea trip was interesting, done in sunny weather, with porpoises sporting about the bows and land in sight all the way. Palms and greenery along shore, and mountains rearing up behind. It took three days. We carried a cargo of lumber, smoked shrimps, and minerals from the province of Sinaloa, headed for Central America. The crew seemed more casual than most people with a boat. The Captain was dressed in a blue coat with brass buttons but had on a straw sombrero and under that a bandanna to keep off the sun. He claimed he had suffered sunstroke three or four times, and the doctors promised that the next one would kill him. So, taking no chances, he only appeared on deck at night, and had his eleven-year-old son do his work in the daytime. But a crewman knocked that story apart, laughing fit to kill, and said the old man was down below playing cards. The other two officers were generally with him, so the ship was left in the hands of riffraff without seamanship or conscience.

They'd rigged an awning for us amidships, after an argument with Lieutenant Morales, in which he distributed some money around. We took our meals there, the stench in the saloon being too brash to endure for more that five or six minutes at a time. Small fishing boats hove in sight pretty often, and the steersmen made no effort to avoid them; it was a kind of game. The closer we came, the more they doubled up laughing, full of fun and high jinks and sportsmanship. I could see the lieutenant trying to fasten a clamp on his temper, and figured he was apt to lose. If we came especially close to a boat, our scum of a crew pelted it with rotten oranges and papayas from the stores; then, at last, they had a burst of real luck and knocked a dory off the stern of a lugger. Another half-second and we'd sliced the craft in two like a melon.

Lieutenant Morales arose, excused himself, stepped crisply up the companionway to the quarterdeck, and addressed the squint-eyed windbag at the wheel.

"Summon the Captain."

The man shrugged, grinning. "Is much too sunshine, I think. I doubt it. No." Then he looked down, mouth open, at the point of a sword touching his throat, and said, "I wonder if I might suggest summoning the Captain, señor. It has occurred to me suddenly."

When the Captain appeared, blinking in the strong light, and scratching, Lieutenant Morales said, "About this crew now—"

"You notice it, señor? *Muchas gracias.* Hand-picked, cream of the crop, by myself in person. Finest body of men afloat."

"Very likely, but they nearly ran down a lugger, on purpose. I want it stopped."

The Captain scratched his head, then under one arm, then under the other, and said, very doubtful, "Maybe is possible, señor. I not know these men very well. Maybe they not like it."

"Are you the Captain here or not? What *are* your duties, by the way? I'll wish to make a full report to the owners. Who does the navigating?"

"*Aha!* All mens navigate—I teach them in person."

"Do you mean to tell me that these piratical guttersnipes are capable of celestial navigation? I doubt if any one of them could successfully row a skiff across a river."

"*Sí,* señor, I teach them in person. I say, 'You see land on left?—fine! On course!' One damn fine trip all the way."

As Lieutenant Morales stood regarding him, he excused himself, stating that he felt a sunstroke coming on, then disappeared below. The next blow-up came halfway to Acapulco when, during a light headwind, the engine gave three or four unusually loud knocks, backfired, snorted, missed a few licks, and exploded. A big puff of black smoke came rolling out of a ventilator and sprayed us with soot.

Lieutenant Morales reeled off the first profanity I ever heard him use; then we climbed down to inspect the damage. The Captain was there, and seemed happy.

"I tell them. Oh, yes, I tell them in person she not make one other trip. *Overhaul!* I say it openly to all."

"That's very well," said the lieutenant, "but where's your engineer?"

"He go to visit his mother, señor."

"Where? You mean aboard the ship here?"

"His mother live in Guaymas, señor. She very sick. He not return in time."

"You villain, isn't there anybody else who can work on this accursed collection of nuts and bolts?"

"It have to cool first, señor. Plainly, since the furnace door blows off onto the deck. Regard the flames inside. We be damn lucky if she don't catch fire and burn up, I imagine."

Well, we proceeded on, by sail, tacking this way and that, tedious and slow, and the next noon we ran out of food.

Up trooped the Captain, wearing his usual half-grin, and Lieutenant Morales says, "When we purchased the tickets for what turned out to be a lunatics' cruise, we planned on surviving the customary shipboard diet—neither good nor bad but adequate and sustaining. Instead, we are presented with"—he studied his plate—"approximately twelve stale beans apiece. My point is—why?"

The Captain looked pleased again. "By Dios, señor, it is the same. Once more, I tell them in person, twice, within the hearing of all—*somebody forget to provision!* Then I add a farcical remark, 'Peoples cannot eat coal!' which is very amusing to me." Then he added shrewdly, "We buy a great deal of fine food in Acapulco, señor. Cheap!"

This time, Lieutenant Morales pulled out a pistol and cocked it. "It amuses me to tell you that we require some food *here*, on this particular patch of ocean, *right now*. Do you see the village on shore? You can run in there, or do whatever else you like, but I'll expect four decent meals—make that five and include the dog—in the next hour and a half."

The activity that took place was wonderful to watch. As it

turned out, we didn't go to shore but reefed down to nothing and fished. *Everybody* fished, including us, at first using smoked shrimps then cut-fish for bait—trolling along very slow.

We ran through a school of mackerel—shoals of mackerel, with silver streaks on their sides, you could have walked on them—then some big jacks which were worthless besides being a nuisance, and some dolphins with blunt heads, a beautiful blue-green when we flopped them up on deck, and finally snagged a sailfish but lost it after two high splashy leaps: the hook was too small.

Well, sir, in a little *less* than an hour and a half, we not only had the fish but that pinchpenny cheat of a Captain had dug down in his private stores and handed the cook some corn meal for bread, pickles, spiced fruit, and wine.

He was mightily worried that he was about to be shot, and I didn't blame him. Lieutenant Morales was a patient and slow-moving man, but once he'd worked out a statement, I figured he meant exactly what he said.

The rest of the trip was calm. Nothing else happened; we got along fine, and the Captain, you might say, now went as far in the opposite direction. He was a pest, and I never could decide whether he was doing it on purpose. He popped up every thirty minutes or so to inquire if things were all right.

"*Qué pasa*, ladies and gentlemens? Wish an orange? Nice slice of fish? Nuts? Pulque maybe?"

Lieutenant Morales finally told him to leave us alone, then felt poorly about it and gave him five dollars, which he quickly put in his pocket, saying he couldn't accept it, wouldn't dream of accepting it, but would place it in the Sailors' Welfare Fund. Then, at last, he disappeared for good. We never saw him again till the anchor went down in Acapulco Bay.

One nice starry night, with a white moon and the ocean hissing by and twinkling twig fires visible way off on shore, Angelina and the lieutenant leaned against the rail, talking low, and the interpreter stood a foot or so behind. I was seated beneath a lifeboat, minding my own business, and tried not to overhear, but failed.

Angelina says, "I should have taken the boy home. I've behaved selfishly."

The interpreter reeled this off without any serious comment of his own.

"Luckily for me," replied the lieutenant, "California is still at war, still Mexican. You had no choice." He took a pull at his cigar, and the interpreter, winding this part up, did identically the same thing; then he coughed pretty hearty. The smoke went down the wrong pipe or something.

"What's to become of us?"

Well, the interpreter delivered this as, roughly, "I shiver when I consider what may happen between us," but Lieutenant Morales took it the right way and replied, "You will like Mexico better when you reach my father's farm. It is very serene, the land is quiet—"

So far, so good, but this came out: "At my father's humble abode we can have great privacy, with no distractions but each other."

There was a wrench lying on deck, and I started to pick it up, but Angelina said, "Perhaps we should stay at an inn. Running a small farm is chore enough without visitors. And a lieutenant's pay, in Mexico—"

Lieutenant Morales' expression stayed about the same, but he said, "It will be all right. My father is very hospitable. He is—greatly esteemed."

No change in the interpretation; everything back on the track. Then Angelina put a hand on his arm, seriously, not like her old self, and said, "I admire you, rising above your class. It's unheard of, a farmer in this country."

I felt a little easier. The girl hadn't improved any. She was so cocksure about her own position, she just naturally figured that everybody else was standing around cap in hand. Why wouldn't she be, keeping five or six darky girls on the jump all day long? One thing you could say about Hyacinth, he never spoiled anybody. On the contrary, you had to outwit him to survive.

Well, all this fakey artificial polite talk begun to grate on the interpreter's nerves, so when the lieutenant turned and said, "The moonlight makes your face even more beautiful," it translated out as, "I love your eager face and the ripeness of your figure—you turned my blood to fire when I first walked into your tent."

If Angelina hadn't been so balky about learning Spanish, she could have spotted this humbug easy enough. As it was she stepped back a little, and murmured something that, translated, proved to be (approximately) "Why, then, do you wait? When my bosom hungers?" and the poor deluded fellow kissed her, doing a bang-up and complete job of it, too, mouth, hands and shanks. She appeared to enjoy herself for awhile, but finally gasped, pushed him away, recovered her breath, and said, "This is a little *too* fast!" and slapped him good and hard.

All right, there you were. It was nobody's fault but the interpreter's, but I never got a chance to say so. Angelina stalked off, though I had a feeling she wanted to stay, and the lieutenant stood rubbing his face, looking downcast and shamed. Then, recovering, he said, *"Qué las norteamericanas son inescrutables!"*

Who could blame him?

Next morning, when we steamed into Acapulco, they had apparently forgot all about it. The place was busy, with lots of ships, sail and steam, in a three-mile-broad bay, and small boats rowing to shore, and chatter and laughter floating across from all these various craft. The water was a brilliant blue and the beaches so white they dazzled your eyes. Big rock cliffs rose up nearby, and twice coming in past La Quebrada, I saw Mexican boys soar out from high ledges in long, lazy, graceful curves, plunging down hundreds of feet, it seemed, to knife into a tiny cove, making no more splash than a few white bubbles. It took your breath away.

What we had here was one of the oldest (and finest) harbors in Mexico, in use as early as 1512, and a main port of call in the China trade, back during the Spanish occupation. A regular *diligencia* line ran to Mexico City, stopping several times along the way, exactly like our stagecoaches, only this outfit used six mules, four leaders abreast. Lieutenant Morales bought all the space in one carriage, coolly informing the driver that we preferred to ride by ourselves.

I saw Angelina stare as if she wondered how a farmer could get so uppity, but she kept her mouth shut for once, and we climbed aboard, then became involved in an argument about the dog.

"The dog goes as a passenger, *paisano,*" said Lieutenant Morales. "He has three tickets to establish his station."

"So—then he must hold them in his paws," said the driver. "I take them from him directly; it lies within the regulations." He was as stubborn a Mexican as I ever encountered. Commonly a small bribe can persuade them to boil down their grandmothers for soap, but nothing could budge this one.

"Very well, my good baboon, how much for your carriage, with the mules, and the book of regulations? Permit me to buy them all," and the lieutenant took out a long leather purse. The weather was blistering hot down here in the lower tropics, and we were anxious to climb up into the cool plateaus.

"Oh, come," said Angelina. "Tie the silly animal to the axle, and stop showing off. In fact, I think I'll pay for our passage myself. You can't afford all this splendor. Three tickets for a dog!"

Things finally got calmed down, but it was one ruckus that Lieutenant Morales lost, and he didn't care for it at all. It represented a side of him that I hadn't seen. Anyhow, the dog trotted behind the carriage.

You start ascending fairly soon from Acapulco, maybe five miles out, where the last of the palms grow. I remember a succession of ridges, a steep, shaded cañon—Zopilote, or Vulture Cañon, maybe—the Rio Papagayo, and a few towns like Chilpancingo, Iguala, Taxco, built in layers up a peak, and Cuernavaca, where the rich Spanish once had country homes. We changed mules now and then, and drivers once, barely in time to avoid a murder, I judged. The truth is, I slept most of the way, out of boredom, mainly. It was a bumpy ride without much entertainment, except dark, grave-faced boys that crept out onto the road dangling iguanas from strings, hoping to sell them for a real or two. They make a very good steak—the iguanas, I mean—but look too dragon-scaly to be enjoyable.

Angelina and Lieutenant Morales buckled down learning English and Spanish, ordering the interpreter to teach it both ways, and the lieutenant, possibly smartening up slightly, told him, "It will be conducted without embellishments, Luis. Get out of line even an inch, and I'll beat you with my saber." So they tucked into that project, up hill and down dale, around the narrow, windey roads, during noonings beside streams, at night in the fondas, everywhere. They became mighty chummy about it, joking and laughing at their mistakes, and me, I commenced to wish I didn't know anything but French. It was that painful. Some people are born with an ear for languages, myself being an example, while others, like these magpies, would do better to stick to signs. Nearly all of these high-born Mexicans finish their educations Abroad, and so had Lieutenant Morales, but he'd skipped English for some reason.

Each night, Angelina squawked about him taking the costliest rooms where we stopped, and generally tried to squash him down to living like a sick Indian. She'd fixed onto this idea of his being a poor downtrodden farmer trying to impress the daughter of rich Missouri planters, and hardly let it rest. He was nice about it, though he often looked uncomfortable and embarrassed. Once he tried to say, "My dear girl, I really *can* afford—" but she broke in like a terrier and insisted, this time, on settling for three dingy little rooms that even the dog sniffed at, and he wasn't used to much. It made her feel virtuous, I expect, but I saw Lieutenant Morales gaze wistfully into some elegant chambers that the proprietor kept for the wealthy Gachupines who traveled this road to Acapulco. Still, he couldn't speak out; not enough to bottle her up. It wasn't in his breed.

For a farmer, he appeared to have a lot of friends. One noon we stopped in Taxco (we had a second driver, now, a man with a sensible attitude toward tips) and trudged up the spiral cobble road to a fonda, where the lieutenant shook several hands at the bar. He apologized, seating the rest of us at a table outside on a flower-draped terrace that looked down across red tile roofs and skinny church spires to the mountains and the plains below. It was a breath-taking place, and we had a wonderful meal. Everything from raw oysters on a hammered silver platter to thick lentil soup to chicken with a darkish sweet sauce called *mole*. And after that, avocado paste, (spicy-hot, with onion, garlic and tomato) and mashed frijoles and on to sugared tropical fruits, or *dulces,* made from papayas, bananas, and oranges. They had ice-cold melon, too, but I was too full to eat it. We fell to wondering about the ice, and found that they fetched hunks from glaciers up in the mountains, here and in Puebla and Mexico City as well.

It was the best meal we'd had on this ride, including the ship's fare, which was swill, and I didn't mind when they told me the mole was made out of chicken blood.

At Cuernavaca, we stopped again, this time in mid-afternoon, and Lieutenant Morales had the driver take us to a part of town where we could see the snow-capped volcano of Popocatepetl thrusting up so high as to seem alone in that long stretch of plateau, nearly eighteen thousand feet, still and withdrawn and maybe brooding, I thought, on the awfulness of some parts of life just now in Mexico. An hour later, when we picked up the lieutenant again, Angelina noticed that he paid all the men's bills at the cantina, so she harped on this while we proceeded, but he was too sunk down in thought to notice. We were getting close to the cities, and I felt a twinge of excitement in my stomach. I had lived a long time with bad luck, and wondered if it would get better or worse. The traffic grew heavier on the highway, slowing us up, but we stopped at Tenango, only a few miles from the capital, climbed down, collected our baggage, tipped the driver again (making five times in the last hundred miles) and hired a private carriage at a livery stable. The owner made a point of shaking hands with the lieutenant, then lifted his hat a few inches off of his head. At an offering of two gold pieces for the rig, he waved one finger angrily, closed the fist on the coin, and said something about "*su padre.*"

Suddenly the atmosphere had changed. The language lessons were over, the chattering and laughing had dried up, and our host's face suggested that his mind was on other matters entirely. The war, the heavy fighting, was going on not far from here, and I commenced to see wounded soldiers—a man on crutches, one with an empty sleeve flapping, another with a dirty bandage across an eye. Then we rolled out on a narrow road that branched off, I figured, into the country that lay between Mexico City and Puebla. No traffic here, no signs of anything except, by and by, cattle in the distance, and, once, a couple of men on horseback, way off. No fences, medium-good grass, cactus, mesquite, chaparral—the usual Mexican plateau growth, but richer and greener, too.

The hours passed and Lieutenant Morales lost his somber look; he sat up to glance around on both sides, interested and alert. His silence finally exasperated Angelina to say, "Well, where *is* this precious farmstead of yours? Does it exist?"

After a moment, he said, "It exists, señorita. You are on it now." She studied this over, and said, "Oh?" Then the situation begun to sink into her backwoods skull, but it was a while before she could bring herself to ask. "How *long* have we been on it?"

"For—perhaps two hours. Seventeen or eighteen miles. It will be eighteen miles when we reach those trees; I was permitted to ride there as a child."

She lay back against the seat and closed her eyes, and frankly, I enjoyed watching her. In the space of three or four minutes, she had learned a whole new set of ideas, and maybe Missouri excluding all others was gone from her bones forever.

We clip-clopped down a slope, crossed a pretty green stream with brown pebbles in the shallows, rode through the cottonwoods, and after a mile or so saw other, bigger trees ahead. A few slow spirals of very black smoke rose up, all separated by some little distance. I hadn't any idea what they meant, but I felt sick inside when I saw Lieutenant Morales' face.

He arose in the seat and lashed at the mules but it was no more than a minute before a wild, hurrying band of horsemen—vaqueros swinging sideways in their saddles—came pounding down on us like the furies.

Lieutenant Morales vaulted out of the carriage, shouting, "What is it? What's happened?"

The leader of this hard-looking bunch said, "El Presidente Herrera, he was here, Don Ricardo. Then the soldiers of the Black One, shooting and burning and pursuing, and also, I think, Santa Anna himself—"

"Where is my father?" cried the lieutenant, seizing him by the shirt.

"Don Antonio está muerto, patrón," said the leader, and taking off his sombrero commenced to weep.

XXVII

CHAPULTEPEC, *September, 1847:* I shall set down the events in chronology, while I await a surgeon's decision whether henceforth I am to walk on one leg or two. Or, perhaps (as the prudent man suggests, rattling his instruments), none at all. In any case, my career as a soldier appears to be ended, and with it many another in this "flying hospital" filled with the penitent, the lachrymose, and the semi-conscious.

The reader should be informed that I am routinely drugged and may be found guilty, with De Quincey, of morbid flights into the personal. As of this moment, I doubt it. My memory is sharp and clear, my outlook cheerful, my bowels open (surgeon's term indicating a hopeful sign) and, altogether, I feel splendidly able and composed. *Nor is this due to morphine.* There are those who have a tolerance for the drug, damn it, and I seem to be among them. Instead of suffering my wits to be dulled, I find them honed and ready, snapped to attention in replacement of the mortal coil fallen. In short, my military duties are, once again, scholastic. Well enough. *Alia tentanda via est. Cedant arma togae.*

Is that you, Carla? The reader must forgive me if I include all pertinent facts, including asides to friends, as I wait. A Journal of War, to have value, should be complete. No, I don't wish a glass of water. Why do you cry? Really, I've never felt better in my life. You must go now. I am busy. Plainly. Return later. There is hardly any occasion to kiss me. Besides, you smell of tobacco again. Later, later.

After the amusing incident of the guerrillas (bandits?), we resumed our search for the Army, my companions only barely maintaining the discipline that I thought necessary to a floating unit—combatant-literary—such as the one I led. Laugh, but a captain with collateral obligations involving the quill, a reluctant sergeant drowning in piety, a renegade nymph from the *noblesse,* and a partially reformed gambler-laundress of tireless carnality do not comprise a command easily managed. Essentially it is non-homogenous, and requires special techniques. In this I flatter myself that I came up to scratch. Rallying the corps for a last forced march toward the action, I ordered one member to remove two petticoats (over which she had been stumbling, as an example); forcibly persuaded another to put one on, out of modesty; ordered O'Hara to quit babbling about Chinamen; then reloaded my rifle and inscribed a few hasty notes. After that, we were off over the still littered road to war.

General Scott was approaching Puebla, which had been announced as ripe for conquest. By quizzing sick or wounded soldiers, and from other sources unmentionable at this time, we learned that he had issued a proclamation, "a crowning act of conciliation," aided by the Bishop of Puebla, and that the people were greatly impressed.

I should say that Puebla was more fully under the domination of a comparatively enlightened Church than any other Mexican city. It was also thoroughly satiated with the military. The whole fabric of Santa Anna's lies began to fall apart. The Americans had proved *not* to be "barbarians, vandals, tigers." They had *not* "branded and sent across the Gulf into slavery shiploads of Tampicos." They had *not* stuck little children with bayonets at Vera Cruz. And, supremely important, Buena Vista no longer stood up as a Mexican victory.

On the contrary, whenever the Americans appeared, taxes were abolished and trade became brisk. The odious *alcabala,* or excise law, which laid a tax on every species of barter and sale, was quickly suspended, causing the Indians to dance in the street for joy. Scott's treatment of soldiers, by contrast to Santa Anna's, made army life seem like a continuing fiesta. And Americans, in the towns, were much preferred to the guerrillas, who were not only eyesores but murderous.

The tide of sentiment was shifting, and, as usual with any change of opinion, it swung to the point of absurdity. Thinking over the destruction at Cerro Gordo, the Mexican populace asked, "Why resist?" A number of American deserters added stories which when sufficiently inflated made this course logical. The average American soldier was capable of killing a Mexican immediately, with one stroke of a sword. It was done over and over. American horses were not only gigantic—three times the size of a mustang and possibly having eight legs—but they could run faster than geese flying. It was difficult for the naked eye to follow one at top gallop. Veritably. Of the American artillery, it was known that the smallest guns could shoot as far as Cuba; moreover, every shell exploded into fifty pieces, each one fatal.

In the face of these depressing statistics, Puebla prepared itself for accommodation. The churchmen, asserting themselves (and their God), replaced a militant governor with Isunza, a man of compliance, and took to the streets with processions, the purport of which was to show that prayer conquers all. (The writer is not qualified to debate this; certainly it conquered Puebla.) The new governor, after a benediction or two, ordered the city's arms and ammunition sent away—"for safekeeping." Then he could "find no funds for military purposes." Suddenly the cupboard was bare, a mystery that the Bishop, not Mother Hubbard, might have cleared up in a twinkling. "Reason prohibits vain sacrifices," stated the Governor, a sophistry that will likely be used by cowards and connivers throughout the history of declining nations. After the arrival of the *Americans,* he said, *no more than three citizens were to meet in public.*

We were told, the day before joining Scott, that this last occasioned open grumbling. What about card games involving two sets of partners? War was war (all agreed) but must it toss a wrench into the city's saloon life by requiring three hands and a dummy? Unperturbed, the authorities additionally decreed that nobody should appear on the streets carrying an unsigned placard. If, that is, a person wished to carry a placard saying, "The hell with both Santa Anna *and* the Church!" he must subscribe it, "Juan Pinga," or "Hector Moreno," or whatever his name might be. The over-all sentiment now became diffused, the people of Puebla apparently being much given to unsigned-placard carrying. Neatly straddling a fence, *Monitor del Pueblo* announced, "We can only await with resignation the terrible blow with which Providence chooses to afflict us." "Catholics or no Catholics," I heard one man remark, "they at least had the gumption to pick on the guilty Party."

It was in this confused atmosphere, a few miles out from town, after weeks and months of unrequited ambition, that I finally caught up with the Army and presented my papers to General Scott.

You again, Carla? No, I don't wish a cold cloth. As you see, I am writing. Yes, I understand; there are a good many waiting for attention, some worse than me. I seem pale? No, I do not prefer to be sick. You will hold the basin? The idea is repugnant. Maybe just a little sick—

Yes, I intend to put it all down, the good and the bad, sickness and health, everything. Why won't I sleep? Because you see me, here, climbing my own heights of Chapultepec, under fire. Rhetoric over and beyond the Call of Duty.

Is there anything you can do? Well, just read it over so far. But withhold suggestions. A writer wants approval, not criticism. And do not under any circumstances say, "Fine, great, absolutely wonderful, but what I didn't like was—"

So. You feel that, at certain parts, I have descended to the frivolous? War is not *frivolous. Neither are the troubles of Mexico frivolous. In some ways, I am typical of what is meant by the term "gringo"?*

Well, I see that I am busy after all, my girl. No, no; there is no need to be sorry. You possess a quick temper; true. But it means nothing. Yes, I agree—I am gravely wounded. Wounded, at least.

Later. Come back later. But not as a critic. Leave the criticisms behind. I'll send word if I need you. But don't wait up. The criticisms are stupid.

I must confess to a rapid thumping of the heart when, after endless argument and explanation, I pushed past two iron-jawed sentries and on into the semi-darkness of the General's Headquarters tent. From a surly, bespectacled, omniscient adjutant, he had at last been given my message. He sat behind what appeared to be a species of folding games table, with inlaid chequers of parti-colored wood: a rough-hewn giant with an expression of infinite fatigue and wearing a worn and faded poncho drawn over his massive shoulders.

I hastened to apologize, in view of his crowded schedule, but he actually *stood up* to shake my hand! I was dwarfed, beaten-down, annihilated by his frame; he stood six feet five and was large in proportion. (He was also a man, as we now know, with many problems, of which the winning of the war was perhaps the least vexing. At odds with a witless Administration, intrigued against by cunning and ambitious political generals like Pillow and Worth, he would eventually be deposed, shamed at a court of inquiry, and, in the words of an outraged Captain R. E. Lee, "turned out as an old war horse to die." Never was Montaigne's description of such tricksters more apt: "Since we cannot attain to greatness, let us revenge ourselves by railing at it.")

"I have Colonel Doniphan's letter, General," I said, holding it forth. "I dislike to take up your valuable time."

"Sir," he replied with astonishing humility, "I can find time to talk to a gentleman from Missouri. The state bears a reputation for truth. I hear far too little such speech in these days."

He took the letter, asked me to be seated and himself sat down, with a demeanor that I could only think of, in a fellow historian's words, as "venerable and majestic."

He read the letter slowly, twice or thrice over, giving himself plenty of time to digest the contents, and looked up now and then to study me politely. For some reason, I suddenly gained an impression of complete confidence in a fellow human being. Then, carefully, he folded the letter and placed it beneath a white stone paperweight.

"You and the colonel are close personal friends, then?" he inquired almost wistfully.

"More properly he is my father's friend. He is also our family counselor."

"I once heard it said by a person of importance that Alexander Doniphan was the only great man he ever met who looked like one."

"The second, sir," I replied promptly, and meant it. To my embarrassment, he flushed.

"Captain, you might lose that impression if you listened to some of my subordinates. They consider me a doddering old fool, superannuated, set in my ways, wrong-headed, over-emotional, prone to regard the common soldier as cut from the same cloth of humanity as the officer, and generally unfit to command. Let me tell you this," he went on, leaning forward, "for I seldom have a chance to unbend—*one or two of those fellows hope to be President*."

He sighed heavily, leaning back. "I sometimes get the notion that they're fighting for that, and that only. Excepting, of course, that they do fight *me*. There we must give them credit." Then, no doubt feeling that he had said too much, he added, "But it's no matter, no matter. We're here to prosecute a war. Let us do so, and ignore the barking of jackals."

"I am flattered by your confidence, sir," I said, "and assure you I'll always work with you instead of against you. As to my position, no doubt you have some company or other, cavalry preferred, whose officer has been incapacitated. I can easily—"

"Yes, sir, we can only try to make the correct decisions, and hope they'll be swallowed without friction. General Quitman commands the Volunteer Division. Worth, and Twiggs—there's a good man, by the way—and, ah, Pillow head the others. Now, sir, Johnny Quitman tells me his muster rolls are in a snarl to frighten an accountant. You knew he lost Meyerbach? Well, now, let's give him a hand. Later, perhaps, after settling in—"

"You mean, sir, that I'm *not* to head up a company? At Sacramento—"

He arose and came round, dropping an arm over my shoulder in fatherly fashion, then propelled me in the friendliest way toward the exit.

"Those things come along in order. I've noticed it time and again. You and John Quitman should hit it off first rate; you'll like him, and he'll like you. Get him out of that mess he's in. It'll tell pretty heavily in the final reckoning."

"General," I said, "will you do me the courtesy of letting me read Alex Doniphan's letter? It's hard to think that he would—"

"Now, now, nothing of the sort; quite the contrary. Colonel Doniphan says here"—patting his breast pocket, where the letter now reposed—"that your courage is so unbridled that you'd like to win the war singlehanded. It wouldn't be fair to the rest of us, would it? *Larkins!*" he bawled to the adjutant. "You can lay off eavesdropping now and come in. I bid you good day, Captain Shelby, and the best of luck!"

It's difficult to explain, but I came away fired with a determination to seize the intractable muster rolls and shake them into submission. In due course, I met General Quitman, an amiable and splendid-looking man, though harassed at the moment, as advertised. He complained bitterly about Meyerbach, calling him "a false friend," "a shifty Semite," and a "genius gone sour," so that, in disgust, I gained an impression that the man had turned coat or deserted. "Getting hit in the arm—the right arm—at a time like this!" said General Quitman, staring me down as if I meant to argue. "I kept telling him to crouch, but he kept getting up. And I'll tell you something else—that ball was meant for *me*. How's that for impertinence?" I murmured something placating, and went to work, using O'Hara as a kind of rough bookkeeper, or filing clerk.

On May eleventh, we heard that Santa Anna was moving his forces from the capital toward Puebla, and an excited bustle stirred the camp. But when the order came to march, as soon as the provision train arrived, we found ourselves opposed, so to speak, by no more than about twenty-five hundred cavalry (with three pieces of artillery) at the village of Amozoc. There followed a confused exchange of shots, and the redoubtable Santa Anna (if indeed he was present) retired, inflicting no casualties but generously leaving behind six prisoners, including his chaplain and a lieutenant, besides eight cavalry horses.

Then, on into Puebla, a glittering milestone of this war. Everybody (except the men suffering from dysentery) was in a carnival humor, and the populace cheered or blew kisses when we passed. On the balconies with the ladies were a great many priests, all wearing black robes and having, on their heads, felt hats resembling a piece of flattened stovepipe. They made gestures blessing us, and then I'm hanged if O'Hara, in his new role of lay brother, didn't begin to bless *them*, as well as everybody else in sight. It was a paradoxical act, for he was dressed in a rig so villainous that, with his bulk, he looked more formidable than a guerrilla. I admonished him strongly, but he scarcely heard me, in the intoxication of his success, replying only, "And not a Chinyman in the lot, sir! It's like a bit of Heaven after what we bin through."

Unlike its counterparts in America, the city has no suburbs. One emerges abruptly from cultivated fields into compactly built dwellings that bear little resemblance to the Mexico of our previous experience. There is a European sophistication here. The broad thoroughfares were swarming with onlookers who spilled far back into the cross streets. Our little army of four thousand was lost, swallowed up, in the surging sea of curious. At the central Plaza we halted, stacked our arms, and rested for two hours while quarters were assigned to the different corps, the lodgings of most being arranged in monasteries.

I obtained permission from General Quitman (with whom my professional relationship is now virtually that of aide-de-camp, which was probably Scott's idea in the first place) to billet our foursome at my own expense, and we dined that first night at the Commercio, an excellent eating house near the Palace, kept by a Frenchman. From my Grand Tour, I could not help but recall that one finds it almost impossible to eat meanly in any French-run establishment.

All was not roses in Puebla, however. The visitor to Mexico, even in peacetime, must keep in mind that the old, old country lies sleeping in primitive torpor, half in, half out of an Aztec culture both ignorant and contemptuous of Western mores. In the morning, we found a girl stabbed dead near our doorstep, the victim of *ladrones* (thieves) who swarm the streets at late hours. She was a person of no account, a trollop and gambler, but we thought it monstrous that she should lie untouched until after ten o'clock. I have noticed that dreadful things often come in twos and threes. That same night, as we returned from a walk, a Mexican man staggered groaning to our door, terribly stabbed and cut about the head. His wounds were attended, but it occurred to no one to summon the authorities. *Sí*, such abominations occur in Mexico, señor. It is best to guard oneself . . . avoid the reckless drinking of aguardiente . . . one becomes accustomed—

But the more we saw of the city, the more we loved and admired it. It was kept almost excessively clean! The streets, paved with square blocks of granite, appeared not only swept but scoured. Early in the mornings, each inhabitant sweeps in front of his house, heaping the accumulated dirt in the middle of the street, from where by sunrise police carts carry it outside the city. Further, we were in the rainy season, and the freshets began daily at about half-past four, continuing for two hours or more. The rest of the day was clear, the temperature delightful.

All around the horizon, looking from this brightest jewel in Mexico's tiara, rose snow-topped mountains—Orizaba, Popocatepetl, the Volcano de Puebla—of which the eye never wearied. Nothing in the scene abraded the senses, beyond the town or in. The upper floors of the old Spanish houses, two and three stories in height, project over the sidewalk, supported by arches resting on a Doric colonnade. The over-all impact is exotic, warm, friendly, Mediterranean, but it is in the interior court, with its fountains and fine paintings, that the life of a Mexican family thrives. Perhaps in no other place on earth does the passion for domestic privacy rise to this same high pitch.

The weeks passed, I looked for Sam, my duties lightened, we wandered the streets like tourists with a guidebook. In the churches, especially in the Cathedral, O'Hara acquired an aura of beatification that struck me as downright offensive. After the pilgrims had entered, knocked aside or kicked a beggar or two, lit a candle, knelt, prayed, then risen to leave, they often found O'Hara at the doorway, beaming like the presiding genie of the establishment, and, as God is my witness, uttering a frequent pious *"Pax Vobiscum."* It was enough to sicken an informed person on religion. In fairness, I must say this for him; *he never accepted gratuities.* Those small coins that he did take (absolving the donor from everything in the process) he dropped in the poor box. He may always have had, as a reputable priest told me, a lurking potential for the cloth; for my part, I hastened him out when I could.

On the Plaza's opposite side stood the Governor's mansion, which housed General Scott and staff during our stay. Along the other sides of the square were rows of shops, smart, filled with wares both native and foreign, and in the center a splendid fountain played from multiple spouts. Around this, hundreds of country people, seated before stalls or lounging in the open, offered for sale the many-hued fruits, vegetables, and flowers of the region. It made a fine splash of color, there in the sun in the clean white old Spanish city. And one's spirits were further brightened by the sight of hackney coaches, rare vehicles, perhaps modeled after that of Queen Joanna the Foolish, who is said to have introduced the first coach into Spain. In the intervening years, they have undergone no change; they are the same lumbering vehicles, suspended on leather springs, that you see in the faded, illustrated copies of *Gil Blas* and *Don Quixote: el cochero,* on his mule, with postilions when they have a team of six or eight.

Sunday is the fete day. The gardens in the park take on a look of special loveliness, and the families high and low spill out from their barricaded retreats to stroll, flirt, romp with children, listen to music, eat dulces and sleep in the grass. The rich and fair ladies of Puebla roll along the roads in coaches, attended by their beaux on horseback. Their dress is magnificent. In the phrase of an acquaintance, "The flash of their diamonds and brilliants is only rivaled by the bewitching glances of their dark eyes. They are noble women, and more noble-hearted creatures never existed on earth."

Do you attend, my good Carla?

Then, always, against this radiance of daytime Mexico, the black night deed casts its shadow on one's rising exuberance.

Acts sometimes so foul as to stagger the non-Latin mind. One evening, walking from my quarters with a Captain Favel, we found a group of Mexicans, horror-struck, standing in the doorway of a fine-looking house. Crossing themselves, they asked us to enter, and in a long curtained room lit with candles—a ghostly sight—we saw the dead body of an old gray-haired woman, all dabbled with blood, her throat cut from ear to ear. On a bed in one corner lay a beautiful young girl of six or seven years whose head was nearly severed.

Outraged to the point of violence, we asked the cause of this frightful butchery, and learned that the girl was an heiress (her parents being dead) in possession of a hundred thousand dollars, which, at her own death, would go to the Cathedral of Puebla. Some monster of an under-priest, irking his superiors, had not been able to wait but had murdered both the child and her dueña. So far as I know, he was never punished. However, a friend engaged in writing a book to be called "General Lane's Brigade in Central Mexico" intends to pursue the subject to its bitter end. So, we shall see.

*You again, Carla? You won't care for this last scrap of narrative. It might amuse your father. No, nothing. Yes, a pain appears to be growing in my right leg; perhaps a spider bite, a scorpion, even. I dislike to complain, but really—*don't move it! *I'm sorry, but that hurt very badly. No scorpion? Hold on—where to?*

It comes as no surprise to me that the creature is impossible. I admire the rest of her family; they have good taste. Hello, who's this? You've bought *me some morphine! Really, my girl, you can't go about bribing our orderlies. This isn't Mexico. It is? Well, the point is moot. Moot. No, I don't know what it means; I never did. Moot, mooter, mootest. You might memorize those, by the way. They've got me out of many a tight jam, cornerstone of my education.*

Carla, if you don't mind, I don't wish to stop writing. It's going very well. I don't need morphine, either, but I do have a pain—by damn, what a pain I have now! *You're certain about the scorpion? Maybe a little sick again. You'd even better hurry . . .* basin, *Carla!*

. . . that's a remarkable experience, like death, almost, or anyway you don't care so much about death while it goes on. It's what some people get out of religion. Dear Carla. I wouldn't kiss me if I were you; I stink of sickness. A very funny thing, and possibly even moot, is that when I'm writing the Journal I notice nothing else. Rx: Syntax, the household nostrum for everything.

What happened to that fellow with the morphine? Why *has he mislaid his bloody pills? No, I don't need them, my boy, so you can wipe that smirk off your face. I see. I suppose my teeth* were *gripping slightly; that's the way I hold my mouth. You can't get the pills down while I grip? Go slack? I tell you again*—don't move me! *Maybe you'd better give them to me now. It'll take a moment?*—yes!

Well, now. All right. Very good. Nothing at all. You see—I didn't need them.

Now we come to the fighting, to the strong part; that is, until the contretemps that led to the above. Our four divisions rode out of Puebla in the second week of August, General Twiggs leading the way. The townsfolk lined the streets, General Scott passed each regiment, moving to the head of his columns, and the regimental bands one after the other played "Hail to the Chief." It was blood-stirring, and convinced me that I would soon meet my destiny as a leader of men. (In all modesty, I had laid a firm foundation: the muster rolls were in the best of order.)

I should append a sad footnote to this occasion: many, many of our troops were left in Puebla, some forever, others stricken less desperately with dysentery—*el vómito*—the curse of bad health that affects most foreigners, sooner or later, in this Janus-faced land where no city's water supply is safe to drink, or, I predict, will be safe to drink for the next hundred years. After all, señor, to what purpose? For the gringos? Well, *mañana*.

We are headed for the capital, there to strike the last killing blows at Santa Anna and restore peace to the suffering land. So we are told, so I believe. The way lies over the valley of Puebla, to the right of Popocatepetl, our course northwest. The morning is clear and cold, growing hot as the sun nears its zenith. The scenery exceeds in grandeur and sublimity anything in our experience. On all sides glitter peaks with white summits buried thousands of feet deep in ice and snow; below, on the plain, are white haciendas, and off in the distance frowns the great pyramid of Cholula.

In two hours we toil up to the pass, eleven thousand feet high; then descend into the glorious valley of Mexico and stand for awhile looking on, overwhelmed, from the spot where Cortez first beheld it: a vast plateau rich with towns, lakes, orderly patches of cultivation, ranches, *casas de campos* of the wealthy, color and life and history, the high-flown kingdom of the Aztecs, Montezuma's toy, a magic domain and princely.

We reach Buena Vista—not Taylor's Buena Vista—then on over broad fields of maize to Chalco, where we camp beside a centuries-old church, built in the shape of a cross and containing in its gloomy, cavernous main vault the inscribed names and histories of all the curates who served in this place from 1606. The walls are hideous with cracked and faded painting and Latin legend. One whole panel is given to the pictorial agonies of persons, not further identified—renegade priests?—who left the world with sins not yet atoned for. If that long-ago artist was working on the right track, they are being kept exceedingly busy, and miserable, at the moment. (Ecclesiastical Spanish, not Latin, was good enough for those fellows):

"HOY POR MY, MANANA POR TY—COMO TE BEO, ME BI—COMO ME BES, TE BERAS. ALIBAME POR TU AMOR QUE OTRA A TI, TE ALIBIARA. CUANTO BIEN HASES POR MI, ES OTRO TANTO CAUDAL QUE CONTREPESADO A EL, ATESORAS PARA TY."

"I today—thou tomorrow—what thou are, I was; as thou seest me, wilt thou be seen thyself. Aid me, for thine own love, that another may aid thee. All the good thou doest for me is so much treasure laid in the balance, in thy favor."

I stand before the wall and transcribe, essentially a non-religious man, impressed a little in spite of myself.

The regiments are strung out. We hear firing behind us; nobody knows what it means. It ceases and we push on. The lake-chain of Chalco and Xochimilco begins here, and there is talk that Scott has commandeered boats in which to transport us toward the capital. But no such order goes out. We move forward in a stinging rain, detouring around the lake in a "feint," the road becoming congested with troops closing up, wagons, ambulances, and heavy artillery. Through the rain, silent and nervous, we view an odd region of contrasts: here green with olive groves, there pocked with the truncated cones of ancient volcanoes; maize; aquamarine fields of maguey—and always, where this last grows, mestizos selling pulque. I am thirsty and would like to drink, but the "whole-swine" containers, with tails and legs sticking out in bold relief, moving at every sloshing of the liquid, prove too much for my stomach.

"Pulque!! Al néctar de los Dioses!"

Softly pleading Indian faces, each man with a headless hog over his shoulder, offering nepenthe, and the *vómito,* for "*dos clacos.*" The contingent of barefoot wretches are given the name of "cracked heels" by our soldiers.

Santa Anna has established the flamboyant General Valencia, his second in command, at a hill breastworks near the suburban village of Contreras, which dominates both approaches to the capital, by San Angel and San Agustín. It also blocks free access to the great highway to Acapulco whereon are carried the rich cargoes of silks, teas, and spices. In the morning, outriders see Valencia himself, reconnoitering to decide on the deployment of troops and guns. He is a man of medium height, but unusually broad and powerful, with a bull neck deep in his shoulders, as if, one observer says, "somebody had tried to force a good idea into his head with a pile driver." To approach his army is all but impossible. It must be done over mile-wide strips of pedregal—old lava flows—black, jagged, tumbled up rivers of plutonic stone. The question: Can the artillery be dragged within range? Horses have no footing in such a rocky morass. Failing this, do we charge? We await orders within sound of the bugles, the laughter, the jeers, the shouts of *"Viva!"* from above.

Now comes the order: Drag up the artillery by hand! We begin, cursing our luck. For hours we push, lift, haul, prize up, and even kick the heavy pieces clumsily over the charred sea, on, up toward the tormentor—all in a heavy rain of iron from the pieces placed in fortification. There is no striking back, not at this stage; the enemy are beyond range of our muskets. To me it is a dispiriting let-down. Though the muster rolls are forgotten, and new arrangements made by which glory can be gained at last, all excitement has vanished. There is no rush, no charge, none of that brisk stirring of the blood which has come to mean war to a former bemused advocate of the quiet life.

We begin to question our commanders' judgment. In the distance we see the towers and spires of the city. When shall we be there? In the afternoon we commence firing, but our pieces are small by comparison with the artillery roaring back. Still, our guns continue to come up—MacGruder with a field battery, dragged a full mile over exposed ground without a shrub for concealment. In place behind a ledge, it provokes a duel with Mexican siege guns, sixty-eight-pound howitzers, at a range of nine hundred yards. Our rockets start a whooshing line of harassment, and an assault brigade creeps up in their cover. We are beginning to move on Contreras.

But at nightfall there is bitterness and despair. A New Yorker who returns with dispatches from the forward positions gives a gloomy picture. The field is a dreadful sight. The men are ready to drop where they stand; they suffer from wounds, fatigue, thirst, hunger, and cold—and in this state listen to the martial music and jubilation above. There a tumultuous spirit of victory prevails. Valencia, feeling that he has surpassed Santa Anna in success, staggers about carrying a bottle, shouting, boasting that he will be the next head of State, distributing promotions to anyone who crosses his path.

After dark the rain falls in torrents. Brought back to aid a staff in the belfry of a church, I think of the men lying in this downpour on the pedregal, and fear that we have lost our first important battle in Mexico. Then we decide on a stroke of psychology. Fires are somehow lighted all along the line, to show that the gringos still hold. It is a brave sight, and at three o'clock Riley's brigade, cursing the now slippery footing, arises in the darkness to attack. Everyone's outlook changes. Scott himself has arrived, imperturbable as he lays out maps to survey the situation, then the much loved General Smith is ordered up with his brigade to help Riley. I myself hear cries of "Here he is! Now we'll have them!"

The battle quickens. All along the enemy system, from Valencia to Santa Anna at the nearby support line of San Gerónimo, our own attack commences, led off, at six o'clock, by a slight, round-shouldered man with a sandy mustache and sandy hair—Smith, who walks slowly to the front, oblivious of the shells, looks at his watch and cries out in a ringing voice, "Are you ready, men?" The thunder of a returning cheer warms our hearts. "Then *forward!*" There is a long, clattering noise of the scramble for a frontal movement; then the busy Lee and Beauregard again find a flanking route—the professional soldiers in action—and Valencia is suddenly in mortal trouble. His men at the breastworks, caught between two fires, throw down their guns, the lancers give way in a tidal wave; infantry, horse artillery, mules, laborers, women flee in wild disorder. A few remain—artillerymen chained by orders of El Presidente to their guns. Our General Smith is a precise man to whom time is always of interest. On the parapet, once more consulting his watch, he remarks, "It has taken just seventeen minutes."

[I wish to insert here that, a few days later, we apprehend and translate a large amount of Mexican mail going into the city. In one piece a writer says of Contreras, "When the rain and darkness came on at night, I supposed the Americans would retire to sleep, but they were too astute. In war the Yankees know no rest, no fear." The letter is addressed to a Congressional deputy and calls on him to attend "the funeral obsequies of our dishonored nation."]

The news about General Valencia apparently sends Santa Anna into convulsions. He is quoted as screaming, "Don't talk to me! Valencia is a vile sot—he is to be shot on sight! Blow out the brains of the traitor!" Then he runs back and forth whipping both men and women who, quite understandably try to escape his panic. At length—too late—he orders Valencia's guns spiked, and retreats in haste toward the city. Deeper in the suburbs he leaves General Rincón to hold the Convent of Churubusco, and orates, sententiously, "I will make the capital a second Troy. I swear it!"

Emotionally, Contreras is our point of demarcation. The capital—Mexico itself—lies only a few miles distant, and the men sense an ending to this war. We rattle and hurry in pursuit of the fleeing Santa Anna. Nobody is content to rest after the arduous battle won. Really, now, there is no hiatus, no break between the fighting of Contreras and the bloody action of Churubusco on August twentieth.

The clear, cold morning of August nineteenth sees the four divisions of our Army, with its incomparable brigade commanders, near San Agustín with the commander-in-chief. We pause to learn the plan of battle, and I write in my Journal. A young colleague beside me follows my example. He is a sensitive, fair-haired youth from the Deep South, Taliaferro by name, cultured, kindly, solicitous of all around him. Of the men I have been thrown with in these last months, he shows the most genuine compassion for the slaves in attendance upon many of our officers. They understand and like him, they dote on him as he rags them about sloth and superstition, rousing them to laughter, then risks his commission to scrounge for the kind of food they require.

So—I perform a sad mission. He writes: "In this country of Mexico, so far as my observation goes, there is wanting the first element of national greatness, *i.e.*, a people. What matters it that a population of nine or ten millions of human beings occupy the same soil, if between them there is no harmony, no fellowship? Such is the condition of things here—aristocracy and dregs—the sturdy middle class, the bone and sinew, ay, *the vital element*, exists not at all. The most important link in the social chain is wanting or defective; the NATION'S HEART, for I may term it so, scarcely throbs. What marvel, then, that the body is puny and sickly?"

To me he says, "One more entry, Shelby, and then I'll ask you to close the book if I fail to survive the fighting ahead." He continues:

"The operation is to commence at three in the morning. Tomorrow will be a day of slaughter. I firmly trust and pray that victory may crown our efforts though the odds are immense. We are outnumbered three to one, and we must fight in the open against strong defenses. I am thankful that my parents do not know the peril we are in. Good night."

Late in the following evening, I find his damaged Journal and add the final italicized line:

"The writer fell mortally wounded early the next morning."

Swiftly, with bayonets, we strike at the Hidalgo and Victoria battalions, in fortification before the convent, and half of the force crumbles, only General Bravo standing fast and, indeed, fighting his way superbly toward the Churubusco bridge. At noon, Engineer Stevens climbs a church tower of Coyoacán to reconnoiter, and reports Santa Anna's main body of troops streaming along a highway into the city. He describes the convent as almost abandoned—gravely erroneous, for when General Twiggs reaches musket range, it bursts into life with men and artillery firing at point blank. The foxy Rincón, gray-haired, Spanish, has adopted a very un-Mexican tactic of withholding his fire, and our men go down like nine-pins.

I grow confused in the noise and uproar of fighting. The Mounted Rifles hurry forward in support, the First Artillery is advanced, then Smith's brigade, and the Second and the Seventh Infantry, led by the unflinching Riley. I find myself in the head-high corn field surrounding the convent. I stumble into a broad ditch of water, and am helped out. "O'Hara?" He replies that the situation is "porely," that the polyticians and Chinymen are fighting like devils, and indeed the garrison in the convent, inspired there by good leaders and with cannon aimed (we find) by American deserters from other battles, hold and repulse our best efforts. From parapets and bastions pour sheets of flame, and the guns at the bridge behind speak out with new authority.

Over all hangs the familiar arid smoke pall, distressing to the nose and eyes, and I am twice kicked by horses down on the ground and struggling. American troops are panicking, someone cries, and O'Hara and I try to wrest ourselves free of the interminable rows of corn. But the earth is spongy after the rains and the fields crisscrossed with deep, treacherous ditches. One must knock down quite a few stalks to shoot at the convent walls and embrasures. Our men, the panicked men, have been confounded to come "butt-end first" upon an enemy that was supposed to have fled. It is true that both officers and privates show every sign of panic. They scatter into the cover of the corn field, which is raked with musket and big guns. We fight on, in disorganized, changing groups. A shell bursts with blinding fury beside me and some others. I am stunned, and, I think, run around in circles. Then I see bodies in grotesque positions on the ground, and cry, "O'Hara, where are you? O'Hara, are you hit?" As the smoke lifts, I trip over a familiar giant's frame, and seize it by the shoulders. "O'Hara—!" The figure is headless, and I lose my wits for a space. "O'Hara," I plead on my knees, weeping, "best of friends, sweet Irish fool, forgive the madness that brought us here. O'Hara—" I shake the body in anguish, watching the blood spurt out of the torn tubes at the neck, and bend over, broken in remorse. "O'Hara—" I can think of nothing else. Then, "Bless you, sir, I'm never done for yit. Glory be—you've got the wrong man!" We stand up and embrace like lovers. It will linger as one of the best moments of my life.

Once again we consider the day lost when in a move so audacious as to invite criticism Scott detaches a part of his left wing to cross the Churubusco River, wade through marshes, and strike at Santa Anna's rear. The troops emerge on the highway near the hacienda of Los Portales. Now, instantly, El Presidente is himself thrown into panic. "Remember Valencia!" is the Mexican cry and he breaks off his crack units, the Fourth Ligerio, the Tulancingo Regiment and the Eleventh Line, to avoid being trapped. The gage of battle shifts, our men rally and re-form, the convent is stormed, and, at the end, inside the walls and with active resistance over, Captain J. M. Smith puts up a white handkerchief to prevent further bloodshed. The Mexicans seem dumfounded at this humanity, and silently lay down their arms. Doubtless some think of the Alamo.

On the highway, permission to pursue is given the wildest, the most impetuous of our cavalrymen. A soldier writes home, "Oh, what a glorious sight it was to see Phil Kearny riding into them! His troops are picked men, with picked horses—all iron-gray—and seem to have supernatural strength. Standing upright in the stirrups, they looked like centaurs." They ride on long after the trumpet sounds recall, until at last a grapeshot proves faster than Kearny; and so, giving up an arm but winning a brevet, he finishes the Battle of Churubusco.

In all, Santa Anna has lost ten thousand men; we lost fourteen officers killed—the handsome Butler, commanding the South Carolina "Tigers," Colonel Burnett of the New Yorkers—and 119 privates; sixty officers and 805 men are wounded, and forty more are missing and presumed dead. But we have more than trebled our ordnance. Surely that is something to think about, but I am curiously unable to mention it when I write to Taliaferro's parents.

No, Carla. Only a little more to tell. They can't take me till early in the morning? I feel nothing. I said it before; I'm all right when I'm at work on the Journal. I wonder—perhaps I am a writer and not a soldier. How sad—not a leader of men. It's a new thought, but I don't wish to be distracted. Near the end now, very near the end, quite possibly the end indeed for me. I'm not a fool. I can smell that leg. Yes, it may be as you say; no doubt I am your pobrecito, *but I'll have to finish this entry. God knows I've done nothing else right, not since—where was it?—Fort Leavenworth, in the State of Kansas. Back when we were somewhat younger. Now put your hand against my cheek and leave—the passing fancy of a visiting military historian of this community.*

We lie without shelter, asleep in a muddy corn field. New quarters are being arranged at the great hacienda of Los Portales, in Churubusco, in Mixcoac, and in Coyoacán. Carla and Mrs. Mendoza come up with the laundresses, but there is no night of carousing. Sleep is the most precious thing on earth.

I am made a Brevet Major! The pieces are falling into place. It seems that I rallied a group of fleeing men and stormed a wing of the convent. I shall never admit it, but I remember nothing, little or nothing after the explosion of the shell.

We bury our dead, a solemn chore. They are laid in the earth in the bloody garments in which they died, many being too torn and mangled to move. Before we finish, a flag of truce arrives from Santa Anna, and we agree to an armistice. But there is discontent and grumbling. Why have we not gone on into the city? A soldier says, "We seem to have won the race but lost the prize." Then, real talk of peace is in the air. Should we negotiate on easy terms? We wait, while Congress and the newspapers argue the subject out. As always, our European friends know best.

There are the usual windy advices from London, a sneer from *Le Constitutionel* of Paris, suggestions, involving a payment of gold (by us, always) from the Mexicans themselves. Their country is up for sale.

We attend to other duties. The Irish deserters are punished. Two hundred of these were with Santa Anna, men to whom the spell of religion was stronger than love of country. One can admire them in part, but it is a sobering thought for the future. We have captured eighty; now we try them, with every consideration of tolerance. A number are found "not guilty," and released. Fifteen who deserted before the Declaration of War are branded on the cheek with a "D." Fifty are hanged.

Our troops have endured harsh privations and fought well. There is noisy complaint that any of the defectors should go free, but Scott states officially that, "I would rather be put to the sword than do an injustice in this matter." So be it. Justice, I think, has been done.

Meanwhile, commissions are formed, usually with strong opposition from one faction or another, and then are dissolved. The negotiations go forward very briskly on August 23 and 24. The people of Mexico appear to be of two minds: reluctant to lie down in defeat and fearful that the tricky Santa Anna will win the war and proclaim himself dictator. It comes as no surprise that he begins to violate the armistice. Our wagons seeking supplies are rudely turned back from the city gates; another group, led by the quartermaster, is attacked by a mob with stones, sticks and lances. Nonplused, our troops hear cries of "Death to Santa Anna! Death to the Yankees!" Armistice makes strange bedfellows!

We camp now on a hill of rich Tacubaya, overlooking the capital. It lies at our mercy, but we are prevented by politicians from entering. Our Headquarters is a mixture of palaces, fountains, luxurious gardens of flowers and fruit—apples, pears, quinces, figs, oranges, pomegranates, peaches, grapes, strawberries—and of ruins, hovels, and squalor. It is Mexico in microcosm, a land of blacks and whites, without the connecting nourishment of gray.

The present Commission has no members friendly to Santa

Anna. Its foremost figure is the popular Herrera, once president and now head of the peace movement. They labor in vain. Santa Anna, stung by the waning of his power, openly breaks the armistice to fortify the heights of Chapultepec, seat of the ancient Montezumas, the capital's pride. He has cleverly used the waiting time to replenish and bolster up his ranks.

General Scott immediately declares the truce ended, and all is changed. We are a military force again; a great and decisive battle impends. The Army, in September, is on the move, a dizzying collection by now of troops and followers: sutlers with their stores; printers with presses; editors; reporters; players; circus riders with fancy horses; gamblers; spectators; brokers; sailors turned teamsters; discharged soldiers proposing to be landlords; and, as a friend puts it, "certain frail but daring fair ones as well as *damas cortesanas* who venture to face the dangers of war."

A separate book could be written about these accretions that attach little by little to any army, as an old hull gathers crustaceans in its voyage.

Lying behind Chapultepec is Molino del Rey, a fortified line of stone buildings with a flour mill and a foundry for bronze cannon. We must take both redoubts. Our intelligence reports that Santa Anna has twenty thousand effective troops; the capital, through which we must pass, is a city of two hundred thousand persons presumed to be hostile. We are eight thousand strong.

We roll along without opposition, the steely clatter of the columns keeping the populace at a safe distance, some men standing with hats in hand, others spitting in distaste. A pretty woman tosses out a rose, and her husband slaps her face. Nearing the far limit, we break apart in preparation to attack. General Worth makes his dispositions; Smith's battalion advances at double time; our division is to assault the heights. And now, for once, Captains Lee and Beauregard fail to agree on a route. The almost omniscient Lee advises the southern front, and four generals concur; Beauregard holds out for the direct line up Chapultepec. A silence falls on the meeting, then Scott arises to say, rather grandly, "Gentlemen, we will attack by the western gates." Even the most valorous turns to stare at the sobering eminence;

the high white walls seem to mock us in our unsheltered state. This can be no simple conquest. General Bravo, not the strutting Valencia, is in active command at the top. He is feared and respected. Pillow says flatly, "We shall be defeated." Even Scott, we learn afterward, admits privately to Colonel Hitchcock, "I have my misgivings."

The troops and ladders are readied. I rejoice in my rank, and lead my men, after the deafening thunder of attack and answering bombardment, through a park-like grove of giant cypress, then shout: "Forward the Tenth!" This is the supreme moment. Glory —fame forever—lies a few hundred yards distant up the slope. In my eagerness, I make a tragic error. I have urged my men far ahead of the general advance, into a withering hail of lead. Amidst the clash and roar, I see my comrades begin to stagger and sink to their knees; far behind, it seems, I hear a terrible cry, "Ransom has fallen—the colonel is shot!"

Something knocks heavily against my knee. The air is smoky; I have charged into a tree. But my legs buckle and I sprawl in a twisted position, one leg beneath me, the other thrust out stiffly. I grope down, bewildered; the knee is not in its usual place. It seems curious. In the end I find it around on the side of my leg, hanging near to the shin. There is no pain, but I feel dizzy, my face waxen and drained of blood. My insides are all gone, in a sense. Instead of strength there is hollowness and perspiration. And suddenly I am thirsty. But my India-rubber canteen, too, has paid the price of war; one side is ripped through by a ball. "O'Hara! O'Hara, if you love me!" I crawl to a tree, dragging the kneeless leg, and prop myself against the bole. Then a blessed peace descends, and I listen to the shouts and the firing, far off, a twilight sound—in the numbness of my mind a schoolboy comfortably at home by order of the doctor.

Ready? Is that you, Carla? It's too dark to see. I finished the Journal, late last night. You were here? You held the light? I may do some mopping up later; no hurry. And, of course, these reflections. Why is it important? It's important for those who come after. Further than that I can't say. (Classified.)

More morphine? Lots of morphine—ah! *No, only surprised.*

Really, now, I'm indebted to morphine for some odd sensations—for example, your hand seems rough and gnarled, twice the size of mine. O'Hara? Well, now—what word from the Chinamen? I hear they're massing the hills for an assault on the laundresses. You're a fine fighter, O'Hara, but there's a Chink in your armor.

Hold on! What are those fools doing? Why *do they move me? Oh,* ah! *Make it fast, boys, or shoot me and get it over. You're here, Carla? Tell me where we are, every step, and what we're doing. In a big tent now, lanterns on poles, buckets, basins, charcoal fire under one basin, little table, long high table—needs a good swabbing—three men, four men. Dr. Everett? How do you do, sir; you'll excuse me for not getting up. This should be simple, I hope. Matter of sliding the knee back in place; I should have done it myself. You look tired, sir, and I regret the levity, but I'm just a little, well, lightheaded.*

A minute, sir—no, it won't hurt me to sit up. God damn it, let go, O'Hara! What are these instruments? Why the pocket knife with the fancy handle? And the saw with the lion's head and ring at the end? Never mind the looks—talk directly to me.

No! *Oh, by God, you won't! You'll never take my leg off. O'Hara, carry me out of here on your back. O'Hara, I'll kill you if I come through this. I promise you, O'Hara.*

I realize that you're a reasonable man, Doctor. It doesn't matter to me if there's gangrene above the knee. I don't care if there's gangrene from feet to chin. This is my leg, and my life, and the decision is mine alone. Yes, it's true that I was in shock for several hours. Well enough; I can't survive a long operation. It's understood—to put the knee back is tedious, and the chances are ten to one on gangrene even so. Then, at best, I'd have a stiff leg, a fused knee, a painful leg, an awkward leg, a leg keenly sensitive to weather, a leg requiring help the rest of my life. Artificial limbs have come a long way? It's only a conditioned attitude that abhors amputations? It's the idea of the thing. I understand that clearly. Dr. Everett, sir, you have indeed made it clear.

Now put the knee back.

Sweet Carla, you're my only friend. I withdraw that, O'Hara. But what a really tough old nut you are, Carla! You're excited;

address the doctor in English. She says, here in Mexico it is the custom to treat rot with maggots. The filthy little beasts gobble up the rot, and leave the wound clean. Quite true; the idea is revolting, but she will see to it personally. I'll agree to that—carbolic and water first, then a cauterization with Nitrate of Silver, Nitric Acid and Chloride of Zinc. All sturdy fighters in the war of asepsis? Very well put. And then, if you don't mind, the maggots.

Do I object if you talk while you work? A personal idiosyncrasy. The scalpel and saw figure in the writing of Ambroise Paré, circa 1550? An enlightened man to be sure, but perhaps a little less of the scalpel and saw, if it's perfectly agreeable. Certainly I'll take a drink of alcohol. I've excited the morphine away? Kentucky bourbon whisky! Your own? You're a very good fellow, sir. Hold it, very sorry, but that doesn't seem to wo— Ah—ah—ah! I'm most awfully sorry; it was too quick. One second fine, and then not so much. Maybe go ahead, now. I've felt much better in my time. Yes, just a little faint—ammonia . . .

. . . for how long? Much improved. You progress? That is a correct diagnosis, sir—there is pain. But it's a long way off. The morphine, to be sure. A heaven-sent boon to man that is born of woman. During the rest of my life, I intend to take a little each day with my breakfast. Why do I watch? So that you don't slip, my friend, and retreat to the previously-prepared line. Of course I'd like to hear about interstitial mastitis—not there!—just in that one place, not there! NOT THERE!

. . . out again? You really must stop that, O'Hara. A great hulk like you. Just grip my shoulders again. Good! but don't crush me. I've problems enough. Dr. Everett, you're a scholar and a patient gentleman. You use a ligature of double silk thread and rely on a forceps to draw forward the cut end of the vessel to be ligatured. I'd have it no other way, sir, I assure you. But NOT THERE! . . .

. . . over? All over? Poor Carla. I'm a different man now; I'm a cripple . . . We did take the heights, O'Hara? I'm unsettled in my mind. Perhaps you told me before. You told me all? They talk of a Lieutenant Grant, who waded ditches under fire to place *a decisive gun on a church roof. Our terrible casualties? Another time about the casualties, O'Hara; I myself caused*—sick, Doctor, sick! *Oh, God! Oh misery! . . . I thought I'd choked to death. No more talking, you won't take the responsibility. Doctor, my thanks.*

XXVIII

Rancho Ciénaga Grande: I'll have to move along fast now, and do my best work, because we're coming pretty close to the end. But a number of events remain—the most important ones—and they need to be explained, fitted in one way or another. (Leave it to me.)

When we rode up to find the lieutenant's father dead, I thought he'd go crazy. That old man must have been mighty nice, for a Mexican, because all kinds of people, the highest and the humble, came in from miles around to pay their respects, war or no war. They were crushed, and sat hatless in the patio, or inside, silent and leaking, the peons in particular beaten down, as if they'd lost their best friend, which I judged was so. Only a part of the main hacienda had been scorched out by fire: some bedrooms and a string of servants' rooms at the far end. I'd never seen a Mexican place as grand as this since we left home. It made the houses in Santa Fé look like privies (which they weren't, nor any sign of one, as mentioned previous, risking the vulgarity of it).

Since I undertook this book, during a concussion or something, I've learned a good deal about that sort of thing. It's called "literary license," and means permission to be as nasty as you please. For example, it's on the order of a Frenchman named Rabbelay, which inserted some remarkable statements in a book called *Gargantua*. The interpreter, Luis, told me all about it, and

I'm obliged to admit that it was too strong for my stomach. Of course, he may have been lying. He lied all the time, regular; he had a gift for it. Such liars are born, not made. An apprenticeship won't do it, and neither will a college education, though Angelina said it might help. They come along once in a century. He would have shot straight to the top in politics; I heard Don Ricardo say so himself, one day after an important translation had gone cockeyed.

Anyhow, this proud family home was enough to make you gulp. You entered from their private road, all bordered by cedars and cypress, through a snowy-white, rose-covered arch with the ranch name engraved ever so pretty, having graceful-looking swans on either side and a cluster of little ones—cygnets—at the top. The hacienda itself was 150 yards long on two sides and half that at the ends; the usual fine fountains played water in the center; four flower beds there in the shape of swans (but their necks stuck out an uncommon length, it seemed to me); stately rows of orange trees—with real fruit, too, not just wooden bulbs tied on, the way some of those frauds do to save gardening; the building made of white-painted stone, not plaster; smooth flagstones everywhere except the flower beds; communicating balconies on the second floors but no passageways down below; just doors. This was a puzzler; I never found anybody that cared to explain it. You take in most of these Mexican mansions, a person, to reach the parlor, likely has to pass through the family boudoirs, and if he stumbles across a woman propped up in bed, combing her hair, maybe naked besides, it's embarrassing. You can say, "Good day," or "It's nice weather we're having," but it doesn't hit the bull's-eye, somehow. You understand, we didn't do that here. To get to the sala, decorated very rich with plush and velvet and crystal and imported mirrors and chandeliers, we went around by way of the piazza, which was overhung by a balcony, thus keeping off the rain.

Back behind was a deep well in a stone cylinder with a slate-roofed house on top that had a recessed religious scene featuring Jesus wearing a black mustache, like a vaquero. He had on chaps, and was carrying a lasso. Don Ricardo said it had been put up by a pious ancestor of his, and nobody had taken it down yet.

He said he judged it would be struck by lightning one of these days; leastways, he hoped so. The water from the well was drawn by mules attached to a long sweep that turned a windlass like an old-fashioned cider mill. The mules walked in one direction till a bucket reached the top, then traveled the opposite way till another came up. This kept going night and day, the water being spilled into troughs and used for every purpose, agricultural and domestic. Somebody said the overseer was humane about the mules, and only used one set for a year or so, but they didn't appear to be much account afterward—continued to hee-haw back and forth like a pendulum till it got on people's nerves.

There were rows of sheds for shearing, and further back, storehouses for corn and barley, and stacks and stacks of straw and corn stalks; they never made hay in this country. On the estate, twenty miles long by fourteen wide, there were herds of cattle, flocks of sheep, droves of mules, horses and swine, and some hundreds of peons, which on most ranches like this lived in a state not much better than slavery, being kept in debt to the landlord from birth to grave.

From all reports, peons prospered at Ciénaga Grande. They were paid for their work, taught how to save, treated free for disease, advised against having too many babies (which appeared to step up the output), and given every chance to buy land. But the unvarnished truth is that none of them ever did. As low-down as they were, they lacked the ambition to rise higher. Each morning before daylight they got up, assembled in a kind of military array beneath a huge cross, then joined in what was called a *matin* song. In the evening, they did it all over again, singing a song to the Virgin, while the overseer sat on a horse nearby. Mostly, their huts were clean, and the food they were given was ample.

Not long after our arrival, we entered Don Antonio's library, where he'd been shot while seated at his desk, and found a half-finished letter he was writing to a titled friend in Spain. It lay on the leather amidst splotches of blood that hadn't quite been erased, and never would be, and talked about what had become practically a mania, people said. Even Blaine owns up that it gives a brand new slant on a breed, in this country, that's denounced by nearly everybody outside—ignoramuses usually—as a form of exercise.

"We wealthy proprietors, lords of immense estates, would sell all for enough to secure a most moderate income in other lands; but who will buy? We are, like the veriest serfs, chained to the soil. The rich man is doomed; now a prey to a rapacious government, now the victim of ferocious robbers against whom the government gives him no protection. So great is the misery of the better classes that many families are preparing to leave forever a land where, tantalized by the gifts of fortune, they have found nothing but the dregs of bitterness. To pretend that all are born equal, or have equal capacity, is the most dangerous sophistry. My forebears won this holding with superior courage and an intelligence trained for centuries; too, they were willing to accept great responsibility, to grind themselves with work by day and lie abed worrying by night. Who will help my poor peon if we leave to him, overnight, bewildered, the herds, the carefully cultivated land, the sensitive and distasteful commerce with politicians, a full exposure to depradors? In this stage of his growth, he is like a child—unfit to manage. He thinks only of Today. I dread—"

The assassin's hand had struck Don Antonio down here, and I for one wished we had the rest of his letter. Common sense is so rare that most people resent it; it comes on them like an accusation.

As soon as Don Ricardo recovered from the first flush of his grief, this place, this Rancho Ciénaga Grande, was turned into a regular headquarters for conspiracy. Horsemen arrived and left at all hours, day and night. There were low-voiced huddles and meetings and rendevoos, as they called them, sometimes not in the house, but at different spots on the estate, and you saw a powerful lot of hand-shaking and kissing of cheeks and embracing. These Moraleses—only the name had a few fancy additions on the end, like rags on a kite-tail, most of them hooked together with "y" such as "Morales y las Piedras y las Montañas" and the like; as I say, the clan had any number of friends and it represented a strong political movement besides. As nearly as I made things out, it had to do with peace, votes for all, and other reforms. That is, I do honestly believe that these people represented the best in Mexico, and they looked it. It's odd how a person's appearance, over the years, generally falls into line with what he is. These visitors—and I never met any finer specimens anywhere—*stood out* as kindly, and intelligent, and knowing, and gentlemanly, and *honest,* and it sort of knocked the wind out of my notions about Mexico. They were thoughtful, and interested, and always took time to inquire after our health and to say what a shame it was about the war.

Well, sir, I never eavesdrop, that being one of the faults my mother taught me not to commit, and Hyacinth stuck in *his* oar on the subject, though he was the nosiest busybody in seven states, snooping all over the place, mostly, then setting up as one of the three wise men in the Bible. No, I never eavesdropped here, but I managed to be where the talks went on pretty often, in spite of myself, and rather than disturb a meeting, I very politely slid under a sofa or a desk, taking care to remember my manners.

Don Antonio plus half a dozen others, elsewhere, had been killed all at the same time by the men of Don Narciso Noriega, who was Santa Anna's sidekick, or political go-between. *Tercero,* as their word went. To hear them talk, this fellow must have been the worst fiend in Mexico, and was generally referred to, outright and open, even by ordinary people in Puebla and Mexico City, as the Black One (on account of the peculiarity of his beard, which left mainly his eyes showing), or El Diablo. It was a handsome reputation, and I saw grown men clench their cheek muscles so hard, discussing him, that they probably ground down the tops of their teeth.

Santa Anna was a man of tolerable size—all agreed, and deplored it—but he was so oily and selfish and treacherous and grasping and ambitious that he'd lost the confidence of everyone but the grafting politicians around him. What's more, his disposition, which was scraping the bottom of the barrel to start with, had sunk pretty rapid after he'd lost a leg in 1838, whilst holding off a French attack on Vera Cruz. He'd kicked out the French all right, but had shed one leg in the process. For some reason, it seemed to make him peevish.

A man like that had his hands full. He'd named himself to be

President, more or less, but he was also Commander-in-Chief of the Armies and preferred to be out among the action, if it didn't hot up too brisk and threaten his scalp. Now the point is, he couldn't be in two places at once, and with the country proceeding on his platform, the Army was busy most of the time: against Texas in 1836, against France in '38, and now against the United States in 1846 and '47. He wasn't President during *all* those engagements, you understand, but he was in and out, back and forth, and lately he'd been in for quite a while. The country showed it; things had never been worse.

Well, Don Narciso did the fixing and the maneuvering and the skullduggering when Santa Anna was away. Blaine says you commonly find one with every government, a foxy sort of night prowler that sits back, out of range, and plots and connives and "advises" and pulls the wires and rigs up this or that scheme, aimed mostly to keep the Administration in and honest people out. He mentioned an upright but easygoing dunce named Othello, of the colored persuasion, that had such a man stuck to him like a plaster, whispering in his ear. I didn't get the whole story, but he finally blew up, which anybody would do in the circumstance, and shot his wife, who had about as much knowledge of politics as their house cat, and then himself and after that the adviser, which recovered and went into slavery. Thinking it over, it may have been poison. Anyhow, it was a gaudy mess, and, of course, typically political.

I dislike to say so, but there's nothing more refreshing to people like the Mexicans than hatching a revolution. As the days wore on, Don Ricardo begun to enjoy himself, but he meant to even the score with Don Narciso, too. His face was as hard and taut and thinned-down as a cinch-strap, his nose was thinner than a wishbone, and he scarcely ever smiled any more. Now and then he caught himself, and was mighty sorry about being tied up and abstracted; he said so very gracious, then buckled down to make life pleasant for Angelina and me. There were some other dwellers in this house, curiosities, mostly. The old gentleman had been educated in Spain, had married there, and held a colonel's commission in the Spanish Army, having fought in the Peninsular War. His wife died in Spain, after which he hustled back to run the ranch, which the Mexicans were threatening to confiscate. The word was overworked around here. There wasn't hardly a day when the Government didn't threaten to confiscate everything. To be safe, a body had to organize his own private army and lounge around the front gate with a shotgun.

Anyhow, there was Don Ricardo, of course; and another brother, which had been studying for the priesthood but died in a duel over whether angels were male or female; and a young sister, Esmerelda, around thirteen that two or three dueñas rode herd on as if she was apt to jump a fence and head for the high pasture; and a lovely spinster lady, a *soltera,* as nice and considerate as they come, except for being a little carp-headed. She seemed especially fond of Angelina, though wary, or alerted, around me, and took the viewpoint that not being Mexican was an affliction. She wished to make it up to us, it not being our fault, and tried to feed us "our own kind of food," on the order of stoking a chimpanzee with wild onions in a zoo. But it generally turned out to be ham and eggs, three times a day, which she'd read about in a book written by a Frenchman and published in England about Americans. She took it to be gospel. After a week, I mired up on ham and eggs and went around to a peon's shack I knew and had a merry old time with tortillas, frijole paste, tamales, six ribs of kid, and a spiced avocado, washed down with pulque. The family refused any payment, and the wife, who didn't eat with us—their women seldom do—gave me a warm kiss besides.

I tripped on the way back, and like to fell in the well, and Angelina was sore as a boil when she picked me out. *She* was half starved, she said, besides feeling bilious from an overdose of eggs, and was planning to walk home to Missouri; said she'd stolen a compass and aimed to strike straight north, moving by night. But Don Ricardo's meetings eased off just then, and when he found out about the diet he waltzed in and broke it up fast.

There were others here, but I never learned their names. In addition to La Ciénaga, the family owned a mansion in town (like others of their set) and the members came and went. The war didn't appear to slow them up much. Business, and the social life, proceeded about as usual.

They had a *sobrestante,* an overseer, who looked after the peons in a way surprising for Mexico, understanding and fatherly and patient; and a chief of vaqueros with fierce black mustaches, a man as tough as a mustang, but laughing and good-natured and good fun to talk to, because he enjoyed showing you how to do things like braid a lariat out of wet rawhide; and a major-domo named Miguel that I couldn't stand. He was too pushy-humble-complimentary. Face lean and sallow—almost yellow—and clean-shaven but he had long sideburns that splayed out at the bottom like pedestals. He wore very tight pants, and considered himself a leading hand with the ladies. Angelina said he made her sick and said what he needed was a pair of trousers with three legs. You could always depend on her: common right down to the wire.

I don't know why the breed of major-domo is so repulsive, but Don Ricardo said it's because they live in service to women. He couldn't stand him either. "They learn to intrigue, and gossip, to pander in small ways, and accept *pourboires* from guests; they protect the masters from the servants, and conspire with the servants against the masters. They do neither man's work nor woman's. Major-domos of intelligence are expected to cheat both the proprietor he represents and the merchant from whom he buys. They live in an uncomfortable land of the non-existent middle, belonging nowhere and hating all. In the long run, even their sex becomes dubious. Still, they are useful in that they possess the knack of keeping a large house running. And in Miguel's case, his people have been with us for three generations. Fundamentally, I trust him, but I don't care to be where he is."

Well, *I* didn't trust him, and had a good reason. One night late, at a secret meeting attended by the former president, Herrera, I found myself trapped on a balcony outside the library. The French windows were open, and I could hear the talk easy enough. A piñon fire flickered in the fireplace, and a couple of lamps were on dim; otherwise the room was shadowed. In the firelight, Mr. Herrera seemed pale, and tired, and uncertain, but he had a courageous look even so, as if there was little chance of stampeding him into a decision. I've got to admit that the conversation was mostly over my head. It was in Spanish of course, and occasionally galloped along too fast even for somebody as fluid as ~~I me~~ myself.

Most of the gathering, including Don Ricardo, were strongly behind Mr. Herrera's well-known policies of peace, and wished to establish them right away by violence. Santa Anna and Don Narciso were violent, it was argued, and could be eliminated only by violence of the same kind, or worse. Then, when the Army was reshuffled, Mexico could be kept peaceful by force. One silvery-haired old fossil with goggles on went further; he was what they called a "liberal reformer," a genuine professor emeritus from out of a college. He expressed himself in favor of complete freedom for everybody in Mexico, and said it should be made compulsory. The statement had such a jackass ring that it caused some uneasy looks, as though nobody quite knew how he'd got in here. These were serious men, with solid, working experience of life, but Blaine says such drooling fools generally manage to shove in and reduce most well-intentioned programs to absurdity.

Altogether, the conference, though largely sensible, presented some odd lines of reasoning, and I saw Don Ricardo's face grow confused, but I supposed it was the usual procedure here with conspiracies. If a government lasted a year anywhere between Texas and Argentina, it was praised all around, then written up pretty lavish in the history books. I heard a visitor introduced, at a tea right in this house, as "Señor ———, the president of Ecuadoro from Tuesday to Friday afternoon, a year ago last May." Angelina said it was meant to be funny, but I didn't think so, because the man, bowing, made a correction and said, "Early Tuesday *morning,* señorita, from the hour of nine-thirty, when the Palace wall collapsed on the administrative offices."

Anyhow, this low-pitched but vehement discussion continued, and Don Ricardo said, in the stiffish Castilian he was teaching Angelina, "Sir, six of our leading men now find themselves dead, murdered in cold blood. As to my father, we have an informer among our people; the intruders could not otherwise have gained the grounds unchallenged at such an hour. His identity is suspected, and he is being watched. Pepe, the *jefe de vaqueros* is the only newcomer to La Ciénaga, my father's folly and his undoing. At the proper moment, I will kill him, slowly, by my own hand."

I was so outraged that I almost cried out—I *knew* that fellow and *liked* him, but hadn't much time to worry about it, because I heard a cough, not quite smothered, directly beside me. I came close to jumping out of my skin; I'd never in my life felt so much like turning tail, and that was something you didn't do, not with our bunch in Missouri. Any one of my uncles would have shot me with pleasure. But the whole setting here seemed suddenly dismal—foreign, far from home and things familiar, the language itself, the talk of death and plots to kill, even the tropical sweetness of the night-blooming flowers crawling along the walls.

I stood still and sweated. I'd got to stay put and see it through. These people were friends, and while he might not amount to very much, that Pepe was no traitor. He wasn't that kind, and I meant to prove it. As slow as possible, I turned my head, then tried to focus my eyes on the objects nearby. Inside the window was a high velvet drape, and against its darkness was a blacker shape: a man standing at the edge, listening. I could have killed him with my knife, but I waited, heart thumping, whilst the talk went on, until the president excused himself and retired, after which some lower-voiced arrangements were made—I didn't catch the details—to dispose of El Diablo sometime during the following week. It was discussed as casual as plans for butchering a pig.

When the last guest had bowed himself out, with the usual handshake and embrace, Don Ricardo was left alone, and I says to myself, "Now, my friend, we'll see what's what. Come out by the balcony, and I'll howl the house down. Or step inside and I'll spot you for sure." I hadn't any handy reason for being there myself, but figured that the Lord would provide; I've noticed that He commonly does when a person's strapped for a lie. That's one of the nice things about religion, the knowledge that help is generally available for a worthy cause.

Don Ricardo lit a cigar, then tampered around with some papers on his desk, then commenced a search for something he'd misplaced, laying down his cigar and pulling out all the drawers one by one. And after that he discovered that he'd burned a groove in the table, so he took a turn at it with a cloth. Then he spent some time dislodging a particle of food caught between his teeth. He let down so far, when he found it, as to muster up a kind of lower-class hawk and spit it into the fireplace. It's curious how even the quality lower their guard when they think nobody's watching.

Well, sir, I'd become so fidgety I couldn't stand still, and I begun to see this fellow in a new light. I never before realized what a real old downright dyed-in-the-wool saphead he was, and resolved to tell him so the first chance I got, when he straightened up, yawned, patted his stomach, bent his knees a few inches, and went out, closing the door behind him. Now it hadn't occurred to me that it might be Pepe, and I stiffened up with a gasp when, after a few seconds, the drape rustled then switched aside and a figure tiptoed into view before the fire. It was all right; the sideburns were the first thing I noticed. Miguel.

I was busting to tell Don Ricardo, but he was absent from his bedroom, having a last jaw somewhere, likely, so I went to my room and lay down, calculating to wait him out, and the next thing I knew it was morning. Everybody gone to town when I got up, and didn't come back till late. Angelina'd left me a note, telling me what to do for amusement, so I did something else. Walking down the patio, I saw Esmerelda sitting at her window, looking pretty and curious, and I stopped.

I says, "Come on out."

"I can't. It'd be wicked."

"Who says so?"

"María. Also Amalia, Carlotta, and Joselita. Also my aunt, but Ricardo says not. He says it's silly. He thinks many of the old customs are silly. But my aunt says I've become pubescent, nubile, and concubitous. I don't know what they mean, but I feel quite well."

"You talk an awful lot."

"Yes, I speak brilliantly in several languages. Luis has taught me for eight years. He once lived in a splendid place called Pittsburgh, and knows the fashionable slang. Skidoo—that has *ton*,

I think. He taught me, of course, in the presence of María, Amalia, Carlotta and Joselita. And, to be sure, my aunt. She is *very* severe. She was jilted. A doctor-visitor, a full-blooded Englishman *très distingué* expressed amazement that I'm not completely neurotic."

"Well," I said, with a kind of ringing in my ears, "I guess I'll take my dog out for a run. He catches small game, and eats it."

"Does he eat the guts? You needn't be shocked. I know a good many words like that. You see, they never lock up the library. It might interest you to know that I'm familiar with the reproductive system of the frog."

"Oh, come on out. You *are* a little crazy, I expect, but it's a nice day, and you can't stay cooped up here forever."

"The windows are barred. That's because of my class. Personally, I'm not wildly class-conscious. I'm studying to be an anarchist."

I tried the rickety iron rods, they screwed right out of their sockets.

"I wish I had known that before. I like to steal outside at night. The moon has a strange effect on me. I have a very passionate nature; it runs in the family. Perhaps you are aware that the moon controls the ebb and flow of we women's emotions? . . . That came out of of the library too."

I said, "I wonder if you couldn't just stop talking for a *minute?* It appears to be a female disease, every one I ever met."

"But you see, I never get a chance to talk at all. My talk in here is mostly trying to find out why I shouldn't do something. I'm a typical case of thwarted frustration."

"Now listen to me. I'll be back here at siesta time, and we'll go off for a romp. We're bound to have two hours at the least."

"Oh, let's!"

I don't like to sound noble, but I did the girl a favor. I felt sorry for her. She was nice enough though not perfect. My dog Bollo appeared to like her almost as well as me, but that was because he'd been shut up. Then I started to teach her how to catch a horse and ride him bareback, but she already knew. I would have taught her to use a lasso, but she roped me around the neck while galloping by on the horse. The truth is that she stopped just short of being a smart aleck. She could ride like somebody glued on; she was slim and hard but the opposite of skinny, if you understand me, and she looked fetching, for a Mexican, when she slid the horse to a stop with his forelegs out stiff then vaulted off like a boy. Her dark eyes were shining, the black hair was flying out behind, and her teeth appeared unusually white and even against the lip rouge she'd put on the minute we got beyond the house. It wasn't any bad afternoon, though slightly boring, and we were going to do it again the next day, but something interrupted.

XXIX

Don Ricardo's plans were set now, and he felt shamefaced about neglecting us. Towards noon, he ordered four thoroughbreds saddled, then took us—Angelina and the girl and me—on a picnic to the river we crossed when we first arrived at La Ciénaga. I planned to tell him my news when we got there; I couldn't get a word in before. The place was two or three miles away, and seemed splendid and soothing now that our travels were over. There isn't anything like a picnic to ease a person's mind. Cottonwoods and willows grew thick on both banks, and nice sandbars and gravel beds curved out at the bends, and the water rippled along green and clear. Don Ricardo said we could swim here; he said the river ran so far on his land that the contamination got purified out. He said you could drink it. Me, I'd sooner drunk out of a hog-wallow. Mountains lay off in the distance, lavender and brown and blue, always in a haze, and the white cone of Popocatepetl rose up overall.

Well, we laid things out on the sand, hidden all around by trees, and pulled up some logs to sit on, and Don Ricardo peeled off to his shirt, more informal than I thought he could get, and the girl and I commenced to throw stones. She was having a lot of luck when we heard a shout of *"Patrón! Capitán! Pronto! Pronto!"* from the direction of upstream, and saw Pepe coming leaning down on us, a-horseback in the shallow water and making that animal hump. I don't think I ever saw a man so disregardful of himself or his mount. His sombrero hung by a thong, and he carried a rifle up high in one hand, held as light as a wand. Don Ricardo sprang to his feet but had time for only a "*Qué pasa?*" before a shot rang out from downstream and Pepe fell like a sackful of laundry, not more than twenty yards away.

It was over in a second. A bunch of riders loped out of cover, Don Ricardo flung himself at the leader, the sun glinting on a knife-blade in his hands, but it was perfectly hopeless; there were too many. Our arms were bound, we were fitted out with masks for some reason, and tied to horses—worn-out plugs—that they themselves had brought. Then we took up a dreary clop-clopping down the stream bed. I'd liked those trees before, but now they sealed us off from view. My mask was loose; I could see daylight out of one side. The greenery was rich and plentiful—we hadn't a chance.

I said, and I couldn't help it, "You see, it wasn't Pepe. It was Miguel."

"Never mind. Everything is the result of my stupidity. I have no future ambitions except to become a good soldier. In a jungle, it is very dangerous to be a bad one."

I heard Angelina say, her voice low and defeated, "Now I've had *two,*" then came the sound of a smack, aimed at Don Ricardo, who spoke up cheery and bright, "Thank you, my friend. That will be repaid with interest compounded. Please assure yourself."

We rode in the stream for two or three hours; then we stopped at what I took to be the outer limit of La Ciénaga, where a mean little road crossed. Here we waited for night. The masks finally came off, we were promised that execution would promptly result from any noise we might care to make, and the ride continued. It was no novelty for Mexicans to see people under restraint in these times, and nobody challenged us. Besides, two of our party had on the flashy uniforms of Dragoons.

After riding all night, it seemed, we entered a city, the hooves ringing hollow and loud on the cobbles at that hour, and at length came to the house, mansion, palace of the worst man I have ever known. Dismounting; rather, being pushed rudely off the horses, we entered—shoved and cursed for our slowness—by a kind of underground passage, dank and cold and smelly and lined with rough-hewn stone.

Don Narciso awaited us in a high-ceilinged reception room with spindly French furniture and windows tightly shuttered. He said, "That will do, Hai-soos. Station your men outside." (I found out later that the scoundrel's name was Jesus, being pronounced as I wrote it, and I never encountered a worse case of miscalling.)

Well, we stood regarding the Black One, like people struck dumb by something in a freak museum. *He,* at least, was *well*-named. He had on clothes of solid black (except for a starchy-white ruffled shirt), his hair shone like shoe polish—either natural or dyed; the second, I think—and his close-cropped beard appeared like some fanciful arrangement in a garden. That is, it took up where his sideburns failed to leave off, crawled in tight around his cheeks, crossed his upper lip to shake hands in a mustache, and dribbled on down over the chin to end in a sharp point like a dart. All the borders, even the curves, were as clipped and precise as geometry. In the center of this horrible-looking outrage his lips seemed uncommon full and ripe and red, and he didn't help matters by wetting them with his tongue. Overall, the mouth gave you the impression of an open wound.

Ordinarily, the ugliest scarecrow has one redeeming feature, but this specimen, I'm happy to say, broke the rule by reporting in empty. His nose was long and sharp and high, his astonishing small ears lay flatter to his head than bark, one pierced for a plain round gold earring, and his eyes were as black and flat and careful as a snake's. He must have stood several inches over six feet, and his extreme thinness would have been thought puny in anybody else. But I noticed that his neck was nothing but cords and veins and sinews and tendons, thrust out in relief as if under pressure, with a constantly moving, embarrassing sort of Adam's apple. I noticed besides that the neck had a small nervous jerk; he lifted his chin now and then and flipped it sidewise and up. What's more his hands kept clenching and unclenching ever so slightly. But none of this registered in his face. It was as close-hauled as a statue.

I failed to mention that this plucked buzzard of a carcass produced a voice that boomed out like a pipe organ. It started way down low, rumbled up deliberate, acquired a considerable boost in his chest, got honed and molded in his throat, and came out with elaborate over-done politeness bordering on a sneer.

I dislike to confess it, but I was awed. The fellow, in the aggregate, provided an exhibit to humble a grizzly. He was that still and intense and unfrivolous. But Don Ricardo spoke right up like a man addressing a tinker. He says:

"You'll answer for these crimes, Noriega. I'll see—"

Our host turned abruptly and opened the door. "Hai-soos, escort the deserter to the cells. He's to be shackled and fed bread and water until his trial for desertion and high treason against the State."

"You lie, you unfamilied scum. My leave papers are signed by General Herédia himself. But I promise that *you*'ll be tried, for murder and worse. And now, sir, I demand that you release these people. Call off your dogs and stand aside."

The bearded beanpole only made an impatient motion with his hand, and the others stepped promptly forward, but Don Ricardo leaped to the window, kicked open the shutters and shouted down into the street, "*Policía! Guardia! Pronto!*" Then the gang was on him, grabbing his arms and banging the shutters closed, but he wrestled free—his temper had mounted so high that he looked like a madman—and lunged across the room to smash Don Narciso into the wall. He wrecked one of those spidery yellow tables and left our elegant friend sprawled horrified on the floor, one hand to his face, which was bleeding. I doubt if anybody had successfully opposed him in years.

Well, the situation had changed in a flash. The abductors were six grown men and mean, but their boss was out of action, and they appeared undecided. Mexicans like that require somebody to tell them what to do. Otherwise they smoke and wait. It suddenly occurred to me that Don Ricardo needed support; the same idea hit the girl Esmerelda, who picked up a vase, examined it like a buyer, then broke it over the head of the man nearest her. Angelina turned to a dark, rat-faced little fellow close by and said, "I didn't enjoy that ride. *Muchas gracias!*" and caught him in a delicate area with the toe of her right shoe. She really kicked him hard, and of course the creature was always in good condition, from riding and man sports and arguing, and additional actions that made her a revolving nuisance. Pound for pound, she was as tough as they come, male *or* female. He let out a species of frog-croak, on the order of "*Oh! Ah-h-hh. Oh!*" and doubled over, hanging on with both hands. As for me, I'd spotted a workable sword on the mantel when we first came in, and I jumped for it. But I never got there. A heavy blow from behind left me on my knees, with everything swimming around in circles. I didn't rightly know anything at all for awhile. When I came to, the scum were back in control. I could have cried, and felt sick to my stomach, too. Still, I couldn't bring myself to throw up on that pale green rich carpet; we're just that crushed down by rules and training and all the humbuggy good manners that tighten people up and make them miserable.

Don Narciso was seated—laid out—on a chez long with his collar wide open, dabbing at his forehead with a kerchief. He was totally dead-white, an unwholesome white, and his neck twitched like a shot rabbit's. For a moment I got my hopes up about apoplexy. Finally he forced out the following, "You struck me. *Me!* You will regret—"

"I suppose you're too great a coward to duel," suggested Don Ricardo, held up on his toes by Hai-soos and two others.

"Stupid young man, it would be no task for me to kill you with a sword, shortly, in a matter of minutes"—curiously enough, I found this to be true; he could have done such a murder in the way of light exercise, as he had on other brutal occasions—"but it would be too quick. I have devised plans more ornate. Hai-soos," he said to the ruffian, "take him below. Have him beaten well and sincerely for his impertinence. We must beat him every day till he begs like a dog for a bone—"

"There aren't so many days."

"—and at the end, as entertainment for certain of my friends, we shall summon Ignacio the Garrotero. I must show you our garroting chamber," he said in a pleasant tone to Angelina, licking his lips before he spoke. "It is old, of historic value, and has a wooden cross mortised into a circular stone pedestal two feet tall. At the junction of the pedestal and the cross is a stone step a few inches high, to accommodate a man's feet. At the cross's extremity are the arrangements for the fastening of hands —but you will have to see it for yourself, to appreciate the deliciousness of its flavor. Such deaths remain our national form of execution, of special interest if the criminal is revived several times before the final twist."

"In the historic old Mexican, I spit on you and your garroting chamber," said Angelina. "Also on your black goat's beard and your absurdity of an Adam's apple. I hope to prune it with a sharp knife soon. There's something—well, prissy about it," she added, looking confused, as if she wondered why she said it.

He sprang up, and raised his arm to strike her; then he screamed a kind of question, in Spanish, to which she shrugged, and he gritted out, getting control of himself, "We shall explore these matters, *juntos,* you and I. Be assured—" But for some reason beyond my understanding, she laughed in his face.

Then the unpleasant scene was finished. Don Ricardo was led away, looking sober I thought; Esmerelda—in tears, now, and crying out to Ricardo, putting me in a murderous humor to hear her—was dragged to a heavily barred chamber of this second story; and Angelina, haughtily, without protest, stalked in her bold style down the spongy carpeting of a corridor lit by dim lamps, in wall sconces, that threw ghostly shadows all around. When she passed the man she'd kicked, he removed his hat, which he had just put on, then bowed slightly and shrunk back; he appeared respectful, even admiring, and murmured something about "*mis pobres cojones*" but hoped to see the señorita another time for his pleasure. Don Narciso struck him with a crop, and I was left alone, as downcast as ever I'd been in my life.

But not alone for long. Presently the black figure returned, shut the door quiet and careful and decisive, and stood looking me over. He'd done up his collar and combed his shiny hair. Then he asked me a lot of questions. What was my name? How did I happen to be here? Angelina? Name, home, age. Was she familiar with men? Large, rough men, or weak, gentle ones? Being too tired to lie, I told mainly the truth, though it went against the grain. I wished I could have another whack at it tomorrow, when I'd be stronger. Well, each answer puckered him up like a storm cloud, until finally he drifted off in reflection, pacing back and forth, brow furrowed, holding a finger against his lips.

"I have it," he said at last, with an icy imitation of a smile. "We must make you the page boy of the establishment. Do you know what that is?"

"I'm an American citizen," I said, "and you better watch out." All things considered, it wasn't much of a statement, but it was the best I could muster at the moment; I was practically dead on my feet.

"Your duties will be to run errands—inside the palace walls—to obey me in all things, and especially never to oppose me. *Do you understand that you are not to oppose me?*" he cried in a kind of nervous shriek. "It is not my disposition to be opposed—you may be gravely injured. Now, Sa— sir, the third door on the right around the balcony leads to your room. It will not be locked."

My expression must have slipped.

"Should you try to escape, the foolish, foolish females of your party will be placed in the cells with your friend. Near the garroting chamber. Do you understand?"

I nodded, with as insolent a stare as I could manage.

"Let this help!" and he slapped me across the mouth. My lips were cut and begun to puff out, and I'm blessed if, on the instant, he wasn't all concern and regret and apology. While I stood dazed, he wiped away the blood, felt my teeth, washed my face with scented water out of a basin, petted me, called me an excellent boy, a pretty boy (and smart), gave me a pink lozenge from a bottle, which I couldn't eat, nor would have, and, at last, warned me never to be noisy.

"I am unable to endure loud sounds," he said, suddenly half angry again. "Now you must go to bed. I seldom meet people without first consulting my physician, and certain things have upset me. *In God's name, get out!*"

There now begun a period that I've tried a good many times to blot out. I kept no record of the days in that gloomy nightmare of a prison in which silent long-faced servants appeared and disappeared, where men called to confer in whispers at late hours, where the sound of weeping was sometimes heard, where, I knew, shameful deeds were hidden away, together with all sunlight, by dark shutters and heavy padded doors. Even the patio seemed to doze in a dimmed perpetual twilight, sheltered beneath trees of thick foliage, and empty, both night and day, of any sound of footsteps.

The house is hard to remember in its details. On one wall of the piazza a fresco ornamented things by showing the Castle of Chapultepec, along with a notice in fancy gold lettering that it was built by a "Count Galves, Viceroy," and was used now as a military school. There were statues with arms and legs or worse busted off, making a person wonder why the artist had stopped to tinker with anybody so piecemeal and sickly; and some big blackish paintings of men in armor and pink-faced women with low dress lines. There were other big paintings in a secret room I opened one time when everybody was absent, but I can't describe those in a book for family consumption. They were enough to stop your blood, vile and sportive and painful, perhaps because so splendidly done. The brazen naked figures seemed to jump out of the canvas; they were that real. I saw the guests at a drunken dinner led there, laughing in excited voices, on a night when Don Narciso had consulted his "doctor," a humped-over, evil-looking Italian, wearing a black cloak, who'd arrived at the patio in a carriage like a funeral hearse, with ruffled silk curtains and rubber tyres on the wheels.

Don Narciso was two people. Sometimes, summoning me to his library, he chatted and told the pleasantest sort of stories, where all the people were nice and kind; he made himself wonderfully agreeable, trying always to address me by name but failing. I never knew why till the end. I noticed that, as he talked, he became more and more keyed up and jerky and nervous, especially if strong emotions were involved, until often, you had the impression he was racing way out in front of himself, no longer contained but blown up and choking from some terrible force inside. Then, as apt as not, for no reason—anything might bring it on—he wound up by slapping and smashing and screaming at me like a maniac. And afterwards, when I lay in my room, maybe genuinely hurt (for he had the strength of any crazy person on those occasions) he'd come in ashamed and contrite, abusing himself bitterly for blowing up over what he admitted was a trifle, going as far in one direction as he'd gone in the other.

On an evening when I displeased him by smudging a ridiculous book he'd set me to translating, by a man named Cervantes, being mostly about a numbskull of a horse, he struck me in the face with an inkstand. One eye was damaged so severe that the Italian doctor came, gliding in soft and silky with a black bag to inspect me. Afterward he conferred in low tones with Don Narciso, the two removed to a corner. Whatever his suggestion, the answer was "No, no! I want the boy alive, eye or no eye. I have my reasons." Wretched as I was, I heard it plain. They laid on a poultice, and Don Narciso sat beside me till daylight, holding my hand. But it was a long time before I healed.

Then I tried hard to see Angelina and the girl, but their doors stayed locked, and the servants never replied when I struck up a conversation. They were a close-mouthed and shifty collection; no normal man would have given them house room. One night I made my way two levels below the ground, descending a steep, musty, twisting stairway, off the kitchens, that changed from tile to wood to smooth flagstone, and then from rough rock to dirt, and reckoned I'd find Don Ricardo at last, but when I saw a light far down a shored-up passage, I stumbled, hurrying, and got caught by a raggedy creature carrying a bunch of iron keys. He appeared out of nowhere, from some dingy tunnel off to one side. Delivered upstairs, prepared to be scalped, I escaped all punishment; I couldn't believe my good luck. It was a matter of humors, you see. Don Narciso listened, sorrowful and patient, then waved away the jailer, whilst very offensively holding a perfumed cloth to his nose, and asked me: "Do you like this place? Do you fancy the life here? Would you care to be in my position as owner and proprietor? Consider your answer carefully, Sam, for a good deal depends on it." It was the first time he'd ever managed to call me by my name. I hadn't any idea what he was talking about, and luckily for me, a messenger arrived with news that put me out of his mind. Then, the next night, matters came to a head.

I was bound and determined to reach Angelina and figure some way to break out of this tomb. My nerves were going to pieces;

moreover, I was concerned about the others. So, I waited until two o'clock, lying awake in the dark, sweating and hearing all manner of noises. Then I got up, stole out, closing my door without a sound, and crept down the corridor. In one hand I carried a big bunch of keys I'd found in a desk that our captor had forgotten to lock. The wall lamps were snuffed out, thanks to goodness—the Black One had what amounted to the horrors about fire—and the house quieter than a tomb. But not when I arrived at Angelina's door. I heard a moan that cramped up my stomach, then a scream that rose and fell, rose and fell, rose and fell. Then something like, "Oh don't, please don't, don't, don't! Not now. Ah, *no!*" I felt so faint I hung onto the wall for support; and after that I heard a low pleading of, "Give me a few minutes, three minutes, two minutes—"

Right there I went berserk. I'd seen a machete hanging on a wall in the kitchen, and I scrambled down two flights of stairs, falling at one turn and hurting my ankle, but snatching the blade free all the same; then back up quick. I have no idea what I yelled, but I commenced hacking at the brass-studded door and shouting threats of murder, and meant them. Everything exploded into life. Lights went on, servants came running, the door flew open to show Don Narciso, whiter, and blacker, than ever, his clothes mussed, holding up a candlestick with a demon's expression, a trapped animal's look of rage, fear and, maybe, embarrassment. In the other hand he had something I couldn't make out, but when he saw who it was he screamed for Hai-soos to grab me, and after that I don't remember much.

I could have been carried, or dragged, down below. There might have been a series of narrow tunnels, some lined by rock, others of earth, moist and dripping. I may have imagined a big wooden cross with leather thongs at the wings. And the skeleton ruin of Don Ricardo, with greasy long hair and beard, shackled to wet rock by iron anklets and wristlets, could have been one of those hobgoblins that skid through a person's dreams when he's sick with fever. But the beating I took, from Hai-soos and two others, was sharp and real, wherever it took place. I must have lost consciousness, then been revived several times by slaps on the face. And then, at last, they were unable to revive me at all.

Just before, I heard one say, "By the Holy Virgin, the boy's dead!" and Hai-soos replying, "Hand me the truncheon; I don't mind flogging a corpse. What's the risk, *compadre?* Our chance of Heaven is gone."

I woke up in my own bed. It was late afternoon; slender fingers of sunlight poked through cracks in the shutters and slanted down onto the floor. My head felt tight and stuffy, as if drugged, but I had no recollection of the night. I tossed back the covers and crawled out, then crumpled to my hands and knees and vomited. I was sick five or six times, until nothing was left to heave up, and that's always the bad part. I was afraid I might hawk my stomach out. I lay abed for a long, long time, maybe all of that day, and night, and into the next day. Servants came and went, but no sign of Don Narciso.

When I felt strong enough to dress, I knew what I had to do, and I wished I'd done it before. In the mirror I looked peaked but not disfigured—that was on my back and chest and stomach, and would be there for good, I reckoned—and when I entered the library, Don Narciso arose cheerily and cried, "Well, my boy, I've missed you. Sit down and we'll talk about Riv—about your adventures. You've never told me the whole story." I knew the exact spot where the gaudy-handled letter opener was, and I lowered myself into a chair, hanging onto the arms pretty careful. Injured or not, I felt entirely at peace, happier than I'd been in all the long time since home (dim now but suddenly very precious). I felt good, but there came an interruption in the form of the principal manservant, who glided in and whispered something in his employer's ear.

He leaped to his feet immediately, hands clutching and unclutching, neck beginning to jerk—all the signs of panic—and cried, "*Who* is it? Who did you say? Speak out, you fool!"

"The Señorita Rojas y las Cruces, patrón; together with three companions of a common order. She is authentically beyond the gate."

The monster commenced to pace back and forth, dreadfully agitated. "I can't see her! Send her away at once. You blundering imbecile, you've said I was here? I'll have you whipped. No, I can't dismiss her. Wait! Tell them to stand in the patio for five minutes." He rushed to a sideboard and swallowed three or four white pills, washing them down with wine from a carafe.

"Leave me—no, stay." He put his hand to his forehead, then smelled some material in a bottle. "Distressing—distressing and thoughtless. I must reconsider everything. Surprises. The unexpectedness of a woman in the daytime . . . I am a night person, the day, daylight"—then here a loud rap at the door, it swung open, and I slumped half through the floor. In walked Blaine—hobbling, rather, on a cane—behind a beautiful proud-looking girl, and then, by George, Sergeant O'Hara and Mrs. Mendoza. O'Hara was twirling his hat in his hand, and seemed uncomfortable. Standing behind Don Narciso, I put a finger to my lips for all to see, but Blaine paid me no attention whatever. He and Don Narciso froze, perfectly motionless, both ghostly pale, both fixed in a sort of trance. I judged they'd taken one of those instant dislikes to each other, and when dealing with this fellow, it was as natural as breathing. A deceased mole would have done the same. Then Blaine shook his head slightly, and our black friend recovered enough to bow. Speaking in a low voice, the girl said, "I have come, Don Narciso, to throw myself on your honor. I ask you to release me from my father's arrangement—in the presence of these witnesses . . . by custom."

His head was bobbing so bad I hoped it might come unhooked, and his lips no longer looked red and over-healthy, but he finally got out, in painful, jerky, disconnected phrases, "To be sure, señorita, a lady's desires, my duty, what you wish—" and then he stepped very fast to a bell-pull in the corner.

I screamed, *"Blaine! He's calling his thugs!"* Then I yelled a lot of other things, many of them not very elegant. All the bottled-up torture of the weeks and weeks in this horrible place came tumbling out like a log-jam breaking. I don't remember exactly what I said—I was sobbing and babbling all at once—but it had to do with Angelina abused in her bedroom, and Esmerelda, and Don Ricardo rotting in the cellars; and at the end I ripped off my shirt to show the condition of my body.

The door burst open again, and the collection of cutthroats poured in, Hai-soos in front as usual. I never knew Blaine could move so nimble; he stepped aside about three paces, drew his revolving pistol from under his coat, and said, in the unhappiest tone I ever heard:

"Somebody should have done it years ago, Dirk," and shot him in the left breast. Before he fell, a red stain appeared in his frilly white shirt, and widened out in a ring. The cutthroats washed back, hesitated, waiting for Hai-soos, who mustered his courage and cried *"Viva!"* starting to rally, and O'Hara now volunteered the first act of violence in his war thus far against Mexico. Crossing himself, he seized Hai-soos by the neck and crotch, lifted him high overhead, trotted him to the window, and threw him into the street, carrying along the shutter, the glazing, part of the sash and the balcony's iron railing. One of the others murmured, *"Nombre de Dios!"* and they scrambled out and clattered down the stairs.

We laid Don Narciso on a sofa, and Blaine slumped down in a chair nearby, holding his head in his hands. The women cried, of course, and so did O'Hara, though he hadn't any idea why, but was happy to pitch in and help, and I watched my brother die. He lay staring at us, his face appearing to smooth out, little by little, becoming easier, and softer, and younger.

Then his chest heaved up in a great gasp, he turned his head and smiled, placed a hand on Blaine's sleeve, and said, "Thank God it's over."

XXX

There's only a brief way to go now, and frankly, I'm glad. When I started making this book, I hadn't realized what a back-breaker I'd tackled. Even with the boneheaded contributions from Blaine, which slowed down the plot and jarred the general tone, it's been a tiresome long grind. The next time they have a Mexican War, I'd sooner sign on as commander-in-chief of everything, and leave the writing to generals. Still, Blaine says I may get a medal, for what he calls "corrupting the English language beyond the call of duty," but I reckon that's some more of his sass.

But I'll skip along and describe what happened. Before many minutes had passed, that house was in a crashing uproar, with bright lights going on everywhere and servants appearing on the upper floors, clustered in the doorways and seeming, I thought, grateful and relieved. Every one of them, every person in the place (excepting Hai-soos, which was out in the street, deceased, with most articles of importance busted, from his ankles on up to his chin) was a poor, petty, small-time criminal on parole to Don Narciso and compelled to work free, under the threat of prison or death or worse. And some of these, we found, had been hustled up on false charges entirely; it was the regular system. The rich and powerful in Mexico could do just about what they pleased.

Anyhow, Blaine had another shocker coming. I felt sorry for him; he'd absorbed nearly all the punishment a sick man could handle. But in the confusion I told him the rest about Angelina, and we started ankling down the corridor pretty fast, leaving Sergeant O'Hara in charge. The door was locked, of course, so he collared a scared servant and said, "Get an axe—*hacha*, pronto!" But the man fetched a key instead, and we pushed on in. She was sitting on the edge of a fancy big bed, dressed in nothing but a perfectly transparent wrapper—her clothes had been removed from the room—looking hollow-eyed and weepy, the smart-aleckness gone, and when she saw us, she got up, still holding onto the bed for support, and cried, "Oh, *Blaine!*" He dropped his cane and limped forward, and she threw her arms around his neck and hung on like a baby that's lost its mother. Then he asked some kind of question, but she shook her head and replied, very low, along the lines of no, not possible except with those of the extreme gutter, impossible, though maybe worse for her, and I decided it was none of my business, for once.

In the doorway, the dark-haired girl watched steadily for a moment, then smiled and lit a cigarrito. When she breathed out the smoke, she gave a little sigh as if it was good to let down and be natural again. That is, her expression was far from happy, but she seemed peaceful, all the same. After that we found the girl Esmerelda, who *was* dressed, praise the saints, and in good condition though she cried, to be on the safe side, and embraced Angelina, which made it possible for them to cry together, and she very nearly embraced *me,* but I pranced around to the other side of the room. I'm not adverse to that sort of moonshine, you understand, but it ought to be practiced in private.

Don Ricardo, when we reached him, was so pitiful a sight that *I* could have cried. Those skunks, the late Hai-soos and his gang, had spanceled him to rock, and his frame had shrunk away to nothing. His hair and beard were long and tangled, like my vision of the beating, so I judged he'd seen it all, if conscious. The fellow was scarcely in his right mind, too weak to notice who we were, and had to be carried upstairs. By that time several officials from the town had arrived, and they trod mighty cautious when Esmerelda stepped forward to tell who we were. I never heard a young girl speak out so blistery and hot. It was curious, but she no longer sounded like an anarchist; she sounded like a Mexican, and a pretty toplofty one at that. She was mad clear through, and addressed those grafters like a bunch of *léperos*. She got by with it, too.

Things had changed during our long imprisonment at Don Narciso's. In the middle of October, General Lane had rudely thumped the remaining Mexican Army in the battles of Huamantla and Puebla—no more than five miles from where we lived—and old Peg-leg Santa Anna sloped out of the country, protecting his hide as usual. Some said he went to Guatemala. The mild-mannered and peaceable Herrera was returning to power, and his friends were in favor once more.

So we went through a humbuggy hearing with Blaine, and everybody agreed that, in view of the fallen Administration and all, he'd acted in self-defense. To be fair, I should add that a number of high-grade Mexicans were also on hand, and they expressed thankfulness to be rid of Don Narciso. There was some excitement about putting up a statue of Blaine in a park, but nothing came of it. Nobody could decide who'd pay the bill, so that in the end they inquired if he would, and he said no.

Anyhow, we removed in two *diligencias* to Mexico City, where the Morales family had a mansion, as stated, and tucked in to recover from our miseries. Don Ricardo in particular required a lot of nursing to get back his health, and neither Blaine nor Angelina was exactly in tiptop form. I myself felt glad of a rest. For a good many weeks I had terrible nightmares over what I'd seen and suffered in that house, and would awake screaming and sweating and thrashing about, often to find Angelina shaking me and telling me it was all right. But people can take an astonishing amount of punishment and work back to normal, and gradually, in this sunny, pleasant home in a beautiful city, we commenced to mend. Meanwhile, Sergeant O'Hara and Mrs. Mendoza left on a pilgrimage to cities nearby, hoping to get some ideas for settling down.

A whole bundle of letters came from home, and we had a good sniffle. Nothing important had happened. In response to an appeal for more volunteers, my Uncle Cassius, sixty-three, had traveled to Fort Leavenworth to sign up, but a harebrained young sergeant said he was too old to fight, so he naturally challenged the dunce to a duel, to chalk him up a liar; they talked him out of it after a little trouble. My mother's scars were nearly gone—she'd ridden over to help out some new poor-white neighbors, named Robert and Zerelda James, who gave birth to a son, Jesse; my father was overworked on the plantation but the price of hemp had soared way up; my sister Claudia was being courted by a man that was suspected of once having lived in the North though he denied it and nobody seemed able to prove it, but there was talk of putting a detective on the case; and Hyacinth had got his foot caught in a rabbit trap, all on his own—I hadn't a thing to do with it—and that was the best news of all.

Afterward, poor old Blaine set about the dreary, dismal task of trying to tell them about Dirk, and he finally got it done, but it required nearly a week. And when it was finished, he shut himself up for one whole day, not speaking to a soul. I felt sorry for him, but couldn't figure out any good way to help.

The period that now began was maybe the happiest I could remember, even with my family in Missouri, and Blaine says it will be as good as I'll ever have; said I'd never be sixteen again and "smitten with puppy love," or words to that effect—talking through his hat. Visitors claimed that this city was more like Paris than something lying in a primitive setting on the outside edge of a forgotten Indian culture. It used to be called Tenochtitlán back then, but the name now was taken from an ancient war god—Mexitli, so they told us. When the invalids started having thoughts of getting out, Don Ricardo—bundled up and with a servant helping him about the carriage—took us everyplace possible.

The house was near the Calle del Puento de Jesús, because at one time boats and bridges were required in nearly all parts of town, and when the neighboring lakes overflowed, floods caused a merry lot of damage. The waterways were replaced by paved streets now, but Don Ricardo had a man dig down two feet to brackish water, in a park, to show that practically the whole works rested on a crust of made soil. The floods had been eliminated by means of an immense drain, tolerably clever, as fine an engineering feat, said Blaine, as the aqueducts that ran in by Belen and San Cosone from Chapultepec. These flowed into fountains, all over the city, from which *aguadores* dipped out water and toted it in earthen jars to the small householders.

By and by we were able to take walks in the fashionable sections, in the Alameda, near the Paseo, a handsome straightaway drive, nearly a mile long, bordered on both sides by noble big trees and sidewalks and stone seats and bootblacks and women selling tacos and young men with slick black hair peddling other commodities. And, always, women with their table and *brasero* from which they furnished a really good and sturdy hot meal, including beef stew and chile, for half a dozen *clacos*—nine cents.

But walking, except, in our case, for health, was not an exercise for Society, so that the Alameda and the Paseo, said Don Ricardo, were thronged mostly by French *modistas* who "were too poor to breathe the aristocratic dust of the Paseo from their coach windows." As in the other cities, Sunday was the great day for amusements, the day when people went to the bullfights, or the parks, or the *misa mayor* at the Cathedral, or the circus, or the National Palace, alongside the Plaza, or to one of the five gorgeous, gilded theaters, like the Nacional, which had just changed its name, hauling down the sign Teatro de Santa Anna only a few hours after its namesake had high-tailed it aboard a boat for Guatemala. No matter what critics say, Mexico is a current place, and has a very sensitive nose for keeping up with the trends.

A number of Mexican homes were being opened to American officers, and anyway we met a good many friends of the Morales family. People were so polite they called for you in their coaches; and they referred to their homes as *la casa de usted*. Public balls and parties were announced almost every night for the special benefit of the Army. They ran advertisements in the newspapers, very curious, in which it was said that "Only ladies of the first respectability will be admitted," but nobody examined the women's credentials very careful, according to Blaine. He said he'd be glad to examine them himself, but Angelina nearly slapped his face. The most exclusive balls were held at the former convent in Belemitas Street, but a bunch of the French *modistas* thronged in one night, shouting, contorting around and smoking, and made a lot of folk mad.

High Society here could get tiresome it seemed to me, and I copied out a letter from an English-speaking newspaper that troops were sending home: "The family circle for a stranger is rather dull, generally, except where music is introduced, as, by the way, it very commonly is. The *muchachos* and *muchachas* (boys and girls), are both better instructed in accomplishments than in practical knowledge; the education of the girls is particularly defective. Music, in many families, is highly cultivated by both sexes; drawing and painting among the boys, and embroidery among the girls, have also many proficients. But when it comes to waltzing and dancing, there is no limitation. Young and old, grave and gay, seem to waltz by intuition; and the American, with his utilitarian views, who has devoted his life to filling his head with such stuff as grammar, geography, and arithmetic, to putting steam in traces, and writing his letters in lightning, all at the expense of his heels, is a *sujeto muy mal instruido,* indeed."

The subject most popular among the women was Tom Thumb —"*un hombre tan chiquito*"—some kind of American circus performer, who they were itching to see, for some reason. I'd never heard of him, myself, but it got to the point where I hated to admit it; so I finally owned up that I knew him well, had grown up with him, gone fishing together, and corresponded regular, but when one lady said, "You must tell me, young man, how big is General Thumb, really?" I pulled a boner, I reckon, because I said, wishing to give him all credit, "Well, I wouldn't say he was eight feet, but I can tell you this much—he's considerable over seven." She frosted right up, and I found out afterward that I'd got it just wrong. The fellow was a midget, drat his hide.

The food in these fancy homes of Mexico City was different from what we'd had elsewhere. Dinner came along at five in the afternoon, when everybody was starved down after a light breakfast and ready to tuck into something solid. First, always, came broth (*caldo*), generally chicken with a Frenchified flavor; then one or more *sopas* of rice, along with *fideos* (vermicelli; like a very soft kind of bread); then the grand dish of the capital—*el puchero,* being a mixture of things like *bouilli,* bacon, cabbage, bananas, garbanzos (chickpeas), a rich tomato sauce and additional ingredients, the whole cooked in a glazed earthenware vessel. It really was good, but was it enough? Not at all. It might have sufficed for a camel, but after it, in these houses, came stewed, roasted, and boiled meats, then a salad, and fruits, and lastly, of course, a round or two of dulces. Any time you stopped to rest, servants whipped away your plate, knife, and fork, and replaced them with clean ones. None of this food was ordinary, either. The hams came from Spain, as well as the wines, and, when the ladies retired, the men smoked *puros* from Havana. *Puros* are cigars made entirely of tobacco, unlike the Mexican variety, which is wrapped in corn shuck, as told previous. Some of the women liked cigarritos, and I once heard Don Ricardo say, studying Carla, "My father disapproved, but I enjoy seeing a girl smoke. A pretty girl. After all, it's—Mexican." She smiled back, her gaze level and cool and understanding. These people lived well, and while they appeared to have an uncommon number of stomach-aches, they wouldn't have changed things for the world.

The dark-haired girl (Carla) and I climbed to the towers of the Cathedral, passing through the apartment of the bellringer's family (above the roof) and into the belfry. Everybody said this view was the best in Mexico, but it made you dizzy to look down on the domes and terraced roofs and over the long, long valley dotted with lakes and mountains, fields and chapels and villages and castles. Beyond the gate of San Lázaro some municipal troops were drilling, as happy as if they'd won the war, and the changing formations, tiny and sluggish, resembled a puppet show. Nearer by, filling the streets and the Plaza, were crowds of pygmy people, pygmy carriages, horses, *padres,* both American and Mexican soldiers, water carriers, women, children, Indians and donkeys—all swarming in and out of the dozens and dozens of vendor stalls beneath the *portales* of the National Palace.

My companion, who struck me as a Mexican version of Angelina (being another know-it-all), said the majority of those were a particularly low breed of léperos—"half-naked mestizos with brown hides blackened by dirt and sun, whose profession consists, at the best, of enough honest labor to add to their gains from begging and thieving." Like most high-class Mexicans, she was contemptuous of léperos, and said they were "the vilest people in the civilized world, with no idea of morality or decency." Possibly. However, something else she told me was true, that lépero mothers often gouge out their babies' eyes, to give them a better chance at begging in later years. Carla claimed that the marriage custom of these people was *"fuera de la iglesia,"* or behind the church. But I heard another person say they simply couldn't afford the hog-gobble fees of the Church, so what was a person to believe? It's annoysome; most arguments appear to have two sides, both one hundred per cent watertight.

Blaine joined a new officers' social club called the Aztec Club, and he hauled Don Ricardo in, too. The two hit it off from the start, and one night they took me to the Bella Union, a bang-up entertainment center, but I was waltzed out in a hurry when they determined the nature of the exhibits. Me, I'd a stayed on to gather material for my Journal, except that my window had an iron grating on it, like all such windows here, and some busybody showed the pushful bad taste to slink up and lock my door on the outside.

We went to the theater to see a visiting Spanish actress named Cañete, who was having a spurt of popularity just then. She played the leading part in a play called *Gamin de Paris,* by a Frenchman written in Spanish. The place was overflowing with thousands of people—biggest theater Blaine said he'd ever been in—and they gave this little lady a rousing hoorah. So she came out after the curtains and made a smiley-curtsey speech of "tanks," in *English,* but her grip on the tongue was so ornery I got lost; I'd been getting along tolerably well in the Spanish, when awake. There weren't any Mexican actors hereabouts; the theater imported all of its companies from Spain, and Italy, and France. Altogether the evening went off well enough, if you enjoy that sort of thing. Between rounds they had a dancer named Gozze, a Spanish Celeste, a troupe of singers called the Sable Harmonists—braying out a group of songs on two favorite themes: children and beating a donkey—about as ignorant as possible—

and two army bands. In point of time spent alone, a person got his money's worth.

My nerves healed up, and after the siesta I took to strolling the city with Esmerelda, peaceful and serene, also armed with a revolver and a sword buckled on by Don Ricardo himself—on account of the ladrones. Robbers. They flourished in spite of General Smith's military police of four hundred picked army men. There was a difference between them and léperos. Socially, ladrones were several notches above léperos, being dangerous and having ambitions to steal enough money to buy an honest business with. No self-respecting ladrón would give the time of day to a lépero, and the latter suffered from it, claiming prejudice. Blaine said all of these social injustices would be ironed out by law some day, so that léperos could hold up their heads with the haughtiest robbers in town; but the statement had just the slightest ring of his customary bilge. Anyhow, if you got caught out after dark, these swine were apt to pounce from a lonely recess and attack you. And it was easy to get caught out, owing to the lunatic system of street naming. The whole city was arranged in squares, and the name of each leg ended right there at the square. Thus, if you asked somebody for, say, the Calle Plateros, and arrived there, conceding that you were born lucky to start with, you'd slide off it in about thirty seconds. Even so, nobody ever bothered us; all ladrones had an awestruck respect for revolvers. The sight of one was enough to send them sprinting out of a neighborhood. It was too bad; I'd been practicing up in a vacant lot and hoped to bag a few. A man told me the authorities were paying a bounty of two pesos a head—captured, plugged or killed.

Around this time I'd worked out some ideas involving the making of money. But the problem came to a climax one day after Don Ricardo regained his full strength. He clapped on his hat—in the strong light his hair now had some gray flecks in it, I noticed—and said we'd journey to Puebla to take up the matter of Don Narciso's property. He had a hard, stubborn streak like a mule's and said he'd be hanged (*colgado*) if *some* one of us didn't benefit from that torture. He said, further, that money, in his family, had always been treated with respect, and his respect had picked up considerable while he was lying chained in the basement.

"But my dear fellow," said Blaine, as we stood in the splendid, leafy, flower-speckled patio, "*I* don't want it. I'd far rather let the whole matter drop."

"My esteemed friend, I dislike—it grieves me—to quarrel with a man who has become as dear to me as my own kin, *but you are not the only person involved.*"

He turned to place a hand on my head, and while normally I'd as soon be bitten by an alligator, I stepped forward and made the expected response. After all, I *was* a guest in his house. "You can count on me," I stated. "Whatever's indicated and right, I'll do it. This is your country, so let's follow its customs—any amount." (I hoped he might wring out as much as a hundred dollars in damages, which would give me the start I needed.)

"I've taken the liberty of summoning the family solicitors," he went on, and I'm jiggered if a troupe of thirteen black-garbed customers didn't sidle up and lift their hats, but not very far—as cautious and calculating and oily-skinned a collection as you'd find by throwing a seine through the City Hall. Nobody with ordinary eyesight could have told them apart. Each had an armful of books with slips of paper sticking out as markers, for referring to "precedents," and most had a number of quills, pencils, erasers, and writs of various sorts in their jacket pockets, to be used in emergencies.

I had forty dollars hid on me, and I ducked down and buried it in some loam at the foot of a tree. I didn't do it on purpose; the action was as natural as breathing.

One says, "In regard to the Cause at hand, before speaking *sub judice,* I might mention *but would deny it if quoted in Court,* that—"

Another, behind him, gave a discreet little cough and remarked, "On the whole, not having *yet* filed for summary judg—"

"You mean—?"

"Precisely."

They withdrew a few paces to confer, and Don Ricardo barked out with impatience, "In the name of sweet Heaven, climb into your carriage. Resolve it later. Play *tresillo,* or divide up a tort and eat it. I'm ready to move." I got the notion that he'd likely been closeted pretty close with these sharks lately, and had maybe wore out a little on their style.

At Don Ricardo's, I read in a book about Mexican lawyers: "Your honored profession (law) is in the hands of unworthy members generally, who, besides a character worse than indifferent for integrity, have neither the reputation for learning or talents so common to the bar throughout the civilized world." And Blaine said, "They don't put you very much in mind of Alex Doniphan, do they?"

Not to dribble on, we rode to Puebla, all those lawyers in one coach, sitting on each other's laps, I judged, while jotting down notes in code—in case anybody broke a leg and decided to sue—and requested a meeting with the Alcalde, three Judges, two Bishops, several attorneys for claimants, and some others I failed to identify.

Disregarding his advisers, Don Ricardo himself made a speech, delivered more like an ultimatum than a plea, and explained our relationship to the deceased. He'd no sooner finished than a Bishop got up to say that he held, in his possession, a will in which Don Narciso left his entire property to the Church.

"Do you have that testament on your person, sir?" inquired Don Ricardo in about as abrupt a tone as I ever heard anyone use to a high and mighty member of the Cloth.

"I regret that it has been mislaid," replied the Bishop.

"Very likely. Now who else has a lien on that happily departed gentleman?"

Twenty-two women, and one man, arose to swear on a Bible that they had lived with Don Narciso as common-law wife, and three swore in addition that they'd been married in secret, the certificates lamentably disappearing in a fire. In each case, the ceremony, by coincidence, had been performed in a building now reduced by bombardment. A woman who seemed unusually confident said she could prove *her* claim with details; said it wasn't generally known, but Don Narciso had a snake tattooed on his ——. But at this, a tearful, pretty young girl, wearing a black veil—his sister and sole living relation—jumped to her feet and hotly denounced that as a dirty lie; she was in a position to know better. For a minute, it looked as though they might mix it, but the Alcalde had them both ushered out. One very refined old lady, on the arm of a distinguished-looking lawyer with an eye as direct as an eagle's—it made me regret my scratchy thoughts about the thirteen—walked up and swore she was his mother; and any number of servants worked in some kind of farfetched claim or another. One man with a twisted foot stated that Don Narciso had hit him with a stove, but it was proved that he'd received the injury while robbing an orphanage when he was twelve.

I don't wish to make this hearing sound absurd, but it *was* a curiosity, mainly because it produced such a rich brand of lying. The participants attracted admiration. These were no run-of-the-mill liars; they were highly talented comers, and one, at least, that had the specialty of weeping to order, was signed on by lawyers to be used as a witness in other cases from time to time.

In substance, Don Ricardo, and his solicitors (who turned out to have some value after all) and the Alcalde, together with the Bishops and Judges, agreed on a compromise, and that was where I came close to fainting. I didn't recover for three or four days.

"What is the approximate value of the estate?" a thin, dried-up prune of an attorney for the deceased was asked, and he replied, adjusting his spectacles and stooping over some ledgers, "Aside from the *palacio* in the Calle Orizaba, whose value I would be most reluctant to appraise *on this market*"—he gave Blaine and me a brief, venomous glance—"besides the house, I say, there exists El Rancho Castanuella, of 314.623 square miles, with its hacienda constructed of, ah, porous amygdaloid and glassy felspar porphyry; certain outbuildings, in the number of thirty-two; cattle in undetermined quantities—I decline to adduce without the exact figure; sheep, swine, horses, to include fifty-five *frisones*, of the northern breed, worth a thousand dollars each—*more or less* (I will *not* be bound to that); ninety-three *peones* indebted for periods from"—he stuck his nose down in the ledger pages—"ten to one hundred and five years—"

"Oh, never mind the lawyer's drivel," Don Ricardo interrupted. "What else? In general. Don't wade off into a morass of decimals."

"My dear sir, I must protest!" cried the man with feeble violence. "Attorneys for the estate will not be held account—"

"Just proceed," said Don Ricardo, with a wave of the hand, and I begun to wonder if *he*'d been elected the new President.

Gravely insulted, the men concluded, stiffly, "And approximately three million pesos—dollars—in specie, chattels, foreign and domestic securities, and personal jewels. There are certain other—"

"That will do. Well, then, let us put our heads together and make a division. But first of all, my young friend Sam, do you have any preferences among these abundant but not overwhelming properties?"

They placed a damp cloth on my head, and I remember Carla rubbing my wrists, and after that, they walked me around the room for awhile. The alcalde offered to summon a physician, but I was all right. It lasted less than ten minutes. When I sat down again, my face a muddy yellow, as Blaine stated later, I said, "I can't think so good just now, but I—I don't want the house in Orizaba Street, nor any part of it, nor—" I felt slightly like throwing up, so they let me stretch out again on a bench. Money does that to some people; I wonder why.

"Enough!" cried Don Ricardo cheerily. "I suggest you leave it to your brother and me." The conference went on for an exhausting long time, and all in all, sixty-three precedents were referred to: it established a record in Puebla, and most of the lawyers thought it had a good chance of standing up for years. They looked pleased. At last the Church expressed satisfaction with its share, the State and municipal people gobbled up what they could in view of the Morales family's influence with Mr. Herrera, and others, even some servants and one or two women, left with jubilant looks.

A great many documents were signed, including some by me, flat on my back, wax was melted and seals called into use, oaths were taken on a Bible that finally collapsed and shed one of its leather covers, and there followed an emotional spree of handclasping, embracing, kissing and congratulations. These people semed profoundly moved, but as for me, it all sounded far off, like actors rehearsing in a dream.

Then Don Ricardo came over, drew up a chair, and said, "Sam, *buen amigo.* Sam—what an abomination of a name!—a part of the debt is paid." As he gazed down, his usually serious face crinkled up around the eyes. "You really are an exceptional specimen, my young friend; your brother and I concur in this, and wonder how you've lasted so long—"

"What do I have, then? I hope it's as much as a hundred dollars," I said, "because I'd like to *stay* here, and go into business, and after that, Es—"

"Poor young Sam," said Don Ricardo in a musing sort of way, "you have an agonizing lot of growing up to do in these next few years. I'll be here to help, but I can't absorb all the pain, the disappointments, the bruises, and slights and compromises, the strife with envious neighbors and shabby politicians. According to Nature's law, we are told, these burdens and others must be borne to toughen your fiber for 'manhood,' a most unenviable and seldom happy estate. And Sam, the passage from boyhood into that nervous region of no-return is the hardest time of all. . . . Castanuella, one of Mexico's great ranches, is yours. With a sum of money to keep it free of debt. You have a large responsibility, muchacho; see that you use it, if possible, *pro bono publico.* On the record," he added briskly, with a reflective expression, "perhaps Mexico should be alerted as well."

On a day in April, Blaine and Angelina and I made a journey 190 miles north to Querétaro, where the war was ending with a treaty at a place called Guadalupe Hidalgo. After the signing, they planned to go home, and me, too, for a little while. From the time we left, almost two years had gone by until this moment. General Scott—Escott, as the Mexicans called him—was removed as head of the Army, thanks to the sneaky back-door attacks on his reputation by the political generals. President Polk had been powerfully impressed by a letter, printed in the New Orleans *Delta* and some others, that was signed by a man named "Leonidas." It described the tragedy of Scott's bad approach to Chapultepec, and went on to praise the amazing high qualities of General Pillow. Nobody (besides, maybe, Scott) much minded when the letter turned out to have been written by Pillow himself.

"People shouldn't be swayed by that. Polk is easily as intelligent as most Presidents," said Blaine, trying to be fair, "and not much brighter than a roustabout." Anyhow, "the Old War-Horse" stepped down, the row continued, truces were signed and broken, armistices drawn up and ignored, negotiations went forward, certain Mexican cliques battled others for control, and Congressmen hee-hawed about this and that (aiming their remarks at the voters, of course), and only prolonged the war about seven weeks, it was estimated. The Government made a record number of wrongheaded decisions, always taking the trouble to deny them first, the way officials do. It's an odd situation; I can't get it fixed in my head. Children are sent to school to learn truth, and honesty, and "character," but the people that vote money for the schools are the shiftiest coyotes on earth. Unless I misread the newspapers, practically anything plotted up by the State Department, for example, is preceded by a barefaced lie that it isn't so. Blaine says you could stretch one of those people on the rack, explain that the truth would set him free, and he'd lie for exercise.

Still, we'd come out on top. California would be ours, after a payment of $15,000,000; and the southern boundary of the United States was fixed as the Rio Grande and the Gila River on west to the Pacific. Nearly two thousand Americans had been killed, and seven thousand Mexicans. Thousands upon thousands of nice young men like Blaine and Don Ricardo would walk about for the rest of their lives with a stiff leg, or one arm, or both eyes gone, or their lower jaw shot away, or a tin hole in their throat, or one side of their face burned blue-red. Added to those, eleven thousand of the ninety thousand American soldiers involved had died of sickness or been killed in accidents since the war started. And all, says Blaine, because a set of rotten, hypocritical, sanctimonious, self-serving, tricky, unprincipled politicians, both Mexican and American, hadn't stature enough to sit down and work things out like statesmen. "Generally speaking, my good ass" (which I didn't care for as a means of addressing a person of wealth, and a *ranchero* at that) "the pushiest available trash wind up running the world. Perhaps it must always be so. The meek may inherit the earth, but the brassy and grasping will plunder it to the point where nobody wants it. How could the ignoramuses in power possibly understand each other across these borders? They can't even converse without an interpreter. Thus the harvest of three centuries of 'education.'"

It was good to hear him. He hadn't been steamed up like that for months, and he said he aimed to write a "hard-hitting treatise" on the subject. Well, it represented a stride on the road back to normal; he no longer seemed interested in attacking conditions with a sword. Then he expressed relief that Sergeant O'Hara hadn't heard his "beautifully chosen political observations"; he might have pulled up a sapling and killed somebody, probably an innocent bystander.

Blaine was mistaken about that. We rode on into Querétaro, and in the doorway of the old, old Iglesia de San Francisco de Fé found O'Hara, dressed in a coarse and patched brown robe, girded round the middle with a rope, wearing a crude pair of half-tanned sandals on his feet; his face appeared emptied for good of all anger against the politicians. He'd been appointed the novitiate guide of this establishment, and he steered us about with pride, pointing out the curious roofs where everything, every inch, was constructed in a series of wavy troughs to carry the scarce and precious rainfall to drains at the corners then down far below to slimy green catch-pools of rock. At the end, Blaine gave him a peso, for the poor, which he bit, saying, "Begging your pardon, sir, but we get a mort of oddities, and the most of them, they ain't silver."

Blaine inquired about his future, and he said, "Why, I'll be getting me Orders in only a few years now"—he furrowed up his brow—"if only I could hustle sommat forwarder on the writing, which, to own up, goes against the nature of me fist [he held it out, the size of a small ham; its back covered with curly red bristles] then me and Mrs. Mendoza—"

"Do you mean she's here? Surely she hasn't been solicited to take vows?"

"Why, no, not exactly, sir, but she's supporting me every step. You see, she's a-operating a prosperous monte game, located handy across the square, and business growing all the time. The blessed woman's been a tower of strength in me work, a-scrimping and putting by for the Lord's holy mission."

When at last he got his Orders, he said, with an extraordinary and quite genuine look of humility, they hoped to open a small chapel of their own: The Church of All Saints except Jerome; during her formative years Mrs. Mendoza had taken a distaste to this meddlesome symbol of her faith . . .

I left them chatting, Blaine soberly taking notes, and strolled for awhile alone through the tidy parks and gardens, past the long familiar sights of lofty, lopsided churches and ragged beggars, past the glittering carriages and deformed children and flowers and starving dogs and markets that flashed like rainbows with tainted and bright-colored fruit. It was awful, and lovely. Something turned over deep in my chest; it would be, forever after, home.

R.L.T.

Querétaro, 1963

ACKNOWLEDGMENTS

THE AUTHOR wishes once again to acknowledge his indebtedness to Sterling Memorial Library, at Yale University, and in particular to the curator of the Library's collection of Western Americana, Dr. Archibald Hanna, whose uniquely expert assistance made possible most of the research here involved.

Thanks are also extended to the State Historical Society of Missouri, directed by Richard S. Brownlee, and the Library of the University of Missouri, for information relating to the early life of Alexander Doniphan in Clay County.

In the course of a winter's travel and residence in Mexico, the author received guidance and help from people too numerous to list, though perhaps Don Esteban Molino y Gomez Palacio, at the incomparable Rancho Siete, should be mentioned especially.

As often before, a great deal of editorial drudgery was skillfully borne by Judith Martin Taylor, wife of the author.

R.L.T.

PRINCIPAL BIBLIOGRAPHY

Trailing Cortez through Mexico, by Harry A. Franck
Memoir of a Tour to Northern Mexico, by A. Wislizenus, M.D.
The War with Mexico, (Volumes I and II), by Justin H. Smith
Letters of Captain E. Kirby Smith to his Wife, 1846–1847
General Lane's Brigade in Central Mexico, by Albert G. Brackett, M.D.
Wetmore's *Gazetteer of Missouri*
A Journal of the Santa Fé Expedition under Colonel Doniphan, by Jacob S. Robinson
Letters of Samuel Ryan Curtis of Wooster, Ohio (63 letters)
Heroes and Incidents of the Mexican War, by Isaac George
Mexican Pronunciamentos, 1846–1848 (Ministries of War and Navy)
Marching with the Army of the West, by Marcellus Ball Edwards
A Soldier under Kearny and Doniphan, by Lieutenant X
Letters of Major M. Lewis Clark
Doniphan's Expedition, by William E. Connelly
A Campaign in New Mexico with Colonel Doniphan, by Frank Edwards
Commerce of the Prairies, (Volumes I and II), by Josiah Gregg
The Conquest of Santa Fé, by a Captain of Volunteers
Official Reports of the Battles of Brazito and Sacramento
To Mexico with Scott, by Captain E. Kirby Smith
The Year of Decision, 1846, by Bernard de Voto
Files of the Liberty, Missouri, *Tribune,* (1846–1848)
History of Clay and Platte Counties, National Historical Society
History of Clay County, Missouri, by W. H. Woodson
The Western Metropolis, or St. Louis, 1846, by W. D. Skillman

Missouri Historical Review
Southern Literary Messenger
Godey's Lady's Book
Ladies' National Magazine
Wild Life in the Far West, being the Personal Adventures of a Border Mountain Man, by Captain James Hobbs
Journal of Doniphan's Expedition, by William H. Richardson
Claim of Manuel X. Harmony for Seizure of Property by Doniphan in March to Chihuahua
Files of the Missouri Historical Society publications at Columbia, Missouri
William Clark Breckenridge, by James Malcolm Breckenridge
When Destiny Called: a story of the Doniphan Expedition in the Mexican War, by Ottamar Hamele
Clay County, Missouri Centennial Souvenir, published in the Liberty *Tribune,* by the Alexander Doniphan Chapter of the Daughters of the American Revolution in 1922
The Female Volunteer, or the Life, Wonderful Adventures and Miraculous Escapes of Miss Eliza Allen, by Eliza Allen
El Puchero, or A Mixed Dish from Mexico, by Richard McSherry
Mexican Treacheries and Cruelties, by G. N. Allen
An Artillery Officer in Mexico, by Robert Anderson
A Complete History of the Mexican War, by N. C. Brooks
Travel and Adventure in Mexico, by W. W. Carpenter
Manifestos, Exposiciones, Broadsides, and other Mexican papers translated for the author by Miss Loraine Lindberg
Intercepted Letters, captured by the American Guard at Tacubaya
Memoires of Agustín de Itúrbide
Apología de Santa Anna en Cerro Gordo, by M. M. Jímenez
Costumbres Mexicanas, by J. M. L. Mora
Mexican Bibliography of the New York Public Library
General Zachary Taylor and the Mexican War, by A. C. Quisenberry
Campaign in Mexico, by B. F. Scribner
Los Gringos, by H. August Wise
The Other Side; or, Notes for the history of the war between Mexico and the United States, by Ramón Alvarez
La Invasión Americana (1846–1848), by Manuel Balbontín
Mexican Letters (1846–1848), by Henry Marie Breckenridge
El nuevo Bernal Díaz del Castillo, ó sea, Historia de la Invasión de los Anglo-Americanos in México, by Carlos María de Bustamente
An Infantryman's Account: Campaigns against the North Americans
The Causes and Justice of the Mexican War, compiled from Official Documents by The New Hampshire *Patriot*

PRINCIPAL BIBLIOGRAPHY

The Conquest of New Mexico and California; an Historical and Personal Narrative, by Philip St. George Cooke

Autobiography of the late Colonel George T. M. Davis, captain and aide-de-camp in Scott's Army of Invasion

Adventures in Mexico, by Corydon Donovan

Extracts from the *Journal* and letters of Captain Samuel F. Du Pont

Biographical Sketches and Ancedotes of a Soldier of Three Wars, by James D. Elderkin

Letters from New Mexico, published in the St. Louis *Weekly Reveille* (1847) by Richard S. Elliott

A Kentucky Soldier's Account of the March to Mexico, His Capture and Imprisonment by the Mexican Army

The Twelve Months Volunteer, by George C. Furber

Peace with Mexico, by Albert Gallatin

Journal of a Soldier under Kearny and Doniphan (1846–1847), by George Rutledge Gibson

Campaign Sketches of the War with Mexico, by Captain William S. Henry

A Review of the Causes and Consequences of the Mexican War, by William Jay

The Adventures and Recollections of General Walter P. Lane

Letters from the Frontiers, by George A. McCall

Down the Santa Fé Trail and into Mexico; the Diary of Susan Shelby Magoffin (1846–1847)

Memoirs of José Francisco Palomares

La Invasión norteamericana en 1846, by Eduardo Paz

The Diary of James K. Polk, (1845–1849)

The War with Mexico, by Roswell Sabine Ripley

Reminiscences of a Campaign in Mexico, by John Blount Robertson

Detalle de las Operaciones Ocurridas en la Defensa de la Capital de la República, by Antonio López de Santa Anna

Camp Life of a Volunteer, by Benjamin Franklin Scribner

Autobiography of Elihu Hotchkiss Shepard

Reminiscences of a Campaign in Mexico (Indiana Brigade) by Isaac Smith

Campaigns of the Rio Grande and of Mexico, by Isaac Ingalls Stevens

Prairiedom: Rambles and Scrambles in Texas, by Frederick B. Page

Pictorial History of Mexico and of the Mexican War, published by *The New York Sun*

A Concise History of the Mormon Battalion in the Mexican War (1846–1847), by Daniel Tyler

Western Wilds of America (Five Years with the Texas Rangers), by Joe Shelly

The Battles of Mexico, by Lucius H. Vermilya

Last Leaves of American History, by Emma Hart Willard

A Narrative of Major General Wool's Campaign in Mexico, by Francis Baylies

Mexico in Miniature, by H. Skinner

A Navy Surgeon in California (1846–1847), by Marius Duvall

Journals of the late Brevet Major Philip Norbourne Barbour and his Wife, Martha Isabella Hopkins Barbour

Address delivered at the United States Military Academy, West Point, by Colonel Alexander W. Doniphan, June 16, 1848

Leyes del Territorio de Nuevo Méjico, Santa Fé, October 7, 1846. Published in Spanish and English by Colonel A. W. Doniphan

Doniphan's Expedition, by John Taylor Hughes

A Doctor Comes to California, the diary of John Strother Griffin, assistant surgeon with Kearny's Dragoons

The Slaveholding Indians, by Annie H. Abel

Report of the Secretary of War; an Examination of New Mexico (1848)

The History of the American Indians, by James Adair

The Treaty Between the United States and Mexico, 1848 (adding the territory of Arizona, California, New Mexico to the U.S.)

Camp Life of a Volunteer—A Campaign in Mexico, by "One Who Has Seen the Elephant"

Mexico vs. Texas, by a Texian, Anthony Ganilh. (First Texas Novel in English, first published in Paris)

Official dispatches . . . connected with the Commission to . . . mark the Boundary between the United States and Mexico, by John R. Bartlett

Recollection of Mexico and the Battle of Buena Vista, by a Soldier

Sketches of the Campaign in Northern Mexico, by Major Luther Giddings

The Statistical Account of Mexico, by Joseph A Villa-Señor y Sanchez

Claims of Mexican Citizens Against the United States for Military Depredations, by Francisco Gomez del Palacio

Andele, or the Mexican-Kiowa Captive, by J. J. Methvin

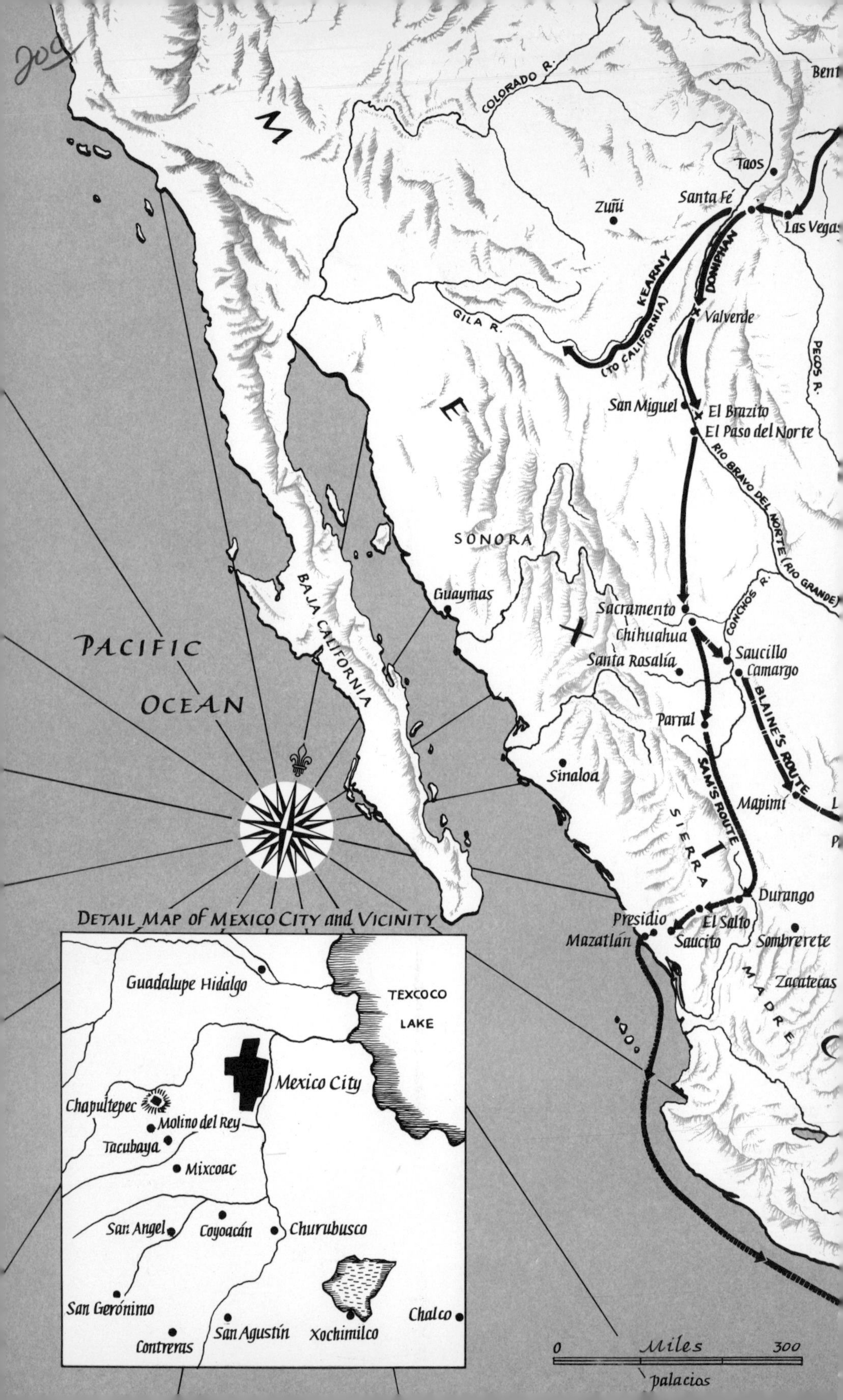

COLORADO R.
M
E
Bent
Taos
Santa Fé
Las Vegas
Zuñi
KEARNY
(TO CALIFORNIA)
DONIPHAN
Valverde
GILA R.
PECOS R.
San Miguel
El Brazito
El Paso del Norte
RIO BRAVO DEL NORTE (RIO GRANDE)
SONORA
BAJA CALIFORNIA
Guaymas
CONCHOS R.
Sacramento
Chihuahua
Saucillo
Camargo
Santa Rosalía
PACIFIC
OCEAN
Parral
BLAINE'S ROUTE
SAM'S ROUTE
Sinaloa
SIERRA
Mapimí
Durango
El Salto
Presidio
Mazatlán
Saucito
Sombrerete
MADRE
Zacatecas
DETAIL MAP of MEXICO CITY and VICINITY
Guadalupe Hidalgo
TEXCOCO
LAKE
Mexico City
Chapultepec
Molino del Rey
Tacubaya
Mixcoac
San Angel
Coyoacán
Churubusco
San Gerónimo
Chalco
San Agustín
Xochimilco
Contreras
0
Miles
300
palacios